WHEN TWILIGHT COMES

Gwynne Forster

WHEN TWILIGHT COMES

Dafina Books

KENSINGTON PUBLISHING CORP.
http://www.kensingtonbooks.com

S

DAFINA BOOKS are published by

Kensington Publishing Corp.
850 Third Avenue
New York, NY 10022

Library of Congress Card Catalogue Number: 2001091604
ISBN: 1-57566-919-6

First Printing: February 2002
10 9 8 7 6 5 4 3 2 1

Printed in the United States of America

ACKNOWLEDGMENTS

I am much indebted to my editor, Karen Thomas, who believed in my ability to write this book and supported me as I did so. My sincere thanks to her.

My thanks also to Nathaniel B. Moore, Public Affairs Manager of *Newsday*, who graciously welcomed me into *Newsday*'s newsroom and explained to me the daily operations of a modern newspaper.

And I thank my husband who supports and encourages me in my work and takes pride in my accomplishments.

Most of all, I thank God for my talent and for the opportunities to use it.

One

An eerie feeling settled over Marge Hairston as she walked through the newsroom that Tuesday morning, the day after Labor Day. She couldn't put her finger on it, but it was there, looming like a hulking figure in the dark. She managed to shake it off, paste a smile on her face, and walk among the cubicles, as she usually did, making sure that everybody had checked in. Marge didn't believe professionals should have to punch a clock, but unless the reporters were covering a story, she wanted them at their desks on time. On that morning, her steps were slow; something compelled her to stop and say a word to each of the reporters and editors who made *The Woodmore Times* what it was—Woodmore, North Carolina's most influential African-American newspaper. Arbiter of social status. Maker and destroyer of political careers. If *The Woodmore Times* printed it, you could bank your money on it, or so its readers thought.

Marge could see that she surprised her staff when she stopped to talk. Instead of being hunched over in their cubicles or staring at their computer monitors, as they usually were, they locked their gazes on her. Each of them looked as if they expected something out of the ordinary. And maybe there would be. She patted Ross Ingersol, her editor in chief, on the shoulder. Ross had stood by her for the twenty-five years since her husband's death, had taught her the fine points of managing an urban newspaper, and she considered him more a friend than an employee. Still, she wasn't used to touching him, and the very act brought a lump to her throat. At least she supposed that was what caused it, since choking up wasn't a thing she normally did. Ross tried to smile, but that fell flat, and he merely looked perplexed. And worried.

"How's it going, friend?" she asked Ross.

"Smooth as a baby's behind."

His stock answer brought a guffaw from Marge, relieving the tension.

"Everything okay with you?" He didn't look at her as he spoke, but kept his gaze fixed on the computer screen, unlike the daring, in-your-face man she'd known more than half of her life.

"Fine," she said. "Same old. Same old."

Marge walked on, stopping at each cubicle to exchange a few words. By a quarter-past nine, she had spoken to all of them. She walked back down to the other end of the newsroom, posted the daily notices on the bulletin board, went into her office, closed the door, and dropped into the nearest chair. Why the devil was she so tired when she hadn't even begun the day's work? After musing over that for a few minutes, she made a mental note to leave work at five o'clock and get to bed by ten-thirty.

"Come in," she said in response to the knock on her door, and made herself straighten up and appear occupied.

"What're you doing sitting over here in this lounge chair?" Ross asked her. He stepped in, closed the door, and handed her one of the two paper containers of black coffee he pulled from a bag. "You looked like you could use a shot of energy. Caffeine does it for me every time."

She took the cup he handed her, hoping he wouldn't notice how her fingers shook. "Thanks. Just what I needed. You know, Ross, it's weird how you always read me like a book."

"I've been around you enough."

She nodded. "You sure have. Way back since before I got this matronly figure, your hairline receded, and my kids got grown and started telling me what to do."

He closed his eyes and leaned back in her desk chair. "Yeah. You were a pint-sized little bantam hen squaring off against a bunch of the toughest guys in this business."

And if she'd known what she was doing, she'd have been scared to death. "When I look back," she said, as much to herself as to Ross, "I can see they let me get away with a lot."

Ross stretched out his legs and sipped his coffee. "With your looks, handling those boys was a cinch." He drained the cup. "I'm here if you need me."

And he always had been. Ross went back to work, but she sat where'd he'd left her, her mind skimming back over thirty years. Ed, her late husband, was her whole life in those days. Good days. They had done everything themselves, from preparing the copy, typing and photographing it, to making the printing plates, taking them to the printer, and distributing the paper to newsstands. Their struggles to build the paper's readership, pay their staff, and make ends meet at home hadn't seemed so tough when they were going through it. Mostly because they'd had each other. She and Ed would come home wiped out. But he'd tell her that all he needed for rejuvenation was her hand touching his, a glance at her soft brown eyes with their twinkling lights, the touch of her full, pouting lips. He'd stroke her cheeks and tell her he loved her chocolate-brown skin and her belly when it was big with their children. She made herself snap out of it when she felt the dampness on her cheeks.

As she'd promised herself, Marge left her office at five and half an hour later wandered around her house, trying to figure out what to do with the time. Finally, she sat in the old-fashioned swing on her back porch and watched the sun through the leaves of her pecan tree. The late-summer breeze rustled the leaves, and a few nuts fell to the ground, but the sun just hung there, a big red disk staring at her through the tree leaves. She stared back at it. Like the newspaper, her garden was one of her genuine sources of pleasure. She loved it, especially the pecan, apple, and pear trees that shaded the garden and back of the house and produced fruit for her and her neighbors. Occasionally, Sharon, the youngest of her three children, would stop by for apples and pecans.

Looking at her beloved garden did nothing to relieve the disquiet that had plagued Marge most of the day. It wasn't cold, or even very cool, but a chill snaked through her as the sun finally slipped out of sight. She wasn't superstitious, and she didn't believe in occult phenomena, but right then she couldn't think of any "natural" explanation of her certainty that something inevitable and unwanted was about to happen.

"What you doing home so early?" Eloise, her next-door neighbor, called from across the back fence.

"I realized I'm tired. You ever been so tired you suddenly didn't care about anything?"

A tall woman with smooth, dark, and velvety skin, braided hair, and large, square hips, like the Hottentot people from which she obviously descended, Eloise was, to say the least, an impressive figure. She rested her forearms on top of the fence, making a cushion for her chin.

"Not even your paper? You don't even care about *that?* Something tells me you in the dumps."

Marge pressed the heel of her right foot to the floor and gently moved the swing back and forth. "The paper. Yeah. Sure I care about the paper, but Ross and the gang can take care of it."

Her own words unsettled her. She waved her hand to encompass all that she saw. "But this. The garden, the house, this diamond ring." She pointed to her finger. "All of it. I worked, sweated, and drove myself to a frenzy for all this. Just like Ed did."

"And everybody in this town, black and white, respects you for it, too. Ain't many women done what you done, Marge."

"Maybe. But wouldn't it've made more sense if I'd just taken it easy and enjoyed life? Or maybe gone to college, something I always wanted to do. Wouldn't it?"

"Girl, you all right? This don't sound a bit like you."

"Of course I'm all right. Just a little tired, and starting now, I'm through driving myself. I got three grown children who don't give a hoot about the paper, don't lift a finger to keep it going, but they all expect to live comfortably off of it after they retire."

"Now, Sharon ain't like that, is she?" Eloise asked in respect to her goddaughter, whom she loved without reservation and as deeply as if she had given birth to her. Eloise had never married, and she had substituted Sharon for the children she craved. Being a God-fearing Baptist, she hadn't considered having a child out of wedlock.

Marge stopped the swing and walked out into the garden. "Not really, I don't suppose. Sharon's struggling to get her career on track. But Drogan and Cassie . . ." She let it hang.

"I wish you wasn't so down. Tell you what. Why don't I put some roastin' ears and steaks on the grill and call Gert. I'll make some iced tea, and after we eat, the three of us can play a few hands of cutthroat."

Marge looked at the weeds choking her rosebush and couldn't make herself care enough to pull the grass. "Some other time, Eloise. I just—cutthroat doesn't appeal to me right now."

"*What?*" Eloise shrieked. "You don't want to play pinochle? Girl, now this ain't normal. If *you* don't want to play cutthroat, something's wrong. I knowed you to play cards when you had a high fever."

In the thirty-some years she'd known Eloise, she hadn't seen the woman hysterical or even mildly melodramatic, so she agreed to the plan, more to placate Eloise than because she thought she'd enjoy it.

Gert, their close friend and card-playing buddy, brought freshly baked corn bread and country sausage, which Eloise grilled along with the corn and steaks.

"My belly sure feels better," Gert announced after they finished eating, patting herself as she spoke. She looked at Marge. "Girl, you too quiet. What you need is a good toss in the sack. It's not normal for a healthy woman to ignore her body's needs."

"Now, Gert, you leave Marge alone," Eloise said, defending Marge as usual. "Sex is your cure for everything. Not everybody is forever and eternally hot like you."

"Maybe not, but she doesn't have to behave as if she's got rigor mortis. Beats anything I ever heard of. I bet you anything that if she got real nice loving tonight, she'd be primed to dance and play cutthroat the whole weekend."

Marge looked at her two friends, women who had stuck with her through tough times—when Ed died suddenly, when she thought she'd lose the paper, through family illnesses and more.

"Y'all go right ahead and talk about me as if I wasn't here," she said, allowing herself one of the few genuine smiles she evinced all day. "You've both earned the right to say whatever you please to me and about me."

"Yeah," Gert replied, "but if we're all that close to you, why don't you do like I tell you? The Lord doesn't require you to sacrifice yourself on the altar of abstinence."

Marge wished she hadn't agreed to their getting together. She wanted to rest. "You'd better be right, Gert, because you're definitely in a fix if he does. I'm sixty-one years old—"

"I'm sixty-two," Gert said, "and girl, you bet your buns not a week passes without—"

"Save your confessions for the priest," Eloise interrupted. "Marge, what's the matter?"

"I'm just plain tired. I think I'll turn in."

* * *

"What do you mean, you'll be in later?" Ross asked Marge the next morning.

"I guess I'm just realizing I'm not made of iron, Ross. I don't feel like rushing this morning, so I'll get there when I get there. I know you'll look after things."

"Yeah. Sure. Uh . . . You get some rest."

Marge started for the shower, realized she'd better not risk it, called 911, and unlocked her front door. Three hours later, she woke up in Woodmore General with an IV in her arm and Sharon peering anxiously down at her face. Assured that her mother would be all right, Sharon kissed Marge and went back to work after promising her she'd be back around five.

That afternoon, Ross, having traced Marge to the hospital, walked into her room where Marge sat up in bed watching Judge Mathis on television. He leaned against the doorjamb and whistled sharply, dragging her attention to him.

"What the hell happened, Marge? Yesterday morning, everybody at the paper figured something was up. What's wrong?"

"I don't know yet, but this isn't so bad. I've been waiting on people most of my life. Now they're waiting on me. All I have to do is push a button and somebody comes running in here."

She'd meant for Ross to smile in that grudging way of his, but not a crease showed in his face. "You leveling with me? You don't know anything?"

"I don't. And I'm not worried, because I already feel better."

He popped his fingers, something he did reflexively, she'd decided, since he knew she hated it. "Take a couple of weeks off, why don't you? You, Mack, and I can hold the daily budget meetings by phone."

The thought of Mack, her editorial-page editor, doing his own thing made her blood run cold. Mack was still hungering for his *time,* but being unkempt no longer went for chic. The sixties were forty years gone, but Mack didn't seem to know that. He also didn't know the whole of Woodmore considered him weird, or if he did, he didn't seem to care.

"Good idea," Marge said to Ross when her mind drifted back to the budget meeting and to him. "And you keep a tight lid on Mack."

"Right. I'd better get going. See you in a couple of days. And look . . . uh . . . you take real good care."

She watched him leave, wondering at his last display of emotion.

She'd barely finished her dinner when Eloise arrived, followed by Drogan, Cassie, and Sharon—her three children—in that order.

"Girl, I knowed something wasn't right when you didn't want to play pinochle," Eloise said as she hugged Marge.

Marge returned her hug. "Well, don't gloat. I expect the devil may even be right once in a while."

Drogan moved to the front of the group, and Marge smiled at her firstborn and only son, dressed in a gray pinstriped suit, white shirt, and yellow tie. She didn't look down, because she knew his ridiculously priced leather briefcase rested beside his Salvatore Ferragamo shoes. Drogan's primary goal was to make an impression. She'd often thought it would have been better for him if he hadn't inherited his father's stunning good looks—his long-lashed black eyes, full bottom lip beneath chiseled nostrils, and copper-colored skin that had turned female's heads since his childhood. And she wished, not for the first time, that Drogan also had his father's character. Ed Hairston had been a man of solid substance and strong moral fiber, but she doubted any truthful person would say that about Drogan. Oh, he wasn't lacking honor, and he had moments of goodness and personal strength, but they came a lot less frequently than she would have liked.

"You gave me a shock, Mama. It's hard to believe you're in a hospital bed even when I'm seeing it with my own eyes. What did they tell you?" Drogan asked her after bending over and kissing her cheek.

"Nothing yet. They've been doing a lot of tests and poking me. Dr. Glick said it would be a day or so before they knew anything definite. So I'm just resting."

"That's ridiculous, Mama," Cassie said. "How can they treat you if they don't know what's wrong?"

"They've given me vitamins, food, and rest, and that's probably all I need. I feel better already."

Sharon sat on the edge of Marge's bed and took her mother's hand. Marge could count on her youngest always to be nearby. Sharon didn't talk much, especially when Cassie and Drogan were around, but she had more depth than either of them. It wouldn't hurt her to be more critical of her brother and sister, Marge thought, remembering the times when the two of them exploited Sharon.

"You don't know how relieved I am to hear you say that, Mama," Sharon said, her relief audible. "We're all so used to you being like . . . well, the Rock of Gibraltar, that it's strange—"

"Yeah," Eloise said, her voice dripping with sarcasm. "Looks like she's human. I'll be back to see you tomorrow, Marge. If Gert comes with me, maybe we can get in a coupla hands of cutthroat." She kissed Marge and Sharon, her goddaughter, and left.

"Mama, that's a low-class game," Cassie said. "I wish you'd stop playing that and learn bridge or chess. Nobody we know plays pinochle except those two."

"And me," Marge said. She wished Cassie wouldn't look down on people and whatever she thought was low-class, that she'd stop scorning people she considered beneath her. Compassion was completely foreign to her elder daughter. Always had been.

Cassie rolled her eyes toward the ceiling. "I don't know what you find so interesting about that woman. She won't even take the trouble to learn to speak properly. She's trying, to say the least."

Cassie's uppity ways, even as a child, had always worried Marge. "Maybe to you," Marge said, "but right after your father died, she looked after you children so I could go to work, and she didn't charge me a dime. I can afford to pay her for it now, but if I offered, she'd be insulted. And another thing. Back then, you ate a lot of potatoes and bacon that she bought and paid for. Why should I care how she speaks?"

"We're only thinking of you, Mama," Drogan said, assuming his favorite role of peacemaker and smoother of tensions. "Imogene said to give you her love. She'll try to get by to see you tomorrow."

Marge nodded her thanks. She wasn't crazy about her daughter-in-law, but she kept that to herself. She had trouble respecting women who weren't willing to chart their own course and who expected a man to hang the moon for them. Imogene was a throwback to the days of willing female subservience, but Drogan apparently liked it, so she'd be the last one to complain.

"If the grocery store's still open when I leave here and I can get a nice chicken on my way home, I'll bring you some hot chicken soup tomorrow evening, Mama," Cassie said in her usual way of showing contriteness without apologizing.

"That would be wonderful, dear. I've been trying to figure out what they do to the food here to make it taste like rags."

Drogan laughed. "Maybe it *was* rags. I gave a course in Windows 2000 at the junior high school, and I never regretted anything so much as I did accepting their invitation to lunch." He frowned, as if the memory of it pained him. "One of the boys, a real little rascal, watched me as I got the first mouthful and said, 'How you like it, Mr. Hairston?' I could've sworn I had lockjaw."

Sharon's laughter filled the room, reminding them of her deep love and admiration for her big brother. "I hope you didn't utter any of your favorite words."

"That stew curled my tongue, and it's a good thing, too, because what I was thinking had no place in young ears. Lord, that stuff was awful." He draped an arm around Sharon's shoulder and smiled down at her. "Not even the first cake you made tasted that bad."

Sharon made a face. "That tale gets worse with the years. By the time I'm fifty, that cake will have poisoned the entire family. You leaving, Cassie?"

Cassie kissed her sister and her mother. "Yep. I gotta run, honey. The *sous*-chef's off, and Kix is working the dinner hour by himself tonight, so he'll be too tired to drive. A friend took him to work, and I told him I'd pick him up. Small price to pay for a husband who's the best cook anywhere around. See you tomorrow, Mama."

"She's not kidding, either," Drogan said. "Kix is the only chef I ever heard of who gets tips from the diners. Big ones, too. Cassie said some of his regulars refuse to give their order to the waiter. They want Kix to come out and tell 'em how he's going to cook it. She said his tips are sometimes bigger than the price of the meal."

"It's a good thing he loves to cook." Marge's dry comment brought a laugh from Drogan and Sharon, as she'd known it would. Cassie's feebleness in the kitchen was a standard family joke.

Drogan reached down and picked up his briefcase. "Can I give you a lift, Sharon?"

"Thanks, but I drove. I think I'll sit here with Mama a little longer. Give Imogene a hug."

"I'll do that. She went to Winston-Salem this morning with one of her girlfriends, and she'll be tired when she gets back. I don't see how women can spend a whole day shopping and not buy anything. I'm going to drop by that new Chinese take-out on Butler Street so Imogene won't have to cook."

"That chauvinistic comment is a chink in your otherwise perfect armor, brother dear," Sharon said. "Men are the ones who go into stores, look around, and then ask a saleslady to choose something for a woman she's never seen. Barring that, they simply leave the store empty-handed, because choosing between black and brown is too much of an effort."

He grinned down at her, displaying his perfect white teeth. "Now who's being a chauvinist? I'll be back tomorrow, Mama. Here's my cell-phone number," He handed her a card. "You can always reach me if you call this."

The arms of her son embraced her. Then he looked into her face and winked. "You hurry up and get out of here; you're ruining your image." He smiled then in an attempt at levity, but she didn't miss the concern he obviously felt.

"How're you going to manage with the paper, Mama?" Sharon asked when the two of them were alone. "I know Uncle Ross can get it done, but won't he have to talk with you about . . . you know, editorials and things like that?"

It didn't escape Marge that only Sharon among her children had asked about the thing that most concerned her. Keeping up the paper's standards.

"We'll have afternoon budget meetings—you know . . . conferences to plan the content and layout of the next day's paper. Keeping Mack in line will be a problem. He's a good editorial editor when he remembers that this isn't the sixties, he's not handing out leaflets on the corner of Haight and Ashbury, and he's fifty-seven years old."

She felt the increased warmth of Sharon's hand as her child squeezed her fingers. "When you put your mind to it, you can make ordinary sunshine seem ridiculous," Sharon said between peels of laughter. "I'd be satisfied if Mack would cut a couple of feet off of the length of his hair. Last time I saw him, it was down to his waist. People make a point of staring at him just to let him know they don't approve of him."

"I know, but he's competent, and he's got a good heart. Well, most of the time he has. Did you go for that interview yesterday?" Sharon nodded. "How'd it go?"

"The chancellor, provost, and all the deans were at that interview, every one of them sitting in judgment. I started to wonder if being an assistant dean of the School of Social Work was worth corroded nerves. They practically scraped my insides. So who knows which way it will go."

Marge patted Sharon's shoulder, suddenly aware of the energy she had to use for that little effort. "You just pray that whatever they decide will be the best for you. You're a good person, Sharon, and only good can come to you. What are you doing about Jeff?"

"That man's not for me. I went out with him several times, but . . .

well, he just doesn't have the music that makes me dance. Worse, he annoys me. I got sick of hearing about his family history. That's one of the problems with this town. People are satisfied to stay right where their ancestors left them. They don't want to change and won't tolerate it in anybody else."

"And it's a pity, too," Marge said. "One black Woodmore youngster won a bronze medal in the '68 Olympics, and almost thirty-six years later they're still talking about it; everybody seems satisfied with that one achievement."

"But right now, Mama, you should rest and not think about the paper, though I know that's like asking bees not to make honey. I want you to promise me you'll do as Dr. Glick tells you."

Sharon increased the pressure of her fingers as if to impress upon her mother the importance of her words. "I don't want you to go back to that paper for at least two weeks. I'll be here every afternoon as soon as I get off from work, and I can take anything you want over to the paper. Okay?"

Marge battled the lump in her throat. "You've been a blessing to me from the day you were born. Not a minute of trouble. Biggest problem I had with you was the way you were always under my feet, laughing, playing, and asking me questions I couldn't begin to answer. Your daddy said you were an angel put here to watch over us."

"Oh, Mama. I'd forgotten that."

"As a child, you were so generous, I used to watch you playing with your little friends to make sure you didn't give away your clothes. Cassie and Drogan loved you, but they could always count on you to share your allowance with them. That is, till your daddy put a stop to it."

"Cassie used to beat up the girls who bothered me. I didn't think they were being mean, but she did."

"I know. Cassie was born with a short fuse."

Sharon's laugh was like that of an indulgent parent. "Sure thing. That and a passion for soap and water. It's a wonder she's still got skin."

"She's got it, and it is flawless."

Marge and Sharon looked up, startled by the intrusive remark, and saw Gert standing in the door, grinning.

"Hey, girl," Gert said to Marge. "I hear you got bored and decided to change the scenery. How're you making it?"

Marge leaned back against the pillow and allowed herself a smile.

If anybody could lighten her mood, it was Gert. "I knew you'd be here."

Gert handed Marge a small brown bag. "The food in this place stinks. I know it's time for them to give you dinner, but I doubt you'll eat it, so you might as well enjoy this ice cream. It's got all the calories you'll need for a couple of days."

"Good," Marge said, opening the box. "If there's anything I can't stand, it's diet this and diet that. You get fat, anyhow, and the stuff that adds the weight tastes like the devil. Hmm. Child, this is wonderful." She looked over at Sharon, who stood and picked up her briefcase. "You going?"

"You'll have company for a while longer, so this is a good time for me to leave. See you tomorrow." She leaned over and hugged her mother. "'Bye for now. 'Bye Aunt Gert."

Marge stopped eating ice cream and watched her youngest walk through the door. "I hope she gets that job," she said, mostly to herself. "You know, Gert, it's time something good happened to that child. Long past time."

Drogan put the cartons of Chinese food on an aluminum cookie sheet and set it in the oven to stay warm. He didn't mind bringing pizza, Chinese food, or Kentucky Fried Chicken home for dinner on the days Imogene went to Winston-Salem; it guaranteed him some consideration, as Imogene liked to call it. He put half a dozen pillar candles on the bedroom dresser, set the table, stripped, and headed for the shower. A man shouldn't have to genuflect to his wife in order to get what she promised when she married him, but when Imogene was tired, she'd say a flat no and mean it. Her tight little nipples wouldn't even stand out when he pinched them. They'd been married a year before he'd realized her brain ruled her libido, or so she pretended. He scrubbed his belly vigorously with a brush, enjoying the sensation, not unlike what he felt when Imogene's fingernails scored him.

When they first married, Imogene had been a willing and ready woman, and when she wasn't tired, she usually came through for him. But she'd fold up on him every time she went with Keisha on one of their all-day shopping trips to Winston-Salem. He stopped cold in the process of drying his back. No. Imogene was too straitlaced for anything devious or treacherous. Besides, she was crazy about him. He put on black slacks and a snug-fitting, short-sleeved red T-shirt that emphasized his pectorals and washboard abdomen, got a glass of bourbon and soda, and sat down to wait for her.

It occurred to him that Imogene hadn't always enjoyed shopping, at least not all day long. He mused over it a bit and finally traced it to her last miscarriage. She wanted a family so badly she could taste it, but the three times she'd become pregnant, she miscarried. He could give her just about anything except what she wanted most. A child. He got himself another drink, but before he tasted it, he heard her key in the door.

He rushed to open it. "Hi, sweetheart," he said, kicked the door shut, lifted her, and kissed her. His libido kicked into high gear when she played with his tongue a little bit before sucking it into her mouth.

"You're ready tonight," she said, and looped her arms around his neck. She liked it when he picked her up and kissed her that way, and he didn't mind not having to bend his six-foot-two-inch frame down to her five feet four.

"I've been ready all day. You want to shower while I get the food on the table?"

"I hope you got Chinese."

"Must have been reading your mind." He laid a playful pat on her bottom. "Hurry, before I explode."

Her giggles plowed straight through him. Imogene had a sexy come-on that could make a lame man dance.

She dropped a small package on the chair, started toward the bathroom, and stopped. "By the way, did you go see Mama?"

"Yeah. It gave me a strange feeling seeing her in that bed, too. Mama belongs on her feet taking care of things."

"I hope she's going to be all right."

He didn't want to get Imogene's mind off of what he'd primed her for, so he skimmed over it, masking his concern. "Me, too. They're doing a lot of tests. From the way she looked, though, she ought to be out of there in a few days."

Fifty-five minutes later, their bellies full and the dishes in the dishwasher, he brushed his teeth and heard her doing the same in the adjoining bathroom. She hadn't said a word about being tired, and he wasn't one to question his good fortune. When she stepped out of the bathroom, he picked her up and took her to bed. Life was good.

* * *

After Gert went home, Marge tried to sleep, but couldn't, so she sat up in bed and watched a 1930s movie. She'd put on a face for Ross, her girlfriends, and children, but she hadn't been able to shake that creepy feeling. If something *was* seriously wrong with her, she could handle it, and she suspected Drogan and Sharon could, too, but she wasn't so sure about Cassie. That one had a tendency to play games with herself.

At the moment, Cassie was doing just that. Kix took his jacket from the closet in his office and felt for his keys. "You think Mama's going to pull through this all right, Cassie?"

Cassie adjusted the front of her jacket so that the lapels lay perfectly flat. She hated disorder of any kind. And Mama's being in a hospital meant that everything was out of place. "She looked pretty good to me this evening. You know Mama. Strong as steel and the Rock of Gibraltar."

"Let's hope so," Kix said, well aware of Cassie's penchant for avoiding any unpleasant truth. Still, she didn't seem down, so he had to believe her.

"Darling, do you want to drive," Cassie asked Kix as they walked to the parking lot behind Gourmet Corner, the restaurant he owned.

Kix Shepherd understood his wife. He also loved her. "I thought the reason you came to get me tonight was because you knew I'd be wound tighter than a bowstring."

She grasped his arm and tugged him closer to her. "Well, I always want to give you the choice. You're head of our home."

He had to laugh, because he didn't doubt for one minute that she was just making conversation. He knew Cassie well enough to realize that if he ever started throwing his weight around, she'd probably take off like a jet plane. A show of authority scared the bejeebers out of Cassie, though she stopped just short of being domineering herself.

"You don't mind changing roles with me tonight and driving us home, do you?" Kix asked her, making sure they understood each other.

He loved her joyous laughter, and she treated him to a good dose of it. "All right. all right," she said. "You know me too well."

He opened the driver's door for her, and she turned to him. "I'm a lucky woman. I don't always act like it, maybe, but I know I am." To his amazement, she kissed him right there under the light, where anyone who wanted to could see her.

He stared at her and, suddenly energized, held out his hand. "Give me the keys. I'll drive." She got in, slid over, and started singing "Band Of Gold," her favorite song.

Excitement rushed through him, revitalizing him. He wasn't any more tired now than if he'd just gotten out of the bed. He didn't ordinarily speed; it was dangerous, and it made Cassie nervous. Tonight, however, his foot was heavy on the gas pedal, and Cassie just kept on singing. He didn't know what had come over her, but whatever it was, he aimed to take full advantage of it.

Two

"How're we feeling this morning?" Dr. Glick asked Marge.

"I don't know about you," she said, showing her disdain for his patronizing tone. "I want to go home."

Miles Glick had known her since elementary school, and she regarded him as a friend, but he could still put on his supercilious I'm-a-medical-doctor airs. Not that she cared or wasn't used to it, but sometimes she couldn't resist putting him in his place.

"I'm sick of this punching and poking," she told him. "If y'all don't know what's wrong with me, why don't you just say so?"

He patted her shoulder. "I don't blame you for getting restless. These things sometimes take a while. Medical science is more precise than it used to be, though it's still imperfect, and these tests tell us what we need to know." He placed his fingers on her pulse, looked at his watch, and nodded his head.

"You been feeling washed out lately?"

"Tired, Miles. Just plain tired. The day they brought me here, I'd got so tired I couldn't put one foot in front of the other one."

He took out his stethoscope and placed it against her chest. "That doesn't surprise me. Inhale deeply and let it out. You got a lot of protein in the urine, and your blood pressure's up. I'm putting you on a diet, and you follow it. Lay off meat. Period. Drink a gallon and a half of water a day, fill up on cranberries, and throw out the salt. For the next six weeks, stay home and keep your feet up. I want you to rest, and losing a little weight wouldn't hurt. Forget about *The Woodmore Times,* and let your kids take care of you for a change. I'm leaving a couple of prescriptions for you."

"You got all that from those tests you been doing?" Two whole days, dozens of needles stuck in her, and pictures taken of just about every inch of her body, and for what? "What would y'all do without all these high-powered machines?"

He poked his tongue in his right cheek. "How old was your grandmother when she passed away?"

Marge thought for a minute. "Mama said she was thirty-two. Why?"

"How old are you?"

"You know I'm sixty-one."

"I'd say that's your answer."

She'd like to wipe that smug expression off his face; not that she'd make a dent. In her mind's eye, she could see it on him as far back as when he was seven years old. And it was even more infuriating back then. Well, acting out wasn't getting her anywhere, so she called on her feminine wiles.

"Miles, you know I'd trust you with my life. Come to think of it, I do that all the time. I need to get back to the paper. Can't we handle this on an . . . uh . . . outpatient basis?"

"I see you weren't listening. Rest at home with your feet elevated. That's final."

"I can sit at my desk and work and still have my feet up."

"Now look here, Marge. You know you're not well, and don't tell me you don't. The whole town knows you go to that paper seven days a week. If you weren't sick, you wouldn't have spent the first night in this hospital. So be sensible about this."

"Are you telling me something's wrong with my kidneys?"

He put the stethoscope back in his pocket, made some notes on her chart, and worked hard at smiling. "Looks like it, but we think it's manageable."

She knew a forced smile when she saw one. "You got all the test results?"

"Not all, but enough to know it's your kidneys."

"I see. When can I go home?"

"A couple of days, I expect."

She glared at him, though she was more anxious than annoyed. "You're not even sure about *that*? What's keeping me here?"

"We may have to do more tests. Besides, I want all the results before you leave here."

She slumped back against the pillow. "Let me be the one to tell my children about this. You make those nurses keep their mouths shut."

"Of course. Nurses don't meddle in doctor-patient relations. Don't worry, Marge. We've been together a long time, and you know I'll take good care of you."

"I know. I just got so many irons in the fire right now, so many things I want to do, and in six weeks . . ." She sighed. Seemed like it was out of her hands. "Well, what will be will be."

He told her he'd see her again in a couple of days and left. She closed her eyes and thought back over the years. Looked as if she hadn't escaped that old family plague, after all. Well, she'd had a good life, done most of the things she'd wanted to do . . . except she hadn't gotten to San Francisco to see the Golden Gate Bridge and Alcatraz, that prison they called *The House Across the Bay*, where George Raft was imprisoned in that old movie. Too busy working and making a living. When the children were out of college, the house was paid for, and she could finally afford it, there wasn't time. She'd put everything into the paper, had made it the most prestigious institution in Woodmore. She took a deep breath and stretched out. How could a person be so tired lying down?

Around three-thirty, Gert and Eloise arrived, bringing hot biscuits, vegetable soup, apple pie, and ice cream. She figured she could eat that and worry about the calories another time.

"What did the doctor say?" Gert asked before she sat down.

Of the three of them, only Gert had a college degree. Marge made it through high school, but Eloise hadn't been that fortunate. Still, Eloise had managed to buy a house and save enough for a respectable retirement, and she'd done all that working as a cook and housekeeper. "If you don't have to pay for food, clothes, rent, or transportation," Eloise had said, explaining why she'd "lived in" for over twenty years, "you save every penny you make." Wasn't a thing wrong with that.

Gert and Eloise didn't need to know everything. That way, they wouldn't have to keep secrets, not that Gert knew what that was. Her tongue was afflicted with the same curse as the average Woodmore citizen's; they all had to be the first to tell something even if they hadn't verified it.

"Miles said I'm washed out. Exhausted. That I have to stay home and rest for six weeks."

She could see the relief on their faces. "Not bad medicine," Gert said. "A good rest once every thirty years never hurt anybody."

"Not unless you're Marge," Eloise said. She turned to her friend. "You don't have to stay in bed, do you?"

Marge shrugged. "He wants me to elevate my feet. What's the difference?"

"Plenty," Gert said. "As long as he didn't say you couldn't . . . er . . . er . . . diddle once in a while—"

Marge figured Eloise's laugh could be heard all the way to the nurses' station. "Girl, you elevate you mind," Eloise said. "In all my life, I never knowed nobody but you whose mind never strayed past way down front and center."

Marge let herself enjoy a good laugh. She didn't know what she'd do without her friends. Gert had been part of her life for over thirty years, as dependable as day and night, ever since Ed ran that flattering story on her. From then on, the locals didn't think about buying and selling property without first getting in touch with Gert. And she'd first met Eloise when she came to baby-sit Drogan one night in order to make five dollars extra money.

"Eloise, you know I don't pay any attention to Gert's foolishness." She looked at Gert. "You must have been one real oversexed teenager."

Gert's laughter was like a welcome summer breeze; you wanted it to go on and on. "Child, it's been so long since I was a teenager, I don't remember a thing about it. You told your children about old Glick's orders?"

"Glick ain't old," Eloise said. "He just act old. If he was old, I'd give him a twirl, him being a widower and all. But he too young for me."

Marge sucked her teeth. "Miles is sixty-one, the same age as I am. If he acts old, it's 'cause he is. I'll tell the children about it when they come this evening."

"Tell us what?" Sharon asked as she walked through the door. "What are you going to tell us, Mama?"

"It ain't no big deal," Eloise quickly interjected. "She's gotta stay home for a while and rest."

"Why?"

Marge released a labored breath. "Drogan and Cassie will be here shortly, and I'll tell it just once. I have to take six weeks off from work."

"But Dr. Glick knows you can't—"

"He doesn't know any such thing apparently, and I'll do what he says. Now, just wait till the others get here and we'll all go over it together."

Eloise got up and put on her jacket. "If y'all gonna have a family conference, I'll be going. I'm putting in a few hours over at the senior center tomorrow, but I'll come by soon as I get off."

"I'll get here when I can," Gert said. "I'm closing an estate deal tomorrow, and only the Lord knows when I'll get away from there. Y'all take care."

The two women hugged Marge and Sharon, and Marge watched them leave, more subdued than when they came, she thought. No telling what they were thinking.

Drogan and Cassie arrived shortly thereafter, and Marge geared herself for Cassie's impatience and what would certainly be a thorough grilling.

"He's making you stay home on that flimsy evidence?" Cassie asked. "He doesn't even have all the tests."

"He has enough to make a diagnosis." She didn't add that the remaining test would indicate the severity of her condition. "And I'm not in the business of second-guessing doctors, Cassie. If you know something Miles Glick doesn't know, let's hear it."

"Sorry, Mama, but this comes as such a shock. You've never been sick."

"You think it's not a shock for me? I'll be in here a few more days until all the tests are in. *Six* weeks isn't such a long time. Maybe I'll get to read something other than *The Woodmore Times,* and that might not be a bad thing."

Drogan moved into the middle of the family group, hugged his two sisters, and took his mother's hand. "Since you'll be here two or three more days, we don't have to make plans now. I'll call Ross—"

Exactly what she didn't want—Drogan making policy and Cassie ridiculing it. "That's all right, son. I'll tell Ross. I'm speaking with him and Mack every afternoon. The paper's covered."

"Yeah," Sharon said, "and they're doing a great job, so Mama, you can relax and rest."

"How do you know they're doing a great job?" Cassie asked her. "Have you been over there?"

Sharon stared at her. "I read the paper every day. That's how I know."

Cassie crossed her knees and leaned back in the chair, the epitome of elegance. "I hardly have time to breathe. You know I have to design something new every day. I did three logos for Baker Mills today, but who knows whether they'll accept one of them. This is the third try. After that, I did a series of Christmas cards and drafted the layout for a new line of personalized stationery. A day of that and I don't want to see black on white, including the written word."

Drogan hugged Cassie. "All right, superwoman, we get the message. You're a hot shot at Cutting Edge Stationers and Engravers, and you don't have time for such a silly little thing as what's going on in the world."

"Aw, Drogan," Cassie said. "You make it sound awful."

Marge watched Drogan turn on the charm, his grin sparkling. Infectious. He didn't spare anybody, not even his mother and sisters. He poured out grace and charm as if they would buy more for him than the U.S. dollar, which he craved. She wondered sometimes how Imogene handled her husband's personality. Right now, he was using his charm to soften his criticism of Cassie.

"It *was* awful, Cassie girl. Kix needs to shake you up a little," Drogan said. "The man lets you get away with murder."

Cassie looked at him from beneath her lashes, mugging the way she did as a child, just as good at hamming it up as Drogan. "He loves me."

Drogan frowned, showing a seriousness that he didn't display too often. "Love has its limits, sis. If you pay close attention, you'll see that it's just as fragile as that fine crystal of yours."

Marge wondered at that comment—what it said about Drogan and maybe about Drogan and Imogene. But since she hadn't seen or heard anything to the contrary, she supposed the magic they'd had still worked for them. She saw her children frequently, but except for holidays, birthdays, and special occasions, she rarely saw the three of them together. She thanked God that all three were successful and respected in the community and that they loved each other. She hoped her beloved Ed, Lord rest his soul, was pleased with the job she'd done.

Sharon perched on the edge of Marge's bed, smiling at Drogan's and Cassie's antics. It seemed to Marge that they hadn't changed all that much since childhood. Sharon had always been content to wait until Drogan or Cassie claimed her for one reason or another, usually making a fuss over her. Even as a small child, Sharon had let them have their fun, as if she knew they enjoyed the contest. Raising them had been wonderful; she wouldn't take anything for it.

* * *

"You're not planning to let your mother stay in that house by herself when she comes out of the hospital, are you?" Kix asked Cassie when he got home that night. "She's not Eloise's responsibility."

"I know that. I thought she could take turns staying with Drogan, Sharon, and me. But if she'd rather stay with us, that's fine. Six weeks is no time, and we can get our cleaning woman to stay with her till I get home from work. Mama deserves all the peace she can get."

"Maybe we ought to bring Drogan and Sharon into this and see what they think."

If she did that, she'd lose control of the situation. She might be able to bring Sharon in line, but her brother was another matter; Drogan was a man, which meant that when it came to Imogene's interests, he'd keep his penis in mind. What Imogene wanted, Imogene got. She suspected, too, that if she held out for her own way, she wouldn't have her husband's support. Kix had a habit of insisting on fairness no matter what was at stake. Might as well give in with grace.

"All right," she said, "but before we do that, let's decide about us. Six weeks isn't a lot of time, Kix, but what if it's longer than that? Then what?"

"She's been like a mother to me. We'll do right by her. She never tells anybody to let her know if they need her; she always says, 'What can I do to help?' You know what I'm saying?"

"I do, and I'm right with you. She's not going to want for anything as long as I'm breathing."

He pulled her to him in a hug that was more friendship than passion, and she had the feeling that she'd scored some points with him. That couldn't happen too often. But why would he think she wouldn't look after her mother? He handed her the cordless phone, and she dialed her brother's number.

"What's up, Cassie? We were just about to go over to see Mama. Aren't you going?"

"Of course I am. But Kix thinks we ought to have a family conference and make some plans for when she comes out. He's right. Can you and Imogene come over on your way to the hospital?"

"Well, sure. Give us about forty-five minutes. Sharon coming?"

"I'm going to call her right now. See you."

"Right."

She was in her element now. In control. And she was always magnanimous when she had things going her way. "Sharon, honey,"

Cassie said when her sister answered the phone, "could you come by here on your way to see Mama?" She gave her reasons and wasn't surprised that Sharon readily agreed.

"I'll be there in about half an hour or so."

"I'd thought Mama could stay here while she's recuperating," she told Sharon, who was the first to arrive. "Kix and I don't think it's right for her to be in that house alone when she's not even supposed to be walking around."

"But, Cassie, if we have to get someone to stay with her at *your* house while you work, she might as well be at home."

"It's not the same. I'll be with her nights and weekends, and Kix is home on Mondays."

"I don't know. Let's see what Drogan thinks."

Drogan presented the problem to Imogene and waited. Imogene was about as predictable as the outcome of the Kentucky Derby, and she regarded hardly anything as a firm obligation. She didn't think highly of herself, and her ego constantly needed oiling, but she was a good homemaker, so he couldn't complain.

"I think we ought to bring Mama home with us, Drogan," Imogene said. "I know Cassie means well, but if we have to get someone to take care of Mama, she might as well stay in her own house. I'm home, and I can look after her."

He'd hoped she'd say that. After all, he was head of their little family. Mama ran the paper, but when it came to other things, it seemed to him that they all looked to him.

"That's good enough for me, baby."

At Cassie's house a little later, Drogan put his hands into his pants pockets and paced around Cassie's living room, his head down and shoulders curved forward. His sister was proud of her home, and he had to admit to its elegance, but for some reason, he never felt comfortable sitting down there, afraid he'd leave behind a speck of lint. He tried to remember whether Cassie had been that prissy when they were kids. He didn't think so.

"You and Sharon are working full time. Imogene is home all day, so it's logical that she stay with us."

"She can stay either place," Kix said, the impatience in his voice surprising Cassie. "Let's leave it to Mama."

* * *

Five days later, at nine in the morning, Marge called each of her children and told them she was allowed to go home. "Gert and Eloise are coming to take me home, so go on to work," she told each of them. They could figure out for themselves that Gert would take the day off from her job in order to help her friend.

Around five o'clock, the three of them arrived at her house, Cassie and Drogan with their spouses. *My Lord,* Marge said to herself. *Anybody would think I was about to breathe my last.* "Sorry I can't offer you anything," she said aloud. "That cake I made is probably stale by now."

"Don't you worry about us, Mama. We don't want you here by yourself," Cassie said. "Kix and I want you to stay with us."

"But Imogene is home all day, so it's best you come over to our place," Drogan said.

Imogene walked over and hugged her mother-in-law, and Marge made a show of hugging her back. "Drogan's right. And I'm a natural nurturer, so I'll spoil you to death."

Marge's smile projected as much brilliance as she could muster. "I know you would, honey."

"I'll hire an aide to be here with her mornings while I'm teaching," Sharon put in, surprising them all. "She's coming with me."

Marge looked at her three children and shook her head. "Y'all don't know how happy it makes me to know you want me to stay with you while I'm recuperating, but I've already decided to stay right home here." She raised her hand as if to ward off objections. "It'll be an inconvenience to each one of you, and you know I love my own home and my own things."

She folded her arms across her chest and gave them a firm, resolute look. "I'm staying home. I appreciate what y'all are trying to do, but I'd rather stay home."

"How're you going to manage if you have to keep your feet up?" Sharon asked her.

"Same way Cassie would manage. I'll get someone to come in. Now y'all stop worrying and fussing. Everything's going to be just fine."

If she had to stay with any of them, she'd rather it was Sharon, because her youngest child didn't try to boss her around, but Sharon needed to concentrate on getting that promotion. Cassie was a control freak, and her big heart didn't compensate for her nagging. As for Drogan, a little of his precious Imogene went a long way with her. Best to stay right where she was. They restated their cases, but she held out, and finally they realized she meant it and accepted it.

On a Thursday afternoon three weeks later, Miles Glick dropped by unexpectedly. He rang the bell and remembered that Marge couldn't open the door. He phoned Eloise on his cell phone, and she went over to Marge's house and opened the door for him.

Marge didn't like the look on his face, and when he walked over, took her hand, and put on his best bedside manners, her heart began to thud.

"What is it, Miles?"

"Well, I've been over your case, and I consulted with experts at Wake Forest University in Winston-Salem. I don't think you're going to be able to go back to work, Marge, so you're going to have to make permanent arrangements about the paper."

She sat up straight. "Would you please come right out and say whatever it is you're trying to say? I know things aren't going too well, 'cause I don't feel a bit better. If anything—"

"You feel worse. That's no surprise. Pretty soon we're going to have to take some serious steps. You can't go back to work, Marge. I'm sorry, because I know what it means to you, but that's all in the past. We're pretty certain it's polycystic."

Marge stared at him, nodding her head back and forward. "I was afraid of that. Polycystic kidney disease is what my people on my father's side end up with." She thought for a few minutes. "You know I've had plenty of experience with this, Miles, and I tell you right now, I'm not going through what my folks went through."

"You may not have a choice."

"We'll see about that."

Eloise came over later that evening with some homemade ice cream. "Thought you might like some. It's raspberry, your favorite, and something you can't never find in the stores." She savored some from the bowl she'd brought over for herself. "What did Miles want? I figured you wasn't expecting him."

They'd know soon enough. Besides, as close as they were to her, they deserved to have answers. She told Eloise what she knew. "I'm not going on any machines, no matter what you, Gert, or my children say. It's out of the question."

Eloise's spoon clattered to the floor, and she gaped, speechless. "You can't do this, Marge. What about the children?"

It wasn't as easy as she made it seem, and her shoulders slumped in resignation. "Eloise, be happy for me. I raised three great children who can look after themselves. They're healthy, reasonably happy, and reasonably well off financially. How many mothers do you know who can say that? Now let's get off the morbid stuff. I intend to enjoy this ice cream. It's delicious." She ate with relish, as if she didn't realize that Eloise didn't eat another spoonful.

She waited until the next day to tell her children, because she wanted them with her when she gave them the news. It couldn't be accidental that they'd stopped asking her how she was, how she felt. She didn't know if they'd assumed she was getting better or realized she was getting worse.

"Dr. Glick says I can't go back to work. He said that part of my life is a thing of the past."

Their gasps filled the room as three pairs of terror-filled eyes stared at her. "You're not serious." Cassie found her voice first. "These small-town doctors can't be trusted. We'll get some experts."

"Miles has already consulted with experts at Wake Forest University in Winston-Salem. We won't get any more experts. And please don't start the matter of my moving anyplace. I'm staying right here. What I can't do for myself, Lizzie can do."

"Well, I suppose Ross can handle the paper," Drogan said, his voice lacking its usual force and timbre.

"If that's what I decide to do."

"What do you mean? Who else could handle it?" Cassie nearly screamed the words.

Marge watched fear erode Cassie's normal self-confidence. She hated to see her daughter's composure crumpled like mangled wire, but she couldn't help her. All of them would soon know the stuff they were made of, and so would she.

She'd thought about that a lot over the past four weeks, what she'd do if it came to this, but she hadn't made up her mind. Not until then. "If you want that paper to stay in the family, one of you will have to run it."

"But *Mama,*" they said in unison.

"I can't," Sharon said. "I'm up for a promotion, and I don't see how I can manage to convince the chancellor I'm serious about it if I have to take leave to learn how to run a newspaper."

Marge knew Sharon had more to lose than Drogan and Cassie. She looked at Cassie. "What about you? You can take your work to the office at *The Woodmore Times*, set up a drafting board, and—"

A look of terror streaked across Cassie's well-made up face. "Are you serious? Mama, you can't be. I'd lose prestige at Cutting Edge. You know that. When the cat's away, you know what happens to the mice. I'm hoping to be division head in a couple of years, but if I'm not there in person, they'll pass right over me."

"Don't look at me," Drogan said before Marge could pose the question. "My clients depend on my expertise. The training center would collapse without me, and everybody knows I'm the best head-hunter anywhere around. My business runs on my personal knowledge, experience, and expertise. No way!"

"I see. I know all about doing two or three jobs at once. After your father passed, I ran that paper, sewed your clothes, managed the house, and kept food in your mouths. I couldn't make excuses, either."

Cassie wrung her hands. "Mama, look—"

She interrupted her. "Believe me, I see plenty. Drogan, I recall you said Bill did such a great job for you the two months last summer while you and Imogene vacationed in Greece that you gave him a raise. Seems to me he can do that donkey work now. Except for your lectures, almost all of your business is over the Internet, so you shouldn't have any problem making the important decisions; you have a laptop computer and a cell phone."

Drogan looked first at Cassie and then at Sharon. "You can see my position, can't you? I'm head of my house, and I'm the one who has to make a living."

"No kidding," Cassie said in a voice punctuated with scorn. "That's the excuse my boss gave me when he promoted Norman Clark to a position that I was more qualified to fill." She mimicked her boss. "Norman has a wife and child, and he has to support his family." Her lips curled in an angry pout. "Put a sock on it, buster."

"Well, he was right," Drogan replied. "Count me out, Mama."

Marge was tempted to ask him what had happened to his famous charm but didn't. "Then I suppose I'll have to sell it."

"All right, Mama," Sharon said. "Tomorrow I'll tell the chancellor that I'm resigning as of the end of this semester. I'll try to run it."

Nothing that had happened in the past hour surprised Marge. She knew her children, and so she knew, had always known, that she could only count on Sharon. She was also aware that if Sharon ran the paper, Drogan and Cassie would pressure her for a regular accounting of costs and for their share of the profits. And just as horrifying to contemplate, they'd try to dictate the paper's policies. And neither of them would lift a finger to help her. She wouldn't stand for that.

"The one who runs the paper will own it. Sharon, the paper is yours, and I'll have it transferred to you legally as soon as I get hold of my lawyer."

"But Mama! You can't do that. It's part of our inheritance," Cassie said.

"I can do anything I want to. Your father left *The Woodmore Times* to me, and you can see the deed anytime you like. It's mine to do with as I please, and I'm giving it to Sharon. She had more to lose than either of you, but she wasn't willing to see someone outside the family take over her parents' life's work. Sharon, it's yours."

"Well, hell!" Drogan said. "The paper was supposed to cover part of my retirement."

"Humph," Cassie snorted. "Your retirement. Always your miserable retirement. That's all you think of. I suppose now you'll stop taking your wife on all those expensive vacations and save your money."

Sharon touched Cassie's arm. "I don't want this to cause problems between us."

Cassie whirled around, stormed toward the door, and stopped. "Spare me. After that half-ass excuse you put up about some kind of promotion, don't speak to me. I'll bet anything you and Mama had this planned all the time."

Sharon recoiled from Cassie's attack. "Look," she said in a strained voice. "You could have had it, but your job's too important. For five years, I've worked my behind off writing research papers, counseling students, and carrying extra teaching loads in order to get ahead. I have the chance now that most professors at that university would give their hair for. I don't like giving up my job and my status to work at something I don't know a thing about. So you lay off me."

Marge watched them as their true faces began to emerge. Drogan left without saying good-bye, but at least he hadn't glared at her with eyes of fire as Cassie had.

Sharon groped for the nearest chair and sat down. "Maybe you shouldn't have done that, Mama."

"What difference would it make if I hadn't? If I willed it to the three of you, you'd be forever fighting over every little thing, because the bottom line is Cassie and Drogan don't plan to put any effort into sustaining the paper. But you believe me, they'd fight the United States Army for every penny it makes. So it was you or Ross, and something tells me he wouldn't have accepted it, anyway. He'll teach you all you need to know, just as he taught me. I'll call him tomorrow."

"What about you, Mama? What will you do now?"

"Soon as I transfer the paper to you, I'm going to San Francisco."

Sharon's bottom lip dropped. "Are . . . are . . . Mama, are you all right?"

"No, child, I'm not, but I don't plan to act like it till I have to."

Three

Sharon left Marge that night with a troubled heart and a mind no less free of worry. Knowing that she needed a clear head, she fought back the anger that threatened to becloud her senses. Her muscles ached and her heart beat erratically as thoughts of her mother's still not fully defined illness, responsibility for her parents' life's work, and possibly ruptured relations with her siblings weighed upon her like murder on a guilty man's conscience. She stopped at the end of the short walkway leading from her mother's white Cape Cod house to the street, turned, and looked up at the place where she'd lived the first twenty-four years of her life. She couldn't recall any unhappiness in that house. Although it hardly seemed possible that she'd known only pleasure, warmth, and joy there, somehow that was all she remembered. The good things. And she'd known plenty of those.

She walked on down Russet Lane, her long shadow preceding her in the clear early-evening moonlight. "Hold your head up and keep your shoulders back," Mama always said to her five-foot-nine-inch-tall younger daughter. But on this night, her shoulders sagged, and her view as she walked with her head down was of the cracked pavement through which weeds asserted their right to grow, inciting in her an abnormal and uncomfortable belligerence. Didn't she also have the right to grow, to follow her own course? How could Cassie and Drogan be so selfish? Furor boiled up in her, but she beat it back. What was done was done.

At the end of the block, she reached her white Mercury Cougar, got in the sports car, and turned toward home. But somehow she didn't want to go home. She wanted—needed—company, someone who'd listen while she poured out her thoughts. That someone had always been Cassie, but her sister had looked at her with scathing regard and denounced her. Cassie was wrong, as she had been so many times in the past, but this time she wasn't going to beg Cassie to accept forgiveness. How many times had she done that when it was Cassie and not she who had trespassed? Cassie had no right to blame her for their mother's action. She didn't want the newspaper, but she didn't want to see her mother's heart broken, either.

Halfway into the intersection, with a red light facing her, she slammed her foot on the brakes. She loved her sister, and she would miss their daily telephone conversations, peppered with jokes, laughter, and tall tales. She had shared everything with Cassie, and maybe that hadn't been wise; no person, not even your sister, should be privy to the color of your insides. The light changed, and she drove on.

"It's time you kept your own counsel, girl," she admonished herself. "Your judgment is as good as Cassie's."

At home, in the small red-brick town house of which she was so proud, she didn't indulge in feeling either put upon or sorry for herself but heated a bowl of chili in the microwave oven, split a bagel, toasted it, and ate her dinner while she watched the evening news.

The phone rang. "Hello, Aunt Eloise. What's up? Mama all right?"

"She ain't no worse, if that's what you mean. But she in there talkin' 'bout goin' to San Francisco, and you know, I think she means it."

"You know any reason why she shouldn't go?" Sharon shoved aside the irritating thought that Eloise knew more about her mother's plans than her own child knew; Eloise and her mother were closer than some sisters. Now that was a thought.

"Well, if she so sick she can't work no more, she shouldn't be roaming round the country by herself."

Her heart pounded with such force that Sharon thought it would beat a hole in her chest. "Aunt Eloise, is there something Mama didn't tell us?"

"She told you she can't go back to the paper, and she's accepted that. What more do you need, honey? She a sick woman."

"I realize that." She said it softly, as if hearing the words from her own mouth made it worse. "But . . . well, I guess she ought to do whatever she feels like doing."

"Marge gon' do that anyhow, child."

Her short conversation with her godmother proved sobering, and she told herself to prepare for the inevitable. As always, she thought first to call Cassie and Drogan, but she discarded the idea. If she called them, who knew what kind of reception she'd get.

Sharon walked into her office at the Woodmore campus of State University, pushed aside the letters on her desk to make room for her briefcase, and sat down. An open window allowed gusts of cold air into the office, and she quickly closed it. Her right hand went to the telephone, but she withdrew it. She had to request an appointment with the chancellor, though she dreaded the finality of what she had to do.

A sudden urge to pitch the phone across the room gripped her, and she controlled it with a pounding of her fist on her desk. *Good little Sharon. You could always depend on her.* That was the way Cassie and Drogan—and maybe everybody else—saw her. Not that she hadn't played up to it; come to think of it, she had. But giving up all she had worked for was too much. Well, what was done was done, but *good little Sharon* was a thing of the past.

She flipped through her Rolodex for the chancellor's number, and her gaze fell upon her incoming box and a letter that bore the chancellor's return address. She sat down slowly, nearly missing the chair, and with unsteady fingers, opened the letter.

"Dear Dr. Hairston," she read, "I am pleased to inform you of your appointment as assistant dean of our School of Social Work. My hearty congratulations."

Damn! A week earlier, she would have danced for the joy of it, but now she only contemplated what might have been. It didn't surprise her that the chancellor agreed to see her at once. Apprised as to why she'd come, his apparent emotions vacillated from seeming discombobulation to suppressed anger, all of which she pretended not to perceive.

"How can you blithely disregard this opportunity? Every one of your colleagues would give anything for this recognition."

"It's not an easy choice, sir, and I don't make it blithely, as you put it, but if I stay here, *The Woodmore Times* will fold, and I can't allow that to happen. My parents worked too hard to make that paper what it is. I'm sorry."

His pursed lips bespoke his lack of sympathy for her decision. "Well, if you must go . . . I'm disappointed, as I'm sure you must be."

The man seemed forever trapped in the lofty heights at which he'd enthroned himself. What a kick she'd get out of telling him to lighten up! She smiled, at first forcing it and then more naturally, for she suddenly believed what she was about to say.

"It's easier to leave, sir, knowing that I've succeeded in what I tried to do here, to have come so far in this short period of five years."

"I wish you well," he said as he stood and extended his hand, effectively terminating the appointment.

As she walked across the campus to her car after teaching her eleven o'clock class, she knew she would miss her associates and that sense of belonging she'd earned with hard work.

"I just heard the news," Mildred Scott, her friend and a teacher in her department, said. "Congratulations. What this place needs is some young blood."

"Thanks, friend." Sharon liked everything about Mildred Scott except that dreadful, sweet perfume she wore. And she wore it as often as she wore her skin.

The wind shifted, taking the odor of that expensive Paris perfume in the opposite direction. Sharon breathed deeply and let herself enjoy the light moment. She hated not being able to tell her friend she intended to resign, but such announcements had to come from the chancellor's office. "Takes all kinds," she said, and headed for the offices of *The Woodmore Times.*

Sharon could count on one hand the number of times in the last couple of years that she'd been inside 761 Eighth Street West. She left the business of the paper to Mama, as did Cassie and Drogan. She walked through the lobby, and everything seemed so different. She didn't recognize the receptionist, and it shocked her that the man didn't know who she was. On the fourth and top floor, she went directly to Marge's office. Evidence of her mother's deteriorated health greeted her in the form of a partly evaporated cup of black coffee, half of a now-dried apple, and other indications that Marge, neatness personified, had been sick when she last left there.

She walked out into the newsroom, and since none of the reporters paid her any attention, she moved past them until she got to Ross. Immediately, she knew she should have called him. His bottom lip dropped, and his eyes widened, and whoever he was talking with on the phone received a shock when he hung up without an explanation or a word of good-bye, stood, and grabbed her hand.

"What's the matter with Marge?" The urgency in his voice startled her, and she realized the disruptiveness of her presence in the newsroom. Every reporter was standing up and staring at her.

"Mama's the same," she said as quickly as she could. "She hasn't called you?"

His gaze bore into her. "Why should Marge call me? I go by her house just about every day. Let's go up there and talk."

She waved to the reporters and editors as she walked with Ross to Marge's office. "What's happened?" Tremors in his voice spoke loudly of his anxiety, his fear for Marge's well-being.

"Please sit down, Uncle Ross. The doctor told Mama she can't work any longer, and when neither Cassie nor Drogan would agree to manage the paper, I said I would, and she gave the paper to me."

His sharp whistle split the air, and his fingers rubbed ruthlessly over the back of his head. "Damn! Hell and damn! I knew it." He jumped up and paced from one end of the office to the other. "I knew it when she left here early that day." He dropped himself back into the chair.

"Did they tell her what the problem is?"

"Kidneys, but she either won't say how bad it is or she doesn't know. She told her girlfriend she's going to San Francisco."

"What?" He screamed the word. Then, to her amazement, the air seemed to seep out of him like a deflating balloon. "She always said that was one place she wanted to go before she— Can she manage by herself?"

She shook her head. "She thinks she can, or maybe it hasn't occurred to her that she might need help." She frowned. This was getting worse by the second. What hadn't Mama told them? "I sure hope she doesn't need any help."

He nodded, absentmindedly, it seemed. "For Pete's sake, don't offer any. That would be a blow; she's always been able to do anything she wanted to." He rubbed his chin, staring at her as he did so. "You mean she *gave* the paper to you? Lock, stock, and barrel? Period?"

"She sure did. I expect she'll tell you about it. I know it's probably going to ruin my relationship with Cassie and Drogan."

He seemed deep in thought for a minute. "Don't get worked up anticipating that. Marge is wise. Always was. She knew exactly what she was doing."

"She said you'd teach me what I need to know. I have to finish up the semester, which ends with Christmas recess, but after that, I hope you'll show me what this is all about." She waved a hand toward the newsroom. "Mama said you would."

"Sure as shootin'. I taught her, and I'll teach you."

Sharon deposited the dried apple and coffee container in a wastebasket, got her briefcase, and left Ross in what had been her mother's office. Mama had been in Ross's life so long that she doubted he'd come to terms easily with the paper's future without her.

On her way out of the building, Sharon stopped at the receptionist's desk to introduce herself, felt a hand on her arm, and turned. "Why Reverend Ripple, what a surprise!"

"How are you, Sharon?" he said, his left incisor shinning blatantly in gold.

She avoided staring at the tooth, a homage to success that blazed against his black skin. Porcelain wasn't only cheaper; it looked a lot better. If she wasn't afraid of insulting half of the senior citizens on the northern end of Mountain Lane, she'd run a piece in the paper about front gold teeth.

"Fine, more or less, Reverend Ripple," she said as she focused on him. That was as close to the truth as she could get.

The reverend smiled, giving her another good look at his gold tooth. "I come every Thursday to give Marge the church's announcement for the Friday paper. If I didn't get it in, those holy parishioners of mine would probably forget about church on Sunday morning and head for the nearest shopping mall."

"Surely they wouldn't; we all need that spiritual renewal for the coming week."

"If that's the case, they must get it by osmosis while they're sitting up there nodding, half-asleep. One of these Sundays, right in the middle of the sermon, I'm going to say the country is under atomic attack and see how many of the people hear me." He grinned as if savoring a precious thought. "Bet you not a person will move."

To her mind, Reverend Ripple often seemed to sleep through his own sermon. "I know you're not serious. By the way, Mama isn't here. She's uh . . . not too well, which is why you've missed her from church."

"When people don't attend regularly, I don't know when to check on 'em."

"Ross will take your ad."

"With his hand out, yeah. Marge doesn't charge me. The man loves money, not that he throws a lot of in the direction of the church. I'll ask Marge to straighten him out."

"Drop by to see her when you get time."

"I'm going by soon as I leave here. God bless."

As Sharon walked to her car, the need to get away from everything, to unload, nearly overwhelmed her. She found herself driving along Parkway Street, which bordered Pine Tree Park, and seeing no one around, parked, got out, and walked along the edge. Squirrels played near the path, and hundreds of blackbirds obscured the limbs of the pine trees that served as their hosts. Signs of the approaching winter. She loved to watch squirrels and regarded birds of all kinds as her friends, but hunger pangs shortened her idyll, and she walked back to her car, albeit reluctantly.

"Why don't I want to go home?" she asked herself as darkness encroached, but admitting it didn't motivate her to go. Instead, she telephoned her mother, learned that Marge had several guests, including Eloise, and with nothing specific in mind, headed her car toward Winston-Salem.

After a so-so meal at Dunes Restaurant that did nothing for her spirit and not much more for her stomach, she wandered over to Tanglewood Park to watch the Holiday Light Show, a famous spectacle that lasted from mid-November to mid-January every year.

Lights in myriad shapes and colors blinked and twinkled from trees, posts, signs, and every place within sight. The pine trees swayed in the soft breeze, so that their lights danced merrily in an otherworldly fashion. She looked up at the sky where stars proclaimed their superiority, and the moon's radiance completed the night's majesty.

A loneliness such as she hadn't previously experienced washed over her, and she was tempted to leave. But she didn't. It was as if her feet cemented themselves to the earth. Only six-thirty and darkness already engulfed the park. Children dashed through the crowd, their balloons high above them and their parents trudging along behind them. She knew then why she stood there and wouldn't leave. She needed to be a part of something, of some *one*, even if that someone was represented by a crowd of anonymous people. She knew now that where her family was concerned, she had to stand on her own two feet. And she would.

"Spectacular, isn't it?"

She resisted the impulse to turn around and get a good look at the owner of that mellifluous masculine voice.

"Once the park is lighted, I come as often as I can," he said. "I wish I lived across the street from it and I could gaze at it from my window."

She made it a policy not to talk to strangers, especially strange men, but the lure of his voice was irresistible, enticing her finally to turn slightly in order to get a look at him. She wouldn't say she had an immediate feminine reaction to him, but even in the eerily lighted night, his strong masculine persona jumped out to her, and as she looked at him from the corners of her eyes, she knew she was in the presence of a strong man. Neither his direct, dark-eyed gaze, chiseled lips, square chin, towering height, nor broad shoulders drew her to him. It was the effect he communicated. That something that proclaimed *man* as God meant him to be.

She shook her head and pulled herself out of the trance. "It's almost mind-boggling," she said, though mostly to herself. She'd bet that display cost a fortune.

The rumble of his voice held a comforting, almost soothing resonance. "Much as I like all this, I can't help thinking how many hungry mouths the money spent on this electricity would feed."

She turned fully to face him then, for he had voiced her own thoughts. "What did you say?"

He repeated it, and she teetered between unease and a sense of well being at having encountered a kindred soul. "Much as I enjoy it, I think it's an indulgence that not even a city this size can afford," he said. "There're homeless people on these streets."

"Making regular trips here to enjoy it isn't sending that message to the city fathers; this crowd suggests a high rate of approval."

"I know, but I can't seem to stay away from here." He put his hands into his pants pockets and bowed slightly. "I enjoyed your company." He disappeared in the crowd.

"Guess I'd better get on home," she said to herself. "I never did *that* before." She walked quickly and purposefully away from the park, irritated at herself for having struck up a conversation with a strange man. And in a park, at that!

When her car wouldn't start, she glanced at the fuel gauge, let out a long breath, and slumped in the seat. For the first time since she began driving, she'd forgotten to check the gas level. Mama would always tell her to be sure she had her driver's license and a tankful of gas. Mama hadn't been there to tell her, and she'd acted like a child.

The pain of knowing they could no longer look to Mama was nearly unbearable. But she knew the futility of moaning over what couldn't be helped, so she took out her map of Winston-Salem and began looking for the nearest gas station. Nothing.

"Excuse me, please," she called to two men who strode past her car. "Where will I find a gas station?"

"What's the matter?" one of them asked as they walked back to her. *My Lord, this is too much,* she thought when she saw that the other one was the man with whom she'd spoken earlier.

"I'm out of gas." She'd done a silly thing, and she couldn't bluff her way out of it.

The taller of the two peered at her through the windshield. "I thought I recognized your voice," he said. "If this isn't the craziest thing! I'd just been wondering about you, and—" He stopped short as if he'd said more that he cared to. "I can get you a couple of gallons if you'll wait here."

His companion laughed. "How far do you think she'll get with no gas?"

He had an attractive grin, she decided. "Right. We'll be back in fifteen minutes or so."

The strange coincidence didn't sit well with her, and she'd have left if she'd had a choice. About fifteen minutes later, a car pulled up behind hers and parked. Immediately, she checked her windows to assure herself that she'd locked them, took her cell phone out of her briefcase, and placed it on the seat beside her in case she needed to call the police. Eyeing her rearview mirror, she recognized the two men who emerged from the Lincoln Town Car and let herself breathe.

She pushed the button to open the gas tank and watched while one of the men emptied a big yellow container of fluid into her car. She didn't trust the situation enough to get out and thank them, but she did roll down her window when the taller man came around to the driver's door.

"I'm sure you know that I thank you," she said. "How much was the gas?"

He studied her for a few seconds. "I don't think you'd be comfortable if I told you it's on me. I brought you four gallons."

"That's six dollars and forty-two cents."

"Glad we walked this way. You could have been stranded here indefinitely. The nearest filling station is at the intersection of Route 40 and Highway 421. You certainly couldn't walk that far." When she put the key in the ignition, he said, "I see from your license plate that you're from Woodmore. Maybe we'll run into each other sometime."

Coincidences with this man were stacking up and beginning to try her credulousness. "We may." *You couldn't be too careful, not even if the man had an intelligent face, a bedroom grin, and a voice that would soothe anything from a crying baby to an angry lion.*

"You live in Woodmore?" he persisted.

"All my life. I don't remember seeing you there."

"I live here in Winston-Salem, but my business interests take me to Woodmore a couple of times a week. I'm . . . with Scenic Gardens, the retirement village out past Pine Tree Park."

"I've read about it, and I've driven past there a few times. I understand it's drawing retirees from as far away as Denver."

"Some from Canada, for that matter. My name is Rafe McCall."

She had no choice but to tell him who she was. "Sharon Hairston."

He frowned, as if attempting to place the name. "I'm glad we met, Ms. Hairston. Get home safely."

"Thanks . . . for everything."

He stepped away from the car, and she started the engine and headed toward Route 40 on her way to Highway 52 and home.

How strange! She slapped her forehead with the palm of her left hand. Where was her mind? Rafe McCall could answer the questions she'd had about Scenic Gardens ever since ground was first broken and . . . *Was she crazy?* She'd forgotten all about the paper. Mama would have gotten an interview on the spot. The thought gave her pause. Mama had lived for the paper; it had filled her thoughts whenever she was awake. Now *she* was owner and publisher of *The Woodmore Times*, and she couldn't afford to forget that. She also wasn't going to tell Mama about that boo-boo. Her blunders, oversights, foul-ups, and mistakes would be her problems, and she'd take responsibility for them. If she was lucky, she wouldn't have too many opportunities for regret.

On Friday, the following day, she managed to leave school without encountering any of her colleagues. She didn't know what the chancellor told them or if indeed he had announced her resignation. Most of her coworkers would think she'd resigned because she didn't get the promotion to assistant dean, and those who knew she'd gotten the post would conclude that she wasn't rowing with both oars. So she didn't go to the cafeteria, library, or professors' lounge but to the offices of *The Woodmore Times.*

"How you doin', boss," Mack said when she met him in the hall on her way to Marge's office.

She had never loved Mack, and that greeting didn't made her like him any better. She stared at his long hair, half curly and half-wavy, legacies of his mixed parentage, and thought how much she'd enjoy whacking it off. Might as well set him straight once and for all. "Hello, Mack. Were you in a habit of addressing Mama as boss?"

His fingers plowed through the offending mane, and he frowned in a way that suggested he disapproved of her words. "I call her Marge."

She let a half-smile drift over her face, a smile that could fool you into thinking it was something that it wasn't. "That's what I thought, Mack. My name is Sharon."

She went in the office and closed the door. "Whew." Heaven forbid she should have to deal with a lot of attitude. And another thing. She'd have to stop thinking of Ross as "Uncle Ross," because he worked for her. Still, she couldn't make herself call and ask him to come to her, so she walked down to his cubicle—all of the reporters and editors worked in open, adjoining offices, low-level cubicles—and waited until he looked up from his writing and saw her standing there.

"Why didn't you call me? Just press number one on your phone. That's me."

"Thanks, but it didn't hurt me to walk down here."

When they reached her office, he closed the door. "If you want to succeed at this, you have to assert your authority. If you don't, you won't be able to control this place."

She sat down and motioned to him to do the same. "Thanks. Who's likely to be difficult?"

He laughed aloud and moved his fingers back and forth across his chin. "Every damned one of them."

She thought for a minute, laid back her shoulders, and narrowed her left eye. The thought of what she was about to say surprised her, but she said it with all the verve of a boss controlling a longshoreman "shape-up." "Ask them how they like their rattlesnake?"

Ross slapped his knees and laughed uncontrollably. When he regained his composure, he said, "Atta girl! If you're gonna sweat, for Pete's sake, don't let anybody see it. If this gang starts acting out, that's exactly what I'll ask 'em. You can count on it."

"I can't give the paper my full attention until school's over, but I can start learning some things."

"Right. We'll begin with the budget meeting—you Mack and me—when we decide the paper's content and layout. The biggest problem is what goes upper right on the front page and our contingencies for breaking news. It might be a good idea to bring in Josh from the plant downstairs. A couple of hours a day ought to do it for now. Reporters must have their copy in by four in the afternoon. No exceptions unless it's breaking news. Between one and four it's a madhouse."

On the way home, Sharon stopped at Just Right Cleaners to get her winter coats. Fall had eased into winter, and Thanksgiving hadn't even arrived.

"Sharon! What a coincidence. I decided I'd better get my coats out of storage, too. I nearly froze last night."

Sharon wondered not for the first time how Mildred Scott managed to keep a size-twelve figure and eat chocolates practically nonstop. Mildred bit into a piece of chocolate candy, chewed it a bit, and rolled her eyes skyward. Relishing it. "Hmm. Girl, this is good. How about stopping at Pinky's for some coffee. I've got to get warm."

She left Mildred an hour later, stunned by the woman's confession of loneliness for the affection of a man and her admission that her passion for chocolates was fired by the heat of her unappeased libido. She thought of her own loveless days and nights.

Alone later that evening, Sharon's thoughts lingered on her conversation with Mildred, of her single-minded pursuit of her own career at the expense of other interests, friendships, a love life. And now she was giving up all that she knew. Her dreams, the self she'd come to know and respect. And what did she have left? A chance to fall on her face unless she succeeded at a task for which she had no skills and in which she had no genuine interest. Nothing. She didn't have one thing or one person capable of making her burst with joy. It didn't take a nuclear scientist to put a name to the hole inside her. For what reason other than loneliness would she have entered into a conversation with a strange man? In a park. At night.

She leaned back on her sofa, sipped from a glass of zinfandel, and gave her thoughts free reign. A good-looking, personable, and intelligent man had pulled her into conversation, and it hadn't occurred to her to want more from him than impersonal words. Nor had she made an effort to prolong her time with him. She was so used to thinking with Mama's mind, of focusing on her career and achievements, that she'd lost sight of her own personal needs and interests. She'd wanted her mother to be proud of her, to respect and admire her. She released a harsh laugh. Mama loved Cassie and Drogan, too, and if she didn't admire and respect them, nobody knew it but her. She was damned if she'd give her life for somebody else's dream. She almost choked on the wine as she realized she'd just made up her mind about something. Something equally as important as *The Woodmore Times*. She'd run that paper, but she wouldn't let it take over her life.

With his right hand still on the keyboard of his laptop computer, Drogan answered the phone on the fifth ring. "Hairston speaking."

"Uh . . . hi. It's me. When can we meet?"

He'd told her not to call him at home, and he certainly couldn't call her, so . . . "I was thinking of going over to Winston-Salem day after tomorrow. We could—"

She interrupted him. "I can't do that." For some reason, her voice irritated him. "I'd be gone too long. And anyway, that's too far off. What about Danvers tomorrow about ten? I'm faking a dental appointment."

That didn't suit him, but it was better than nothing. He was beginning to wonder if sneaking around was worth what he got out of it. "Right," he said. "And don't call here, because she's the one who answers the phone."

"Where's she now?"

Resentment flared up in him. Imogene's whereabouts wasn't her business. "She and her girlfriend went shopping," he said, hiding his annoyance to guarantee him her favors. "See you tomorrow morning."

"Right. And you be there on time. You hear?"

He hung up, propped his elbows on his desk, and cupped his chin with both hands. He loved Imogene and wouldn't think of exchanging her for Irene or any other woman, but Imogene had gotten so stingy with sex that he had to go elsewhere for his needs. Once he'd done it, he'd kept it up. Dropping Irene wasn't child's play; the woman was pure fire in bed.

He ate lunch, a cold chicken sandwich and a glass of milk, packed up his laptop and papers, and drove to his office. He ought to go see Mama, but what the hell! He didn't feel like it. The phone rang as he opened the office door.

"Hello."

"Hi. Where were you? I called you at home."

"I was between there and here. Where are *you*, Imogene?"

"I'm in Winston-Salem, but Keisha wants to go over to Danvers, and we don't know which highway to take from here."

Damn! Suppose he'd arranged to see Irene there that afternoon. He had to stop playing so loose like that, risking his marriage. "What's in Danvers that you can't find here or in Winston-Salem?"

She hesitated so long that he wondered if she'd hung up. "Keisha wants a studio photograph, and she heard there's a good photographer over there who's cheap."

He plowed his fingers through his hair. "I don't care what Keisha wants. I'd like you to spend more time at home."

"I know, and I will. Which highway do we take?"

He stared at the phone, wondering if it was useless to reason with her. Couldn't she see that what they had together was slipping away from them? Oh, what the hell!

"Highway 52. See you later." He hung up without waiting for her reply.

$\mathcal{F}our$

Marge rolled up the last of the six pairs of panty hose she planned to take with her to San Francisco and tucked them into the bag that contained her lingerie. As she had done so many times in her sixty-one years, she ignored the water that accumulated in her eyes.

"If you ask me, this whole idea is plain crazy, Marge."

She avoided eye contact with Eloise; if she looked at her, she'd lose composure. "I always wanted to go, and I'm going."

Eloise spoke to her in soft, motherly tones, her voice dark with concern. "Child, ain't nobody sightseeing this time of year."

"Maybe nobody's got my problem, either, which is probably their reason for not sightseeing. No point in trying to dissuade me."

Eloise pulled the green plaid skirt down to cover her knees and leaned forward as if to emphasize the urgency that she felt. "Couldn't you wait till spring when it's warm . . . and . . . and not so dreary?"

And what if she wasn't around when spring came? "I don't know that it's dreary in San Francisco, and neither do you. Don't all the travel ads talk about sunny California? Anyhow, if it's dreary, it's dreary." She walked over to the window, looked out, and spoke with her back to her friend. "If you want to be helpful, Eloise, please stop imagining things. And don't nag."

"All right. You know it best."

"And you know I hate sarcasm." She went to the closet to get her gray cardigan sweater, and her gaze caught an old leather jacket of Ed's that she hadn't had the heart to give away. A piece of her past that had hung in that closet for over twenty-five years. She folded the jacket and put it in a shopping bag, not giving her action or its implications a second thought.

"One of the folks at the senior center might make some use of this," she said, handing the bag to Eloise. A bag that contained the last personal item that belonged to her late husband. Two months earlier, she wouldn't have considered doing that. However, she'd done it, and without even a twinge of emotion.

Eloise stared into the shopping bag, her lips quivering and her face lined in a frown. "You sure you ain't gonna be sorry? If you kept it this long, why you giving it away now?"

Marge drew up her shoulder in a quick, dismissive shrug, making light of what she knew was a serious question. "I should have given it away long ago. A lot of people could use a good warm jacket."

Eloise shook her head slowly but didn't voice her concern. "I'd best be getting over to the senior center. Old man Moody will be happy to get this." She pointed to the shopping bag. "He needs it, too. Come in there yesterday practically threadbare. By the way, when you see Drogan and Cassie?"

Marge pushed the cranberry juice Eloise brought her to the other side of the table. She was sick of cranberry juice, and having to drink a gallon and a half of water a day was getting next to her. "I haven't seen either one of them since I told them I couldn't go back to work."

Eloise stared at her. "You kiddin'?"

"Wish I was."

Marge watched her leave, the dearest friend she'd ever had. Maybe she ought to tell Eloise of her premonitions, but she couldn't bring herself to do it. She answered the phone on the fourth ring after contemplating ignoring it.

"Marge speaking." She hadn't meant to speak sharply, and the long silence told her the caller hadn't appreciated it. Finally, he spoke, and she listened for a second before interrupting him. "I appreciate that, Ross, but you don't have to assume responsibility for me. I'm doing fine."

"Great. In that case, meet me for lunch at Pinky's. Twelve-thirty."

"What if I have other plans?"

"What other—Listen, Marge, you're not acting like yourself. You love eating at Pinky's. Come on. Meet you at twelve-thirty."

"Who'll run the paper while you're hanging out with me?"

"Same ones who always ran it when you and I went to lunch. See you later."

"Now, look—" She stared at the receiver. Ross had hung up.

Her chest swelled with impatience. All of a sudden, everybody and his aunt felt qualified to tell her what to do. She bit back an expletive. First Eloise and now Ross wanted to prove to her that she shouldn't go to San Francisco. Tough! She didn't intend to let them or anybody else stop her. And another thing . . . She had a few words for Cassie and Drogan, especially Cassie, who hadn't yet learned how to forgive what she regarded as an injustice or a transgression. She dialed Cassie's office phone number.

"Ms. Hairston-Shepherd speaking."

"Cassie, this is Mama. I'm calling to tell you I'm going to San Francisco . . . in case you're interested."

"In case I'm—Mama, what's come over you? San Francisco's on the other side of the continent."

Marge pulled a chair closer to the telephone table and sat down. "I know where it is, but I don't know why you'd be concerned. I haven't heard a word from you since you flitted out of here the other night."

"That was a big pill you asked me to swallow. Like you don't have but one child." Trust Cassie to go on the attack. She always put her accuser on the defensive, and it didn't matter whether she was guilty.

"You wanted something for nothing. The paper sent you and Drogan through college. Sharon went through school on fellowships that she earned. The paper paid the down payments on your house and Drogan's house, and neither of you mentioned paying back. Sharon saved her money and was able to close the deal on her house."

She heard Cassie suck her teeth in disgust, and it wasn't the first time she'd wondered about her elder daughter's conscience. "Since when does a child have to repay her mother?"

"When she borrows something from her." The futility of the discussion pressed on her like hardened concrete. She expelled a long, deep breath. "Of the three of you, Sharon had the most to lose. You and Drogan work for yourselves, and you could have continued doing that while you managed the paper. But Sharon has resigned as assistant dean, given up the career she worked so hard for in order to—"

"What are you talking about?" Cassie shrieked. "Sharon was never a dean."

"She resigned the same day she got the promotion. Would you have done that? Never. You're old enough to stop pouting whenever something happens that you don't like, and I wish— Honey, if you could just stop hiding your insecurity behind that crust of superiority.

What I'm asking, Cassie, is that you try to be more gentle. I'll call you before I leave." She said good-bye to Cassie and hung up. The conversation left her dissatisfied, and she didn't feel like going through that with Drogan. She'd deal with him later.

Twelve-thirty. After showering and applying Vaseline Intensive Care liberally on every part of her that she could reach, she put on her best ecru underwear and a robe, got out her old-fashioned curling irons, and went into the kitchen. Marge didn't believe in paying anybody to do for her what she could do for herself. And she could certainly wash, straighten, curl, and set her own hair. After all, it was hers, and she knew more about it than anybody else. She didn't consider herself stingy, but she didn't waste money, either, and it didn't make sense to buy electric curlers when the curling irons you'd had for years were still serviceable and you had a gas stove and matches.

She hadn't dolled up in years. Being sick was nothing to be thankful for, but it *had* caused her to lose some of her surplus behind, as she thought of it, and she could get in that red dress Cassie gave her for her fiftieth birthday.

"I look pretty good," she said to herself as she gazed into the mirror. "Won't Ross be surprised."

And surprised he was. The heads of Pinky's diners snapped around at the sound of Ross's whistle. He took his time sitting down. "What's the meaning of this?" His head moved from side to side, seemingly of its own volition, like someone denying a disturbing apparition.

She feigned ignorance about what his question implied, though she didn't expect him to let it pass. Ross was too clever a man. Still, she laced her voice with innocence and affected a breezy air.

"Sorry. I know ladies wear hats to lunch—or they did when people still called us ladies—but I don't own one."

Ross popped his fingers and rolled his eyes toward the ceiling. "Cut the crap, Marge. You're up to something."

If she was, it was her business. "Everybody's telling me what to do. I'm doing as I please."

He looked into the distance, and she imagined his mental clock hard at work. After a few minutes, he stunned her with "I'd like to go to San Francisco with you. I've never been there."

She gasped aloud. Eloise and Cassie told her outright not to go, but he was going to control her by tagging along. "What would . . . ?"

"Don't finish it." He frowned and felt the breast pocket of his jacket for the cigarettes he gave up nearly a dozen years previously. "What do you care what anybody thinks? You and I know it won't be a tryst. Wouldn't you like to have company? At least you wouldn't have to talk to me if you didn't feel like it."

She surveyed him with narrowed eyes, partly annoyed and partly touched by his gesture. "Like the rest of them, you don't think I can make it alone."

"So now you're a mind reader. Knowing you, I figure you'll do whatever you set yourself to do."

"Why?"

"I've got my reasons."

And pressing him wouldn't do her a bit of good. She couldn't think of a more agreeable traveling companion. Still . . . "What about the paper? Who'd take care of it while you're gone. Sharon isn't ready to deal with it."

"Who'd do it if I got sick? They know their jobs. How long you planning to stay?"

"A week, I guess." She leaned back in the chair and studied the menu, though she knew it from memory.

Ross watched her, his gray eyes sharp for his sixty years, as he tried to discern from her demeanor what she wouldn't tell him. But his quiet, reflective manner didn't fool Marge. From hooded eyes, she observed his serious mien. A slender man about three inches taller than her own five feet six, with a prominent hooked nose, graying hair, thick black eyebrows, and fair skin, Ross wasn't any more black than he was white. She wondered about his lineage, and not for the first time. She knew from his famous half-grin, the signal to expect his mulelike stubbornness, that he was going to press her about her plans.

"So when do we leave?"

The more she thought of the idea, the more agreeable it became, but she wasn't about to let him think she'd jump at the chance to take a trip with him.

"I'll uh . . . I'll think about it."

They gave their orders to the waitress, and she worked hard at hiding the tiredness that overcame her. She had to admit that having Ross along wouldn't be a bad thing.

"Didn't you ever think of marrying?" she blurted out.

His fingers brushed over his thinning gray hair. "You could say I *did* marry. I've been as faithful to the paper as any man ever was to a woman. For the last thirty-four years, *The Woodmore Times* has practically consumed me."

She nodded, remembering the early days when she, Ross, and Ed worked twelve and often many more hours a day to keep the paper going. "I know. If it hadn't been for you, we'd have gone under. You think Sharon will make a good manager? She's giving up so much. I'm anxious for her."

"I wouldn't worry about it, Marge. Sharon's tender, but she's strong enough to do whatever she wants to do. I'm not sure about Drogan and Cassie."

"Neither am I. They're interested in short-term gains, and they're selfish. Drogan less than Cassie. I worry about her. She's substituting that job of hers for something vital."

Ross popped his fingers again, looked around for a waitress, and beckoned her. "This is lunch, not dinner. So would you tell the chef we've only got an hour."

"Yes, sir."

"The trouble with Cassie," he said, turning back to Marge, "is she's so damned superficial. I never know which Cassie I'm talking to."

The waitress brought their meal, and they ate silently for a few minutes. Marge hadn't thought Ross possessed such insight about her children. She'd have to give that a lot of thought; understanding was a result of caring.

"She was always full of make-believe, but her primness is something new. I wonder how Kix handles it."

Ross shrugged. "Good question. You know, I used to think Drogan would be good for the paper."

"Workwise, yes, provided he didn't alienate the staff with his doggedness. But his editorial policy would be too avant-garde. He thinks people ought to do whatever they please as long as they don't hurt anybody but themselves. And he can wade into a person. Drogan isn't what he seems."

A laugh bubbled up in his throat, overlaying the gruffness of his voice. "He can hit you all right, and he coats every stab with that charm of his. You made the wise choice when you gave the paper to Sharon."

Ross drove her home in his old white Cadillac, and less than ten minutes after she got inside, Drogan called.

"Yes, I'm going to San Francisco," she said in response to his question.

"Come on, now, Mama. When Cassie told me that, I didn't want to believe her. Where'd this notion come from? If you're too sick to work, you're too sick to go traipsing across the country by yourself."

"Thanks for letting me know you care." Drogan hated sarcasm from anybody but himself. Too bad; she figured he deserved it. "Why do you think I'm going alone?"

"You're taking Eloise?" The tone of his voice bespoke his distaste for the idea. "If you do, you'll have to pay her way."

She breathed a tired sigh. "And I would, too, but she didn't suggest going with me. I'll let you know when I'm leaving."

Had concentration on her work all those years blinded her to her children's shortcomings? How could Drogan and Cassie have forgotten that Eloise fed and clothed them when their own mother hadn't possessed the means?

He seemed unaware that her last remark was tinged with frostiness. "Yeah. I guess you *would* pay her way. Has the princess taken over the paper?"

Marge banged her fist on the table. What had happened to her warm, loving family? "I'm not going to wrestle with you over that. I asked you to take over the paper, and you refused. It's a closed subject."

"You're up to something, and I'm going to find out what it is. *California, for Pete's sake!*"

She hung up and for a long time leaned against the desk. Strained relations with her two older children didn't sit well with her. She had hoped shame would force them to yield, but it hadn't. When she returned from San Francisco, she'd try to do something about it.

"Marge and I had lunch at Pinky's today," Ross told Sharon when she walked into the newsroom.

Her lower lip dropped, and her briefcase slid from her hand to the floor. "How? What happened?"

Ross put the empty pipe to his lips—for comfort, he usually explained to anyone who asked. "I invited her to lunch, and she came. Looked like a million dollars, too."

"You don't know how glad I am to hear that. I wish she'd come back to work."

Suddenly, the computer seemed to take on magnetlike powers, for he lowered his gaze and fixed his attention on it. When she repeated her wish, he took an imaginary puff of his pipe and continued to stare at the computer. "Not a chance," he said at last. "So don't let your mind dwell on it. By the way, a guy named McCall phoned here this morning and asked me how he could get in touch with you."

Why would her stomach roll like that—as if she were suspended in the air? She let herself breathe, but she avoided looking into Ross's all-seeing, all-knowing gaze.

"What did you tell him?"

"Told him I'd give you his number." He handed her a Post-It note. "Who is he?"

Remembering that she shouldn't treat him as Uncle Ross, to whom she told all of her business, she allowed herself a shrug of nonchalance. "He's somehow involved with Scenic Gardens."

Ross sat forward, all business. "We tried to get a lead on whoever's backing that development. Think you can interview him?"

Her stomach settled. Maybe he hadn't phoned because he wanted to see her but for business reasons. "I'll give him a call. Would you rather K.C. interview him?"

Ross pounded his right fist in his left palm and gave her a stern look. "You don't ask me such questions, Sharon. Around here you *tell* people what to do. If you want K.C. to do it, say so. If you'd rather write the story yourself, you don't have to ask a soul."

"Oh, no! As editor in chief, you're responsible for assignments. If I want to do a job, I'll run it past you."

He grinned. "That's the ticket. Whatever you say goes."

She went to Marge's office and opened the windows wide, releasing the stagnant odor of nonuse. Then she sat down and telephoned Rafe McCall.

"McCall." His voice, deep and mellifluous, yet authoratative and commanding, sent a strong message to her, one that reminded her of her feminine self.

"*Yes!*" This time it was an order, and she quickly checked herself. "Mr. McCall, this is Sharon Hairston. You called me?"

"Yes, I did. No one named Hairston is listed in the telephone directory, and I'd begun to think you were married and had given me your maiden name."

She wasn't about to bite that one. "Then how did you find me?"

"Cabdrivers know just about everything about the people in a town this size. After a week of disappointing searches, I flagged one and asked him if he knew any Hairstons."

So he hadn't called for business reasons. "What's on your mind?" She wanted to kick herself; Cassie would never ask a man such a question, but she didn't have her sister's skill at dealing with men.

"I see you go dagger straight to the point. I haven't managed to stop thinking about you. What about dinner tonight?"

The word *no* sat on the tip of her tongue, but she remembered Mildred Scott's 365 nights alone each year. "Where would we meet?"

A short silence. "At your home, if you don't mind. I'll call for you at six-thirty. What's your address?"

She checked herself as she was about to give him her mother's address and gave him her own instead. "Two fourteen Butler Street."

"I thought we'd go over to Winston-Salem, if it's all right with you. Shaffner House Restaurant serves great food. I'll get a reservation for seven-thirty, unless you prefer eating early."

So he was thoughtful. So far, so good. "Seven-thirty's fine."

"Then I'll be at your place at six-thirty. I'm looking forward to seeing you."

Nothing else. No small talk. No cunning seduction. What an intriguing man! Seconds after she hung up, Ross knocked and walked in.

"Anything interesting?"

Embarrassed that she hadn't thought about the interview with Rafe, she gulped. "To tell the truth, I didn't think about the interview. He wanted to have dinner."

Ross's left eyebrow shot up, and he fingered his chin, a habit she realized she'd do well to understand. His chin appeared to represent to him the most important part of his face. She'd seen him stroke it in at least three different ways—up and down, across, and in circles—and she wondered how he'd stroke it if he was angry. He left with a bemused expression on his face.

Half an hour later, she heard the pounding of a hammer and the buzz of an electric drill, stepped out of her office, and looked around.

"You like it, miss? Super, if I do say so myself," the workman said.

He stepped back to look at what he'd done, and she saw beside the door a brass plate on which was engraved: SHARON HAIRSTON, PUBLISHER.

Her head snapped around, and she stared at the man. "Who on earth—?"

"Mr. Ingersol ordered it."

Just like Ross to do that and end the pretense that it was Mama's office. As the workman congratulated her, she realized at last that she had taken her mother's place.

"Thanks . . . I . . . Thanks."

"You like it?"

She hadn't seen Ross walk up. "I . . . Yes. I guess so," she told him.

As if he understood the turbulence of her mind and the sorrow in her heart, Ross touched her shoulder in what she knew was a gesture of support.

"You'll get used to it, and don't forget you're making your mother proud."

"Get used to it? I wonder." She started back into her office, but he stopped her.

"I'm supposed to give you this."

She took the legal-size envelope that Ross handed her, went into what was now her office, and closed the door. Inside, she examined the notarized deed to *The Woodmore Times* that made her its legal owner in exchange for one hundred dollars. A note from Marge explained that the small payment was intended to prevent her siblings from winning an ownership suit against her. She studied the documents, wrote her mother a check for that amount, and mailed it on her way home.

There was no getting around it or over it now. She owned *The Woodmore Times* and the Woodmore Press, and nobody had to tell her she'd embarked on a new career, that she'd changed the course of her life. As she walked toward her car, store windows mirrored her silhouette. Flat-heel shoes, hair bouncing untamed around her shoulders, coat midway between her knees and ankles. She'd never paid attention to fashion, but . . .

Impulsively, she walked into Bessie's Beauty Salon. "I'd like a decent haircut. Somewhere just below my ears."

"You bet, Miss Sharon. You just sit right down."

When she left, her permed hair curled downward in back and swung forward beneath her chin in a fashionable cut favored by the New York models. Anybody would think Bessie had been waiting for a chance to make her over. The woman had thinned and shaped her eyebrows, elongated and blackened her eyelashes, and dusted her face with blushing tones of powder. She gazed at herself in the mirror of a store front. Who was this woman?

"Oh, what the heck!" Sharon said as her steps slowed in front of Clara's Hollywood Boutique. Resolute, and emboldened by the effect of Bessie's wizardry, she squared her shoulders and walked in. At five-twenty, she ran into her house and spread the contents of her packages on the bed. Later, dressed as a modern, fashionable woman, she bit the flesh of her cheek when she looked at the three-inch heels on the black suede shoes she'd acquired during her shopping spree, eased her sheer-stockinged feet into them, and stood up. Hmm. Not bad, and great for the shape of her legs. Minutes later, the peal of her doorbell sent jitters racing through her. Tripping down the stairs in those heels wasn't as difficult as she'd expected. She opened the door, and the expression on Rafe McCall's face, the glint in his eyes, told her that everything she'd done since leaving the paper at two-thirty was more than worth it.

"I'd whistle if I wasn't sure you'd knock me down a peg for it."

He wasn't the only one who felt like whistling. Feeling friskier than she'd ever dreamed of being, she looked at him from beneath slightly lowered lashes and said, "Go ahead and be yourself. I like to know who I'm dealing with."

She'd hung her coat in the closet by the door, making certain that he wouldn't have to come any farther into the house than the foyer. After all, she didn't know the man. He helped her into the coat and stepped back to let her pass. So far so good.

As he steered the big Lincoln Town Car away from the curb, he responded to her quip. "I make it a point to know who I'm dealing with, whether it's an adversary or a friend, and I'm not sure I pegged you right."

Sharon settled down beside him in the butter-soft leather seat, folded her arms, and mused over his words. "Did you overlook something?"

He glanced over his left shoulder, made a U-turn, and headed for the Market Street underpass. "I don't think so. You added something."

If he spoke his mind, she'd do the same. "And that bothers you?"

"Not in the least." He pushed a few buttons, and strains of Louis Armstrong's "Mack the Knife" floated over them. "I like both of you."

So he had a sense of humor. She liked that, and she let a smile play around her lips as her mind focused on his barely veiled accusation.

"So do I." And she realized she meant it, though the woman she appeared to be would take some getting used to. She hadn't cultivated her feminine self as thoroughly as she probably should have, but if the look Rafe McCall gave her when she opened her door earlier was an indication of what she'd get by reforming, reform she would. She liked Shaffner Restaurant, but his confident air when they walked through it and seated themselves impressed her even more.

"What would you like to drink?"

"Tonic with a twist of lime." At his inquiring expression, she explained, "I'm not much of a drinker, and I certainly wouldn't drink alone."

He leaned back and studied her with such thoroughness that she all but squirmed under the intense scrutiny, even as the scent of roasting turkey, herbs, and buttermilk biscuits—wafting in from the kitchen—comforted her.

After a minute, he leaned forward with an air of urgency. "What makes you think I won't drink?"

"Because you look like too sensible a man to drink and drive."

He appeared to digest that. "The cabbie told me your family owns *The Woodmore Times*. That so?"

"Not exactly. *I'm* owner and publisher." At his raised eyebrow, she told him how that came about and asked him what he did at Scenic Gardens.

"I own it until I sell all of the co-op units."

She wasn't sure she liked that. "Does ownership of that housing development have anything to do with your inviting me to dinner?"

He glared at her, unmistakably annoyed, then quickly changed his facial expression. "If you own that paper," he said, his words slow and deliberate, "you must have known my connection to Scenic Gardens. I could ask if that had anything to do with your accepting my invitation."

She bristled. "How could you think that . . ." Her voice drifted off as she followed his gaze. He stood as two tall women of questionable ethnicity approached, obviously twins, beautiful and fashionably dressed.

"I didn't even hope to see you here in Winston-Salem," one of them said.

Sharon looked from Rafe to the women and back, saw nothing personal in his face, leaned back in her chair, and waited.

He gestured to her. "Sharon Hairston, these are two of my clients. They own a unit in my Asheville homes. She greeted them and enjoyed the fact that he didn't remember their names. The women looked at her, and the one who spoke to Rafe seemed to size up the competition. After a few minutes of what was clearly empty, hatched-up conversation, one said, "See you later, Rafe," and they walked on to a table in the back of the restaurant. The word *bitchy* flashed through her mind.

"Didn't you remember their names?" she asked him.

"Actually, I did, but I decided not to let them know it."

She'd have to think about that. Later, as they walked out of the restaurant, he asked her, "What's your pleasure?"

"I wouldn't mind a quiet boat ride."

"What? Did you say 'boat ride'?"

She couldn't imagine where the idea came from. "Yes, I did."

"Give me a rain check for that. Anything that's a possibility right now?"

"I enjoyed dinner with you, but I'd better get on home. I have to get up early."

His face clouded with a quick grimace, and she knew he wasn't pleased. His mocking gesture verified it when he bowed from the waist in acquiescence. At least he's honest, she thought.

"You're disappointed?"

"I'd hoped you might want to take in some jazz or check out one of the night festivals, make an evening of it, but . . ." He let it hang. "As you wish."

She would have loved to hear live jazz, but she'd told him she had to get up early, and she'd stick to it.

As he sped through the moonless night, she wondered if he'd kiss her and whether she'd enjoy it if he did. He walked with her to her front door and stood there until she opened it. Then, with his hands in the pockets of his trousers, he gazed down at her until she feared her nerves would rearrange themselves in her body."

"I want to see you again, Sharon. When? And please don't put it too far in the future."

"This weekend?"

Like the sudden piercing of moonlight through dark clouds, his smile quickened something within her. "Good. How about Saturday morning. We'll make a day of it. If it's cold, we can do museums. If it's warm enough, we can enjoy the outdoors."

"Either one is fine with me. This was . . . Well, it was super. Night." She turned to go inside, but his big hands cupped her shoulders.

"I enjoyed this time with you. See you Saturday morning." A light, quick brush of the backs of his fingers beneath her chin and he dashed toward his car.

He must have felt *something*, she told herself, or he wouldn't have caressed her. Maybe he wanted more. As for herself, she wasn't sure. She liked all that she saw of him, but he'd stirred up urges in her that she didn't feel like dealing with right then. On the other hand, the man excited her, and she wanted to know what was behind it.

Rafe McCall hadn't wanted any more; if he had, he'd have let her know it. Silent suffering wasn't his style. In due course, he'd find out where this second, glamorous Sharon Hairston came from and whether she was a permanent fixture in the life of the woman who didn't remember to put gas in her car.

Cassie worked until eight o'clock that evening and rushed home to get a bath before Kix got there around nine-thirty. His new waiter lived nearby and drove him to and from work, easing her guilt about the times he'd had to use public transportation. Although she kept their car, she worked only seven blocks from their home, compared to the fifteen miles he traveled. They didn't have much time together, and though she loved him, that suited her. She didn't much like spending a lot of time on her back. In fact, she wished somebody would tell her what the fuss over sex was all about.

Kix usually brought home their supper, so she didn't have to cook. She indulged in a long bubble bath, put on a pink silk jumpsuit, fastened her hair up in a French knot, set the table, and sat down to read.

She raced to the door when she heard him put the key in the lock and greeted him with a quick kiss on the mouth. He dropped the bag of food on the floor, pulled her to him, and kissed her, but she knew that if she parted her lips, he'd have her in bed in minutes, the food would be cold, and she'd be furious.

He picked up the bag of food and headed for the kitchen. "How'd it go today?"

She followed him and leaned against the doorjamb. "Great. Just great. We got a contract to design a logo and all the paper products for Wellingford Industries. I'm definitely asking for a raise."

"And you deserve one. How about us spending Monday in Asheville. It's fantastic this time of year. Trees look like somebody painted them. Every earth color you can imagine. We'll spend the day doing whatever you like. What do you say?"

She tried not to frown. That definitely wasn't what she wanted to hear. "Kix, I don't think I can. I've got so much to do that—"

"When do you think you'll have time for me?" He braced his left hand on the wall just above her head but didn't touch her. "Next year? Or maybe the year after?" It hadn't escaped him that she didn't ask how his day went. He narrowed his eyes. "We can be together one day a week, but in the last month you couldn't get one day out of seven away from that office."

She wasn't accustomed to seeing him in a threatening stance; disconcerted, she looked down at her feet. "You don't understand."

He sucked air through his teeth, got the food, brushed past her, and put it on the table. "No, Cassie. I don't understand. But one day I will, and then it may be too late for you to correct the conclusions I've reached. Let's eat."

They cleaned the kitchen together, and she wondered at his silence, though it occurred to her that he usually didn't talk much.

"I think I'll turn in," he called down half an hour later, still dripping from his shower. "Coming?"

Her fingernails scored her palms as she balled her hands into tight fists. "I thought I'd read for a while," she called up to him, and hastily picked up the biography of Frederick Douglas that he'd left on the coffee table.

"Humor me, Cassie."

Her head snapped around. How long had he been standing there?

"What do you think marriage is?" he asked. "A chance for grown-up girls to play house?"

She grabbed her head with both hands. "Kix, please. I need to relax. I . . ."

"Oh, no," he said, slouching against the wall. "When girls play house, they have dolls. But not you. Did you ever play with dolls?"

Still holding her head, she closed her eyes. "Please. You're giving me a headache."

"Sure. If I even hint about you having a baby, you freak out. Now, let me tell you something. You're thirty-two, already past the best ages for having children and getting too old to have your first child. When are you planning to start our family? When you're fifty? Everybody has options in this life, Cassie, and that includes you and me. Sleep well."

She jumped up from the sofa, ran after him, and grabbed his arm. "What does everybody want from me? I have to work to get ahead, because I'm not taking a backseat to Sharon. She's got the paper, and I have to make a name for myself. I can't do that and stay pregnant."

His harsh laugh and steely eyes as he stared down at her gave her a tense moment. Kix had never acted that way. But she knew he wouldn't touch her, that he admired her. He looked up to her.

"You'd better straighten out your head. You had a shot at owning that paper, and you didn't take it. I don't want to hear about it. You give me a date when you're ready to start our family." He headed up the stairs, stopped, and added, "And be here Monday evenings when I'm off."

Her hands went to her hips in defiance, but he didn't see the gesture, and she could only stare at his back. Damn him! She'd do as she pleased, and he wouldn't do a thing about it.

Saturday morning, when Sharon answered her front door, a sense of relief shot through Rafe as he saw a return of the girl who first attracted him. The thinker whose social consciousness matched his own, whose fine brown skin was flawless without makeup, and whose skirt covered her knees. Not that he minded being with a woman who made other men jealous of him; he certainly did not. But the prospect of having a woman companion who was his soul mate, solidly on his wave length—as he'd thought Sharon might be—gave him a Colorado high.

They hiked and rode horseback in Pine Tree Park, and shortly after noon, he made a fire beside Wade Lake and roasted corn, red potatoes, and clams while they warmed themselves. They sat in silence beside the fire, eating the food he cooked, drinking the coffee he'd boiled, and looking at each other. Nine hours, and he wasn't ready to leave her.

"I could do this again tomorrow," he told her when he took her home.

"Me, too, but I'd better see about my mother. She's not too well, and I usually visit her every day."

"I'm sorry. She has my good wishes. May I call you tomorrow?" He gazed into her eyes, sending her the message that he'd call until she answered. "Hope I didn't wear you out today."

Her smile eased over her face. A face he could get used to. "I had a wonderful time."

His eyes widened, and he couldn't have moved if he'd tried as she reached up, brushed his cheek with her hand, and casually strolled into the house.

What the hell! He let the back of his hand graze the spot where her fingers touched him. Damn! He wanted to go after her, but prudence decreed that he keep his hands off that doorbell. Talking about a bag of surprises! He didn't know how he could stand the wait until he saw her again.

After church Sunday, the next day, Sharon headed straight for Marge's house, as she usually did when leaving the service, though in brighter times she went for her mother's fresh-baked buttermilk biscuits, stuffed pork chops with gravy, candied yams, and collards. The same things that drew the Reverend Ripple, who arrived soon after she did.

With his fingers on Marge's forehead, he said a short prayer. "I'm not about to preach another sermon, Marge. My throat's already dry from pouring precious words on deaf ears."

Marge propped her hands on her hips, lay her head to one side, and challenged him. "Are you saying preaching to me is a waste of time?"

The reverend sat down and draped his right foot over his left one. "Waste of time and words, too. You've been ignoring what I say for years. Did Sister Eloise bring over any of her cheese biscuits?"

"Sorry. She went to the senior center. I don't expect I'll see her before around five."

"Sure would appreciate a glass of water, Sharon." He looked at Marge. "Is Sister Eloise doing good or trying to hook up with one of those old fellows?" His laughter rang out, a man who enjoyed his own jokes. "Tell her I said half of some old man's social security won't compensate for her nightly disappointments. Least I don't think so."

When Marge leaned back on the chaise longue and grinned, Sharon expected a good round of irreverence, and her mother didn't disappoint her.

"I guess you know whereof you speak, Reverend Ripple. Still, I wouldn't broadcast it if I were you."

Gilford Ripple let go a roar of laughter. "I hope not to be accused of that for the next thirty years. Then I won't care. I'll just thank the Lord for my blessings, and with nobody expecting nothing, I'll finally enjoy a good rest."

Marge sucked air through her front teeth. "Thirty years? Shucks!

You're already sixty-five. If you ask me, you gonna be resting before you know it."

Sharon didn't know when she'd had such a good belly laugh. It had never occurred to her that a man might regard sex as a tiring job or a duty.

"It ain't a question of running out of steam," the reverend said. "It's more a matter of realizing your time could be better spent doing something else."

Marge sent Sharon a quick glance. "Thank God that view's not universal. I bet it's not even widespread."

"Don't worry, Sharon," the reverend consoled. "What puts one man to sleep will make another one stand up and dance."

Getting up from her seat on an old Moroccan pouf, Sharon looked directly at him, then headed for the kitchen. "Thank the Lord for that," she flung over her shoulder.

After putting on one of her mother's smocks, Sharon began cooking dinner. But she couldn't give the meal her full attention because her thoughts hovered over the previous day spent with Rafe McCall. She'd felt like a starry-eyed girl while they biked and rode horseback together through the forest. At the edge of the lake, he cooked for them, chiseled chopsticks from the branch of a tree, and fed her the meat of a roasted clam. He made the day so special. She couldn't help wondering where their friendship would take them.

As she expected, the reverend didn't leave until he sated himself on the soul food she cooked. She stayed with her mother until Eloise arrived, then headed home. He said he'd call, and her instinct told her he'd do that and everything else he said he'd do. However, the voice she heard when she answered the phone after she got home belonged to Drogan.

"I thought you'd finished with me," she told him. "What's the idea of behaving as if I don't exist?"

"Nothing so dramatic as all that. I need time to reconcile myself to this new scenario. Mama's retired and you of all people publishing the paper. Next, I'll see dinosaurs strolling along Market Street."

"If you do, keep it a secret. I'd hate to hear that you'd been carted away in a straitjacket. Seen or heard from Cassie lately?"

"Sure. I get to listen to her harangues about you and Mama at least once a day."

She figured that was an understatement and said as much.

"Well, you know Cass," he said. "She'd bitch about the sunset if it happened earlier or later than she thought it should. Don't be too hard on her; flexibility isn't one of her strong points."

He dismissed Cassie's shortcomings in that cavalier fashion, as if nothing more were to be expected of her, though his own behavior hadn't been circumspect. Nowadays, talking with her brother and her sister was like communicating with strangers.

"We've always been so close, Drogan. A couple of weeks went by and you didn't call me. I never thought that would happen, especially when we're in the same town."

"You could have called me."

She wound the telephone cord around her wrist until it pinched her flesh, and she grimaced from the pain. Didn't he remember what happened that night? "Why would I? You left Mama's and didn't tell any of us good night, not even Mama, and she'd just told you she had to retire because of poor health."

In her mind's eye, she saw him slap his fist into the palm of his right hand when he said, "Regurgitating that scene will do about as much good as an umbrella in a hurricane."

In other words, he was still sore about it and didn't intend to discuss it. *What had happened to her wonderful Drogan? Be charming. Sweep it under the rug. Pretend it's not there.* For the first time, she understood Drogan's modus operandi. Smile. Do anything you like; no matter how much it hurts, don't show the pain; and don't concern yourself with those you hurt. Just grin like hell and let calm prevail. And she'd worshiped him all her life. Her precious big brother.

She told herself not to dwell on the negative. "A least you and I are talking. Cassie hasn't called me, and I miss her a lot. Maybe she's ashamed."

"Don't bet on it."

They talked for a while longer, and when she hung up, her phone rang immediately.

Personal shame was not an emotion with which Cassie had more than passing familiarity, though she was often ashamed of others. Indeed, Cassie rarely allowed herself strong feelings of any kind, and almost six years of marriage to Kix Shepherd had done nothing to change that.

Cassie didn't look up from the birthday card she was designing, though she knew someone had entered her office. Her colleagues had to know and accept that her work was important and tedious and that she was not to be disturbed.

"Guess what," Marlene said.

How many times had she told that woman not to bother her when she was working? "All right. All right. What is it? I'm terribly busy," Cassie said with the crayon poised inches above the sketch pad for effect. "Well!"

"I'm pregnant, and Jake's so happy, he's about to lose his mind."

"Just what I've been waiting all my life to hear," Cassie said under her breath as she rolled her eyes. "How wonderful." She put as much enthusiasm as she could into the remark, but what she managed wasn't much. "Great, honey. Now let me work," she said.

Cassie stared at the door after Marlene closed it. *What was so great about getting pregnant? She was sick of hearing about it at home, and she was damned if she'd listen to it at the office.* The phone rang. Now what?

"Mrs. Hairston-Shepherd speaking."

"Hi, babe. How about leaving work on time today and we make use of my night off."

She gritted her teeth. "Oh, Kix. I'm so sorry, but I have to finish this sketch, and I'll never manage it before five. I know you said you wanted us to have the evening together, but I'll make it up to you. Honest."

Kix's voice had the ring of impatience. He snorted, surprising her with the sound of it. "One of these days, Cassie, you're going to have to make some hard choices. If you're not home by seven, I'm going out."

Fear streaked through her. Kix had never said anything like that before. He appreciated her and was proud of what she'd accomplished. And he looked up to her. Surely, he wouldn't . . .

"Look. I didn't mean to give you the impression that I'll be working late. I—"

He interrupted. "Just be here by seven."

"Well, of course. Do you want me to bring in something to eat. I could—"

"I'll cook. You know that."

What was wrong with him? "All right, then. I'll . . . uh . . . I'll be there with . . . with open arms. And you be sweet. Love ya."

"Right." He hung up.

"I won't do it. I won't. My whole life would change," she said aloud. But she wondered how long Kix would wait for her to start their family. She was thirty-two years old and—Well, what the heck! Maybe he wanted her home because he was lonely for her. She could handle *that*.

At home alone as the winter afternoon slid into dusk, Sharon lifted the phone's receiver, heard Rafe McCall's voice, and her loneliness melted away.

$Five$

Cassie raced up the walk and stuck her key into the lock of her front door. Her watch said six-fifty, and she prayed that Kix hadn't left, because his watch was faster than hers.

"Honey?" she yelled, and was immediately annoyed at betraying her anxiety. When he didn't answer, her heartbeat shifted to a dull thud, and sweat dampened the palms of her hands.

"Kix!" The silence battered her nerves, and she raced to the kitchen and stopped short, trembling, when she saw the darkened room.

"You made it by a minute."

She flipped around, barely missing the corner where the dining room joined the hallway, a scowl marring her usually perfect face. She had never let him get the upper hand, had always made certain that he looked up to her, that he didn't forget he'd married a professional woman who was a member of Woodmore's most prominent family. People looked down on a woman who couldn't hold her man, especially if he wasn't in her own class, and she'd come close to letting him think she was vulnerable to him. She wanted to kick herself.

"Supposed you'd missed a red light and had to wait for the light to change. You played it close."

She caught herself just before her shoulders lifted in a shrug. He was there. A little annoyed, maybe. But if he'd wanted to leave, he'd have done so, and she knew it. She was a Hairston, and she didn't intend to let him forget it.

She strolled over to him, pressed her lips to his, and let her left hand drift down to his crotch. "Honey, you know I'd have died if you hadn't been here. I barely made it to the printing shop before it—"

He stepped away from her. "That shop always closes at seven and opens at nine in the mornings. You risked a lot for nothing because nobody will touch your copy tonight, and the shop opens about the time you pass by it tomorrow morning. You'd better straighten out your priorities, Cassie."

What was wrong with him? It wasn't like him to challenge her. "Let me change into something comfortable," she said, looking at him from beneath lowered lashes, the way she did to let him know they could make love.

But he ignored her signal, turned away, and headed in the direction of the kitchen. "We can eat in ten minutes."

She froze in her tracks. Ten minutes. That meant she wouldn't have time for a bath, and she told him as much. "I need at least twenty-five minutes."

"Ten minutes, Cassie. One of these days you're going to scrub your skin off. And I wouldn't mind not smelling that ten-dollars-a-bar soap of yours."

Gaping at him, she imagined she looked anything but her normally cool self—more like a stupid woman—as she tried to fathom the meaning of his words, his attitude, and his demeanor. "Kix, for goodness' sake, are you all right? I mean, this isn't like you."

She heard the lid come down on a pot more resoundingly than was necessary. "No, it isn't," he said. "I'll have the food on the table in six minutes."

They ate in silence, for her intuition told her she'd better not mention her work and that was all they usually talked about. She couldn't affect an interest in cooking, and she didn't think that, as a professional chef, he'd be interested in much else. At least in the more than five years they'd been married he hadn't started a conversation about social or cultural things, or if he had, she didn't remember it.

"I'll clean the kitchen," she said, wanting him to see her as cooperative, a helpmate.

"I'll do it."

She dashed to the bathroom, brushed her teeth, and took a shower. She hated showers; she'd have to get her nice hot bath later.

"I have one day off a week, Cassie," he told her when she joined him in her white satin gown, robe, and mules, "and I neither relish nor intend to spend those evenings alone. Not anymore."

"But darling, you know—"

"No, I don't know. I want you to enjoy your work and to be successful at it, but I also want a life with my wife and my children. If you can't come home at five o'clock one day out of seven, you tell me right this minute."

She didn't want to tie herself to that stricture and searched her mind for an escape, but she couldn't think of anything he was likely to accept.

"All right, if that's what you want." She sounded grudging even to herself, and sensing that he wasn't placated, she went over to him, sat on his lap, and held his head to her breasts. She let her robe gape, exposing the smooth beige flesh of her ample bosom above the low-cut gown.

Cold shivers shot through her when he ignored her attempt at seduction, refusing her the control she sought, picked her up, and strode to their bedroom. She writhed beneath him as she always did to let him know how anxious she was to get him inside of her. Once he entered, she had him in her clutches, where she wanted him, and moaned and yelled his name, begging for release. She let it go on for about five minutes and began contracting her vaginal muscles, faking an orgasm and moaning as if in ecstasy. He released himself within her, but she couldn't help noticing that he did so with no apparent emotion. *Lord! Something was definitely wrong.*

"Darling, that was so good," she said, and waited for him to roll off her. But he didn't. "I need to get up," she pleaded. "I'll be right back."

"Not this time."

It frightened her that he might be on to her machinations, and she worked hard at controlling the trembling of her lips as he stared down at her, his expression unfathomable. And when he lay his head on her pillow, imprisoning her, tears seeped from the corners of her eyes. She had to bathe. *She had to!*

Well after midnight, he moved off her and turned on his side, his back to her. She waited half an hour, then eased out of the bed, tiptoed to the bathroom, and drew a tub of hot water. "Thank God for good, cleansing water," she said aloud as she cleaned herself inside and out.

When she awoke at eight-thirty that Tuesday morning, Kix had left for the restaurant. The first time in their five and a half years of marriage that he hadn't cooked her breakfast. Well, what the hell! Wasn't he from a peasant family somewhere in the middle of Mississippi? What could she expect? She slipped out of bed, put on a robe, and headed for the bathroom.

* * *

Kix got busy with his day's work. The restaurant didn't serve breakfast, and the *sous*-chef took care of lunch. He only had to concentrate on the dinner. His skills as a chef had made Gourmet Corner the region's finest restaurant, and his renown extended beyond western North Carolina. To his peers, the media, and many of his patrons, he was a celebrity, but to his wife, the woman he loved, he was a cook. Period. And Cassandra Hairston-Shepherd thought she deserved better. One of these days, he'd give her a reality check that she wouldn't forget.

Working on the dinner menu, he shaped the quennelles and dropped them into simmering salted water, but one by one they broke apart. Fifty dollars' worth of sea scallops down the drain. Since walking into the kitchen that morning, nothing he'd touched had turned out right. His mind was on his marriage. He wiped his hands, went into his office, and called Cassie.

"Mrs. Hairston-Shepherd speaking."

Her officious tone of voice didn't put him off. Given an opportunity, she would downsize the Angel Gabriel. "Ever since Mama gave the paper to Sharon," he began without identifying himself, "you started acting like you have to prove how important you are. Every stinking day of the week, Sunday included, you have to go to your office, or so you—"

"But honey," she interrupted, "you don't understand. I'm doing this for us, so we can have—"

"Cut the crap, Cassie. You're doing it for you. And no matter how hard you try to convince yourself, you'll never justify turning Mama down when she needed you. You even have the gall to sulk because she made you take some bad medicine." He imagined that she was standing now with one fist knotted at her hip, because she hated a challenge and he'd just handed her one.

"Kix, I'm a Hairston, and that's the Hairston newspaper, part of which is mine. I'm not sucking up to them after they disenfranchised me."

He wondered sometimes why he bothered trying to penetrate that thick attitude of hers. "I'm talking about your mother, Cassie. She wouldn't have given up the paper if she wasn't terminally ill. Doesn't that mean anything to you?"

She sucked her teeth. "Hogwash. She's hoodwinked you, too. If she's terminally ill, why would she be going to California?"

That was the first he'd heard of it. He'd always tried to protect Cassie, but now he didn't spare her. She had to face reality. "Maybe because she's always wanted to and it's now or never."

"Oh, Kix, you don't mean that. You're just guessing. Excuse me." He assumed she'd placed her hand over the mouthpiece, because he didn't hear anything. "Sorry, darling," she said a few minutes later, "but it gets awfully hectic in here."

"Yeah. Don't let me add to the confusion." He told her good-bye and started another batch of quennelles, but his heart wasn't in his work. Cassie had blinders on. He'd never been rough with her, but he knew he'd have to take strong measures if he was going to have a life with her, and he wasn't afraid to do it.

About that time, Marge locked her suitcase and sat down. What she was doing might seem crazy to her family and friends, but she couldn't think of a single reason to conserve her energy. She was going to have less of it every day, and she intended to use what she had while she had it. She answered the phone after its first ring.

"Marge speaking. Hello."

"Mama, this is Kix. Just calling to wish you bon voyage."

"Well, *merci,* as they say in France. Sometimes I forget you graduated from that famous Cordon Bleu cooking school in Paris. I appreciate your calling me, Kix. I sure do. It's more than my own son I gave birth to has done."

"Thanks, Mama, but you know children take their parents for granted."

"Some of 'em. Yes."

"If you need anything, don't forget you can count on me."

"I know it, son, and I . . . I thank you."

"You have a great time and come back safely. "

She hung up. Kix's call didn't surprise her, but if Imogene had phoned to say good-bye, she'd probably have passed out. Imogene concerned herself with Imogene. Until recently, she had posed as a subservient clinging vine—the type of woman for whom Marge had little use—and her drastic change during the past few weeks from that to a woman who practically ignored her husband bore watching.

The doorbell rang. Thinking it was Ross, she yanked it open without checking and got a surprise when the Reverend Ripple strolled in.

"Thought I'd check on you before you left," he said.

Marge sat back down and rolled her eyes toward the ceiling. "Hmm. And here I thought you came to pray."

He grinned, his gold incisor sparkling as if he'd just had it polished. "We can do that, too."

"Too?" Her eyes widened. "What else did you have in mind for us to do?"

"Now, now, sister. Take it easy. You could've had some of those good old collard greens and corn bread wasting in the refrigerator."

It was no longer funny. Hadn't anyone told him? "Reverend Ripple, don't you know I'm terminally ill with my kidneys. I haven't cooked collards in over . . . let me see, weeks and weeks. I don't cook any longer."

His bottom lip dropped, but he quickly closed it. "Well, I declare, Marge. I'm so sorry. Let's have a word."

After he prayed, he patted her on the shoulder. "I don't much believe it, Marge. The Lord's pretty choosy, and I figure he'll postpone having to deal with you up there reorganizing things for as long as he can. I'm pretty sure of that. Still, I wouldn't mind if you'd give my wife the recipe for those collards before you leave for California. Never can tell," he added, his golden grin at work.

He was trying to amuse her, but she wasn't sure he'd managed. "I see Ross is here with the car," she said, glancing at the window. "You'll have to wait for it till I get back. I expect you have faith, don't you, Rev?"

He scratched the back of his head and grinned. "Sister, I always try to ask the Lord for what I'm likely to get. You take care." He opened the door for Ross and left.

"Ready?" Ross asked her.

"Ready as I'll ever be. You're really coming, aren't you?"

"I wouldn't miss it." He set her bags outside and locked the door. "Come on."

She stepped down the walk, turned, and looked back. She might have faltered, but he took her hand and spoke, not in his usually gravel-like voice but in one soft and solicitous. "We'll work with what we got, Marge. We always did." She nodded, got into the front seat of the 2002 Cadillac he'd rented to take them to the airport in Winston-Salem, and turned her thoughts to California.

*   *   *

In *The Woodmore Times* building, Sharon walked into her office and sat down at her desk, on her own for the first time. Without the props. Mama was in California, and Ross Ingersol had gone with her. Almost immediately, the door opened, and Mack sauntered in. She knew it was he before she looked up. Not that she was attuned to his special scent; she didn't even know if he had one, but anyone else would have knocked. From the day she became publisher, he'd served notice in various ways that he meant to test her—arriving at work as much as an hour and a half late, leaving the office for hours at a time during the working day without indicating his whereabouts, and coming late to budget meetings.

"I didn't hear you knock, Mack," she said without looking up.

"Yeah." He sat down. "We need a budget meeting, and you oughta call Larsen in; he's good on features. If we can get it started right now, I can—"

She tried to stare him down, but he didn't fidget or squirm, though she knew he couldn't mistake her expression for friendliness. "I'm busy, Mack." She looked down at her watch. "The meeting will be at nine as usual, and Larsen is not invited. Be back here at nine sharp, and knock before you enter." She picked up her pen and began to write.

"Now, look—"

"You look!" she said evenly. "Incidentally, I understand Larsen thinks he'd make a good editorial-page editor. So, since you think so highly of him, perhaps—"

He threw up his hands. "Oh, all right. All right. I'm only thinking of the paper."

"Your thoughts will be welcome at nine o'clock."

He strutted out, and she didn't doubt that she was in for a week of jostling and challenges. She only hoped those newsmen wouldn't force her to take harsh measures, for she was determined to manage the paper as she saw fit.

She checked the wire services and finished jotting down her own ideas for the day's layout. Satisfied with what she wanted, she called in her reporters, got their suggestions, and learned, to her astonishment, that they had never been involved in the paper's layout. She accepted several of their ideas and reserved others for another day, and it didn't escape her that the three reporters regarded her with new respect. When Mack arrived at five after nine, she told him she had what she wanted.

His shoulders slumped, and his bottom lip dropped, for he realized that his show of insolence had merited him nothing. In fact, she'd let him know that he was expendable.

"B . . . but Marge never did a thing like that. She planned the paper with me and Ross."

Sharon leaned back in her high-back leather chair, draped her left knee over her right one, and said, "I doubt you were foolish enough to be rude to the previous publisher. I don't have to do what she did. If you want to remain as editorial-page chief, show your publisher some respect. Mama was sentimental about this paper. I am not. This is a business. Wilson will act as editor in chief till Ross gets back." *Let him digest that.* She phoned Woodmore Wines and Spirits and had a bottle of champagne sent to each of the reporters.

She wrote Drogan a note suggesting that they meet for lunch, but it seemed so cold and formal compared to the warmth they'd always enjoyed. She read and reread it and finally shredded it and tossed it into the wastebasket. Then she lifted the receiver to dial his number, but what would she say? They hadn't had harsh words; in fact, they hadn't had *any* words since she called him three weeks earlier. She hung up. And to think, he used to telephone her almost every day. She propped her elbow on her desk and supported her forehead with her hand. How could Drogan push her out of his life when he knew how dear he was to her?

She hadn't spoken with Cassie. Maybe . . . On an impulse, she dialed Cassie's number.

"Mrs. Hairston-Shepherd speaking."

"Hi, sis. How are th—" She stared at the receiver as the dial tone droned in her ear, and though she attempted to shrug it off, tears pooled in her eyes and finally flowed down her cheeks. The phone rang, and she grabbed a tissue and dabbed at her eyes. Maybe Cassie had hung up by mistake.

"Hello." The words came out in a whisper.

"Sharon! What's wrong?"

His voice came to her as the sweetest sound she'd heard all day. Still reeling from Cassie's rejection of her overture, she worked hard at controlling her emotions. "Nothing. Why?"

From his long silence, she knew he didn't believe her. "Sharon, what is it? Is your mother all right?

"Yes. Yes. She's fine as far as I know. She's in California. How are you?"

"I'm all right, but I have a feeling you aren't. I was hoping you'd have lunch with me."

"I'd love to. One o'clock?" He agreed, and she hung up wondering at his solicitousness.

She walked over to the window and looked down on Eighth Street at the pickets who stood in front of City Hall protesting the mayor's plan to build a city jail three blocks from the high school. She slid the window open in order to hear the shouts, and the smell of roasting chestnuts and grilling shish kebabs stirred in her a yearning to get out of there, to do as she pleased. The paper be damned.

Realizing that Cassie's rudeness was at the root of her discontent, she closed the window and went back to work. Drogan and Cassie weren't her reason for breathing, and if they could get along without her, she wouldn't let herself need them, either.

"I won't let them tear up my insides like this when I know there're deliberately being mean because they know how important they are to me," she said aloud.

She went over to the window on the Market Street side of her corner office and looked down on a different scene, at the dreary December day, the leafless trees, the debris hurtling along the sidewalk in the brisk wind, and the waterbirds—habitues of Wade Field—that drifted into town in search of food. People rushed along, hunched over against the wind, and a young boy ran up to an old man and guided him across Confederate Avenue. Two different views of the town's center. She snapped her finger. She had her feature story for the paper's weekend edition.

"Oooh!" She spun around as a hand touched her shoulder. "Rafe!" Grabbing her chest with her left hand, she steadied herself and restored her poise. "How'd you manage this? My secretary didn't buzz me."

His eyes sparkled with devilment. "I marched past her as if I belonged here. Works every time. Besides, she was talking on the phone."

On the phone, eh? She'd have to set Nadine straight about that lapse in efficiency.

Rafe ambled to the other end of her office, rubbing his right hand over the backs of the chairs at her conference table as he did so. She watched him. Pensive and seemingly full of something that needed to come out.

He stopped. "I like things—problems, relationships . . . whatever—neatly tied, Sharon, and you didn't level with me when I called you. All right. It was none of my business. Say so. But you were distressed."

She looked him in the eye and said nothing. Little Sharon had ceased to exist, and she wouldn't let anyone pressure her into doing and saying things contrary to her will.

He paced around the conference table and stopped in front of her. "I need to know this. Did whatever happened have anything to do with a man in your life?"

"Not that kind of man. "I have a brother and a sister, and we've always been very close, but they've cut me out of their lives because of this newspaper."

"I imagine that's tough, especially with your new responsibilities. I take it something happened a short while ago that brought this to a head."

She nodded. "I phoned my sister, Cassie, and as soon as she heard my voice, she hung up. I hadn't spoken with her since the night Mama told us that I would publish and own the paper."

"I'm willing to bet they've always been selfish and that they accepted your love as their due. If I were you, Sharon, I'd let it go. I'm a firm believer in that old adage, 'Never let 'em see you sweat.' If they know they're hurting you, they'll pour it on thick." A harsh veneer eased over his face. This man was tough, and she'd bet he could be hard. He shrugged. "Show them you don't give a damn and get on with your life."

Probably the best advice she could get. Still, the thought of cutting them out of her life gave her a chill. "That's what you'd do?"

He flattened his lips but followed that with a quick, jolting grin. "Damn straight. You don't get love by begging for it. Can you get away?"

She looked at her watch and allowed herself a refreshing laugh. She was her own boss, and she could do as she pleased. She called Wilson into her office and gave him the layout. "The reporters will give you their copy no later than three o'clock, at which time you take it to Mack. He should have it back to you by five-thirty. It should be at the plant no later than six. You're editor in chief till Ross gets back."

His smile eclipsed his whole face, and she knew he'd see it done properly if he had to take it from one step to the next himself. "I know the routine, ma'am, and I'll get it to the plant by six. Put your life on it."

She thanked him, and his enthusiasm for his new assignment was so great that she could barely detain him long enough to introduce him to Rafe.

"I can leave whenever you like," she said to Rafe.

From his six-foot-four-inch vantage point, he gazed down at her with large, almost black eyes, studying her intently, seemingly unaware of his effect, of the hard strength and the majesty he projected. She'd never seen a more handsome, mesmerizing brother. The man was a knockout. But so were a lot of other men, she reminded herself. She imagined the titters among the women in the newsroom when he passed through there.

"By the way, how'd you get to my floor?" she asked him. "The receptionist didn't ring me."

His left shoulder lifted in a quick shrug. "I told her I had an appointment with you." When she raised an eyebrow, he didn't grope for words. "Well, I did, though we didn't agree to meet in your office." The man had a fast tongue. "Come to think of it, we didn't say where we'd meet." His gaze seemed to bore right through her. "I want to get to know you, and that includes knowing where and how you work. Everything."

Fortunately, he couldn't divine her thought. *Don't get off of the subject. You smiled at the poor little receptionist, and she withered like a morning glory at high noon in midsummer.* She let his comment about getting to know her pass. While he was doing that, she'd be learning a few things about him. "I'll have to caution the receptionist about letting a good-looking man turn her head."

As far as she could tell, his only reaction to that was a raised eyebrow. "Ready to go?" he asked her.

"Yes."

"Where do you usually eat?"

She told him.

"Then, let's go there."

With her shoulder bag slung over her shoulder and a feeling that destiny was taking over her life, she walked with Rafe McCall to Pinky's Restaurant and inched a little more solidly into Mama's footsteps.

The waitress got their orders straight after several attempts, and Sharon resisted telling her that if she paid more attention to her work and less to Rafe she'd save herself a lot of trouble. They refused the wine list—only Pinky's and Gourmet Corner in the Woodmore area offered wine with lunch—and he leaned back in his chair, focusing on her intently. But as if he were content to communicate without words, he said nothing. She was deciding whether she liked that when she glanced up and saw Drogan, accompanied by a woman she didn't know, walking toward them.

She wanted him to stop, and he did, but she soon wished he hadn't. "Well, whatta you know? Damned if you didn't pick up Mama's habits right off," he said, referring to Marge's preference for Pinky's Restaurant. He showed his perfect white teeth, but his grin didn't reach his eyes, and she knew he was still irritated about Mama's giving her the paper.

Forcing a smile, she said, "Right. It wouldn't hurt *you* to adopt some of her habits, especially her sense of propriety. She turned to the man who sat in front of her. Rafe, this is my brother, Drogan Hairston. Drogan, this is Rafe McCall."

She gulped as Drogan switched personalities with the speed of Mercury. "McCall! How you doing, man? Glad to meet you. You wouldn't be the McCall who owns Scenic Gardens, would you?"

Rafe towered over Drogan, himself a tall man. "Sharon was just telling me about you."

According to her ears, he hadn't said he was glad to meet Drogan, and he hadn't denied that he owned Scenic Gardens. Hmm. So he didn't lie, not even to be courteous. "How do you do, miss?" Rafe said, putting Drogan in his place for not introducing his companion.

"Sorry. This is Miss Hunter, one of my staff. Business lunch." Drogan looked at Sharon. "Probably the same as yours."

Before she could respond to the safety net her brother had thrown out for himself, Rafe said, "No. This is purely social. Sharon and I are friends."

A little of Drogan's self-assurance cracked. "We'd better get started; we have a lot to get through." He handed Rafe his business card. "Good to meet you."

Rafe nodded, and Drogan walked on with Miss Hunter, who now frowned and pursed her lips in obvious displeasure.

"I was going to ask him if he'd like to join us," Sharon said, "till he acted out. He's one surprise after another."

Rafe put Drogan's card in his pocket and stroked his chin with his right index finger. "I don't think either of them wanted that. Besides, I got the sense that he infuriated her for misrepresenting her. If that's a business lunch, I'm president of this country."

"You're right, but if you knew his wife—"

He waved a hand in dismissal. "So he's having his cake and eating it, too. He must be one slick brother; this is a small town."

She didn't try to hide her reaction to that. "You mean fooling around is all right; just don't get caught?" For the second time that day, she was less comfortable with him than she wanted to be.

"I said nothing of the sort. Merely stated a fact."

She changed the subject. "Did you say you were an agent for Scenic Gardens or that you owned it?"

He waited until the waitress placed their food before them and left. "I told you that I was *with* Scenic Gardens. I develop co-op and condominium properties and sell the units. You promised to spend another day with me. How much longer do I have to wait for that?" he asked, shifting from the impersonal to the personal.

"I'll think about it." For the first time since meeting him, she felt the need to hedge.

As they were about to leave Pinky's, she glanced at the window. "Good grief! Would you look at that sky."

He stood and reached for her hand. "We'd better make a run for it."

A deluge drenched them before they reached the other side of the wide avenue. She thought the sky had opened. Soaked, they dashed into a bakery. She pulled at the sleeves of her red woolen suit, one of her favorites, that seemed glued to her body, looked up at him, and laughed.

"What a mess! I hate getting wet in my clothes."

"Tell me about it," he said. "I'm soaked to my skin."

"Me, too."

A grin settled on his face but didn't reach his eyes. "Why don't we . . . go to your place and dry off."

She stared at him, not quite sure she'd heard him correctly. "What was that?"

He repeated it, adding, "Nice way to pass the afternoon."

She gazed at him for a long minute, raised her head, adjusted her shoulder bag, and grinned right back at him. "I don't think so."

With that, she stepped out into the rain. She didn't care if she got wet, and if he called her again, he'd get a good piece of her mind. She went home, changed, and an hour later was back at the paper.

Mack intercepted her as she headed for her office. "I gotta talk to you, Sharon. That act you pulled this morning sent me down a few notches with my reporters."

His reporters! Maybe it was her disappointment in Rafe. Or perhaps the din in the newsroom—the regular afternoon chaos—with reporters and messengers shouting at each other across their cubicles. Or the phones. One rang, and Wilson yelled at K.C., "Pick up, buddy girl." She yelled right back from the other side of the huge room, "Right here, my man." Phones ringing, reporters shouting, and the round of choice expletives that gave the place character could be nerve shattering.

She glared at Mack. "You remind me of an old movie I saw. This man was so guilt ridden that he pestered and spewed invectives at the police authorities until they deprived him of his ability to speak. Get my message?"

Apparently, he didn't. "I know how this place works, and you're going about it all wrong."

She opened her office door. "Come on in."

He didn't wait for her to speak. "You can't let reporters decide what goes in the paper. They'll be unmanageable. They'll—"

She interrupted him. "Have a seat, Mack." He sat facing her desk, crossed his knees, and leaned back, obviously aiming to intimidate.

"Let's get this straight. I can do anything I want to, because I own this paper. If you don't like my style, you have options, and one of those is to walk. Is that clear? You want to work here? Great. But we do things my way."

She watched him leave and knew he'd be back with more of the same. She ground her jaw teeth. In another six months, she'd be so hardened she wouldn't recognize herself. If any of them pushed her, she'd push right back.

Her intercom buzzed. "Mr. McCall coming up, Sharon."

Now, what. "Thanks, Nadine." She flipped off the intercom and waited.

"What can I do for you, Rafe?"

"From your greeting, I suspect you're annoyed with me."

Disappointment was more like it, not that she'd let him know it. She leaned back and smiled. "Do women hop in the hay with you as soon as they meet you? You snap your finger and they just keel over. Right? Have a seat."

He remained standing. "I didn't suggest that, but to tell the truth, I hadn't ruled it out, either."

Taken aback, she said, "You couldn't be a little more blunt, could you?"

She didn't bother to figure out why, but his quick shrug annoyed her. "Sorry," he said, "but I don't see the point in lying about it. I realized when you took off in that downpour that I'd said the wrong thing."

"Did you ever!"

"Something tells me I'll have to start all over with you."

She picked up a pen and tapped it rhythmically on her desk, appraising him. "It wouldn't hurt."

He looked her in the eye, unflinching, letting her know he could stand the heat. "Look, Sharon, I apologize. I'm genuinely sorry. I was surprised when I heard myself say that. Give me a chance to make amends."

She wanted to see more of him, because he attracted her, and when she was with him, she had a warm, feminine feeling about herself. What the heck! Who could blame him for asking for what he wanted?

"I'll think about it."

He leaned toward her with a look of urgency. "Tell you what. I'm going over to Spencer next Saturday. How do you feel about riding with me on my Harley?"

"On your *what?*"

"My Harley Davidson. It's fun to ride, and I'm a seasoned driver. Bundle up, though."

"My Lord! You're a ton of surprises. Can you see me on the back of a motorcycle?"

He rubbed the back of his neck and lay his head to one side. "Why not? Sharon, I'm a Texan. I love horses, the rodeo, big powerful cars, and whatever moves fast. I've kept a Harley for the past ten years." He smiled at the thought. "Closest thing to flying."

She would never have imagined it. The man was the picture of tradition, from his button-down shirts to his argyle socks. "Next, you'll tell me you have a plane and a pilot's license."

His eyes lit up. "I'm taking flying lessons, and I hope to get a plane within the next four or five years. What do you say? We'll leave early in the morning and be back here before dark."

She thought of herself as conservative, but the pull of temptation to do it gripped her, shocking her. She found an excuse. "Mama will be back next Monday, and I need to shop for her that weekend."

He leveled another bomb at her. "I'd like to meet your mother. Mind if I go with you to see her?"

"Wha—?" she sputtered. She imagined he enjoyed the shocks he was giving her, and his laughter confirmed it.

A frown slid over her face. "Are you laughing at me?"

"I . . . uh . . . I guess so. Why would my going with you to visit your mother make you lose your cool?"

"*My* cool? I was thinking that if I walked in there with you, she'd lose a lot *more* than her cool." At his raised eyebrow, she said, "Don't you know that matchmaking is a mother's chief occupation? 'When are you going to find a nice young man?' she mimicked. After I passed twenty-five, it was 'When are you going to find a young man?' Recently, it's been, 'When are you going to find somebody?'"

His laughter wrapped around her like a warm blanket. When he sobered, his eyes flashed a wickedness that made him exciting and desirable. "There's something about you, about being in your company, that makes me a different man," he said. "Right now I don't even care whether we sell another condo or co-op this week. Sharon, are you attracted to me?"

If he was handing her a line, it was certainly a cut above what most men managed, at least in her experience. She let him wait a full minute and then said, "These sudden jolts of yours have the same effect on me as a sudden flash of lightning, and I'm afraid of lightning."

He anchored his body with the pressure of his palms on the top of her desk as he leaned forward, dead serious. "Are you? I need to know."

He wasn't getting that without implicating himself. "Why?"

"Because I don't like the idea that it might be one-sided. You blow my mind."

She grinned in spite of herself, because hearing it gave her a delicious high. And to think, Mama had tried to palm Jeff off on her. "What does that mean exactly?" she asked him.

"You devil. For two cents, I'd show you."

Her grin widened. "Don't tell me you're broke. Too bad. I was always a visual person. In fact, I almost never forget what I see. It's wha—"

"Watch it, Sharon. I don't want to make another mistake with you, but I'm not used to passing up that kind of dare."

She couldn't remember having so much fun at verbal sparring, or flirting, which was what they'd been doing. "When I met you, I thought you were starched stiff as Colin Powell's white shirt collars. Most erroneous conclusion I ever made."

"Look now, I'm not exactly jelly-jelly."

She poked her tongue in her cheek, a habit she'd had since childhood. "No, but you shake well enough."

He communicated his frustration with a kick at the carpet. "Too bad I slipped up and sent you rushing off. I'm sorry, Sharon. I really am. That was a dreadful miscalculation. I want a chance to know everything about you. Every single thing."

This man didn't bite his tongue. "That may take a while, Rafe."

"Yeah. I'm aware of that, and it suits me to a tee. What about next Saturday?"

She hadn't dared to hope he'd forgotten about it. "I don't have any leathers."

"It's a week away."

"I'll think about it. By the way, how'd you manage to change? Do you have a flat in Scenic Gardens?"

"No, but that was simple. I went to Dillards, bought some things, and changed. We'll talk."

She nodded.

After he left, she pulled off her shoes, opened the bottom drawer of her desk, stuck her feet in it, leaned back, and began reading the reporters' copy. She was already getting the feeling that K.C. was a notch above the others. She marked her place and answered the phone.

"Drogan! What a pleasant surprise!"

"I sure was surprised to see you having lunch with that guy McCall. What's he after? Publicity?"

She couldn't believe he said it. Rafe had made it clear that they were friends. "I'm sure he can buy all the publicity he wants. Radio, TV, or print. If you called to insult me, please hang up." She wasn't used to jostling with her brother, and it didn't feel right. She switched gears. "How are you, Drogan. And how's Imogene?"

"Uh, she's fine. Great. And for goodness' sake don't mention to her that you saw me having lunch with Irene Hunter. You know how Imogene is."

She didn't know any such thing. What she did know was the reason for Drogan's call. He was covering his flank, and she decided to let him know she was aware of it. "She won't learn about it from my mouth, but don't forget that Woodmore isn't Winston-Salem. What one person sees here, everybody soon knows."

"It . . . uh . . . we're just colleagues, but that kind of thing is easily misunderstood."

"Yeah. Right. Did you talk with Mama before she left?"

"I thought she'd call, but, well, it slipped me, and when I thought of it, I suppose she'd gone."

She decided to make a stab at reconciliation. "Want to have lunch tomorrow?"

"That won't . . . Not tomorrow."

"Then when? You're not very far from the paper. We could—"

He didn't let her finish the suggestion. "I'm too busy for social lunches. It's all I can do to increase my income, now that I don't have the paper to fall back on."

"Since you haven't once been in the Woodmore Building in the past ten years other than at Christmas parties, why did you think the paper would support you?"

He ignored that. "Mama was damned unfair, and you know it. Thanks to you and her, I'm busting my ass seven days a week trying to catch up. But you wouldn't know about that. I can't socialize during the working day."

"You want me to believe that wasn't a social lunch you had with Irene Hunter? I'm breaking up laughing."

"What do you mean?"

She ignored his stab at innocence. "You know Mama's supposed to come back Monday, don't you? That is, unless they decide to stay a few days longer."

"They who?" His voice rose markedly. "Don't tell me she took Eloise with her."

"Ross went with her. I'll be in touch." She hung up. If he didn't know Ross was going to California with Mama, he hadn't spoken with her for a long time.

That evening, Drogan stretched out on his living-room sofa and waited for his wife to come home. For a woman who didn't work outside the house, she spent an awful lot of time commuting. He hadn't wanted to call Sharon, but he had to know whether she suspected him and Irene. Something told him he'd raised her suspicion himself. But he couldn't risk it getting back to Imogene, and if Sharon said she wouldn't tell, she wouldn't. He loved his wife, but a man needed steady sex, and these days he couldn't count on Imogene. She had al-

ways been crazy for him and never turned him down, but lately . . .
For the past couple of months, she'd become obsessed with her shopping excursions to Winston-Salem with her friend Keisha. He knew
he'd been pushing himself to the limit, building his business. Without
the paper to fall back on, he had to work harder. He hadn't bothered to
save because he had regarded the paper as his nest egg, and now he
was thirty-four years old, with a hefty mortgage on his house, practically no money in the bank, and no nest egg.

Over the past two months, he'd worked long hours, six and sometimes seven days a week to make up for it, and he hadn't paid
Imogene the attention she craved. But on the other hand, when he was
home—like now—and not too tired, she was likely to get home from
her shopping expedition after eight o'clock at night with a bag of fried
buffalo wings, a plastic container of cole slaw, and corn bread. A look
at that was as good as a cold shower, and he couldn't understand why
Imogene hadn't figured that out.

Irene never turned him down, but he was beginning to question
the wisdom of continuing with her. She'd begun making demands
that he had no intention of meeting. He could opt for marital fidelity,
and he knew he ought to, but at thirty-four, he didn't have but about
sixteen more years to enjoy good, hot sex, he rationalized, and he intended to make hay while the sun shone. He sat up quickly when he
heard the key in the door; Imogene hated for anybody to lie down on
the sofa.

"Hi, sweetie," she called from the foyer with a breathlessness that
could make a man think he had a tasty dish waiting for him.

To his surprise, he felt his mean streak coming on and couldn't
make himself get up and greet her the way he always did. "I'm in
here," he said.

She breezed into the living room and pressed a kiss to his cheek. "I
didn't realize it was windy," he said, observing her high color.

"What do you mean?"

"You look like you walked a mile with the wind whipping in your
face." He spread his arms out on the back of the sofa, stretched out his
legs, and looked at her. Imogene was what they used to call "high yal-
low," and every emotion showed on her face. She couldn't fool him.
He stared at her and shrugged it off; she was too naive, too much of a
homebody, to get into trouble. He just wished she liked sex the way
she used to.

"I brought us some dinner. You know, I meant to get home before four, but we went to a shopping mall, and I bet you we walked from here to Winston-Salem right inside that mall. We hadn't been there before, and—"

At least twice a week, he listened to that same thing. He interrupted her. "What did you buy?"

"I . . . uh . . . a pair of shoes and a . . . a little bracelet."

"What kind of bracelet?"

"A tennis bracelet."

Jewelry? He'd given her diamonds, rubies, sapphires, and even an emerald, for heaven's sake. *Keep a lid on it. Otherwise, you won't learn a thing.* "Show it to me after we eat."

She cleaned the kitchen while he watched CNN. Something wasn't kosher. Imogene strolled into the living room, sat on his lap, kicked off her shoes, and put her feet on the sofa. *Don't look a gift horse in the mouth, man.*

She nuzzled his neck and ear and stunned him with the pressure of her fingers on his genitals, something she never did unless he guided her hand there and held it.

He angled his head so that he could see her face. "You're not tired?"

Her lips brushed the flesh beneath his chin. "I'm fine."

The words "Have you been drinking?" rested on the tip of his tongue, but he caught them just before they spilled from his mouth. Imogene didn't drink. What the hell! She was offering, so he was definitely taking. Still, his mind told him he ought to get to the bottom of her bizarre behavior.

He took her to bed and got more fire from her than she ever gave him in the first months of their marriage. He liked—no, he loved it, but he wasn't sure he should. Afterward, when she sank into a deep sleep, he got up and examined her purchases. A pair of black patent Ferragamo shoes and a— What the hell! He stared at the diamond bracelet in its blue velvet box, and when he could bring himself to do it, he unfolded the sales slip. *Good Lord!* Twenty-one hundred dollars. She'd lost her mind. No wonder she'd been so hot in that bed.

Something was rotten in Denmark, and he wasn't going to waste any time finding out what it was. But first he had to cancel her credit cards, and he'd do that as soon as he got the bills. Twenty-one hundred dollars for a bracelet when he was killing himself trying to save money to make up for Mama's high-handed treatment of him and Cassie. What else had she bought? Window-shopping. She always claimed she and Keisha just window-shopped. Well, in the future that was all she'd be able to do.

Imogene got up the next morning, ran to the table in the foyer, opened the elegant little shopping bag, and heaved a big sigh of relief. He'd left home without seeing the bracelet, and she prayed he wouldn't remember it. She'd certainly done all she could last night to take his mind off it. She stashed it beneath her sweaters in the bottom of her chest of drawers along with her other treasures.

Back at his office in the Scenic Gardens housing complex, Rafe sat on the edge of his desk, swinging his right foot. Worried about his relationship with Sharon Hairston. Uncertainty as to his chances with a woman was foreign to him. He was just short of forty, and he'd had his pick of females, but he had never misled one of them about his intentions. From the time he could remember, a yearning to rise from the bottom rung of the economic ladder was the one thing that drove him. And it propelled him when hunger might have enticed him to fold up and quit trying. He hadn't let anybody or anything hinder him.

Miller, his senior salesman, walked in and sat down. "You raised the price of those two units, and I just sold both of them. A couple of minutes after I closed the deal, a woman called and offered me ten thousand above the sale price. I gotta hand it to you; you're resourceful."

He had learned that people wanted to boast about the high cost of their homes, and he was too happy to oblige them. Resourcefulness? The man didn't know the half of it. "That's the name of the game, Miller. Sixteen years ago, I walked around with holes in the soles of the only shoes I owned."

He enjoyed Miller's appreciative look, because be remembered the days when the man would have scorned him. He knew he was an enigma to many people—a conservative in business and in his relations with people, yet a lover of stock car racing, fast cars, and the elegant life. He'd come a long way, and he made certain that a good portion of his income went to help people who were down and out.

"How'd you do it, man?"

He moved away from his desk and shoved his hands into the pockets of his jeans. "Selling newspapers, washing dishes, cleaning stables, herding cattle. You name it; I did it. My first building had four units." He could have anything he wanted now—except maybe Sharon Hairston. The first woman he'd wanted for more than fun or casual friendship and as best he could tell, her interest in him was merely lukewarm.

Six

Sharon dialed Eloise's number and waited. Eloise treated the phone as if it were a torture instrument; she took her time answering it, didn't talk long, and almost never picked it up to make a call if she could avoid it. Eventually, after at least a dozen rings, she answered.

"Eloise Rouse speakin'. If you selling somethin', you wasting your money calling me. Hello."

"Aunt Eloise, you've been answering the phone like that as long as I can remember. Did anybody ever hang up on you?"

"Plenty of 'em. Saves me a lot of phony politeness."

"I thought I'd buy some groceries for Mama, air out the house, and have things looking fresh when she gets back tomorrow. You going to be home around eleven or so? I'll make you a cup of cinnamon coffee"—always good bait for Eloise.

"I already bought groceries for Marge and aired out the place, but you come on over and I'll make you a nice breakfast. We can visit for a little while."

"In that case, I'll be there around ten."

"It sure surprised me that Marge let Ross go with her," Eloise said as they sat at her table that Saturday morning eating grits, scrambled eggs, sausage, and buttermilk biscuits. "Me and Gert was just about knocked off our rockers."

"I guess he knew how to ask, because I don't believe she invited him."

"She sure didn't. Here, child, have some more of this sausage."

"I wear a size twelve, Aunt Eloise, and if I live to be a hundred, that'll be the size they bury me in. No, thank you."

"This piece right here's got a little more red pepper in it. Try it." She took it, mostly to please her godmother. "Good, ain't it? Now who was that man I saw standing with you in front of the Woodmore Building? Never seen him 'round here before."

She gave Eloise a summary of her knowledge of Rafe McCall. "He wants me to bring him over here tomorrow when I come to see Mama, but I'm not that crazy. Twenty minutes after he gets in the house, Mama will know what the inside of his veins looks like. And after an hour, she'll have pronounced us man and wife. Oh, no."

"No, she won't. But she'll be impressed, 'cause from where I stood across the street, I knowed I was lookin' at a genuine man."

"Mama wants me to get married."

Eloise heaved her large square hips up from the chair, went to the stove, and got the coffeepot, a gray speckled enamel vessel that she'd had for more than thirty years and considered one of her prized possessions. She insisted that coffee was best perked in an old-fashioned coffeepot over an open flame.

"Sure she does." She stood with her back to Sharon and spoke softly. "And she'll want it now more than ever. Things don't look good for Marge, Sharon."

Sharon nodded slowly, reluctant to acknowledge the inevitable. "I know, and she drove it home to me when she let Uncle Ross go to California with her."

"I don't believe in miracles, child, least not the kind Marge needs. So I'm just going to love her as much as I can while I still have her. That's the way she seems to want it."

"This is true." She worked at steadying her voice. "Mama can't stand people acting maudlin."

"You tellin' me. She didn't mope when Ed passed, and if anybody starts gettin' a long face, they better not show it to Marge. She'll send 'em packin' in a minute."

Uneasy at the implication of Eloise's words, Sharon changed the subject. "Mama will definitely get unhinged if I bring Rafe here with me tomorrow. She'll give him a taste of what it's like to be in a police station interrogated by a battery of cops. Mama knew Jeff because he went to our church, but I never brought a strange man to meet her."

"If she gets uptight, straighten her out. You ain't been a child in years. You bring him. If you don't, he gonna spend a lot of time makin' up his mind about why you didn't."

"I'll tell him why."

"You go ahead and do that. You can tell a man it's rainin', and he'll stick his hand out to see if it gets wet."

She hugged her godmother. "Thanks for a great breakfast. It's been years since I took in that many calories in one meal."

"You oughta do it more often. That's a couple of bones I see there at your throat."

Sharon couldn't help laughing. "I see yours, too. 'Bye."

"What'll it be?" Rafe asked her that afternoon when he met her in the lobby of the Woodmore Building. "I'd like to spend the day with you tomorrow."

She told herself not to let him confound her with his disconcerting behavior—dropping by unexpectedly and calling almost as soon as he left her. "I wasn't expecting you to come by here."

If he detected her displeasure, he didn't show it. "I like to look at people when I'm talking with them."

"I'm on my way to my mother's right now, so—"

His voice was urgent as he interrupted, almost as if he put his foot in the door to make certain she didn't lock him out. "You don't want me to go with you?"

"She might get the wrong impression."

He stared down at her, seemingly perplexed. "What does that mean?" But she knew he got the message.

"I know her. She'll assume that you and I are closer than we are."

A grin softened his mouth, and she felt herself relenting. She had an awful, scared feeling that she was ripe for Rafe McCall, and she didn't want to be. She meant to be her own woman, to run that paper and gain the respect of everybody who worked on it. But she couldn't do that and flap like a puppet on strings, if she let Rafe McCall pull them. She opened her mouth to tell him she'd see him some other time, but he beat her to it.

"Look. We can do this another day. I'd still like to meet your mother. Marge Hairston is an institution in this region, and I'd enjoy meeting her."

She mused over that. He had a second motive, no doubt about that, but he'd just ruled out acting on it, at least for the present. "All right," she said, unsure as to the wisdom of relenting but doing it nonetheless. "Mama loves people, and I expect she'll enjoy meeting you."

"Thanks for the vote of confidence." The remark had the ring of sarcasm, but she wasn't sure he intended that, so she didn't comment on it. "And after that?"

She liked him a lot, and she wanted to spend time in his company, but she didn't intend to be overwhelmed by his charisma and his strong masculine persona—a trait in men that always attracted her. "Let's play it by ear," she said. "See you tomorrow."

Why didn't he say something? The silence strung out till she felt herself suspended between annoyance and excitement. When he did speak, she got a shock.

"Do you happen to know anything about that property north of Wade Lake?"

She stared at him, taken aback by the shift in conversation. "You mean Wade Field? Sure. We're hoping the state will make it a wildlife preserve."

His demeanor changed; whereas he'd been relaxed and jovial, she was suddenly looking at a predator whose claws were barely concealed. "Who, may I ask, is behind this?"

His question triggered an alertness in her, a news sense with which she was becoming familiar. "Half the town of Woodmore and a lot of smaller communities around here." She heard the frostiness in her voice, and she imagined he did, too. "What did you have in mind?"

She interpreted his shrug as an effort to be casual, but she didn't believe it. "Just curious," he said. "It's an attractive place."

"And very valuable," she replied, letting him know she was willing to cross swords with him if he tried to claim it.

"Who owns it?" Tenacious, was he?

"The city owns it, but the state disagrees. The birds that loiter there aren't interested in the dispute. If you're thinking of acquiring it in order to build condominiums or co-ops for the rich, forget it. The people of Woodmore would be outraged."

"What side are you on?"

She looked him in the eye. "The side of right."

He looked into the distance, then fastened his gaze on her and smiled. "Let's leave that for another time. Are you going to let me go with you to visit your mother?"

Why not? Mama could read people, and she could use the added insight. "I told you she'd enjoy meeting you, didn't I?"

A smile seemed to drift over his face. "Fine, I'll come by for you around noon. Okay?"

She agreed. He left, and she wondered about his desire to meet her mother. But there was one thing about which she had no uncertainty. If he tried to build anything in Wade Field, he'd have to do battle with her and *The Woodmore Times*. She suspected that he'd made up his mind to own Wade Field, but he wouldn't have her support.

Sharon used her key to let herself and Rafe into her mother's house. She found Marge reclining on the chaise lounge that faced the wood-burning fireplace, centerpiece of the spacious living room, sat on the edge of it, wrapped her arms around Marge, and scrutinized her face, looking for signs of change.

"Well, now, who'd you bring with you?" Marge asked when Rafe strolled into the living room. He'd waited in the foyer for what he considered a reasonable period of time while the two greeted each other.

"Oh! Mama, this is Rafe McCall."

"Well, how do you do, Mr. McCall. Sharon never once mentioned you to me."

He walked over to Marge and shook hands with her. "I'll have to speak to her about that. It's a pleasure meeting you, Mrs. Hairston. You're a legend in this part of the country."

"Which means I'm old. Have a seat over here in this chair. What kind of work do you do, Mr. McCall? I don't remember seeing you or hearing about you."

Sharon shrugged. He wanted to meet her mother, did he? She sat back to watch while Marge interrogated him. He, too, leaned back in the chair, as comfortable as she'd ever seen a man.

"I build houses, Mrs. Hairston, and I live in Winston-Salem for the time being, which is probably why you haven't seen me here."

She imagined the bullets shooting off in her mother's head. "Hmm. For the time being, eh? Where do you come from?"

"Mama, could you hold off on the third degree? I don't think it's called for."

"I don't mind, Sharon," he said. "San Antonio, Texas. My family still lives there."

"I see. You're not married, I hope."

"If I was, I wouldn't be here with your daughter."

"It's hard to believe a man like you isn't married. You must be all of thirty-five."

A grin flashed across his face. "Thanks. I'm thirty-nine."

"Any children? Anywhere?"

A rumble of laughter rolled out of him, and he let them know he could give as good as he got. "All things are possible, but if I have any, their mothers haven't been gracious enough to apprise me of that fact."

"I see you can hold your own. Sharon's never brought a man to meet me before. If she's sending me a message, I want to know exactly what it is."

"I practically twisted her arm. She didn't think bringing me here was a good idea, but I wanted to meet you."

"So it was *your* idea." She looked at Sharon. "You're owner and publisher of *The Woodmore Times*. That's all. The paper is not your husband. When you get to be my age, I hope you'll look back, as I can, and say you had it all. I mean *all.*"

Sharon didn't want Marge to get on her soap box about the efficacy of love and marriage with that special man, and her conversation was headed in that direction. "We'd better be going. I'll be over tomorrow afternoon to hear about your trip. By the way, where's Uncle Ross?"

"Ross didn't stay. Soon as he found out Eloise was home, he checked the kitchen and left. He may come back later. I don't know."

"I'm sorry to miss him," Rafe said. "I promised him we'd talk."

Marge sat forward. "About what?"

"He wants to interview me."

Both of Marge's eyebrows shot up. "Don't think you're leaving here without explaining that."

A grin flashed over his face and settled in his eyes, and Sharon pulled her gaze away from his face. Nobody had to tell her that Marge was watching her daughter's reaction to Rafe McCall.

"I'm owner of Scenic Gardens. He wants a story on it."

Marge leaned toward him. "Tell me my daughter arranged for that interview."

"She'll tell you all about it," he said in what was obviously a move to protect Sharon.

Standing, he shook Marge's hand. "I wouldn't have missed this opportunity to meet you, not for anything. Don't worry about Sharon and me. I treat women the way I'd want a man to treat my sister."

Marge let her gaze stroll over him, taking in his full six feet five inches, square chin, and strong countenance, judging his demeanor. "I never doubted it. I know a man when I see one."

Sharon opened the door to leave and came face-to-face with Cassie.

"Well, I didn't—" Cassie's eyes rounded, and her bottom lip dropped when her gaze fell on Rafe.

"Rafe, this is my sister, Cassandra Hairston-Shepherd. We call her Cassie."

"How've you been, Cassie?" He offered to shake, but Cassie didn't see his hand, and Sharon watched, fascinated, as the *femme fatale* in her sister kicked in and went to work.

"Well, this is pure pleasure, Rafe. Surely you don't live around here, because if you did, that fact would never have escaped me."

What a flirt! Rafe's hand went back into his pocket, and Sharon watched in horror as his face reflected an opinion of Cassie that made her squirm. She groped for a way to save the moment.

"Rafe, Cassie's husband owns Gourmet Corner."

That did it. His face lit up. "You're Kix Shepherd's wife? He's one of the reasons I decided to settle in Winston-Salem. Gourmet Corner is only about fifteen miles from where I live. Kix is a celebrity; for my money, he's the best chef there is. Give him my regards."

It was hard to tell whether that pleased Cassie, because her smile seemed perfunctory. "I'll certainly do that."

"We ought to be going, Sharon," Rafe said, clasping her shoulder in what appeared to be a possessive embrace. She told herself to think nothing of it, that he was probably sending a message to Cassie.

"Call me sometime soon, Cassie," Sharon said.

"I'll get to it, but I'm terribly busy with a new client. I was on my way out the door, headed for my office, when Ross called to tell me that Mama was back and that I ought to come over here. After I leave here, I'm going straight to work."

"On Sunday? Well, call when you can. 'Bye."

"See you, Cassie," Rafe said.

"She's your only sister?"

"Yes," she answered, fully aware that he had to be wondering what kind of family she had.

His words confirmed the verity of her thoughts. "Then it was she who hung up on you," he said. "Back there, she was reasonably friendly, though I detected some negative vibes. Strong ones, too."

"My sister is a man's woman. She isn't going to let a man, *not any man*, see a kink in her ultrafeminine armor. If you hadn't been with me, she might not have stopped. I'm just getting to know Cassie, and every layer I peel off brings another surprise and a little more pain."

"Don't stop trying. Trust me, the day will come—"

"Don't say it. Mama must have lost ten pounds while she was away. I have to say, though, that she seemed to have plenty of vitality."

"Enough to give me the third degree." He let a smile slide over his face. "She's an interesting woman. I don't have either of my parents, Sharon. Just love her while you have her. She's a spicy gal, and I got the feeling I'd like to spend a lot of time with her. Now, Cassie . . . I'm not sure about that one. Going to Winston-Salem with me?"

His thinly veiled plans for Wade Field didn't bode well for a meaningful relationship between them, and although the thought depressed her, she had to accept that fact. Might as well put the brakes on right now.

"Let's make it another time. Okay?"

He let his disappointment show. "Whatever you say. Mind if I call you?"

"Of course I don't mind. See you."

She imagined that the smile she plastered on her face betrayed her irresoluteness about him, masking, as it did, her desire to be with him and to enjoy the camaraderie and warmth they usually shared. No matter what she said to him or how she behaved, the truth was that she was drawn to him, and if she didn't use her head, she'd be with him as often as possible. But Rafe McCall seemed in no hurry to reveal himself. Until he did, she had to keep a distance between them. She didn't know what she had accomplished by refusing him other than the certainty of a Saturday night alone.

Right then, Cassie was questioning Marge about Rafe. "Did she meet him here? He didn't come with her, did he?"

Marge folded her arms and scrutinized Cassie. Very little that her daughter did or said would ever surprise her. "I never laid eyes on Rafe McCall till he walked in here with Sharon."

"Is he interested in her?"

"Very much so, and I'd bet this diamond"—she held up her third finger, left hand—"it's mutual. There's something special going on there."

"Well, I'll be. He looks like a . . . a . . ."

"A prince," Marge said. "He acts like one, too. She's found a good man, and I hope she keeps him."

"Well, I'd better be going. I'm getting a contract with a new client, and . . . Mama, there aren't enough hours in the day to get my work done, so—"

"What does Kix say about you working every day of the week?"

She shrugged. "He doesn't like it, but I've got to make a name for myself, and I will if I have to work twelve hours every day."

"Really! Mind you don't fool around and lose your husband. Kix is a jewel. When you wake up to that fact, it may be too late. He's every bit as much of a man as Rafe McCall, but he cooks for a living, and you can't see past that."

"Oh, Mama, for goodness' sake. I've been married to Kix for over five years, and I—"

"And you're thirty-two. If you don't give him a family, another woman will be glad to."

"My Lord, Mama, I get enough of that at home. I'll be over again soon. You look great." She kissed Marge and let herself out. If one more person mentioned babies to her, she'd . . . she'd . . . All she wanted was her own place in the sun. Sharon had the paper, but she didn't even get to put her name on her designs. She got in the car and headed for Cutting Edge Stationers and Engravers.

In her office that afternoon, Sunday, Cassie pulled the little radio out of her desk drawer and tuned into a station that played classical music, something she wouldn't even have contemplated if she hadn't been alone in the building. She hummed along with Borodin's Concerto for Cello and Orchestra—proud that she knew every note of it—as she sketched a set of face masks, the logo for a women's club in Danvers, Virginia.

"Ooooh!" she yelled, and grabbed her throat as the door opened.

"Sorry, ma'am, but I didn't know anybody was in here. I'm supposed to put some new electrical outlets in the rooms on this floor. The new machines are grounded."

"Sorry, but I'm terribly busy, and I'm not going to stop my work so you can put in some plugs or something that I don't need."

"Fine with me, babe. If you don't want one of the new computers, printers, and fax machines the company ordered, it's no skin off my teeth."

"Oh, for goodness' sake. Can't you do it some other time? And don't call me babe."

"Believe me, it's nothing personal. I'm just in the habit of admiring pretty women. 'Scuse me."

"Can't you see I'm . . ." She looked up then and did a classic double take. The man oozed sex. She wanted to kick herself for that slip, letting him know she thought he looked good. A slow, knowing grin covered his face, and she dropped her hands into her lap to hide their trembling. Her heartbeat accelerated like a V-8 engine in overdrive. What the devil had come over her? She was used to good-looking men—she lived with a handsome man—but something about this one . . . A tall man, well over six feet. And that dark blue T-shirt the maintenance man wore, threatening to burst from the pressure of his prominent pectorals. But it was his eyes that got to her, greenish brown with lashes long and curled above a straight nose and lips that half-pouted and half-mocked. She stared at him in frank admiration. At his corded neck, silky black eyebrows, and clean-shaven skin the color of shelled walnuts.

"If you don't want one of the new machines," he said, walking all the way to her desk, staring down at her as if to make sure she got a good look at the merchandise, and dropping his voice to a lower register, "I'll just leave."

Heavens! The look of him! Flat belly and marble biceps. Rough and hard and . . . and masculine. Wild looking. She wanted to . . . She pulled herself together. "Oh, all right. I'll . . . I'll work in the lounge till you finish." She gathered her pocketbook, briefcase, and papers and got up. He didn't move. "Would you mind letting me pass?" *Oh, Lord! Please don't let him touch me.*

"No problem, babe. You sit right here and I'll do your office last."

With that, he turned and gave her a good look at his sexy saunter. She stared at his flawless physique and his sculptured behind, sweetly enticing in skin-tight jeans. She swallowed hard.

"Bastard!" she said under her breath. "Who is he that he should be so arrogant?" She tried to work, but with little results, because she knew that what got to her wasn't the electrician's arrogance but her reaction to him. Her mind conjured up all kinds of steamy things about him. Unfamiliar with her unladylike feelings, she crossed her legs in frustration.

At four o'clock, he opened her door again without knocking. "I thought you might have left by now." He walked into her office and closed the door. "It's almost four o'clock. What does your husband say about your working on Sunday afternoon?"

"I don't ask his opinion."

He pulled off his baseball cap and scratched the back of his head. "Whew. I sure asked for that."

She didn't want to look at him, but she couldn't help it. Without that silly cap, he was even more gorgeous. A state-of-the-art brother in a blue workman's uniform and dirty-brown brogan shoes. She pulled her wits together.

"Give me a second and it's all yours. Please put one outlet right here by my desk." She snatched up her things, and in her rush to get away from him, hit her kneecap against the corner of the wooden desk.

"Ooooh."

She reached for the desk to support herself, and he grabbed her. "Steady, babe. I hope you didn't hurt yourself."

But his hands were on her body, hard and masculine, the first time a man other than Kix had touched her in eight years.

She twisted away from him. "Thanks, I . . . I'm fine," she told him, and bounded out of the office, hardly caring what he thought. At the elevator, she leaned against the wall, hyperventilating, sweat soaking her blouse and underwear.

"You all right?" he asked.

Alarmed because she hadn't heard him approach, she turned and pressed the call button with all the strength she could muster.

"Sure you're all right?" he persisted.

She whirled around and glared at him. "You go to hell."

The elevator arrived, and she dashed into it, heaving a sigh of relief. She sat in her car for fifteen minutes before willing herself to drive home. She'd planned to go to Gourmet Corner, have a drink, and spend a few minutes with Kix before the dinner hour began, but she doubted she could look him in the face without showing guilt. She hadn't done a thing, but she'd wanted that man, a common laborer, worse than she wanted a promotion. She hadn't ever felt that for Kix or anybody else. In near panic, she went home, drew a tub of hot water, and scrubbed herself furiously. Then she downed two jiggers of bourbon and curled up on the living-room sofa.

Here she was hot after a man who wore a skull-and-bones baseball cap, tight jeans, and dirty workman's shoes, and Sharon had that fantastic-looking, elegant man that she had no idea what to do with. What Mama hadn't given Sharon, God had made sure she got. Everything! That morning, Kix had signaled he wanted to make love when he got home, and she had intended to comply, but now . . . she wanted to forget about men. Especially that . . . that electrician. She curled up in a fetal position and fell asleep praying she'd never see him again.

Contrary to Cassie's opinion, Sharon did know what to do with Rafe. She had decided to decelerate their budding relationship, not because she wanted to see less of him, she didn't. But considering the clash that was bound to come, prudence demanded that she go slow with the man. She remembered Drogan's longtime interest in Wade Field and called him.

"What would you say if I told you somebody might put a housing development in Wade Field?" she asked him after their short, cool greetings.

He released a bristling expletive. "With all the problems I've got right now, I can't even think about that place. Anyhow, I was on my way out when the phone rang, and I have to get out of here."

"But would you please think about it. That's a real possibility."

"Look. You got the paper. Print some editorials or something. The publisher of the illustrious *Woodmore Times* ought to know how to whip up public sentiment. I gotta go."

She was sick of his grumbling. If his financial position was precarious, it was his fault. "Drogan, you're beginning to sound like a broken record, and I'm getting tired of hearing it. I'm not responsible for your problems, and you know it. If you don't care about Wade Field, I'm not about to lose a minute of sleep over your attitude."

He hung up without responding, and that surprised her, because she had never criticized him. What was so pressing that Drogan didn't take time to defend himself—a trick for which he was well accomplished—and so urgent that he didn't care about the one concern for which he'd been a dedicated political activist—preservation of Wade

Field as a wildlife preserve? He was in such a hurry that he was civil to her.

Drogan didn't think about the impression he might have made on his sister. Racing to get out of the house before Imogene got home from wherever she'd gone, he put his arms in the sleeves of his coat as he ran down the walk to his car, the wind whipping him through his shirt. He didn't relax until he turned from Salem Court—the street on which he lived—onto Highway 52 and made it through the underpass. Meeting Irene in Danvers at the home of her sister wasn't the smartest solution he could think of, but with Imogene hanging out in Winston-Salem and every other nearby town too small for anonymity, they didn't have a lot of choices.

Driving well above the speed limit, he emptied his mind of everything but what he knew awaited him in Danvers and did his best to kill his conscience. Every time he went off to meet Irene, he promised himself he wouldn't do it again. Then she'd call, he'd be sore at Imogene and think, What the hell, he didn't have much of a marriage, anyway.

He pulled up to 119 Charring Lane, swung into the garage, and the door closed behind him. He entered the kitchen through the side door, as he had done more than a dozen times in the past two months, and looked around. With a sultry smile, Irene got up and walked to meet him, and he nearly tripped over his feet when he saw that she wore nothing but a blue chef's apron. What a way for a woman to greet a man! She kissed him on the mouth and began loosening his tie. Irene made good use of every second they had together. She had never even told him she liked him, to say nothing of love; for that, he knew he ought to get on his knees and give thanks. She claimed her marriage to a man years her senior left her with unmet needs, and he believed her, because appeasing her sexual hunger was as much as he could manage.

"Take me upstairs," she whispered, her warm breath playing havoc with his libido. He supposed he ought to be flattered that she had her hands all over him within seconds after he got in the door. He wasn't. There was something masculine about her that bugged him. He wished she'd let him take the lead just once.

"We've got the rest of the afternoon, haven't we?" he asked her, hoping to enjoy her at leisure.

"Oh, Tina won't be back until late tonight, but *he* will be pacing the floor and watching the windows till I get there. Besides, I'm going crazy to get you in me. Come on. Take me up to the room."

With her 160 pounds, he risked a hernia, but hell, she'd have him so far gone within minutes that he wouldn't feel the discomfort. He'd barely gotten into her before her fire-hot tunnel began clutching and gripping him, straining to deplete him of his essence. He let himself succumb to it, but he was damned if he would give *himself* to her. Even as he shivered with release, he hated himself for letting her use him.

And what about you? his conscience needled. He needed what she gave him, but he was willing to dress it up with the niceties most women liked and needed. However, Irene neither needed nor cared for the window dressing. All she wanted was a hard penis on a man strong enough and knowledgeable enough to use it properly.

An hour later, after a second and then a third romp, he lay beside her, trying to regain his senses and himself. "I can't keep this up, Irene." He hadn't previously told her how he felt about their trysts, and he didn't expect her to like hearing it.

She sat up and leaned over him. "You enjoy it, and don't try to pretend you don't."

"Oh, I enjoy it while it's happening, but afterward, I have a hard time dealing with this thing."

She rubbed her breast over the hairs on his chest. "For goodness' sake, Drogan. We're not hurting anybody. Besides, you never had a woman like me, and you know it. What's gotten into you?"

He'd like to have the answer to that himself. Why was he contemplating breaking it off when she'd just singed every nerve in his body? If she knew what she'd done to him, she'd start dictating the terms of their relationship. He couldn't tolerate that.

Her tongue trailed slowly down his body from his left areola to the apex of his thighs, where she meant to guarantee that she'd be able to make him do whatever she wanted. He grabbed her shoulders and jerked her aside. No woman was going to control him, not even Imogene.

"What's gotten into you, Drogan. You're a barrel of laughs today. I take a hell of a chance running off to meet you, and if this is what I want, I'm entitled to it."

"Look, I had a rough morning. Okay?"

"No, it's not okay. Has she caught on?"

"Of course not. She's too busy doing her own thing, whatever the hell *that* is."

"In that case . . ." She went at him then, leaving nothing unimagined or unsavored until she took his will and what remained of his energy.

She crawled up to him, her face beaming with triumph. "You liked it, and don't tell me you didn't."

He slid away from her and got up. "Yeah. You should write a book." With that, he went into the bathroom and locked the door. He wanted a shower, and he wanted to have it in peace.

"Hurry up," she yelled at him through the door as he dried off. "I told him I'd be home by six, and it's already after five." She never called her husband by his name. It was he, him, and his. Maybe that was her way of pretending she wasn't cheating on the man.

He draped a towel around his waist, tied it, and stepped into the hallway. "It's all yours. Drive carefully."

"You, too," she yelled out.

Fifteen minutes later, he was in his Buick, headed for Highway 52. He drove up to number 930 Salem Court, parked, and looked at the darkened house he called home. Why had he been in such a hurry to get there? Nothing dissipated his guilt about Irene so quickly as Imogene herself. Whenever his conscience flailed him about his unfaithfulness, he would remember that his wife was rarely at home when he needed her. Right then, the thought made him feel better.

Wondering how late shopping malls remained open on Sundays, he ignited the engine and headed for Pinky's. When Imogene rushed into the house, out of breath, with a bag of tasteless buffalo wings, cole slaw, and fries, he was going to get a charge out of telling her he'd already eaten a first-class dinner at Woodmore's best restaurant.

"You missed your sister, Miss Sharon, by about ten minutes," the maître d' told him. "She's doing great with the paper."

Just what he needed to hear. "Yeah. She's a bag of surprises."

After leaving Pinky's Restaurant a few minutes before Drogan got there, Sharon parked in front of her house, got out of her car, and received a surprise of her own when Rafe's Lincoln Town Car parked right behind her Cougar.

"I'm not satisfied with the way we parted," he said. "Could we talk for a few minutes?"

Their parting hadn't satisfied her, either, but she could see the big wave coming, and she meant to get out of the water. He seemed less in command than usual, even anxious. Less sure of himself.

"All right," she said, albeit reluctantly, and he followed her into the house.

"Orange juice is all I can offer you."

He seemed to ponder that and finally shook his head. "I suppose you'd think that. No thanks. This afternoon, you came close to giving me the brush-off. Maybe you did. Was it the Harley Davidson or my inquiry about Wade Field?"

The thought that occurred to her was that it didn't matter. She didn't see him as a man who would alter his course to please others, and it occurred to her that if he was, she would be disappointed. "What would local citizens think if the publisher of their most influential paper gallivanted around in black leather pants on the back of a man's motorcycle? This is a small town, and gossip fuels its cylinders."

His facial muscles appeared to relax, and a smile darted around his lips. "So it was the bike. You had me worried."

She gave him a level look "I didn't say that." Might as well give it to him straight. "Have a seat." She pointed to a chair, and the phone rang. "Excuse me."

"Hello." She listened, horrified.

"This is Ross. I just brought Marge to the hospital. Eloise Rouse is here, too."

"Uncle Ross! Is she . . . What happened? Oh, my Lord!"

"Who is it, Sharon. What's wrong?"

"It's Ross—Ross Ingersol—about Mama." She heard the tremors in her voice but couldn't control them.

Rafe was beside her then, and in spite of her decision to stay away from him, she liked his being there. "What did he say?"

She placed the phone in its cradle with exaggerated care. "He said he couldn't stop the nausea. The doctor's with her now."

The muscles of his jaw twitched. He shoved his hands into his trouser pockets and stared down at her. "I want to go with you."

"But you have to go back to Winston-Salem tonight." If he insisted on being kind and thoughtful, she'd be that much more firmly into the net that her emotions were spinning for her.

"Right. But I want to go with you to the hospital."

Seven

By the time Sharon and Rafe reached Woodmore General Hospital, Marge was resting comfortably in a private room, and Ross sat in a chair beside her bed, a distraught expression clouding his face.

"She just won't do a damned thing you tell her to do," he said to them when they walked in. "I told her not to eat all that fried chicken, but did she listen?" He threw his hands up. "Did you?"

Sharon hugged her mother. "How're you feeling, Mama?"

"Better. I told Ross I didn't need to come here, but he and Eloise know best."

She hadn't seen Eloise, and she remembered that Rafe hadn't met either her or Ross. "Aunt Eloise, Uncle Ross, this is Rafe McCall." She explained that Eloise was her godmother.

Rafe greeted them, walked around to the other side of Marge's bed, and spoke to her in barely audible tones. "I'm sorry you had a bad spell. I hope you'll be all right soon."

She nodded. "Thanks. It was that chicken. Happened soon as I finished eating it. Don't worry; that was just a bad episode, and please don't let Sharon worry about me, Rafe."

He reached for her hand and held it. "I'll encourage her not to, but you're her mother, so she's bound to be concerned. Don't you worry. I'm learning that Sharon is a strong woman."

Marge patted Rafe's hand. "Yes. She's surprising a lot of people, but not me."

"Ross, did you phone Drogan and Cassie? Do they know their mother's back here in this hospital?" Eloise asked. "Not that it would surprise me if they knew it and still didn't show up."

"Cassie wasn't home," Ross said, "but I sent a message to Kix at Gourmet Corner. I 'spect he'll tell her. Drogan said he'd be here shortly."

"What you want to upset all of 'em for, Ross? I'll be out of here tomorrow or the next day."

"Stop being noble, for goodness' sake. I did what was right. The nurse said you could have low-fat ice cream. I'll go get you some from that machine in the waiting room. You're hungry, aren't you?" He didn't wait for her answer.

"Ross is upset," Marge said, "and if there's anything that can send me clear up the wall, it's an upset man." She looked at Rafe, and Sharon's heart soared when she saw the look of devilment in her mother's eyes.

"Don't, for heaven's sake, ever let yourself get upset, Rafe. You're supposed to be superhuman, or at least you men would have us women believe that. So grin and bear it." Rafe, smiling as one would when indulging a child, seemed enchanted by Marge.

"Superhuman? Pshaw," Eloise said. "They can't even stand a little pain. If men had to have the babies, there wouldn't be no population problem. 'Deed, there wouldn't be no population." She allowed herself a hearty laugh. "Men gets upset if they sneeze more than twice in a hour, and Lord, don't let 'em come down with nothing serious."

Ross came back with the ice cream, opened the cup, and gave it to Marge, along with a spoon. "How's it taste?"

Marge sampled it and then savored several spoonfuls. "Delicious. Real good. How'd you know I like raspberry?"

"How can somebody know you as well as I have for thirty-five years and *not* know it?"

Sharon glanced at Rafe and saw in his eyes the question that mirrored her thoughts: Ross and Marge had an unusual friendship.

"Mama, I'm so sorry to hear you're not doing so well," Imogene said, rushing ahead of Drogan when the two of them entered the room. "Nobody'd know it, though. You look terrific." She sat on the side of the bed and enveloped Marge in a hug.

Both of Sharon's eyebrows shot up when Marge rolled her eyes toward the ceiling with a look that said she could hardly breathe. In the four years during which Imogene had been Drogan's wife and a part of their lives, she hadn't guessed that Mama might not like her daughter-in-law. True, she wasn't full of love for her sister-in-law, but she didn't dislike her. She wasn't sure now that Mama could say the same. It wasn't easy being around Imogene; she was overly sensitive and either wouldn't or couldn't discuss anything but recipes, supermarket prices, and the places Drogan took her on vacation. A glance at Rafe and she could see that he, too, had questions about the little drama going on between the two women.

Drogan eased to the center of the group. "Glad to see you're sitting up and feeling better, Mama," he said, moving close to the bed and draping his arm around his wife's shoulder. "Ross gave us a few unsettling minutes."

"If you was all that unsettled," Eloise asked him, "how come it took you so long to get here? You ain't foolin' me none."

"Now, Eloise," Drogan said, his charm hard at work, "why're you always so rough on me? I'm here when Mama needs me. You know Imogene was upset when Mama didn't come stay with us while she recuperates. Our home is—"

Marge interrupted him. "You think that's what I'm doing? Recuperating?" She looked at Ross. "You been giving Reverend Ripple free ads every Friday? I meant to tell you I never charged him."

Ross popped his fingers. "You didn't have to tell me. When the man got through giving me a lecture about where my soul was going if I didn't support the Lord's work, I'd have given him the ad just to get him out of there."

"He sure is good at persuadin'," Eloise said. "The whole congregation is scared they'd go to hell if they missed a week puttin' that ten percent in the collection plate." She cleared her throat and crossed herself to emphasize her contriteness. "Course, he do a lot of good work. He sure do."

"And he eats a lot of my collards, fried chicken, and corn bread, too," Marge said. "Faithfully as you please, every Sunday afternoon, he's over there looking for soul food. Anybody would think I was running a boardinghouse."

Sharon relaxed and let herself breathe deeply. Mama was her normally irreverent self, which meant she felt good. She moved through the group to where Rafe stood beside her mother's bed.

"We can leave now if you'd like."

Imogene stared at them. "I thought you were the doctor," she said to Rafe.

"Imogene, this is Rafe McCall. Rafe this is my sister-in-law."

"Glad to meet you, Imogene."

Imogene straightened up. "Hi. You're here with Sharon? Really? Well, I'll be doggoned. Who'd a thought it?"

Sharon stopped. Riveted in her tracts. Two or three months ago, she might have let it pass as one more insensitive remark from a person who didn't have too much under her cap. But with Drogan and Cassie behaving as if they hardly knew her and Mama wasting away before her eyes, she was standing up for herself. She was a woman doing a woman's job, even if she was the youngest in the family, and nobody was going to treat her as if she were inconsequential. Certainly not an airhead like Imogene.

"If you're smart, Imogene—and I know that's asking a lot of you—you'll leave me alone and pay attention to your husband. And while you're changing your ways, learn to do something other than shopping."

Rafe's arm went around her and squeezed her to him. "Why should it surprise you, Mrs. Hairston, that a woman as beautiful, intelligent, as well educated and accomplished as Sharon, publisher of Woodmore's most prestigious newspaper, would be in my company? She's my kind of woman. Or perhaps you think I'm beneath her level."

Ouch! If he'd wanted to pour pepper on an open wound, he couldn't have found a better spot. Best they get out of there. "I'll be back to see you tomorrow, Mama. Rafe and I had better be going, since he has to drive back to Winston-Salem. Can we drop you home, Aunt Eloise?" She looked at Drogan, who was obviously dissatisfied, but with whom, she couldn't tell. "Drogan, please call me tomorrow, and let's have lunch."

He nodded. "I'll be in Winston-Salem tomorrow, but I'll call when I get back."

She knew him now well enough to understand that he wouldn't brush her off in the presence of that many people. He believed in putting up a front.

Imogene's head snapped around in Drogan's direction. "You're going to Winston-Salem tomorrow?"

"Yeah." he said in a voice that suggested his mind had wandered elsewhere. "Why? Say, I'll be there all morning, and you can shop while I'm keeping my appointment. We can do a movie and make a day of it. How about that?"

"Uh . . . I wouldn't want to disappoint Keisha. She hates going shopping by herself." Her face brightened, but Sharon could see that she forced the smile. "I'll call her soon as we get home."

That bore watching. She hugged her mother and, with Rafe beside her, turned to leave.

"I'll be back to see you, Mrs. Hairston," Rafe said. He looked at Ross. "If you'll give me a call, we can set up that interview. Ready to go?" he asked, looking at Eloise.

"I sure am. A nice ride beats trucking it home by foot. Ain't no bus between here and home. Me and Gert'll be over tomorrow after she gets off from work, Marge, and we gon' play cutthroat, so just fix your mind to do it."

"Good night, everybody." A couple of months earlier, she'd have kissed Drogan and Imogene, but Drogan was still nursing his grudge, and since she couldn't box Imogene's ears, she'd rather not touch her.

"You shouldn't oughta let Imogene get on your nerves," Eloise said to Sharon as Rafe drove her home. "You know she don't row with both oars. Over thirty years old and don't do nothin' with her time but run to Winston-Salem and shop. She don't even have to clean her own house, though she ain't got chick nor child."

"I always try to make allowances for her, Aunt Eloise, because she doesn't have much self-esteem."

"Then she oughtna have such a nasty little tongue. You were right she should pay attention to her husband. From what I saw when I was leaving the postoffice Friday, she got plenty to fill up her mind."

Rafe turned into Russett Lane and stopped at number eighteen. "What did you see, Miss Eloise?"

"Drogan alongside a tall woman so close they was touching. I still wouldna thought a thing of it, but after he got in the car and closed the door, he rolled down the window. She stuck her head in the car, and whatever they did lasted a couple of minutes."

"Too bad," Rafe said. "I wouldn't touch that. Besides, they were probably just talking."

"Child, I won't even whisper it in my prayers," Eloise said. "Thanks for the ride home, Rafe. Sharon, honey, you bring him to see me sometime so he can get some good stick-to-the-ribs cooking." She patted the seat beside her. "This is some car," she said of the Lincoln Town Car. "First time I remember being in one of these." She got out. "Y'all come see me, now."

"Don't think I won't," Rafe said. "I love to eat. I'm from Texas, and I love good southern country cooking."

"Well, you'll be coming to the right place. I worked in service for years, and if it's worth eatin', I learned to cook it. Good night."

"My family isn't what it was before Mama got sick, Rafe. We were close and loving. Imogene wouldn't have said that to me."

"Probably not. Drogan's not happy because your mother gave you the paper, and she feels free to show you the animosity she knows he feels."

"Mama gave him a shot at it before she asked me. He and Cassie wanted what the paper earns, but they didn't want the burden of making it pay."

"It's my guess they're angry at themselves and taking it out on you. If not, what you had with them was superficial. Let time test it, and try not to worry about it."

As he pulled away from the curb, she told him, "That's Mama's house right there beside Aunt Eloise. They were friends before I was born."

He put the car in drive, then reached over and put a Brook Benton cassette in the tape deck. "I'd give anything for a friend like that. I have some solid ones. But thirty-some years? That must be precious. A grin swept over his face. "Maybe one day I'll be able to say you've been my best friend for thirty years."

She heard herself say, "Only your best friend?" and clamped her hand over her mouth.

He glanced over at her. "What about best friend, lover . . . Shall I go on?"

"Your imagination is very busy," she replied, but her calm voice belied the turbulence that his words set off in her nervous system. Ideas of Rafe McCall as a lover filled her head, and in spite of her considerable effort to banish those thoughts, she couldn't erase the images from her mind's eye.

"What're you thinking?" he growled as he brought the car to a stop in front of her house.

"What do you . . . why do you ask?"

"I'm looking at that expression on your face, and if you're not thinking about me, I want to know who he is."

She laughed, releasing the sorrow she left in that hospital room and rejoicing in the joy of being with him and knowing he was there for her. The thought of Wade Field entered her mind, but she pushed it aside.

"I could have been thinking of the last great sunset I saw."

"Could've. But you weren't. Is it possible that you were thinking of me?" He had his left hand on the door of the car, but his body was turned toward her. "Well? Give a guy a break."

"I was thinking of you."

He released the door handle and put his arms around her. "I'd be in trouble if you'd said no. You seemed deep in a really sweet dream."

"I was."

"Think there's a chance it'll come true?"

"I don't know, Rafe. I was beginning to think we could have something, but you and I are going to be at loggerheads, and I don't want the frustration of being torn between my feelings for you and what I see as my civic responsibility. I don't need that."

He got out of the car and walked around to the passenger side to open her door, but though she appreciated it, she couldn't make herself sit there like a helpless doll waiting for him. "So what cooled you off wasn't my motorcycle but my interest in Wade Field. Right?"

She put her hand behind her when he seemed to reach for it; just looking at him caused her as much exhilaration as she could cope with right then, and she knew better than to give him the advantage. "Your roots aren't here in Woodmore, and you don't know what Wade Field means to us. So, before you commit yourself to anything final, go to the library and read the files on Wade Field, the state, the city, and the people of Woodmore."

"And you'd break off with me when all I've done was ask a question about the place? Don't you have any confidence in my social consciousness, my sense of decency?"

Her slight shrug reflected the hopelessness she felt about them. "I don't see what decency has to do with it. To me, it's a question of values. Thanks for going with me to the hospital."

"It was nothing. I needed to do it."

He stared down at her for a minute as if searching for something deep inside of her. "Good night, Sharon."

He left her, and she sat on her sofa in the dark as scenes of the day shuttled through her mind. She could handle Cassie's meanness. Though she loved her sister, she'd always been aware of Cassie's self-centeredness, but Drogan . . . From her earliest memory—when she'd trailed him around the house and he'd smile, pick her up, and hug her while she laughed and giggled with joy—she'd loved him unconditionally, idolized him, and he knew it. But this thing with Mama—just when they needed each other, they were like strangers. How could a relationship she'd thought so solid prove to be so fragile? The ringing phone ended her trip back through time, and she hurried to answer it.

"Hello." She flicked on a light.

"This is Rafe. I couldn't leave it like that. In my thirty-nine years, I haven't met a woman who interests me as much as you do. Before you sentence me, don't I at least deserve a trial? Before you consign me to oblivion, wait till I commit a crime. I never heard of anybody being convicted for what he *might* do."

"I think a lot of you, Rafe, but if I learned you planned to build anything in Wade Field, I'd castigate you daily on page eleven of *The Woodmore Times*. We can't be friends with that prospect looming over us."

"*Friends?*" He sounded as if she'd shocked him. "I can be more to you, Sharon, and I will be if you'll let me."

"Don't lead me to expect the improbable," she said, thinking him a man who refused to concede. "If it's a question of your bank account or me and my interests—"

"Don't say it! You don't know me well enough to suggest that I'm unprincipled."

"I didn't, and I wouldn't. I'm just protecting my . . . my feelings. I'd be foolish if I didn't."

She heard him suck in his breath. "Thanks for that much. Don't you expect me to give up till I'm satisfied you're not for me. You reciprocate my interest, and that's what I'm going on. If you're fair, and I expect you to be, we'll get through this."

She nodded and then remembered that he couldn't see her. "The ball's in your court, so be sure to read what the library has on Wade Field."

"I'll get on it tomorrow."

"That's all I ask . . . for now." She fought to catch her breath. Doing battle with him was tantamount to climbing a mountain bare-handed and without a rope.

She wondered at his silence. Then he said, "Why don't you take me out to Wade Field and explain its importance. I'd prefer that to a ton of library reports."

In for a penny, in for a pound. "All right, but first go to the library."

"I will. Then we'll take a look at it together. Sleep well."

He'd said he moved at a snail's pace. She'd begun to wonder what kind of snails he was used to. He was going faster than she thought wise, and he was trying to pull her right along with him. If she didn't watch herself, she'd be head over heels in love with the man, and she didn't know one thing about him except what he'd told her and showed her. If he had any friends, he hadn't exposed them to her.

At the hospital that same night, Imogene and Drogan prepared to leave Marge. "We'll be back, Mama, but we'd much rather know you were home," Drogan said, helping Imogene into her coat. "You don't belong in this place."

"Tell the doctor that, and while you're at it, let Ross know. Those two don't agree with you."

As if he hadn't heard her, his face bloomed into a smile, and he bent over and kissed her forehead. "You take care, now, Mama. We'll be back."

Marge held her breath, knowing she wouldn't be able to avoid Imogene's hug. "You take care, Mama. We're here for you."

"That woman doesn't have a real bone in her body," Ross said of Imogene when he and Marge were alone. "She's every reason why a man should stay single."

Marge leaned back against the pillow. She wanted her family and friends around her, but she was as tired as if she'd run a mile. She'd never liked Imogene, mainly because she couldn't stand women who didn't want to work and were content to do nothing, who didn't know the meaning of sharing responsibilities. But she'd kept that to herself. Drogan's wife was his business.

"Imogene wasn't so shallow when they first got married," Marge said, "but the poor girl's had three miscarriages in three years, and the doctor doesn't think she should try again anytime soon. You never know what makes people act the way they do."

"That doesn't account for how bitchy she was to Sharon. Where'd that come from?"

"Drogan's still mad at me for giving Sharon the paper and mad at Sharon for having it. His wife is reflecting his attitude."

"I didn't get anything negative from him."

If he had, it would mean that Drogan's famous charm was in jeopardy. "He was loaded with attitude," Marge said. "If he spoke to his sister, I didn't see or hear it, and he wasn't brimming with love for his mother. I know when affection is perfunctory. Drogan is like a piece of glass—at least to me. I can see right through him. Always could."

Ross got up, bracing his back with his hands as he did so. "It's time I headed home. I'll be by to see you tomorrow, but I'll call first in case you want anything."

She knew he was worried about her, so she smiled her best smile. "I'll look forward to it." Then, to impress upon him that she still thought about the paper, she asked, "How's Sharon coming along?"

He laughed and knocked his right fist into his left palm. "Wilson left a message on my pager. Seems she rolled heads, walked over Mack when he got out of line, and made Wilson editor in chief till I got back. From then on, everything went as smooth as a baby's behind. I'd say she takes to it like a duck to water."

She couldn't help grinning. Ross loved that expression. "I'm glad. I want her to succeed, Ross. She's given up so much."

"But she's getting a lot. What do you think of McCall?"

"He's right for her. I hope they make a go of it."

"I checked him out. He's a good man, all right, and he's got a solid reputation as a builder." He looked at her till she wondered if she had something out of place. "Want some more ice cream?"

"Yes, but I shouldn't eat it. Maybe tomorrow."

"See you, then." She watched him leave without his usual swagger and wondered if her being sick brought home to him his own mortality, as it did hers. She looked at the clock on her little night table. Nine-thirty. Where could Cassie be that time of night that her husband couldn't get a message to her? And why would Imogene rather go shopping with her girlfriend than spend a day in Winston-Salem with her husband? Worrying about it wouldn't do a bit of good. She turned out the light and tried to sleep.

Marge wasn't the only one skeptical about Imogene's preference for going to Winston-Salem with Keisha rather than her husband. Drogan spoke little on the way home, but as soon as he locked the door behind them, he grabbed his wife's shoulders.

"What's so important about your shopping trips with Keisha, and why would you rather disappoint me than her?"

"You're hurting my shoulders."

"Bull. I am not hurting your shoulders; I'm barely touching you. You're going with me or you're not going at all."

"Let me go. You don't know I exist till you want sex."

He couldn't believe she'd said that. After four years of marriage, didn't she know him better than that? *"What did you say?"*

He shoved his hands into his pockets to avoid shaking her. "I work on weekends. I have to in order to save money, now that we don't have the paper for retirement. You know that. Most days I'm home by six, but three out of five days a week, and lately sometimes more, you're not here when I get home. You're shopping with Keisha, and when you get here, you're so tired you don't even want me to kiss you, much less make love. You don't cook. You don't clean. You don't offer companionship. Why the hell are you here?"

"Even when you're home, you're hunched over that computer. Ever since Mama went crazy and gave that paper to Sharon, work is all you do. When did you last take me to a movie? I want a life while I'm still young. I'm not going to waste away here in this . . . this house."

"I'm trying to keep you in the style to which I've accustomed you. The reason I don't have any money now is because I've given you everything you imagined you wanted, including trips to Greece, Italy, and Scandinavia. If I sold the jewelry I've bought you, I could pay off the mortgage on this house, so don't hand me that crap. Before you married me, you didn't have a pot to piss in. Another thing. Don't think you're putting something over on me just because I don't say anything. You get your act together."

He watched her fold up and realized he'd hit her where she was vulnerable. It didn't give him any pleasure, because he loved her, and if she used her head, she'd realize it. *What about you?* his conscience prodded. *Is whatever she's doing worse than your having an affair?* He threw up his hands.

"This is stupid. What are we fighting about, honey?"

She locked her arms around him, as he'd known she would, grabbing at the reprieve he threw her. "I don't know. I don't want us to fight. I want us to be like we were before all this . . . this anger and hatred . . . this business with Sharon messed up our lives."

Even in his irritation at Mama and the events she'd spun, he wasn't sufficiently annoyed to blind himself to their own responsibility for what happened in their marriage. But if he attempted to straighten her out on that score, they'd soon be back in the argument, and he'd go to bed hungry, hard, and hurting.

"Let's defrost a pizza, get a beer, and eat," he said, knowing she'd agree to most any arrangement that meant she wouldn't have to cook.

She rewarded him with a kiss that suggested she would welcome more later. "Good. I'll get that together while you get your shower."

"What about you? Aren't you going to—"

"I'll do that when you're straightening up the kitchen." With a wink, she stroked his genitals to emphasize her point and rushed toward the kitchen. He couldn't help wondering if women had turned out the way the Lord meant them to be. He was damned if he believed they did.

He finished showering, dried off, and put on the silk paisley robe Imogene gave him for his birthday. When he sat down to the pizza and beer, he heard himself say, "Would have been nice to have a salad along with this."

Her fork clattered against the plate. "Why didn't you say so? I could have ordered the whole meal from Pinky's Take Out Service."

"I didn't want that, honey. This is just fine."

He made it through the meal, and for the first time since he'd been married, he didn't look forward to going to bed with Imogene. Not because he'd been with Irene hours earlier. The satisfaction he got with her never lasted long, because it didn't fulfill him. It was a snack, light fare while he awaited his meal. And it was perfunctory, because Irene put no soul or heart into it, only skill and gymnastics.

Imogene had gotten a lot of mouth recently, a far cry from her sweet, congenial self. And tonight. First, she shocked him with that attack on Sharon, and then she plowed into him like a shrew. Neither put him in an amorous mood. He wondered what was giving her all that courage. In the past, she treated him with respect, but now . . . He didn't like thinking she didn't respect a man just because he had to work his ass off in order to provide for her.

He pasted a smile on his face, took her to bed, went through the motions of making love to her, and suffered the exhilarating agony of pouring himself into her. Ashamed of his weakness, of his failure to stand up to her, to Irene, Mama, and the world, he lay there berating himself. Imogene lay beside him, exhausted from her orgasms. Resentment welled up in him, and he wanted to get into his car, open all the windows, tear up the roads at eighty miles and hour, and get some fresh air. If he did that, the way he felt right then, he might never come back.

He rolled over and quietly spilled himself off the bed. He didn't want Irene Hunter, hadn't ever wanted her as a person, only for what he got from her. He wanted his wife, but he didn't want her on the terms he'd been getting her on for the last couple of months. When the sun came up, he was still sitting at his laptop computer, playing solitaire.

Half an hour after Drogan left for his office at seven-thirty, Cassie phoned his house. "He must have left early this morning," Imogene told her, still in bed.

"I need to talk with him," Cassie said in her best no-nonsense voice. "I'm on my way to work." Cassie liked to remind Imogene that she didn't do anything important. She managed this by innuendo, since she wouldn't risk insulting Drogan's wife outright, especially not now that she and her brother had to stick together.

"Oh, my goodness!" Imogene said. "He's supposed to be in Winston-Salem this morning, and I was supposed to go with him. Good Lord, I hope he didn't forget."

"If you talk with him, tell him to call me."

"Okay. Say, did you go see Mama last night?"

"No. I was asleep when Kix came home, so I didn't know till this morning that she was back in the hospital. Why? Were you there?"

"Of course. We went as soon as Drogan got the call from Ross."

She hated it when Imogene played one-upmanship and won. "Oh, please, Imogene. I'd worked long hours all week, including Sunday, and I fell asleep on the living-room sofa, exhausted, almost as soon as I got home. Kix didn't consider waking me, just picked me up and put me in bed."

"What do you want me to tell Drogan?"

"I want him to call me. I told you that."

"I'll tell him, but you can call him at his office. See you."

Cassie stared at the phone as the dial tone hummed in her ear. Something had happened to Imogene. Until recently, she'd hung on to every word Cassie uttered, revering her like a hero-worshiping schoolgirl. She hadn't wanted her brother to marry a girl who hadn't bothered to go to college and was so lacking in self-esteem that she created her past to suit the occasion and didn't bother to remember the different versions she offered. Well, he had to live with her; she didn't.

As soon as she got to work, Cassie phoned Drogan at his office. "Do you know whether Mama has a will?" she asked him after they greeted each other.

"No. I've thought about it, but . . . look, it doesn't seem right to . . . to ask her about it as if we think she's going to . . . to die."

"We can't afford to be sentimental about this, Drogan. If Sharon has the paper, that house and everything in it belongs to you and me."

"Is that what Kix thinks?"

She rolled her eyes to the ceiling. "Kix? He hasn't shown a bit of interest. You'd think there wasn't a problem. I was thinking maybe you could talk to Ross and get him to ask Mama if she's made a will. Look, I know he's blind as a bat about anything that concerns Mama, but even he can see why she ought to have a will."

"I'll feel him out and see if he's willing to bring it up to her. Okay?"

"Great. You sound busy."

"Actually, I am."

"Well, I won't hold you. Be sure and talk to Ross." She told him good-bye and hung up.

So he was supposed to be the heavy and make himself look like a jerk to Ross Ingersol because Cassie didn't have the guts to do her dirty work herself. He picked up the phone and dialed the probate officer, his buddy since high school. Twenty minutes later, he sat staring at the wall in front of his desk. Neither his mother nor her lawyer had probated a will. He sucked air through his front teeth and dialed Cassie.

"There is no will," he told her when she answered in her usual, officious voice. "I called the probate's office. Now what?"

"You'll have to call Ross and get him to see that she makes one."

"You really think Mama won't give us what we're due?"

I wouldn't have thought she'd give the paper to Sharon. Would you?"

He was getting sick of the whole issue of Sharon and the paper. It was a done deed. He had to prop up his business. He ran his hand over his tight curls and leaned back in his desk chair. "Cassie, I've got more problems facing me than you're ever going to see," he spat out, "so cut me some slack here and let me work. If you're so upset about Mama writing a will, you call Ross or talk to Mama. I gotta work."

"How could you . . . I mean . . . you're the man in the family," she sputtered, "and you're the one who should be responsible for these things. Now, you call, Ross. You hear?"

Cassie hung up, her own near hysteria echoing in her ears. *Why should one person have everything?* Maybe if she called Kix and begged him to— No, she couldn't do that and give him the upper hand. She wrung her hands. What was wrong with her? She no longer recognized herself.

"So you get in early, stay late, and work weekends!"

Her head snapped up at the sound of that voice, and her heart began racing as if it would fly out of her chest. "What are you doing here this morning? Didn't you finish what you had to do yesterday?"

He sauntered up to her desk. "I have to install the machines. If you want to keep your old ones, be my guest."

The man had the ability to madden her. "Then put them in and let me do my work."

"You have to choose the kind of laptop and printer you want. Or maybe you'd rather have a desktop. If you'll be still, I'll tell you what you can expect from the ones we're offering."

"Look, I don't have time to—"

"I can come back about five if that'll suit you better." Smooth, low, and suggestive. Lord, she couldn't be imagining things. If he'd just leave and let her get her breath back.

"Anything, just leave me be."

He stared down at her, his dark, long-lashed eyes sultry and his whole demeanor that of a stud who'd earned the right to the title.

"Just go!" she said, her breath short and shallow.

"Okay. See you later."

Her gaze lingered on his arrogant swagger, clung to his broad shoulders and tight, mobile buttocks, perfectly proportioned to his height of at least six feet two inches. If he didn't have on that awful skull-and-bones cap, dirty brogan shoes, and sweaty plaid shirt, she'd— She slapped her hand over her mouth and put her head on her desk. Then she heard the door close and knew he'd witnessed her turmoil. Oh, Lord! I won't let that man make me cheat on my husband. I won't!

At five o'clock, she put her designs in her briefcase, made notes on what she'd do first thing the next morning, and lifted the phone receiver to call Kix. The door opened, the electrician walked in, and she hung up.

"I see you waited for me."

"I . . . I didn't wait for you. I just finished my—"

"Why bother to lie about it," he said, slowly closing the distance between them.

"Why, you—"

"I know when a woman wants me. You're so bottled up inside and so scared of yourself that you're—"

"How dare you speak to me this way? Who do you think you are?" If he touched her, she'd incinerate. And if he didn't, she'd die.

"Get off your high horse. You knew I'd be back here at five o'clock, because you consented to it."

"Let me alone," she whispered.

One of his hands gripped her back, and the other one claimed her breast. She should scream, kick, bite. She did neither. The feel of his fingers stroking her breast electrified her.

"Open your mouth."

His tongue slipped between her parted lips, and his hands, like steel bands, hooked her body to his. Fire such as she'd never imagined plowed through her, searing her feminine center. She heard her moans and then her sobs.

He pulled back. "What the— For heaven's sake, are you crying?"

"Just please . . . please don't touch me anymore."

"Are you telling me that if I put my hands on you I can have you? That's what you practically said."

"I just want you to leave me alone."

"Look, lady. The minute I looked at you yesterday, I wanted you, and you let me know it was mutual. Standing beside that elevator, if I'd picked you up and brought you back into this office, we'd have been on this floor for hours."

"You d-don't know what you're talking about. Just take your hand off of me, please."

He stepped back. "If I had on an Armani suit and Hugo Boss shoes, you'd see it differently. But let me tell you something, lady. You're not going to rest until we have it. Go on home, Cassandra."

Her eyebrows shot up. "How'd you know my name?"

He shrugged. "It's right here on this order. My name is Judd. Next time, if you don't mean business, don't wait for me. See you."

She flopped down in her chair, unstrung. Yes, and so alive, she feared she'd float up to the ceiling. Maybe she could get Kix to take a short vacation and give them a chance to warm things up between them and she could get that electrician out of her head. But it was nearing his busiest season, and besides, he wasn't too happy with her. Maybe she should agree to . . . *No! She was damned if she was having a baby at a time when Cutting Edge was expanding and four of her newest designs were being considered for awards.* Damn Judd whatever-his-last-name-was; she didn't kowtow to Kix, and she wouldn't give in to him, either. But what was she going to do? She'd nearly died of pleasure when his calloused hand held her buttocks, and Lord, his tongue slipping in and out of her mouth while he stroked and pinched her nipple . . . Frustrated and hungry for him, she crossed her legs.

"The hell with him and his sweaty clothes," she said aloud then pulled herself up from the chair and left. Oh, Lord. It was Monday. Kix was off and at home waiting for her. What was she going to do? If only she could get a nice hot bath, she wouldn't feel so— How could she face him?

"McCall's in his office at Scenic Gardens."

She punched the reporter's number on the intercom. "K.C., may I see you, please."

"Sure thing, Sharon. Be right there."

She told the reporter what she wanted and added, "Ross will set up the appointment. Call Allen and tell him to get a driver for you."

K.C.'s eyebrows shot up. "You mean to take me over to Scenic Gardens?"

"Right. A good reporter doesn't do her own driving."

"Yes, ma'am!"

K.C. rushed out, and Ross smiled his approval. "Now that, my girl, is the way to be popular. I'll telephone McCall and set it up."

Ross had his hand on the doorknob when she said, "I want Wilson to attend budget meetings along with you, Mack, and me. He writes well, and he's stable. One of these days, I'll get fed up with Mack."

Ross half-laughed. "If Wilson starts attending budget meetings, you won't have any more trouble out of Mack." With his right thumb pointing upward, he left.

Her phone rang, and having learned that she irritated her secretary when she answered it, she waited. "Mr. McCall on two. Shall I click off?"

Hmm. So the news was out that she and Rafe had a personal relationship. "Always click off, Myrna, unless I tell you to stay on and take notes."

"Hello, Rafe. I hear you're in Woodmore."

"I am. How about dinner? I know you want to see your mother. If you'd prefer, we could visit her and have dinner after we leave the hospital?"

"I suspect Mama would love to see you, but I went by this morning, and I hadn't planned to visit her again today. Do any research on Wade Field?"

"I said I would, and I did."

"Well?"

"I want to see the place. I read microfilm until my eyes burned, and I still don't have a clear idea of what that area is used for now."

She looked at her watch. "It's ten-thirty. If you can get away at three, we'll go out there today. But if you read that much, what do you expect to learn by looking at it?"

"A lot. I'm an engineer. I'll be over there at three. If nothing else, I'll get to spend some time with you."

Eight

Later in the week, Ross walked into Sharon's office in response to her invitation and took a seat. "I just spoke with McCall about that interview. He's willing, and I think it would be a good feature story for the weekend edition. That doesn't give us much time, but I expect K.C. could interview him today and give it to me by press time Friday. What do you think?"

"Fine with me provided she's free to—"

He sat forward. "Listen here, Sharon, if you tell anybody in this shop, including me, that they're free to do something, they're free whether they like it or not. I thought that was understood."

With a level look, she asked him, "Whatever happened to old-fashioned democracy? I wouldn't think being a dictator would make me popular."

He got up and paced from one end of the office to the other. "Sharon, if you need to be popular, you're in the wrong business. There're seven men and four women out there, and six men at the plant. You start being popular and they'll drag in when they feel like it, stay out when it suits 'em, and turn in sloppy work."

He stopped pacing and stopped in front of her. "Ed, your father, was just like you, and he had to learn to crack the whip and smile while he did it. Marge learned from what she saw him go through. Nobody is more liked than Marge. But not a person here played with her or took her for granted. When she wanted something done, she told one of us to do it. If you want K.C. to do that story, tell her to interview him and get the story to me by two o'clock Friday."

"Are we sending her to Winston-Salem?"

At three, she stepped off the elevator and into the lobby of the Woodmore Building, and her gaze caught him lounging against the receptionist's desk. Quintessential male. If I let him, she thought, he'd take my breath away. "Hi. I hope you didn't drive."

"Hi. I figured you drove to work and we'd take your car."

Because she wanted to keep their conversation impersonal, she asked him," How'd the interview go?"

"Great. She's a skillful interviewer. I'm waiting to see what she writes."

She drove them along Court Street, around Wade Lake to its western edges, and stopped. "Look at that, Rafe. Geese, waterfowl, ducks, herons, all kinds of birds. It's spectacular. In the summer, groups of children come here to learn about the birds, conservation, the environment, and nature."

They walked around the lake, watching the birds dive for fish and fighting among themselves for the catch. Geese waded in the field and swam in the lake alongside the ducks.

"I'm told we've even had a few cranes here; I didn't see them. What do you think?"

"I was out here only once before, last winter, and the area was icy. I didn't see any birds."

"They go farther south and come back in March. Can't you understand what all this means to us?"

"If it's so important to everyone, why would anybody sell it to me or to any other builder? Maybe your concern is misplaced."

"You know money can buy most anything."

"I get the idea, Sharon, but I also see homeless people sleeping on the streets. What about that?"

She stopped walking and faced him so he could see how she felt. "Are you going to build free lodging for the homeless? If you are, I withdraw my objection."

He locked his hands behind his back. "I have to give this a lot of thought. I admit it's . . . well, interesting and maybe even . . . I'll think about it."

Days were short in December, and darkness began to shroud the area, so they only stayed at Wade Field for about an hour and a half. "It's too early for dinner; we could drop by Mama's for a few minutes," Sharon suggested.

"Fine, but take me by my office so I can get my car." He looked at her with both eyebrows arched. "Unless you want to take me to Winston-Salem tonight."

"Don't even go there, Rafe."

"Can't blame me for trying, and don't expect me to stop, either."

She'd be disappointed if he did. A woman wanted persistence in a man. He said he moved slowly, and she intended to encourage that, but if he made a bid for Wade Field, his pace wouldn't matter.

"What do you say we eat at Gourmet Corner? Is seven thirty good for you?" She agreed, and he used his cell phone to make the reservation.

Gilford Ripple's laughter greeted them as they neared Marge's room. "That old fox," he was heard to say. "I'd kick him out of the church if it was my house, but I don't think the Lord would take kindly to my turning people out of *His* house."

Marge sucked her teeth. "You mean you don't want to give up those big bills he puts in the collection plate every Sunday. You preachers remind me of those congressmen in Washington: pour the money into their campaigns and you got a free ride."

"Now, Marge, that's no way to talk to a man of the cloth." He noticed them for the first time as they walked toward Marge's bed. "Sharon, my dear," the reverend said, "who is this fine gentleman?" She introduced Rafe to her pastor. "Haven't seen you in church, young man."

Rafe raised an eyebrow, a twinkle dancing in his eyes. "I don't suppose you have." He walked closer to the bed and took Marge's hand. "How're you feeling?"

"'Bout the same," she said, smothering a laugh.

"What's funny, Mama?"

Marge patted Rafe's hand. "It isn't often I get to see Gilford stopped dead. After all these years, I've finally seen him speechless."

"You're kidding," the minister said. "I don't cross swords till I know who I'm fencing with." He looked at Sharon. "You bring him to church . . . that is, if *you* ever get back there."

"I'll take your innuendo . . . I mean, your advice under consideration," she said, expelling laughter that she knew was a mildly hysterical reaction to seeing her mother in a heightened, jocular mood, so much like her old self.

"We're going to Kix's place for dinner," Sharon told her mother, so we'd better leave. Rafe has reservations for seven-thirty."

"Kix is pure gold," Marge said. "The more I see of him, the more I wonder how Cassie got so lucky."

"Yeah," Gilford Ripple said. "She got a lot luckier that Kix did."

Rafe's head snapped around in the minister's direction, and he stared at the man. Sharon supposed he was wondering why she or her mother didn't correct the pastor, but how could they? Kix deserved better than Cassie gave him. As they left the hospital room, they met Ross.

"How's she doing?" he asked

"Much brighter today," Sharon said. "I know she'll be glad to see you."

Ross popped his fingers and cocked his head to the side. "I come here to see Marge every day. I'm not concerned about her being glad. See you in the morning."

"Why would that question irritate him?" Rafe asked Sharon.

"Who knows? I was asking myself the same thing."

"Your table's this way, Mr. McCall," the maître d' said when they stepped into the restaurant. She loved the ambience, especially in winter, when logs burned and the fire crackled in the big stone fireplace. Red brick walls, polished parquet floors, round tables of varying sizes, and chairs upholstered in dark green damask that matched the curtains at the windows gave the room a homey atmosphere. But its table settings of linens, porcelain, silver plate, and seasonal flowers created an aura of sophistication. As she followed the maître d' to their table, she couldn't help recalling how Kix had built the place by himself, with his hard work, grueling hours, sweat, and skills and with no help from his wife.

"Kix will be out in a minute," the waiter said, and placed a plate of tiny crab cakes on the table.

"I wouldn't mind eating here twice every day," Rafe said, savoring an hors d'oeuvre. "It's the best food within more than a hundred miles, which is why you never see an empty table at dinnertime."

Sharon looked up as Kix came to them dressed in white shirt and slacks, a tall white chef's hat, and white apron. "I heard you were coming, Rafe," he said after greeting them, "so I made a few quennelles for you." He smiled at Sharon. "Haven't seen you here since I first opened. I'm glad you came, Sharon. How's Mama?"

"She seemed better tonight than yesterday."

"Glad to hear it. What can I cook for you?"

After taking their orders, he said, "If you'd drive by one day, Sharon, I'd send your mother something nice to eat. I can't imagine she'd like hospital food."

If *she'd* drive by. What about Cassie? Not that she'd dare ask him. In any case, Rafe saved her an answer. "I can stop by tomorrow," He said. "What time?"

"Between four and five would be good."

They'd finished one of the best meals she eaten in years and moved to the lounge, a smaller room adjacent to the dining room and decorated as a living room. They sat beside each other on the brown velveteen sofa that faced the lighted Christmas tree, whose bells and trinkets reflected the flame and sparks from the wood-burning fire blazing in the fireplace.

Sharon lifted the coffee cup to her lips and stopped, nearly spilling its contents. Her left hand gripped Rafe's right wrist.

"That's Cassie's voice. What on earth?"

"If it is, she's mad," Rafe said. "I mean, furious."

She uncrossed her ankles, braced her right hand on the sofa, and moved forward. But he stilled her. "If she's arguing with her husband, it may be best to pretend we don't hear it or . . . we can leave."

"But . . . but she's so upset."

"That isn't your business, Sharon." His voice had a harshness that surprised her.

Her head snapped around. "I beg your pardon."

"Her husband is back there. Let him handle it."

"I don't think I asked your opinion, Rafe."

"That's right; you didn't, but you'd be wise to take my advice. If they're arguing, stay out of it and they'll patch it up. But if you butt in—"

She jumped to her feet. "What do you mean by speaking to me this way?"

Firm and unyielding, he looked her in the eye. "Ease up, will you? I'm telling you for their good and yours. Let them handle it."

At that moment, Cassie charged through the lounge. "You don't care, because it's not important to you," she flung over her shoulder. "All you care about is this glorified—"

She stopped short as her gaze landed on Rafe and shifted to Sharon. "What are *you* doing here? Trying to take over this . . . this . . ."

She waved her hand around to encompass all that she saw. "Whatever."

"Rafe and I just had dinner here. What's wrong, Cassie?"

Her chin went up. "What would you care?" With head thrown back, she flitted out of the lounge in the direction of the front door.

"I'm sorry about this."

They turned to see Kix standing in the doorway with both hands on his hips, staring at Cassie's departing back.

"Is there anything I can do?" Rafe asked him.

"No," he said, pulled air through his front teeth and then let out a long breath. "I'll deal with her when I get home." With furor blazing in his eyes, he knocked his right fist into his left palm several times and went back into the kitchen.

"Boy, is she angry!" Sharon said. "She didn't even bother to put up a front for you, and that's not a bit like her. I'll bet anything it's got something to do with me and that newspaper."

Rafe narrowed his eyes. "You sister is older than you, and it's not you but she who should hold the family together now that your mother can't do that. Or your brother. You're the youngest, and if anything, they should be concerned about you."

There's nothing easygoing about this man. "I'm not standing on what's right. I'll look after Mama for as long as she needs me, but I'm getting sick of Cassie's hostility and of Drogan avoiding me. If they want the paper so badly, they can have it."

"If you gave them the paper, what do you think would happen to it?"

"Mama said it would die a quick, undignified death."

"That's your answer. If they're strong enough to persist in behaving this way, you have the grit necessary to ignore it. What do you say we run into Winston-Salem and go to Tanglewood Park for a little while? It's only about fifteen minutes from here."

She welcomed the chance for a change of mood, and as soon as they entered the park, she joined in the singing and merriment with the revelers who frolicked in the park every evening beneath the man-made lights and the stars that blanketed the sky. And she welcomed the comfortable warmth of Rafe's nearness. Very soon he would want to push their relationship to another level, but as slow as he claimed he traveled, he was, nonetheless, a few steps ahead of her.

* * *

After they left the park, he stopped the Town Car in front of a modern, detached house that had a tan-colored stone exterior and huge windows. They walked up the winding path embedded with scattered stones of varying sizes, and she concentrated on his face. His pride was evident when he opened the door, turned, and looked at her.

"I've wanted to see how you looked here and to know what you'd think of my home. I'll give you a tour."

The house was like the man, conservative and elegant, yet distinctly individual. From the foyer, bare but for an enormous painting of a black family picnicking by a lake, they stepped down into the living room, whose cathedral ceiling reached the second floor. Huge overstuffed leather sofa and chairs in beige, brown, and rust-colored tones rested on a Tabriz carpet of complementary colors that covered most of the area. She couldn't imagine where he found such a large carpet and nearly swallowed her tongue when he said he ordered it from an Iranian merchant in New York and waited sixteen months for it.

"That tells me you know what you want and you're willing to wait till you get it."

He seemed to reflect on her words for a minute. "I'd say that summarizes me in one sentence. Want to see the rest of it?"

She did indeed. The kitchen, a cook's dream, with yellow brick walls, black tile floor, and stainless steel appointments, was large and airy, with windows that faced a sprawling wooden deck. She thought about the fun she could have cooking in that kitchen. The dining room brought another surprise. A huge stone fireplace was the centerpiece of a very formal setting that she wouldn't have associated with his ultramodern living room. She saw him watching her in a way that suggested he wanted her approval.

"What's upstairs?"

"Three bedrooms."

"Why so many?" she asked as they climbed the spiral stairs.

"I want at least two children, and I need a guest room."

"What if the children aren't of the same sex?"

His smile suggested pleasure at the thought. "I can add on two more rooms if I need them."

He took her to the master bedroom last. It equaled the living room in size, and she noted that he used one end of it for an office. The king-size bed seemed small in that setting. Modern paintings by Beardon, Price, and Johnson mingled with works by more traditional artists.

"I buy what I like and hang it where I like. I don't believe in decorators because I've never known one to express my exact taste. There're four baths in the house and one Jacuzzi. Anytime you want a hot tub . . ." He left the rest to her imagination.

She walked over to the window and looked out at the trees and garden at the back of the house, then strolled around and examined the paintings, the mantel above the big stone fireplace, and the massive armoire, obviously an antique. Then, for reasons she couldn't explain, not even to herself, she sat on the bed, patted the mattress, and looked up at him.

"Hmm. This is comfy. I could—"

"Get up from there, Sharon. Get up right this minute."

Stunned by the harshness of his tone, she gaped at him. "I was just . . ." Her heart began a fast gallop in her chest as his whole demeanor changed, and she could almost feel the heat that blazed in his eyes. Aware of the message she'd sent him, she jumped up.

"Rafe, I didn't mean to suggest that I . . . that you . . . that . . ."

He took her hand. "Come on. I didn't bring you here to seduce you." He locked the front door, turned, and gripped both of her shoulders. "When we get to your house, where you can tell me to leave whenever you like, the playing field will be level. Do you like my home?"

She remembered that she hadn't commented on it. "I love it. It's wonderful. You haven't told me where you went to school or what you studied," she said, regaining her equilibrium. "Are you an architect?"

"An architectural engineer. I studied at Morehouse in Atlanta and at Columbia University in New York."

With her hand in his, he walked them to his car and stood with her beside the big gray machine. "By now, you either care for me and trust me or you don't, and if you don't, you never will. I know how I feel about you, and if you're on track with me, I'm going to pursue it."

From then until they walked into her house, she spoke only to answer his questions, not trusting herself to say more.

She hung his coat in the foyer closet and walked into the living room with him. He'd given her a tour of his house, but she wouldn't even think of showing him her bedroom.

"I know you wouldn't consider a glass of wine, but would you like some coffee?"

He shook his head. "I don't want coffee or anything else in your kitchen. We've been fencing long enough, Sharon. You told me that if I wanted sweetness, I should provide the sugar. I want sweetness, and I want it from you. Come here, sweetheart."

His heat shot out to her, charging her up the way a transformer stirs a battery. She wanted to move. Why couldn't she move her feet?

"Sharon, I need to hold you, to . . . If you want me to make the first move, I'll do it."

She sped to him with open arms, and he gripped her to him with stunning force, stared into her eyes, and lifted her into his embrace. His mouth was on her at last, and he let her feel the fire that burned in him, sizzling, as if it couldn't be controlled. Her nerves went on a wild rampage in her body as he claimed her.

"Open your mouth and let me in. Don't hold back on me."

She parted her lips and knew what it was to have him possess her.

While holding her in a gentle caress, he eased her to her feet. "Are you committed to a man? Any man anywhere?"

She found her voice with difficulty, for she hadn't emerged from the storm they had created. "There's no one. What about you?"

It seemed to please him that she'd asked. "If there was another woman in my life, Sharon, I wouldn't be holding you like this. As a youth, I witnessed firsthand what a man's philandering can do to a woman, and I hope never to be guilty of it." An expression suggestive of pain flashed across his face.

She needed to know a lot more about him, she realized. His thoughts had obviously opened an old wound, a serious one. She didn't doubt his worth as a man, but . . . "I'm not ready to start a . . . something with you."

"It started the night we met."

"I don't want to get in any deeper, because I can't afford to compromise on—"

As if fearing the finality of her remark, he didn't let her finish it. "If I ever ask you to do that, feel free to walk away."

"By then, it would probably be too late."

He paced a few steps, turned, and walked back to her. "Are you willing to concede that we care for each other?"

At least he had committed himself. "Uh . . . yes, but that doesn't change anything."

The seductive gleam in his storm-filled gaze threatened to make a liar of her, and his half-smile stunned her with the measure of her vulnerableness to him. He raised an eyebrow.

"Doesn't change anything, huh? Well, not for you, maybe." He kissed her quickly on the mouth. "A sensible man doesn't give up when he's winning, so don't think I'm going anyplace. We'll be in touch."

She watched him leave. Now what was she supposed to do? Stay away from him after he'd fired every nerve in her body? She sat down on the sofa in her living room and relived that short minute.

Later that evening, Cassie—less contented than her sister—paced the floor of her dining room, furious with herself. She'd tipped her hand, and she wouldn't be surprised if Kix told Mama and Sharon that she planned to sue for property rights if Mama didn't leave a will. He hadn't understood and refused to intercede with Ross. She filled the bathtub with water, added bubble bath, stripped, and climbed in. Too bad she couldn't linger and enjoy it; she wanted to finish her bath and put on some clothes before Kix got home. No point in giving him ideas, though considering his recent behavior, she might be rushing for no good reason. She dried off, put on a blue caftan, and piled her hair up on her head, one of her signals to Kix that lovemaking wasn't on her mind. Then she browned some frozen french fries in the oven and ate them like snacks while she read *The Carolina Times*. She hadn't looked at a copy of *The Woodmore Times* since Mama gave it to Sharon.

To her chagrin, Kix walked into the house and laid a copy of Sharon's paper on the coffee table right in front of her. "I hope that's not your dinner," he said. "Why didn't you eat at the restaurant?"

"The food's too rich. Besides, I wanted to get out of there."

"What do you mean, 'the food's too rich'? If the governor of this state entertains at my restaurant, it should be good enough for you."

"I didn't want to eat there because you refused to understand me."

He sat down and rested his hand on her thigh. She wanted to move it, but she didn't dare. "Cassie, you're my wife. I love you, and I'll protect you. But I will not, you hear me, *will not*, hound your sick mother about making a will. You've been married to me almost six years, and you don't know me. I will treat Marge Hairston just as I would treat my own mother. Don't ever ask me to do anything to another person that you wouldn't want me to do to you."

"Please spare me." She folded the paper and put it on top of *The Woodmore Times*. "I've had enough self-righteousness for one day."

He tipped her chin with his left index finger, wordlessly demanding that she look at him. "We're still married, Cassie, and I want us to remain married, but if you want a change, tell me. I don't plan to lap up your occasional crumbs as if I were a lovesick puppy. I could use a normal married life, and so far, I can't say I know what that is. Sleep well."

She propped her hands on her hips and glared at his retreating form as he headed up the stairs, but when she heard him coming back down, a nervous shiver raced through her. He hadn't finished.

"And another thing," he said. "As long as I pay the mortgage on the house you live in and you share my bed, don't pull one of those stunts you pulled in the restaurant tonight. Pay attention, Cassie, because I mean this. If you ever have another tantrum with me in the presence of my employees, I won't forgive you. You either respect me or I'm out of here. And for good."

She stared, nonplussed, as he strolled back up the stairs, whistling with the air of a man who didn't have a care. How could he talk like that? In her mind, she didn't deserve it. She'd only been trying to get her due. Exasperated at his action, she dialed Drogan.

He stopped midway up the stairs. "Who're you calling? It's eleven o'clock."

She sniffed to let him know how miserable she was. "Drogan. I want to talk with Drogan." Without another word, Kix continued up the stairs.

"Hello? Hello? Drogan, this is Cassie."

"Nothing's the matter that hasn't been the matter all day. Kix refuses to speak to Ross, and he yelled at me when I told him I was going to talk to Mama about a will. You'd think I was some kind of ogre the way he behaved. Drogan, what will we do?"

"Cassie, it's almost midnight. Climb into the bed and give your husband some attention. If you're already in the bed, give him a kiss. I'm sleepy. Good night."

"Of all the—" She stared at the receiver, frustrated and with no means of releasing it. Damn Kix; he was turning her into a shrew.

Kix walked out of the bedroom wearing boxer shorts, a towel slung over his shoulder. She stared at him when he leaned against the doorjamb, his face bearing the kind of expression one uses with a recalcitrant child.

"You're working yourself up unnecessarily. Your brother doesn't appear to be upset about it. If you don't calm down, I'll call Miles

Glick and ask him to prescribe a sedative for you. I don't like seeing you this way."

"I wouldn't be so upset if you'd show a little more interest." She assumed her favorite pout. "This is so important to me."

"Sure. Everything you want is important to you. Never mind what anybody else wants or is entitled to. I told you at the restaurant that what you're after is vengeance. You're not a cruel person, Cassie, and if you succeed in this, you'll still be unhappy."

"You don't understand." She walked past him and, knowing that he'd take a long, hot shower, quickly changed into her gown and got into bed. Nobody understood what she was going through, with Sharon, her kid sister, making waves all around her. She was tired of hearing at work about the wonderful innovations at *The Woodmore Times*. She'd show them all. Judd—she realized she didn't know his last name—would understand her, and he'd look up to her because he wasn't used to women like her. She turned over on her belly and rubbed her nipples. They ached a lot recently. Lord, she hoped there wasn't anything wrong with her breasts. She loved her breasts, full and standing straight out even when she didn't wear a bra. Wonder what Judd thought of her breasts? She'd never let Kix play with them, because she wanted them to remain perfect and not sag. Oh, what the hell! She fluffed her pillow, turned on her side, and went to sleep.

When she groped her way into the kitchen the next morning to get her caffeine fix, Kix was taking popovers out of the oven.

"Popovers? You made popovers! You know how I love those."

The laugh didn't quite make it to his cheeks. "If you're in too much of a snit to eat these, I'm calling the doctor."

"You're too good to me." She stood behind him and wrapped her arms around his chest. "Stubborn, but you're mine, and I love you."

He turned and gazed down at her until she thought she'd shrivel with guilt. "Funny, you always talk this way in the mornings or when we're someplace where discretion dictates behavior. One of these days, I might surprise you, so watch it. He loosened her hold on him and poured a cup of coffee. "Orange juice, popovers, raspberry jam, real butter, double-smoked bacon, and strong black coffee."

She thanked him. "I don't know what I'd do without you." She savored a popover on which she'd slathered butter and jam. "Honest, I don't."

"For one thing, you'd probably starve, or at least you'd lose a lot of weight."

"I can cook if I have to, now."

"Yeah? A week in bed sick would be worth it just to prove my point."

"If you think I'm going to smart-talk you right now, you're out of your mind. I want some more of these popovers."

He laughed then, and she knew she'd pleased him. If only . . . She wasn't going to think about that awful electrician with his dirty fingernails—she hadn't looked at them, but of course they were dirty. She was going to get him out of her head if she drove herself mad trying.

"Honey, can we take a vacation? I mean, I . . . *need* to get away for a while. Things are just crowding in on me."

He pulled out the other chair at their little kitchen table and sat down. "I can't take you on a vacation till after the first of the year. You know I take in a quarter of my annual profits from Thanksgiving through New Year's. I charge higher prices and get bigger tips."

"Oh, Kix. You're too important a person to accept tips. People tip their underlings. I don't like it."

His jaw worked furiously, and she knew he was fighting off anger. "You haven't always felt this way. You used to meet me at the door practically with your hand out, asking me how much I made in tips. Cassie, if you don't get rid of this shallow . . . this superficial posture you've adopted, this marriage may not survive."

"Oh, pooh. You don't mean that. Besides, I refuse to be socially inferior to Sharon. Being publisher of *The Woodmore Times* is something in this town. I won't have her looking down her nose at me."

He got up, but he didn't move from the table. "I wish you could hear yourself. This crisis is something you've created because you have to be the top of the heap. Well, you had your chance, but you didn't take it. Don't mention this mess to me again. I'm sick of it."

Instead of tidying the kitchen as he usually did, he walked out and left the job to her. She stared at his departing back, sucked in her breath, went to the stove, and got two more popovers. *He wouldn't have the nerve to leave me.*

Marge wondered at Cassie's absence. She'd been in the hospital three days, and Cassie hadn't shown her face. "What do you make of it?" she asked Ross. "Kix sent me a fantastic dinner today, so they know I'm in the hospital."

"You mean Cassie didn't bring it?"

"Rafe brought it. Made me wonder why he had to send it by Rafe."

"I'll get a phone put in here. Then you'll be able to call her and find out if she's lost her mind. Be right back."

"You don't think she's sick?"

"Kix would have told you. I'm going downstairs and order that phone. They ought to have 'em in all these rooms. If this is luxury, it must be luxury by 1800 standards."

In his haste, he bumped into Eloise and Gert at the door. "Sorry. Hope I didn't hurt you."

"No, indeedy," Gert said. "Don't think a thing of it."

"What you grinning about, Gert?" Marge asked her as the two women took a seat on either side of the bed.

Gert's grin broadened. "Ross worrying about whether he hurt Eloise when he bumped into her. I came close to telling him she probably wished he'd bumped a little harder. I bet it's been years since she got that close to a man. How you doing, girl?"

"I'm so-so."

"Ross sure is a loyal employee." Gert said.

Eloise rolled her eyes toward the ceiling. "Gert, you gotta do something about your mind. If you got any questions for Marge, ask them and stop all that 'sinuatin'."

"Marge, don't you think it's strange your editor in chief comes to see you every day?" Gert asked.

"Oh, for goodness'—Here he comes. Ask him."

Ross didn't give her a chance. Focusing on Marge, he sat on the edge of her bed and busied himself plugging in the phone. "Now you're back in civilization."

"How do I pay for this?" Marge asked him.

He glared at her. "By keeping your mouth shut about it. It's taken care of. The nurse said you're probably going home Sunday. I'll come for you about ten."

She supposed her gaze held many questions, for he said, "If you want Sharon to come, okay. But in case you don't feel like walking to the car, I'll uh . . . I'll be here to help.

"Why wouldn't I feel like walking that little distance? You walked me all over San Francisco less than three weeks ago."

"You haven't been out of bed in a couple of weeks. Lying down makes you weak." He popped his fingers and then ran them through his hair.

"Don't look a gift horse in the mouth, Marge," Gert said. "If it was me, he could carry me all the way."

"Yeah. I'll bet. Don't let Gert embarrass you, Ross," Eloise said. "Her mind focuses on one thing. Reminds me of a chicken pecking corn. That's all it look at. Head just goes up and down, up and down."

"I've known Gert half my life," Ross said. "First time she surprises me, I'll lower the flag over the Woodmore Building. Well, Marge, I'd better be going. Pinky's will stop serving in about forty minutes. You need anything before I go?"

She shook her head. "Thanks, but I'm fine."

He stood beside the bed, looking down at her, a habit he seemed to have developed recently. She didn't understand it. "Well, you take care. Night, all," he said.

"How's the weather out?" Marge asked. "I've been stuck in here so long, I bet I'm beginning to molt."

Eloise's laughter rang out. "Don't you think it, girl. You still black. If you done any shedding, you must've had two layers."

Gert kicked off her size-twelve shoes and wiggled her toes. "I used to wonder why you and Ross didn't get together. You had the looks, Marge; still got 'em, for that matter. You should've roped him in. He didn't look at you fawn-eyed for nothing."

"Or, for that matter, Miles Glick," Eloise said. "I know I ain't up to his standards, but you coulda nailed him."

"Telling me?" Gert said. "All these years letting a good nest dry up. You won't catch me doing it."

Marge sucked her teeth in disgust. "Could we please talk about somebody else's sex life?"

"Not mine," Eloise said, letting out a snicker, "'cause I ain't got none. And it's been so long, my imagination don't even cover it."

"Well, don't expect me to entertain you," Gert said.

"Of course not." Marge grinned. "If you did that, we might be tempted to believe you."

"How 'bout that! I don't pay no attention to her, Marge. Gert just talking."

"Unless she's been feeding old man Hayes Viagra, and a lot of it, I'm not about to believe this once-a-week business, either. Talks easy done; it takes money to buy land." Marge looked at her friends, appreciating the joy of being with them more and more as the days passed. "You know, I thought I'd be bored here, but I've been fairly contented."

"That's because you needed the rest."

"Maybe, Gert. But it's strange. Like I've been through some kind of metamorphosis. Things that used to have me running around in circles don't matter." Neither of them looked directly at her.

"What do you make of Ross?" Gert asked Eloise as they rode down in the elevator on their way out of the hospital.

"He a nice man and a good friend to Marge. You didn't know them when Marge, Ed, and Ross worked sometimes eighteen hours a day to keep that paper from folding. And when Ed died, Ross stuck with her through some hard times. They're close friends, but that's all."

As soon as Gert and Eloise left her, Marge dialed Drogan.

"You home, Mama?"

"No. I'm still in the hospital. Ross put a phone in my room."

"How's it going? I mean, how're you feeling?"

"No better and no worse. Drogan, do you know of any reason why Cassie hasn't been to see me?"

"What do you mean? She hasn't been to the hospital?"

"That's what I mean. I haven't seen her."

"Well, I'll be. She knows you're there. Want me to call her?"

"Don't worry. I'll call her. She always pouts when she's displeased, but this is outrageous. When she gets over being mad with me, she may find it's too late."

"Too late for what, Mama?"

"For everything, Drogan. Everything."

Mad as he was with his mother, it hadn't occurred to Drogan not to go to the hospital to see her. He had a hunch that Cassie was experiencing an emotional upheaval that involved more than Mama, the paper, and Sharon, and he'd give a lot to know what it was. A woman like Cassie didn't shriek in fits of hysteria as she had about the lack of a will. Even as a teenager, she didn't let herself lose control and act like a crazed banshee. He'd ask Kix about it if he wasn't afraid he'd open a kettle of worms. And he didn't feel like mentioning it to Sharon; he hadn't forgiven what he saw as her insensitivity to his loss of status in the family. She and Mama would deny it, but that's what giving the paper to Sharon rather than to him amounted to. He made up his mind to call Cassie in the morning and find out what was going on.

"Honey," Imogene called to him. "Come here and look at this."

He hurried to the living room, where he found his wife curled up on the sofa munching Terra Chips and sipping zinfandel. "What is it?"

"Just listen to this," she said, giggling, though he couldn't figure out why she should laugh. What he saw on the television screen was a woman in an impoverished environment modeling expensive lace lingerie on a body that was considerably less than voluptuous for a man who scratched his head in obvious perplexity.

She reached for another handful of the vegetable chips. "Isn't that wild? That hag wouldn't look sexy if she wrapped herself in pure gold. Funniest thing I ever saw."

"Yeah? I imagine the poor guy's wondering how he's going to pay for it."

"Oh, don't be a drag. It's just a TV situation comedy." She poured more wine into her glass. "What happened to your sense of humor?"

"I'm a drag, huh? Where'd you get your brazenness? Come to think of it, you got a lot of chutzpah these days. A year ago, that scene might have been funny, but right now it's too close to home. What did you buy when you went shopping Monday?"

She sipped the wine and gave herself the luxury of savoring it before she answered. He watched her closely. Or maybe she was stalling for time while she made up her answer.

"I thought I'd be going to Winston-Salem along with you, but since you didn't go, Keisha and I didn't leave until around noon. We just . . . uh . . . had lunch in Old Salem at the Mayberry Restaurant and fooled around in the old town. By the time we got out of there, it was too late to go anyplace other than Dillards. We just looked around there and came on home."

He scrutinized her face as she spoke, her gaze glued to the television screen. He didn't quite know why, but he didn't believe a word she'd said. And at the moment, he didn't think it prudent to show his hand by questioning her. A fool could see that in the last couple of months she'd undergone better than a 180-degree personality change.

"You're not going to Winston-Salem on any more of your all-day shopping trips with Keisha."

She jumped up, spilling wine on the coffee table and sofa. "What do you mean? You can't tell me what I can't do."

"If you're planning to spend the night in this house and in my bed, you be here when I get home, and if I find you've been to Winston-Salem, I'm through."

Her lips quivered, but he didn't care. Crying wouldn't move him. "I'm not going to be a prisoner in this house while you pinch pennies and won't take me anyplace. If you were half a man, your mother would have given that paper to you instead of your baby sister. We should be the ones getting a Cadillac, but now she'll be cruising around in one."

"Spew all the venom you like. Go to Winston-Salem with Keisha and it's over." He wasn't risking much, because Imogene didn't believe in getting a steady job and working.

She crumpled up on the sofa. "You can't do this to me."

"And you can't do what you've been doing to me, either."

Her head snapped up. "What're you talking about?"

"Since you know, I don't have to spell it out." When she failed to protest, he was certain that her trips to Winston-Salem involved more than shopping, but he wasn't a man who felt the need to rush into a fire. He'd take his time getting to the bottom of it, and he meant to stand his ground.

But first he had to clean out his own closet. He went upstairs and telephoned Irene, the first time he'd phoned her from his home.

"You shouldn't have called me here," she hissed when she recognized his voice. "He's downstairs watching TV, but he's going to ask me who called."

"I know, but I had to. I've got to break this thing off. I can't do it anymore."

"What do you mean, break—" He heard her draw in a sharp breath. "Has she caught on? Don't you dare admit anything. He'd cut out of here in a minute if he found out."

"I'm not foolish enough to implicate you. I'm calling it off because I'm ashamed of . . . of cheating, and I can't deal with this stress."

"You dealt with it for two months," she said, her voice rising with every word. "So don't hand me that shit. You got another woman."

What had happened to her cool nonchalance? "Listen here, woman. We agreed at the outset that if either one of us wanted to walk, it would be over, no explanations and no hard feelings. So where do you get off acting like a jilted wife?"

"You're not going to dump me like I was a sack of—"

He interrupted her. "It's over. I'm sorry if you're upset, but I can't live with myself and keep this up. I need to get my marriage back on track."

"Your marriage. I don't give a damn about your marriage."

He looked over his shoulder to make sure Imogene hadn't walked into the room. "If you give a damn about yours, you'd better lower your voice. I wish we could end this more amiably, but—"

Her whispers reached him as little more than tremors, and he realized she feared having been overheard. "Later for you, pal. I don't trip over men; they're too easy to get."

Silently, he waited for her to hang up. Finally, she did, and he let out a long, heavy breath. Thank God, it was over.

He went to the top of the stairs to call Imogene and heard her sobs. She could cry, but he refused to relent. If she pushed him, he'd call Keisha's husband and have a talk with him. Imogene's "shopping" trips to Winston-Salem were a thing of the past.

N*ine*

Sharon braced her elbows on her desk and cupped her chin. A week had passed since she and Rafe witnessed Cassie's embarrassing performance in Gourmet Corner's lounge. Each time she picked up the phone to dial her sister, she saw in her mind's eye Cassie's face contorted in hatred and misery and couldn't bring herself to make the call. She didn't want to burden her mother with what could only depress her and, after musing over it for half an hour, decided to discuss it with Ross.

She walked out to his cubicle and waited until he completed his phone call. "I thought we agreed you'd use your intercom buttons," he said.

"This isn't about the paper, Ross. Well, maybe indirectly. Could we talk for a few minutes?"

"Sure thing."

The Reverend Ripple walked in and intercepted them on their way to Sharon's office. "Just the two people I need to see. Ross, I can't afford to pay for these ads. Marge always did them free as a contribution to the church, but you keep sending me these bills."

"Marge goes to your church," Ross said, giving his fingers a good loud pop. "What do you need ads for, anyway? All of your parishioners know when service is, don't they?"

He turned to Sharon. "My ads have been in this paper every Friday for the last thirty years, and . . ." Suddenly, he laughed. "Looks like I just shot myself in the foot. Doesn't it. Come on, you two, be a sport."

Ross raised an eyebrow. "A sport, huh?"

"Well," the minister said, "I can promise you a free funeral and a classy service, too. And if you get married in the meantime, your wedding'll be free. Let's see. I can testify to your good character if you get in trouble with the law."

Sharon folded her arms and watched the show. It had occurred to her, as she took in his Sunday sermons, that Gilford Ripple was probably capable of award-winning acting, and she was certain of it when he let a grin sweep over his face. "And, of course, I'll pray for you without ceasing."

"Is that all?" Ross asked him.

Ripple stretched himself to his full height of five feet eleven inches. "Man, what do you want for a few lines in your paper? You want me to stand guard against the Roman soldiers?"

Ross laughed aloud then, something he rarely did. "Yeah. And be there Easter Sunday at dawn, too. Give your copy to Wilson over there where the U.S. flag is flying."

"Bless you, brother."

"Where were we, Sharon?" Ross asked her.

"On our way to my office." That short exchange between Ross and her pastor left her with a lighter feeling; nonetheless, she needed to share with someone her problem with Cassie. She recounted it all, beginning with the night Marge gave her the paper.

Ross listened intently while she poured out the story of her broken relations with her brother and sister, omitting nothing. He'd been resting his slight frame against the wall beside the door, but he suddenly shoved his hands into his pockets, kicked at the taupe-colored, wall-to-wall broadloom carpet, and walked over to the window.

"You oughta change the furniture in here. The place doesn't look like you. It's still Marge."

She realized then that it cost him a lot to go into her office and not see her mother sitting where she now sat. When she would have commented on that, he whirled around and faced her. "Straitlaced and uptight as Cassie is, I never thought she'd act out in public. Something's going on with her, and it's not good." He turned back to the window and looked at the street below.

"Drogan's another matter. He squandered his chance to head up both this paper and the Hairston family, and he's not likely to forgive himself. Still, you can talk to him. And get him to speak to Cassie." He ran the fingers of his left hand through his thinning hair. "From what you said, I suspect she's spinning out of control."

"Don't bother Marge with this," he went on, popping his fingers several times. She almost asked him why he did it. He walked over and stared down into her face. "Watch your own behavior. Be sure you don't exacerbate the situation. If it gets worse, tell me. Whatever you do, please don't let it get back to Marge. I don't want to see her hurt."

"I'll do my best, but if Cassie's not speaking to me—"

"Then tell Drogan to talk to her."

She didn't think Drogan would listen to her, but she kept that thought to herself.

His shoulders drooped when he left her, but half a minute later, he pushed open the door. "Don't forget to order some furniture. A smart CEO wastes no time putting her stamp on everything." He winked at her. "Forgot to tell you. K.C. just handed me a great story on McCall and Scenic Gardens."

What a switch! "Smooth job, huh?"

"Yeaaaah. Smooth as a baby's bottom. The gal's brilliant."

Anxious as she was to see the story on Rafe, she knew better than to break precedent and ask for it. But her mind wouldn't rest, so she dialed Rafe at his office in Scenic Gardens.

"McCall."

"Sharon Hairston, Mr. McCall." She meant that as a tease, but it hadn't sounded that way to her. "I'm told our reporter turned in a great story on you and Scenic Gardens."

"What a nice surprise. You never call me. I imagine she did a good job, because she certainly got enough material. No topic is off limits to that woman, and she's so engaging that before you realize it, you're about to spill your insides."

"I notice you said 'about.'"

She loved his laughter, and he treated her to a good round of it. "Sharon, you're talking to a thirty-nine-year-old. How could I let a reporter outfox me?"

She opened the bottom drawer of her desk, kicked off her shoes, and put her feet in the drawer. "I've gotten the impression that you're full of smarts, but my reporter is a cracker jack. Can't wait to read her story."

"Hmm. I'd like to get in some quality time with you before you read it?"

"Why? You think it'll make your star flicker? I mean, am I going to find out something I won't like?"

"I shouldn't think so. I want more from our relationship, but on the basis of what you see in me and not what you read. Am I making myself clear?"

She didn't want to make a mistake with him, so she had to understand him, and that meant seeing him with a clear head and an open mind. "Not really," she said, and it was true. "Nothing I read about you can influence me more than what you show me over time."

"What about if I cook dinner for you tonight . . . in my home?"

She nearly dropped the phone. There was more to that question than the words he used. "Come again?"

His voice darkened. "You should trust me by now, Sharon. I am what you've seen, talked with, and shared some troublesome experiences with. Sharon, the car's bought and paid for."

She pulled her feet out of the drawer and jumped up from her desk. *"What?* Honey, as far as I'm concerned, you're still leasing."

For a full minute, silence burned the wires. Then sounds of mirth rumbled out of him, a joyous, full-throated laugh that she got caught up in, and she joined him in the merriment. She'd have given anything to be with him right then.

He soon sobered and, when he stopped laughing, repeated his suggestion. "Well, what about it? I'm a good cook."

She cleared her throat. *His to ask and hers to deny.* "Didn't I tell you? So am I. I'm moving slowly, Rafe, and I'm not going to remind you of your professed habit of doing the same."

"I drag along till I'm sure of my course."

"And you're sure?"

"As I am of my name."

"I have a hunch that it would be foolish of me to ask what it is you're sure of."

He didn't respond to that, but said, "If I can't cook for you, will you risk having dinner with me at Gourmet Corner?"

When she hesitated, he asked, "Aren't you interested?"

"I'd . . . uh . . . I'd like that a lot."

"But you were hesitating."

"You could say that."

"Still worried about Wade Field?"

Was he testing her? She wished she could see him right then. "Worried? No. Concerned? Yes. And I don't take the topic lightly."

"Neither do I," he replied, "and I wish you wouldn't behave with me as if I've already broken ground there."

"Tell me you're never going to and I'll let up about it."

He took his time answering. "There are certain things I can say I will never do, but this isn't one of them. I am trying to weigh both sides of this issue. When I'm satisfied I have all the facts, I'll make up my mind."

"Meanwhile, I can sweat it out. Right?"

"In the meantime, I'd appreciate your patience."

Fast on the lip. She'd bet he could state a better case for himself than a politician on the campaign circuit. "Give me some assurance."

"All right. If I do make a bid, I'll forewarn you so you'll have a chance to fight it. Now, how about dinner?"

"Okay. Meet me at six-thirty."

She met him in the lobby of the Woodmore Building, and the first thing she noticed was his solemn demeanor. The absence of the smile with which he always greeted her.

He kissed her quickly on the cheek. "My, but you're prompt. Scared I'd go upstairs and your staff would see us walk out of there together?"

"If that's what you think, we needn't go any farther."

"All right, but why didn't you let me come to your office?"

"It's being painted. If you have a special fondness for the smell of fresh paint, be glad to accommodate you."

"Sorry. I waited all day for at least a hug, but down here— He waved a hand. Come on. I thought we'd spend a few minutes with your mother before we go to dinner. Is that okay?" He took her hand for the short walk to his car.

"I'd hoped we could do that. Thanks."

No sooner had they greeted her than Marge launched into the subject of Cassie's bewildering behavior. "Ross thinks she'll see how mean she's being and stop acting out. If she doesn't, I'm going to give her a shock."

Sharon felt the draft of fear blow through her body. "What kind of shock are you talking about, Mama?" Her mother had been scheduled to leave the hospital on Sunday, but nothing more had been said about it. Her breath seemed trapped somewhere in her nasal passage, and she couldn't breathe. As if he could divine her every move and experience, Rafe grabbed her shoulders and shook her until she gasped.

"Sharon, child, it's time you faced the truth just as I have. I'm not going to get well. I knew it when I went to San Francisco, and I'm not worried. Let me be the one to tell Cassie and Drogan. I think Ross has figured this out, but still, I want to tell him myself."

She'd sensed it. No, she'd known it intellectually, but her emotions hadn't dealt with it. She sat on the bed and put her arms around her mother. "Oh, Mama. This is . . . it's awful. Don't think this way. The doctors don't know everything."

"You're so right, and that's the problem. I don't want to see any tears and no long faces. When you come here, bring me some smiles. I want to be happy these last days, and I will be whether or not Cassie and Drogan get their act together."

"Drogan? I thought he was in touch with you regularly."

Marge shrugged. "He's still angry, but Drogan never did let his anger control him. Wish I could say the same for Cassie." She looked at Rafe. "Thanks for those chocolates. I love chocolates as much as I love collard greens."

Sharon looked up at him. "You didn't tell me you sent her candy." Then she turned back to Marge. "Are you supposed to have that?"

Marge nodded her head to the side and squinted, and anyone who knew her would have no doubt that she thought the question ridiculous. "I can have anything I want, and I thank God that Rafe knows it. Where y'all going to eat?"

"Over at Kix's place," Rafe said.

After pulling a hefty volume of air through her front teeth, Marge said, "He's first class, but you tell my elder daughter that. She has no idea what a gold mine she has. Don't you be that foolish, Sharon."

"I keep telling her what a great guy I am, but if she's listening, she keeps it to herself."

Sharon winked at him. "When it comes to men, I keep my thinking cap squarely on my head."

Marge stared at her. "Thinking cap? Well, I've yet to hear of one that'll keep you—She stopped and patted the sheet on her bed. "Well, you get my message."

Rafe leaned over and kissed her. "You bet she did. See you tomorrow if I'm in Woodmore. Come on, honey. Kix said he has roast pork this evening, and my mouth's watering for some."

"I hate to leave Mama here by herself."

"You go on. Ross'll be here shortly, and Gert and Eloise said they'd be by. Anyhow, I don't mind being by myself. Ross brought me a copy of Forster's *Scarlet Woman,* and I still have a few pages to go on Donna Hill's *A Scandalous Affair.* That'll keep me busy till some of them get here. Y'all enjoy your dinner, and Sharon, don't forget you promised to bring me *Once and Again*, that book by Savoy."

When she and Rafe got to the door, Marge called her, and Rafe waited there while she went back to her mother. "That's a wonderful man, and he cares for you. Try to see him as he is, Sharon. I'd be happier if I knew I wasn't leaving you all alone."

She didn't want to hear that, but she pulled on her strength and stroked her mother's cheek. "I care as much for him, Mama. I'm just hoping I don't care more than he does."

"You don't, so stop worrying."

When she got to Rafe, she made herself smile. "Ready?"

He nodded. "I've been ready almost from the night we met."

She'd have to digest that slowly. Best to get his mind on something other than her. "What do you think, Rafe? She was telling me she wasn't going to make it, wasn't she?"

"She was, but you already knew that when she deeded the paper to you. She did that to eliminate the likelihood that your brother and sister would raise a stink with you about it. What else is there to drive a deeper wedge between the three of you?"

"The family home, what's in it, and Mama's car. I hadn't thought about that. They can fight between themselves; I'd rather not have any of it."

"Doesn't your mother have a will?"

She thought for a minute. "I've never discussed it with her, and I don't want to."

"I probably wouldn't, either. It doesn't seem appropriate. Sure you don't want a gourmet dinner, McCall style?"

"I'm sure it would be a delicious meal, but this time, I'll settle for what Kix can throw together."

"Delicious meal. You're sure, huh? Want a rain check?"

She couldn't help laughing. "How long can I hold it?"

He pressed the accelerator. "As long as you need to."

She wasn't stringing him along just because she knew he cared for her, was she? She'd hate to be thought guilty of that. As he drove past the naked trees and the fields, hardened with the winter cold, desolate and forbidding in the dark, she recalled her loneliness before she met him, her sense of drifting, of not belonging to anyone. She'd had her family, but they didn't give her what Rafe gave her.

"You're awfully quiet."

"I . . . I was just looking at things . . . the way they are."

"Did you see me?"

"Don't take this the wrong way, but I was looking at myself."

His voice held a distant quality, reflective, but he spoke easily. "We all have to do that sometime. A good hard look at yourself can be like a kick in the face, but I doubt that applies to you."

"Hope not." She turned to look at him in order better to gauge his mood. *Why's he so somber,* she wondered, and changed the topic. "Have you been back to Gourmet Corner since we were there together?"

"Couple of times, but if you're thinking of that episode with Kix's wife, well . . . he hasn't mentioned it, and I don't expect him to."

"If he knows Cassie as I do, he won't suffer in silence; if he does, she'll give him plenty to suffer about."

At that moment, Cassie struggled with a more profoundly moral issue than whether to fight over their mother's property, though she focused on that. Day and night she grappled with her inability to erase from her thoughts a man who represented everything she despised.

If she had the emotional energy, she'd get up and go home. Cassie closed her top desk drawer, locked it, and went to her closet for her coat.

"What're you doing in here at seven o'clock in the evening?"

She whirled around, her heart thundering like horses' hooves. "Oh, my Lord. Where'd you come from?"

"I saw your light from the street."

She didn't want him near her. If he touched her, she knew she'd crumple like yellowed paper, dry and fragile with age. "You frightened me."

"I imagine I did."

He swaggered toward her. Rhythmically. Sex in motion. A guided missile certain of its target. Cold sweat dampened her blouse and goose pimples scattered themselves over her arms and neck. She watched, transfixed, as he captured her willpower the way a magnet subdues a nail. Suddenly, his big hand shot out to her and she jumped away from him. "Don't touch me, Judd. Don't put your hands on me. Get out of here."

What he obviously meant for a grin didn't materialize. "I know a woman denied when I see one, and I know when a woman wants me. You're both of those, and you know all the way to your gut that I'll give you what you've been missing. But you think I'm not good enough for you. When I get you, and I will, you won't think about anything but what I'm like inside of you. See you." He walked out and closed the door.

She dropped into the chair beside her desk, propped her elbows on it, and lowered her face into her hands. The door cracked open, and her head snapped up.

"Crying about it won't help, Cassandra. If it's sin you're worried about, you sin every time you think about me, so since you gotta pay for sinning, at least enjoy it."

"I wouldn't waste a tear on you."

The door slammed shut just before the paper weight she kept on her desk crashed against it. She washed her face, refreshed her makeup, and put on her coat. A glance out her window revealed no trace of him on the street, so she got her briefcase and pocketbook, turned out the light, and ventured slowly into the hallway. When she made it to her car without having encountered him, she got in, locked the doors, and let out a sigh of relief.

"I'm behaving like a teenager. I should get a restraining order against him." She gritted her teeth, disgusted with herself. That would be foolhardy, not to mention unfair. The man wasn't guilty of anything but recognizing her attraction to him. "I can't do that." But oh, how she'd enjoy seeing him crawl!

She'd meant to go home but found herself driving toward Gourmet Corner instead, and she didn't have to think hard to find the reason: guilt. And she hadn't done one thing wrong. She didn't want to face Kix, but she was there, so she got out, went around to the side door, and rang the bell.

When the pastry chef, and not Kix, opened the door, she quickly recovered from her repentance over her moral malaise and flashed the man her most seductive smile. She was back in control, where she was admired and her status unquestioned.

"Is Mr. Shepherd real busy right now?" She asked him, though she knew that Kix's employees called him by his first name. But the more they respected Kix, she reasoned, the more in awe they would be of her.

"He's working on a lobster sauce right now, ma'am. If he leaves it, it'll curdle. You can wait in his office if you like. Can I get you something?"

"Why, thank you, Carl. A glass of nice, cold Puillez Fuissé Latour." He raised both eyebrows. "Yes, ma'am."

Let him gape. She'd asked for one of the best wines in Kix's cellar, and if she didn't drink all of it, the remainder of that thirty-five-dollar bottle of wine would go to waste. She crossed her knees, reached for the paper, and recoiled. *The Woodmore Times* and its front page carried a full-length picture of Rafe McCall leaning against a bookcase filled with what looked like leather-bound volumes. In spite of herself, she yielded to her curiosity and read the story.

Stunned, she folded the paper and put it back on the coffee table. Dull, colorless, dowdy Sharon had hooked herself one hell of a man. A professional man. A graduate of an Ivy League university. Rich and important. Sharon Hairston had a good-looking, filthy-rich man tailing after her. She kicked the coffee table and groaned in pain. All that and *The Woodmore Times*, too. If Carl hadn't already seen her, she'd go home.

The door opened, and Kix strode in. "Say, this is a nice surprise." He looked at his watch. "We can have dinner in another, say, forty minutes, provided none of my regulars show up at the last minute. By the way, Sharon and Rafe are in the dining room. Why don't you join them?"

"I . . . I'm too tired. Honey, I don't feel like talking to anybody. I can't handle small talk tonight."

He stared at her. "Small talk? With whom? Not Sharon and Rafe."

"Oh, I'm . . . just mentally washed out."

"In that case, seems to me you'd want to be surrounded by people who care about you. Look, give me half an hour. We can eat here in my office. Okay?"

If only he wasn't so nice, so kind and . . . and . . . If he'd only scream at her. She nodded. "I'm sorry I'm such a wreck, but it's been a rough day."

He hunkered beside her. "Nothing can happen, Cassie, that we can't make it through together. Open up and let me be what I can be to you. That's all I've been asking for these five and a half years, honey. Whatever it is, talk to me. I'll always be here for you."

If only he'd go back to his work before she broke down. She didn't want him to see her come apart. If he did, he wouldn't respect her and look up to her. She put an arm on his shoulder. "Thanks. I'll be all right."

He eased from his crouched position and kissed her lips. She caught herself just before her hand went to her mouth to wipe it. She loved him. She knew she did. But his mouth on hers was like an alien thing, planted there to punish her for wanting that electrician. She put her arms around her husband's waist.

"Sorry I'm being a wimp, but I'll be out of this stupid mood by the time you get back. You go on and do your work."

Kix answered the knock on the door and looked at the wine bottle Carl carried.

"Mrs. Shepherd asked for it specifically, so I—"

"Give her whatever she wants, Carl, and thanks."

He glanced at her, a quizzical expression on his face. "See you shortly."

Now she'd done it. She hadn't meant to be so extravagant, but that story on Rafe McCall, extolling his virtues, was rolling around in her head like marbles in a washer. Sharon had a corporate bigwig, and she had a cook. Sharon also had the paper.

Kix may have wanted to make her feel better, but he accomplished the opposite. He drove her home and, once there, hovered about her, seeing to her comfort. Little things. Playing her favorite Nancy Wilson CD, building a fire in the fireplace, pulling off her shoes and massaging her feet. She leaned back against the sofa and worked at keeping the tears in abeyance, for at that moment, she saw Kix for the gem that he was and loathed her inability to accept. *I must be some kind of intellectual eunuch. Right while he's being so nice, my mind's full of Judd.*

She dozed off, or pretended she did, using it to circumvent lovemaking, if that was on his mind. From where she stood, men never thought of much else. He carried her to their bed and undressed her. She kept her eyes closed and her breathing deep and even, knowing that his gaze feasted on her naked body, her firm, big breasts, flat belly, and shapely hips and limbs. She wanted to open her eyes and watch him salivate with desire for her, but she didn't dare. She tensed when he parted her folds, then relaxed when she thought he only wanted to look at her. But when his tongue flicked there, she bucked in surprise.

"Sorry, baby. I didn't mean to wake you up."

She turned on her side, pretending to sink deeper into sleep, but she couldn't have been more wide awake. What had gotten into him to do such a thing? It wasn't *nice*. Was it? He pulled the bedding over her and kissed her cheek. She wanted to get up and take a bath, but if she did that, she'd have to have sex.

Morning came, and when she realized he hadn't been in bed, she slipped on a robe and ran down the stairs, where she found him asleep on the living-room sofa.

"What're you doing sleeping down here?" she asked when he sat up, rubbing his eyes.

He leaned forward and dropped his head in his hands. "Do you really think I could've slept beside you last night with you wearing nothing but your skin? I couldn't have done that when I was twelve."

She wrapped her robe as tightly around her as she could get it. "You telling me you were sexually awake at that age?"

"A hundred percent. Good Lord, look at the time. I have to check stock this morning. I hope you don't mind getting your breakfast."

She put a pout on her face and hoped it looked real. "Honey, you know how I love your breakfast treats, but if you have to hurry . . ."

Twenty minutes later, the front door closed, and she raced to the bathroom to fill the tub with hot water and scrub herself clean. Thank God she could work in peace that day. She got more work done on weekends than she did during the regular workweek. She was applying perfumed lotion to her legs when the phone rang.

"Cassie, can you meet me for lunch today?"

"I'd love to Drogan, but I have to go to the office. I'm right in the middle of a new project, and it's giving me a fit."

"Lunch will take an hour. Meet you at Pinky's at twelve-thirty. 'Bye."

The dial tone hummed in her ear. She quelled her annoyance and let herself think. He hadn't sounded like his usually laid back self. It could be anything.

"I wasn't sure you'd come," Drogan said, standing as Cassie approached him. "I discovered long ago that it's no use arguing with you. Hand you a done deal, or get nowhere with you."

"I'm not that bad. Did you order?"

"No. I waited for you. I'm going to have some broiled salmon, spinach, and hush puppies."

"No catfish?"

He lifted his right shoulder in a slight shrug. "Left to Imogene, I'd eat fried something or other, coleslaw, and french fries for supper every single, solitary day."

"Are we speaking the same Imogene who is my sister-in-law?"

He nodded. He wasn't used to spilling his guts, not even to Imogene, but life with her had become so difficult. He needed somebody's take on it other than his own. Not that advice about his personal affairs from someone as self-centered as Cassie would make sense, but she'd always been able to read people. And for once, he couldn't understand his wife.

"One and the same," he answered. "That's what I wanted to talk with you about. For the past . . . I'd say, nearly three months, she's been practically unrecognizable."

As she listened quietly, he realized he'd forgotten how patient she could be when it suited her. He didn't divulge the problems that he and Imogene had recently begun to have in bed, but he told her everything else.

"Why does she have to shop in Winston-Salem three times a week? Seems it's escalated from twice a month, which was certainly reasonable. Does she show you what she buys?"

"She and Keisha mostly window-shop. A few weeks ago, she bought a diamond tennis bracelet for twenty-one hundred dollars. Cheap compared to the quality of jewelry I've bought her, but with me busting my butt trying to save money, I don't want to buy such stuff." They placed their orders.

"Hmm. Drogan, don't you know the stores don't change their displays three times a week? Usually not even once a month."

He stared at her. "Run that past me again."

She repeated it. "And another thing. A man shouldn't expect his wife to do dirt work, but why do you need someone to come in three times a week when Imogene isn't working. I have a once-a-week cleaning woman."

But you spend your life in the office, and Kix spends his at the restaurant. "She was always such a wonderful homemaker, sweet, gentle, and cooperative in whatever I wanted to do. Not anymore. Now she ignores the house, rarely cooks, and worst of all, she's full of sass. I forgot to mention that she pounced on Sharon when we were at the hospital to see Mama. I mean she tore into her for no reason."

Cassie finished her shrimp and avocado salad and pushed the plate aside. "Give her the benefit of the doubt. Are you going to ask Mama about her will?"

He didn't want to get on *that* again. "I told you, Cassie. She hasn't probated a will, but I can't make myself ask a sick woman if she's made a will. That would be tantamount to telling her I know something about her that she doesn't and that it's not good."

"Then I'll get somebody to tell her she has to do it."

He signaled the waiter for the bill. "Leave me out of it."

"What did I expect? Ineffectual men disgust me," she said, putting on her coat.

So that's it, he thought in a moment of intuitive discovery. "As far as you're concerned, that covers every guy wearing pants. Including your husband. Right? Wake up, Cassie."

Without a word, she tossed her head, squared her shoulders, and strutted out, leaving him standing at the table, watching her leave.

He paid the bill, turned left down Market Street when he walked out of Pinky's, and headed for his office, thoughts of his crumbling marriage drumming in his head. *What I did was wrong, but I stopped it. She's still at whatever she's been doing.* He walked into his office with feet of lead and sat down. He had to do something. But what?

While Drogan worried as to how he could salvage his relationship with his wife, Imogene was plotting with Keisha to circumvent his order that she not go back to Winston-Salem.

"I can't be calling you all the time, Keisha, because he might start checking the numbers on our phone bill."

"Oh, don't be a worrywart. That's only possible with long-distance calls."

"I'm not going to let him get away with telling me what I can't do. Does he know your car?"

"Why would he? I'm not even sure he knows me," she said, bubbling with giggles. "We'll go in my car, and we'd better get started."

Imogene wound the telephone cord around her wrist so tightly that it pinched her. "Okay. But you can't come here. I'll walk down to Court Street and meet you on the corner of Hyatt. And be on time, because I don't want him to catch me standing there. You hear me? Keisha, Drogan was madder than I ever saw him. I told you we'd better stop staying over there so late. Doesn't Brian ever say anything to you about it?"

"Sure he does, but I treat him real nice and make him forget he's annoyed with me. Try it."

Imogene stared at the telephone receiver. "Girl, what do you take me to be? I can make Drogan think it's thundering and lightning when it's as calm and sunny as you please. Child, I know how to handle my man."

"I hope so. Listen. We have to find time today to go in a store and buy something. I don't mean that jewelry you're so crazy about. I mean something I can show Brian. He's started demanding to see what I bought. That's something new."

Laughter poured out of Imogene. "Buy some expensive perfume."

At that, Keisha screeched, "Are you out of your mind? I don't have a credit card. He'd quiz me for weeks about where I got the money. We'd better get started."

"How long can we stay?"

"We can't leave Winston-Salem before four."

Which meant they wouldn't be able to leave until six, and Drogan would be ready to shred himself. What the heck? She'd tell him they went to Danvers or anywhere except Winston-Salem.

"You sure you want to take a chance, now. You know what he said."

She knew how to get next to Drogan, and she could count on his libido to get her out of trouble. "Yeah," she said to Keisha. "But he ain't laying out nothing, so I'm gon' do my own thing."

Luckily for Imogene, Drogan decided not to check on her. He figured if he had to do that, he might as well call it quits right then. Still . . . He sat at his desk, staring at the wall in front of him, trying to understand Imogene's behavior. He wouldn't be surprised if she ignored him and went to Winston-Salem, anyway. If she did . . . He didn't let himself think of what he'd do. He sat there, puzzling over how they had all changed so much in so short a time.

Although Sharon's life had changed, Sharon had not. She picked up the Saturday edition of *The Woodmore Times* in front of her door as she left home to go to the Woodmore Library. She had an idea for a series on the changing status of slaves in Old Salem from around 1760, when they were first introduced into the area, and up to the Civil War. She knew that at the beginning those who converted to Christianity were baptized in the Moravian Church, worshiped along with their white Christian brethren, and were buried in the same graveyard as they. She wanted to know when and how the change to absolute segregation took place.

As she reached the library, she remembered that K.C.'s story on Rafe was in the paper she carried, and when she sat down in the reading room, she unfolded it. Rafe's full-length likeness greeted her on the front page beneath the caption "One Man's Rocket Climb to the Corporate World." Builder and owner of housing settlements in four states, Rafe McCall had accumulated considerable wealth. Son of a janitor and of a mother who worked as a cleaning woman in the homes of well-to-do African Americans, he'd struggled at every step and excelled at every plateau.

The story chronicled his successes beginning with his college scholarship—academic, he'd emphasized to the reporter, not basketball or football—and followed his life up to his recognition by the NAACP for an outstanding contribution to the improvement of inner-city life. When she finished reading, she leaned back in the chair and closed her eyes, deep in thought. He'd wanted to cement their relationship before she read the story, and now she knew why. She wondered how many women had courted him for his material worth and not for his worth as a man and whether he would know on which side of that line she walked? Best to deal with that head-on.

She left the library, went home, and dialed Rafe's cellular phone number. "Sharon. What a pleasant surprise!"

If her vote were the only one that counted, Caller ID would be abolished. "I just read the piece on you in our paper. It gave me new information but no surprises. I have always known that you are successful and accomplished. I just didn't know to what extent. And your ease with Aunt Eloise, my godmother, told me that your origins were as humble as mine."

"Good, but why're you telling me this?"

"Because you weren't sure that my having the information K.C. put in her article wouldn't influence my attitude toward you. Well, it doesn't, but if I'd known all that when we first met, I'm sure I'd have been wary of you."

"You've lost me. If I had a prison record and you read about it in that story, I'd understand, but—"

"Rafe, you did not meet a sophisticated, self-confident woman of the world. You met a cloistered professor whose most reckless act up to that time was going to a Buddy Guy concert with thousands of screaming fans. I'd never been two steps with a man as smooth as you."

"What about the woman who met me at her front door, fashionable from her head to her three-inch heels the first time we went to dinner? Huh?"

"The result of impulsive behavior three hours before you got to my house and the second most reckless thing I ever did."

"Whew!" His soft whistle floated to her over the wires. "And what a metamorphosis it was! It takes longer than that for a caterpillar to turn into a butterfly."

"It wasn't that I didn't know *how* other people behaved or that I was naive; I knew what polish was, and I'd been exposed to plenty of it. I just hadn't bothered to indulge in high style. I don't go with the flow."

"I see. Want to drive into Winston-Salem tonight, have dinner, and take in a concert? Or just hang out together?"

"What does one wear for hanging out?"

She couldn't get enough of his laughter, and to her delight he let it flow. "Honey, you don't want to know."

She curled up in the big overstuffed chair and put her imagination to work. "Are you talking about what I'm talking about?"

"I thought I was, but now I'm not so sure. I imagine you can do that a lot of ways."

She unfolded herself and sat up. "Do what a lot of ways?"

"Well . . . any number of things. Practically anything. At least that's been my experience."

"What are we talking about here, Rafe?"

She imagined his eyes held that wicked gleam she'd seen when he resorted to playfulness and deviltry. "Me letting it all hang out with you. A man can dream, can't he?"

And so could a woman. "Okay. What'll it be? Jeans or an evening gown?"

His roaring laughter filled her with a joy so exquisite that if he'd been with her, she probably would have granted him anything. "Whatever makes you feel good. Can I see you around four-thirty?"

"I'll be here." She hung up, realizing that she'd taken a giant step in that conversation, half-promising more than she was ready to give. She'd have to correct that. She thought long and hard about it and, half an hour later, wasn't sure she'd have spoken so loosely if she hadn't known his life story. She'd bet he had her under a microscope right then.

Ten

As she mused over her conversation with Rafe, Sharon's gaze fell on the paper that she'd dropped on the floor beside her chair. "Dr. Margaret Scott elevated to assistant dean of the School of Social Work." She'd been so involved with her own life and its problems and changes that she'd neglected Margaret. She read the article, a short, matter-of-fact story that hadn't rated a by-line. Margaret deserved a full profile, and she made a mental note to put K.C. on it. She dialed her friend to wish her well, though she wasn't sure she didn't begrudge her the job. Maybe if she succeeded as publisher of *The Woodmore Times,* she wouldn't miss her old position, her colleagues, and her feeling of belonging in the academic setting in which she'd worked, but at times, she longed for it.

Margaret answered after the fifth ring. "Hi, Sharon. What a surprise. It's been ages."

Caller ID again. "Hi. Congratulations, Margaret. I just saw that little notice in today's paper. It's wonderful, and I'm happy for you. We have to get together and celebrate."

"Thanks. Your loss turned out to be my good fortune. From the changes you've introduced in the paper, anybody'd think you were a journalist instead of a professor of social work. You're doing great, girl."

"Thanks. I'd like to have a full profile on you like the one on Rafe McCall in today's paper. How about it?"

"That would be great, but the dean will probably disintegrate from jealousy."

"Tell me about it. She's one of the reasons I'm not sorry I resigned.

Should I send the reporter to your home or your office? An interview in your office would make a better impression."

"The office between three-thirty and four. By that time, the old hag will be home drinking her afternoon tea."

They'd often joked about what the dean considered her day's greatest pleasure, her soda biscuits and Fortnum & Mason's Earl Grey tea at three in the afternoon. Heaven help the woman whose days offered no greater joy than tea. They agreed on an interview Monday afternoon at four o'clock.

"I forgot to ask how your mother's doing."

"It's hard to tell. She was supposed to come home from the hospital last Sunday, but her doctor's behaving as if he never mentioned it."

"Well, I hope she can get home for Christmas."

So did she. After they arranged to meet and said good-bye, she phoned her mother.

"Mama, what does Dr. Glick say about you coming home by Christmas?"

"Miles is talking about starting a new treatment. I know what he means, but I'm not hooking up to any of these machines, and I mean it."

She didn't like it. When Mama put her foot down, there was no moving her. After hanging up, she called Ross at home, but when he failed to answer, she dialed his number at the paper.

"The Woodmore Times. Ingersol speaking."

No point in reprimanding him about working on weekends, so she didn't mention that. "Uncle Ross, Mama is refusing to go on dialysis."

"I know, Sharon. I had that out with her a week ago. She said it's her life and that she intends to finish it with dignity."

"But how can she do this?"

"Don't fight her on this, Sharon. You'll only make her miserable. I've wrestled with it till my mind aches. I see she's happy when we're playing chess and when she's winning at cutthroat against Eloise and Gert or refereeing their risqué innuendos."

Horrified, she accused him of complicity. "How can you support her in—"

"I don't support that position she's taken, Sharon; I support her as her friend. No matter what she does, I'll be there for her, and you should do the same. It's her life. Not yours!"

Ross had never spoken so strongly to her, and it didn't require genius to understand that he was battling stress.

"Sorry, Uncle Ross. I know I'm thinking of myself, but I can't help it."

He released a long breath. "We have to support each other. All of us." His mercurial shift of mood hit her like an unexpected blast of frigid air when he said, "What'd you think of the story on McCall? My eyes nearly popped. Now *there's* a man. From the bottom to the top in sixteen years."

"I'm trying not to let his feats impress me."

"Yeah? If you tell me what he's done doesn't influence you, I'll give you A plus for phoniness. He's what you need, gal."

Since childhood, Ross—as her godfather—had demanded honesty and straightforwardness from her, and she learned early to try to give him the facts as she understood them. "I wouldn't pretend that, Uncle Ross, not even to Rafe. But I don't intend to act as if that story made him a better man that I thought he was."

"Of course not, unless you want to get rid of him in a hurry. He's too smart to be fooled by that."

"I know. Look, if Mama's not going through . . . all that, she should come home."

"Yeah," he said after a considerable lapse of time. "I've been thinking the same."

On their way to Winston-Salem later that afternoon, Sharon and Rafe detoured by the hospital for a visit with Marge, as had become their custom. She hadn't told Rafe of her mother's decision; indeed, she'd tried to push it to the back of her mind and hadn't mentioned it to anyone. Somebody had to tell Drogan and Cassie, and she couldn't bring herself to do it.

She'd had a day of bewilderment, stress, and not a little fear, but her mother didn't seem to have a care.

Marge peeped into the thermal box Rafe handed her, sniffed, and let a beatific expression crawl over her face. "Rafe, if you're not an angel, you'll do till one comes along." She zipped up the box. "I'll put this over there till Ross gets here."

Sharon exchanged glances with Rafe. "Does Dr. Glick think you'll be home for Christmas, Mama?"

She rolled her eyes toward the ceiling. "I haven't asked him, and I'm not going to. When I get sufficiently fed up with Miles's shilly-shallying, I'll check myself out and go home." Then, as if she'd said nothing of note, a grin broadened until her face radiated a smile. "I bet that'll put the wind in his sails. He's been pussyfooting around the edges of medicine for forty years and still hasn't gotten a grip on it. Some of these doctors are full of it."

Nonplussed, Sharon couldn't think of a response to her mother's seeming indifference to the inevitable result of her decision. She knew she'd better get out of that room, but she didn't want to leave her mother alone.

"How y'all doing today?"

Sharon whirled around at the blessed sound of Eloise's voice. She hugged her godmother. "We were just getting ready to leave."

Rafe kissed Marge's cheek. "See you soon." He shook hands with Eloise. "I'm still waiting for my soul-food dinner, Miss Eloise, and the longer you make me wait, the more demanding I'll be."

"Ahem. I sure do hope that don't apply to everything," Eloise said. And then, as if to reestablish her image as a woman of delicate manners, she went on: "You just tell me what you like to eat and I'll cook it. I'd cook for Marge, but her son-in-law sends her these gourmet meals every day. I ain't about to compete with that. Y'all have a good time."

"What did your mother mean about checking out of the hospital?" Rafe asked as he drove them to Winston-Salem. "I didn't like the sound of that."

She repeated her conversation with Ross. "If we get into that right now, I'll go to pieces and ruin your evening."

"You won't ruin my evening, as you put it. When did you learn this?"

"This afternoon."

"You're handling it as well as anyone has a right to expect. We've had warnings, but her attitude and manner are so upbeat and she's so cheerful that I don't focus on the seriousness of it."

"I don't think she does, either, and that's a good thing."

"Try to think on the positive side, sweetheart. With my parents, it was totally different. Months and months of dreariness. Your mother isn't planning to put her children through that. She's an admirable woman."

"Intellectually, I know that, and I appreciate it, but my emotions haven't caught up with my intellect."

"Something tells me your intellect's been working overtime on *me*. I fare better with you when your emotions take over."

"If you didn't, you've been climbing the wrong tree. I know you're trying to divert my attention, but—"

"Look, sweetheart, I think I'm going to change our plans if you don't mind," he said, pulling up to a supermarket on the outskirts of Winston-Salem and stopping. He draped his right arm across the back of his seat and stroked her cheek with the back of his hand. "How about using that rain check I gave you? I need to look after you. If cooking for you is the only way I can express it, please let me do that."

She turned to face him. He meant what he said. That and no more. "All right." With Drogan and Cassie behaving as if she carried the plague, she couldn't imagine what she would do without him. She said as much.

He looked at her for so long that she had to guard against fidgeting. "If they were behaving as siblings ought to, would you still need me?"

It wasn't a time for diffidence or coyness. "I'd still need you. Because I don't cling to you doesn't mean you aren't important to me. You are."

"You know, the chances of our meeting were so slim, and yet . . ." He shook his head as though unable to fathom the mystery of it. "You're what I lacked, what I knew for a long time that I needed in a woman. I just can't believe it was an accident, finding you that way. Come inside with me. It's never safe for a woman to sit alone in a car at night."

She laughed at the irony of those words, as the gloom that had hovered over her since they left the hospital lifted. "Very funny. If I hadn't been sitting alone in a car at night and near the edge of a park at that, I wouldn't know you."

A grin crawled over his face. "You were lucky there wasn't a full moon. That's when I turn into a werewolf and have my way with pretty women."

His eyes twinkled with merriment, and she pointed to the full moon that shone proudly and majestically in a star-filled, cloudless sky. "What about tonight?" she asked him.

"That only happens in September. You're safe. It's almost Christmas."

"So much for your mystical powers. What are you going to buy?"

"I thought I'd get some lobster tails, baking potatoes, and broccoli. Other stuff is in the house. It won't be as fancy as if I'd known in advance, but it will definitely be edible. Does that suit you?"

Nodding assent, she slipped an arm through his and gloried in his reassuring touch as he hugged her to him. Watching him make his selections, carefully examining each item, she thought, *This man knows what he wants.*

"As host and cook, you leave nothing to be desired," she told him two hours later, when they'd finished cleaning the kitchen and he turned on the dishwasher.

She thought he'd laugh or, at best, joke about what she said, but he did neither. Instead, he observed her with a seriousness that she found unsettling.

Without saying a word, he flicked off the overhead light, took her hand, walked into the living room, and sat with her on the sofa. He filled two liqueur glasses with the Tia Maria that sat in a silver tray on the coffee table and handed one to her.

"In what respect do you think I come up short?"

She hadn't expected such a question and didn't like the agitation it stirred in her, but she was learning from her experiences at the paper that one of the best ways to deal with an attack was to counterattack.

She put the liqueur on the coffee table and faced him. "Have I given you the impression that I've found you lacking?"

He crossed his right ankle over his left knee, locked his hands behind his head, and leaned back against the sofa, affecting an air of nonchalance. She wasn't fooled. "I'm not trying to put you on the spot," he said. "I want to know what there might be about me that you don't have any tolerance for."

Cat and mouse, eh? Though she knew he spoke seriously, she decided not to settle into that mood and assumed the same pose as he. "If you're trying to get me to tell you I think you're perfect, I refuse."

He bolted upright and stared down at her. "I was serious. I want you to care for me, and I want to know what my chances are."

"Really? I listened to the radio as I drove to work Friday morning, and I heard a woman singing a song, obviously to a man. What do you think she was saying to him, probably in response to the kind of question you just asked me?"

"How would I know? What?"

She curved her index finger and rubbed his nose. "Don't be stupid."

"What do you mea—"

"That's the title of the song."

He grabbed the hand that rubbed his nose and leaned closer to her. "What were the words that followed "don't be stupid?""

Laughter bubbled up in her throat and spilled out until she thought she'd laugh herself to death.

He shook her gently. "You're not getting hysterical, are you?" She moved her head from left to right. "Okay. What are the next words to that song?'

"You know what they are," she said. "Otherwise you wouldn't be so anxious for me to say them."

"Tell me. You started this." Suddenly, he changed tactics, leaned over, pulled her into his arms, and kissed her forehead. "Why can't you tell me those words? I want to . . . I need to hear them."

Her arms went around him, and she whispered, "Don't be stupid. I won't tell you the exact words, but she's saying, 'You're number one with me.'"

His arms tightened around her. "Say it again. I want to hear it in your own words. I'm so full of you. Can you tell me what you feel for me?"

She wanted to relax and let go with him, but common sense told her to move slowly. "I just told you. You're man number one with me."

He leaned away and stared into her face. Then, suddenly, his smile caressed her, and she asked herself how she could have lived without him.

To him, she said, "It's getting late." Reaching for her liqueur glass, she heard herself say, "Drink up. It's after eleven."

The weight of his hand stilled hers before she lifted her glass to her lips. "Don't you remember that I don't drink if I have to drive?" The fire of desire blazed in his eyes, he breathed in deep, short pants, and his fire singed her as his masculine aura captured her senses and throttled her willpower.

She could taste him and feel him as the man in him ensnared her. Never had she experienced such jolts of electricity as plowed through her veins or the icy needles that crawled at a snail's pace along her limbs. The gentleness of his smile sent to the winds the resolve that remained in her. Resolve to stave off intimacy with him until she was certain she wouldn't have to do battle with him over Wade Field, until she was sure he was the man for her life. Thoughts of K.C.'s story and what Rafe might believe was her reaction to it flitted through her mind. She pushed that aside.

She had no doubt that in spite of the terrible hunger, the longing she saw in his eyes, the decision was hers. His hands, his beautifully tapered fingers and broad palms, captivated her senses and provoked in her a longing to feel them all over her naked flesh, his arms, long and strong, holding and loving her. She glanced up at him and gasped at the raw passion, the naked desire, mirrored in his eyes. The air between them snapped and crackled as the tension of desire slowly but inevitably engulfed them in its net of flames.

He reached for the glass, never taking his eyes from hers. "Go on," she whispered.

"Will you stay here with me? More than anything, it's what I want, but if you'd like to leave, just say so."

She drained her glass. "Hold me. I need you something awful."

"Are you telling me—?"

"I'm saying I want you to hold me and . . . love me. Really love me."

"Do you know what you're saying?"

"Yes. Yes."

His hands gripped her body to his, and then he was standing and lifting her to him until she felt him hard and strong against her body. His tongue flicked her lips, and she opened to him, took him in, and lost herself in him.

"This isn't a casual thing for me, Sharon. If you go into that bed with me, you're making a commitment to see whether we can make a life together."

"I'm already committed to that."

He picked her up, carried her up the stairs to his bed, and changed her life.

That Sunday afternoon after Sharon and Rafe left, Marge looked first at the sunshine streaming through her window and then at Miles Glick, the man who had been her family doctor for more than thirty years. She could read his face the way she read the funny papers when she was six years old. The picture he presented said more than his words.

"Miles, you've done all you can, friend," she said, "and I'm satisfied. Now, please get that look off your face. This isn't judgment day when you have to pay for all the sinning you've done."

It didn't take genius to see that her words relieved him. He put the stethoscope into the pocket of his white coat, walked to the head of her bed, and sat in the chair. "Just because you've been sinning doesn't mean I have."

"Aw, come on, Miles," she said. "If your wife knew how many of your female patients you—"

"Hold it there. I've been true to Rose."

With the help of her left hand and right elbow, Marge eased herself up into a sitting position. "In your fashion, no doubt. It's me you're talking to, remember? When you invaded Ada Monroe, it sure wasn't with a surgeon's scalpel. No, sir. She was so exhilarated by the . . . er . . . re . . . experience that Eloise, Gert, and I threatened to plug her up if she let it get back to Rose." She hadn't expected him to laugh, but he did, and she joined him in it.

"She was a wild one. From then on, I stuck to the Golden Rule."

"Hmm. I'm not a priest, so don't confess to me. Anyhow, I don't believe you. The ladies always went for you, and you tried to make every last one of 'em happy. Who'd have thought little cross-eyed Miles Glick would grow up to be a handsome ladies' man?"

He threw back his head against the chair and laughed. "You haven't changed since we were in the sixth grade. Nothing was sacred to you then, and even less is sacred today."

He stood when Ross walked in after a soft knock. Marge looked from one to the other, two of her closest friends, wonderful people who cared deeply about her. She had a lot of blessings, and she intended to savor them.

"Come on in, Ross," she said. "I was just jostling Miles about his youthful sins."

"Yeah. These kids today think they invented *making out*. Miles was way ahead of 'em."

"Give me some credit, man. These kids aren't in my class. I was discreet."

Ross popped his fingers and laid his head to one side. "So was Casanova, and far as I know, his wife didn't hit him over the head with a black iron skillet when she caught him at it."

Marge sat forward. "Do tell! My Lord. Nobody ever told me about that. You mean you knew that all these years and never told me?"

"Miles bribed me. He's been my doctor ever since and can't charge me a cent. It all happened twenty-five years ago, and I see him regularly. That's why I'm so healthy."

Marge laughed aloud. "Doggoned if you haven't found the answer to the problem of national health care. Well, I'll be."

Miles left as the messenger arrived with dinner from Gourmet Corner. "Mr. Shepherd said he'll be here tomorrow to visit with you," the messenger said.

She thanked him and added, "Tell him to call here first. I may be home."

"You won't change your mind, huh?" Ross asked after the messenger left.

"Miles said all that treatment isn't worth more than six or eight months." She patted his hand. "I don't have any regrets, Ross. If Drogan and especially Cassie would straighten out their attitudes, I'd actually be happy."

"Sharon's doing great at the paper. She has to crack a few skulls occasionally, but she's getting better at that."

"I don't suppose I could ask for three like her. The other two are giving her a hard time."

"I know, but they'll come around."

"Sure they will . . . after I'm gone."

Later that evening, Cassie finished her bath, put on her night clothes, and sat down to revise the sketch she'd begun at the office.

She hesitated to answer the telephone, not wanting to be interrupted. After half a dozen rings, she relented. "Shepherd residence."

"Cassie, this is Ross. I want to talk with you."

She sat down, shivering as cold chills snaked down her back, but her words belied her fear. "Something wrong with Sharon?" Cassie had sarcasm down to a fine art. Ross knew he could match her rudeness for rudeness, but he didn't feel up to it.

"Sharon's fine. She's doing great. Circulation's up, and we're getting a lot of letters complimenting us on the changes she's made."

"You didn't call me to tell me this. I'm busy."

"No, I didn't. I called to ask you when you last visited your mother."

"Look, if that's all you have to talk to me about, don't call me. I am not going to beg Mama for favors. She as good as published the fact that she prefers Sharon to Drogan and me. I refuse—"

He interrupted her. "How in hell did you get so warped? Your mother gave you an opportunity to manage the paper, though I thank God you refused. You're mad at yourself for blowing an opportunity and taking it out on your family. Well, if you really hate Marge, you can relax. She'll soon be out of the picture." He hung up.

She called him back. "What do you mean by that last remark?"

"You're not deaf. I mean just what I said, and let me tell you, Cassie, you're going to rue the day you mistreated your mother and your sister the way you're doing."

"She doesn't even have a will. That house and everything in it belong to Drogan and me. If Sharon has the paper, the rest is ours."

"So you've started fighting already."

"I told Drogan to speak to her, but he refuses to do it."

"That's because he's a human being. He may be mad at Marge—though I don't know why—but he won't go out of his way to hurt her. If you even threaten it, I'll tell Kix to straighten you out. Leave Marge at peace in her last days."

She wanted to hang up, but her finger wouldn't press the button. "What do you know about what I'm going through?" she heard herself say. "You can sit in judgment on me, but you don't know the hell I'm in."

"What did you say?"

She caught herself, furor welling up in her at the knowledge that she'd come close to exposing herself. "I'm working my fingers to the bone trying to get ahead, and all I can hear is Sharon, Sharon, Sharon. I'm sick of it, and it's all Mama's fault."

"I don't think you understood what I said a minute ago, Cassie."

"No? Then kindly enlighten me."

"Your mother has refused dialysis treatment. She's planning to check out of the hospital and cut off medical care."

She gasped as shock rattled her. "That's ridiculous. She wouldn't do a foolish thing like that."

"She said it's her life and that she intends to die with as much dignity as she lived. And since you've stayed away from her, you've missed your opportunity to persuade her to do otherwise."

She blew out a long breath. "You're not going to lay a guilt trip on *me*. I'm the victim here. Besides, Mama's not serious, and you know it." She hung up and phoned Drogan, but the line was busy, and she figured Ross had called him. She guessed correctly.

"You're joking," Drogan said after hearing Ross's account of his mother's decision concerning her health.

"No, I'm not, and she's signing herself out tomorrow morning."

His pulse skittered wildly as apprehension robbed him of intelligent thought. "Who's going to look after her? Imogene's taken leave of her mind, and I can't count on her. Mama'll just have to stay in the hospital. That's all there is to it."

"Don't count on it. If Marge wants to go home, I'll see that she goes and that she doesn't want for one thing. So don't worry. You won't be out of pocket. Anyway, that isn't why I called you. I wanted you to know your mother's condition. You're head of the family, and you should look after your mother and bring Cassie in line. She doesn't care enough to visit Marge, but she wants me to nag her about making her will. I won't, and I won't stand for anybody else doing it. That's all I have to say."

"Oh, yeah? Me bring my sister in line? If I'm head of the family, why did Mama give the paper to Sharon? Who're you kidding?"

"You had your chance at it. So did Cassie. The two of you don't want to take responsibility for your unwise and selfish choice. You'll regret the way you're acting. And soon."

Drogan stared at the receiver after he heard the click. Ross had hung up. He threw the mobile phone across the bed and walked over to the window. If anybody had told him a year ago that his marriage would be on the rocks, his mother terminally ill, that his docile, unsophisticated baby sister would be running the paper and from all accounts doing it with élan and imagination and that she'd be consorting with a rich corporate CEO, he'd have said that person was insane. He considered his tattered world and made up his mind to fix what he could and get on with his life. If Mama gave part of the house to Sharon, he'd go to court. If she didn't leave a will . . . He shrugged. He'd think about it later.

Right then, he had more pressing problems. Nine-thirty at night and he had no idea where his wife was. She was acting out, all right, but as soon as this month's credit-card bills came in, he'd close her accounts and put a stop to it. He had patience, plenty of it. If she was letting him know she no longer cared, it would hurt—hell, it already hurt—but it wouldn't kill him. He prayed she hadn't been stupid enough to go to Winston-Salem, because he'd meant what he said.

He heard the door open and dreaded what he might learn. She walked upstairs, calling him.

"Drogan. Honey, where are you? I'm so sorry I'm so late, but we had a flat tire, and neither one of us knows how to change one, so we had to wait till a trooper came along and helped us."

"The trooper changed the tire for you?"

"He did, and you can believe we were glad he came by."

That did it. The state police would call a tow truck, but they did not change tires, not even for little old ladies. He didn't turn around from the window. "Weren't you lucky!"

"I'll say. I'll have dinner on the table in a couple of minutes."

He wasn't having it. "I ate dinner at Pinky's. I'm going out."

He was almost sorry he'd broken off with Irene, but on the other hand, he figured it was good that he had; he might have guilt about the past but not about the present. He went to the basement, got the bedroll he used for camping, put it in his car, and went to his office. For the first time in the four years of his marriage, he didn't sleep in the bed he shared with his wife. Sleep wouldn't come, not even after he'd counted thousands of sheep, horses, and goats. He got up and opened his computer. His business had never been so good. If only his personal life wasn't such a rotten mess!

His phone rang at quarter past seven the next morning, and it didn't surprise him when he heard Imogene's voice.

"You didn't come home all night. I've called everywhere. I've been so upset."

What a pity that he no longer believed what she said. "When I left there, I didn't plan to come home. You behave outrageously, and then you use sex to smooth it over. I didn't want it. You think I like myself after I succumb to your little tricks? One of these days you'll parade yourself butt naked, and the only response you'll get out of me will be a laugh."

"How can you talk this way?"

He heard the pout and the threat of tears in her voice, but that didn't move him. He needed for them to level with each other and mend their marriage. He loved his wife, and he detested their superficial relationship. He hadn't realized until then that Imogene was a master manipulator. Maybe that's the way women were. How would he know? The only one of them he'd ever loved was Imogene.

"It's not fair what you're doing," she said, bringing his mind back to their conversation.

"No? Well, you haven't been leveling with me. Furthermore, you're flagrantly disrespectful. I'm sick of it. You were away from home twelve hours yesterday, and you didn't offer an explanation. At least not one that made sense. You and I are going to sit down and tell each other the truth. That's right. Your truth and my truth. It's that or nothing."

"What am I supposed to do while you hang over that computer and ignore me? You want me to stay in the house all day and never go anywhere. You didn't even take me for a vacation this year."

She talked about vacation as if that were her right. He was damned good and sick of it. "How do you expect me to provide for you if I don't work, Imogene? I'm working when I'm using the computer. Another thing; if I hadn't been spending so much money giving you what you want, I wouldn't be broke. You know I don't have the paper to fall back on."

"No. And why? Because your mother knew you couldn't handle it."

He told himself to cool off before he said words he'd regret for the rest of his life. He sat on the edge of his desk and took a few deep breaths. "And while you and I are having our honest talk, you're going to tell me how you got the nerve to talk to me this way. And you're going to convince me it's not related to what you're doing on your shopping trips."

He wasn't sure, but he thought he heard a gasp. If he was right, it meant he'd come close to the truth.

"Honey, you're imagining things. Lots of women love to shop. I was reading somewhere that about—"

"Cut it, Imogene. I don't want to hear anything about lots of women. I'm just interested in what you do and why."

"When are you coming home?"

Now that she mentioned it, he realized he didn't want to go home. "I'll go home when I have assurance that my wife will be there. Not before."

"I'll be here."

"Yeah. For how long? I won't live but once, and I mean to do a good job of it while I'm here. That doesn't include sitting around the house by myself waiting for you to come home, and I'm not doing it."

"I always make it . . . well, nice for you."

"You think that fixes everything? There's no shortage of good sex, Imogene. Let me know when you're ready for married life. But don't wait too long."

Drogan walked into Marge's hospital room at noon, minutes after commencement of visiting hours, and pasted a perfunctory kiss on her forehead. "What's this I hear about you ignoring Dr. Glick and signing yourself out? You can't do that."

"Sit down, son. I would have preferred to tell you this myself, but I understood why Ross did it. I've seen what some of my relatives went through with this ailment and to what end. So if you care about me, accept it—as I have—and show me a good face. All I've wanted is to have my children around me and to see them loving and caring for each other the way they used to."

"That isn't an easy thing you're asking."

"Maybe not, but would it make you feel better to see me with a bunch of tubes and pipes stuck everywhere?"

He kicked out his right leg and adjusted his pants at the knee. "You drive a hard bargain."

"I've been given sixty-one more years than my mother's firstborn, who didn't make it past a year, and seventeen more than my mother got. And anyhow, I always prayed to the Lord to let me live well and die easy. He did his part with the living well business and gave me a great life, so I intend to help him with this last. That's the least I can do to show my appreciation for what I already got."

He couldn't help staring at her. "How can you joke about it?"

She squeezed his hand. "Who's joking?" When he didn't respond, she said. "How's Imogene?"

He leaned forward in the chair and braced his forearms on his knees. "Imogene. I guess she's home, but I wouldn't swear to it."

"That doesn't sound right."

"And that's not the half of it."

"Which one of you's fooling around?"

His head snapped up. "What do you—" A long, tired breath eased itself out of him. "I was for about two months, but I never felt right doing it. I don't have any idea what's going on with my wife. I do know she's dissatisfied because I can't pamper her the way I used to. Anybody would think a European summer vacation was her right as a wife."

"Does Imogene know about your . . . er . . . affair?"

"I'm not that stupid. Besides, I wasn't involved; I just took care of my needs."

She raised herself up and glared at him. "Drogan, if you were ten, I'd smack you. Nothing she does justifies your . . . your cheating."

"I guess you're right. That's why I quit it, but I saw everything slipping away from me. Imogene wants the best of everything, and a lot of it. But there I was all of a sudden with nothing to show for the seven years of hard work I'd put in. Nothing but used airplane boarding passes, receipts for expensive hotel bills, Imogene's designer clothes, and expensive jewelry. The car, the house, and half of what's in it aren't paid for."

"I always thought you were mortgaging your future, but it wasn't my business. What changed?"

With his fingers punishing the back of his head with his furious rubbing, his stare was barely short of hostile. *"How can you ask that? The paper was something I could fall back on, and I didn't have to worry about saving. Now I have to work my butt off ten and twelve hours a day."*

"You could fall back on the paper, although you didn't do one thing to keep it going?"

He shrugged. "Imogene resents that and the fact that Sharon has the status, the paper, and the money."

"And that accounts for her rudeness to Sharon when she was here. If you had agreed to manage the paper, Sharon would be assistant dean of State U's School of Social Work. That's what she gave up, but if she resents it, she hasn't let me know it."

"It's not the same, and you know it. I'd better be going."

"So you're still angry. Get over it, Drogan, before it's too late. As for hard work, your father, Ross, and I used to work sometimes eighteen hours a day building that paper. And we had none of the amenities you have, not even air-conditioning. Who is it?"

He got up and opened the door. "Come in, Reverend Ripple. I was just leaving."

The reverend shook his hand. "Glad to see you. Nothing makes a mother prouder than a good-looking, successful son. Think you could give a couple of scholarships to some of our kids at church? The Lord will certainly bless you."

"Scholarships in what?" She looked at Ripple. The man could apple-polish his way out of Folsom Prison.

"You're a professional," the reverend said to Drogan. "Whatever you're handling right now will do just fine."

"I'll be in touch with you on that." What else could he say? If he hung around there, Ripple would have him making contributions to something. He got a hamburger at Pinky's Take Out and headed back to his office, thinking he should order a small refrigerator and maybe an electric hot plate to keep there. Who knew when he'd sleep at home again?

Eleven

"How you feeling?" Ross asked Marge as he pushed her wheel-chair down the hospital's exit ramp.

"Same. I could've walked, but they won't let you out of here unless you're in a wheelchair, probably because they're scared of somebody slipping and suing them."

"Yeah," Ross said, almost as if he were relieved to have a safe topic of conversation. "Everybody's protecting his own behind. *Your* tail isn't their problem."

"Tell me about it." She wanted to ask him why he wasn't at the paper at that time of the morning. At ten o'clock, that office was usually a mad frenzy. She didn't voice her thoughts. A blood brother couldn't be more faithful . . . or more caring. Indeed, he was a better brother to her than Drogan was proving to be to Sharon.

His thoughts seemed to reside in the vicinity of her own. "Sharon would've come, too, but Mack's acting out again, and she had to make him redo his work. You should have seen the editorial page he handed me. She hit the roof. Wouldn't let me do it for him. I wouldn't be surprised if she fired him. She's already given Wilson the job of under-studying Mack."

Marge laughed aloud. "I'd love to see her fire somebody. You talking about *my* Sharon? Soft as she is?"

"I don't think you know this Sharon. She's developing into a competent manager, and let me tell you, she won't take no tea for the fever. Our gal is up to the job."

She felt her chest swell. She didn't want anything more than for

Sharon to succeed. "I'm happy to hear it. Sharon rolling heads? That's something!"

"It was them or her, and she let it be known right away that it wasn't gonna be her. She let 'em know who runs the show, and brother, she does it, too. Smooth as a baby's bottom."

Ross opened the back door of his ancient but perfectly running Cadillac and looked at her. "I know you think being stubborn is a part of your normal breathing, Marge, but not this time. I'm going to lift you, put you—head and body—in the backseat, and you swing your feet in. Got that?"

"Oh, Ross, for Pete's sake! I can get in the car."

"You're gonna do as I say."

He got her into the car, closed the door, and took the wheelchair back to the hospital receptionist.

"Since Sharon's busy, why didn't you just tell Drogan or Cassie to come get me? They may be off the wall right now, but they'd do it just to let me know how magnanimous they are."

"If I had to tell them to come and get you, they didn't need to know."

She admitted to herself, though not to him, that he had a point. "How're you going to get me in the house?"

"Now listen. If you're gonna be a pain in the rear, you should've stayed in Woodmore General. Being around a snapping turtle isn't my idea of pleasure."

She laughed with the joy of seeing his in-your-face attitude back in place. "If I haven't fought with you once in the thirty-five years we've known each other and worked together, starting now wouldn't make sense. Still, you could try being a little less bossy."

He parked in front of her house and cut the motor. "I'm not chang-ing myself at this age, not even for you. You're going in the house in this wheelchair I put in the trunk for you."

She'd always known that Ross's gruff manners and often acerbic tongue masked a gentleness of which he didn't seem too proud, but the soft center she'd seen in him since she left the paper had come as a surprise, indeed almost a shock. She knew better than to mention it.

Eloise opened the front door. "Girl, it sure is good to see you back home here. I got the place aired out, and me and Ross got the kitchen crammed with food. Sure is a good thing this is a one-story house and you ain't got no stairs to worry 'bout. Ross, you're a saint."

Why would Eloise rattle on like an old, empty wagon? The woman hardly ever uttered an unnecessary word. And then she knew. Her friend meant to be cheerful if it killed her. She was having none of it.

"Eloise and Ross. Both of you listen to me. When it clouds up, don't grin at me and swear the sun's shinning. We all know what's happening, so let's just be ourselves. You are both precious to me, and I want you both near me, but not if you're going to tiptoe around here looking like you're getting root canal without Novocaine. It's not like either one of you. Happy as I am to be back home, I'd dance right now if I had the strength."

Ross popped his fingers, flexed them, and popped them again.

Eloise rolled her eyes. "You better lie down for a spell. You talkin' like the blood done left your head. I declare . . ."

After the two of them helped Marge get into bed, she looked around, patted the sheets, and said, "Maybe I'll lie here and finish reading *Beyond Desire,* but don't y'all think I'm going to stay in this bed."

With his hands braced against his hips, Ross glared at her. Then, to her surprise, he suddenly softened, sat on the edge of her bed, and took her hands in his own. "If you get a bad attack of bitchiness, babe, just let it out. I got thick skin."

Chills slithered down her nerves. She'd rather have him gruff and bossy. As if he realized how far out of character his behavior was, he released her hands, sprang to his feet, and grabbed the phone.

"I forgot I promised Sharon I'd let her know when you got settled in."

He dialed Sharon's number at the paper. "Yeah. Went off without a hitch. Smooth as a baby's bottom. Naah. You call Drogan and leave Cassie to me. Marge is fine, lying here holding court. Right. I'll tell her."

He walked back to the bed. "I'm going to work, Marge. Sharon said she'll be here as soon as we finish the budget meeting. I'll be back about five." She nodded. "He stuffed his hands into his pockets and kicked at the carpet. "I'll call before I leave work. See if you need anything."

"Bless the Lord. That man's a true friend," Eloise said after Ross left. "They don't make 'em like that no more."

"No," Marge said, mostly to herself. "They don't make them like you, either." Sleep crowded in on her, and she dozed off, happy to be at home.

* * *

With Ross out of the office looking after Mama that morning, Mack decided to act out, and she was having none of it. "If you ever walk into my office again without knocking," Sharon said to Mack, "look for another job." She leaned back in the chair and tapped her Mount Blanc pen rhythmically on the desk. "You come to work when it suits you and leave when it pleases you. Friday, you left before the reporters handed in their copy, and Ross did your work." At his raised eyebrow, she said. "Oh, yes. I know what goes on here, and Ross is not going to cover for you. If I hadn't checked you this morning, your page in to-morrow's paper would be a disaster."

He lingered there, seemingly uncertain as to whether he should leave. "Take a walk, Mack. You've got work to do, and please close the door."

It seemed seconds before she heard the door close. He could lean on her all he pleased, but she refused to let him make her a nervous, stressed-out, and fist-pounding boss. And he was going to do his work properly and on time. Or else.

She phoned Drogan, as she'd promised Ross. "Drogan, Mama's home," she said after greeting him.

"Home? She belongs in the hospital. Who brought her home? You shouldn't have done that without getting my consent. I'm a member of this family, too, in case you've forgotten."

She took a deep breath and called on her patience, remembering when a conversation with her big brother was a pleasurable experience. "Drogan, I did not, repeat did not, bring Mama home. Uncle Ross did." And what if she had? "But I would have if I hadn't been in a meeting with the sheriff's people."

"The sheriff? What do you have to do with that crook? He'd sell his mother for fifty cents."

"Are you serious? He'd give her away if anybody would take her." Normally, he'd have laughed at that, but he remained silent so long that she wondered if he'd hung up.

"What are you planning to do about Mama? You know I have to work to make up for . . . for . . ."

"Please, Drogan. You're beginning to whine, and I can't stand that in a man. I didn't call to ask you for anything. I'm prepared to take care of her, and it won't be a burden. So relax."

"Look, I'd help if I could, but you see how it is with me. You've got the paper to fall back on; I only have what I can earn. So I can't do much."

She wished he could hear himself. The man who always took charge was having trouble producing a reason why he couldn't discharge his responsibility to his mother. Her beloved brother, the joy of her childhood, a chameleon who had been posing as her source of strength and rock-solid dependability. Now that she needed him, he was as flaky as French pie crust. For two cents, she could dislike him. And it hurt. Nobody on earth knew how it hurt.

She couldn't remember ever having allowed herself anger at Drogan, not even when, as a child, he teased her until she cried. In those days, he hugged her, carried her on his back, told her little stories, and placated her in other ways after he made her cry. Sometimes she cried in order to get his precious peace offerings. But she was no longer that child, and she didn't need those dribblings of affection.

"Don't explain it to me, Drogan," she said, hating the sound of her own bitterness. "Explain it to Mama. And while you're at it, have a little chat with your conscience. Get familiar with it, because you'll have it for company years from now. Be seeing you."

"Wait a minute. What's come over you?"

"If I thought you'd understand, I'd tell you, but I wouldn't make a dent. 'Bye."

She told herself not to worry about Drogan's attitude, that he had to live with his conscience, and got busy preparing for the budget meeting. She knew she couldn't count on her sister. Cassie's resentment was far deeper than Drogan's. *If I'm alone in this, so be it. I'm not afraid.*

However, Sharon would learn that she wasn't alone. Ross called her on the intercom. "You want Mack in the budget meeting, don't you? He said you threatened to kick him off the paper."

"I didn't threaten, Ross. I promised him, and I mean it. If he walks out of this building without handing in his work or if he saunters into my office again without knocking and sits down as if it is he, and not I, who belongs there, he needn't even go back to his desk. This insolence is his way of showing disrespect, and I don't have to tolerate it. Wilson is almost as good as he is and a heck of a lot more congenial."

His soft whistle reached her through the wire. "I'm in your corner. Do whatever you think's right. Nobody's indispensable."

She didn't need his approval, but having it gave her a good feeling.

"Mama said you're the Rock of Gibraltar, Uncle Ross, but to me, you're more than that. Thanks."

"Humph. Marge can get carried away."

He protested, but she knew from the way he said it that having her mother's approval pleased him. She thought of her mother's friends—Eloise, Gert, Miles Glick, and Ross. Loyal. Caring. One such friend was a rarity. She punched the intercom and heard herself ask Ross, "Uncle Ross, why do people love Mama? Why are her friends so loyal, so faithful, to her?"

He cleared his throat several times. "Marge is . . . Marge loves people. I mean, she really loves them, and her friends know it. Even these old hardheads here in the newsroom know she loves them. It's . . . I don't know. I guess it's her heart. Bigger'n she is." His voice softened, and he spoke almost in a whisper. "Marge is *some* woman. There isn't a thing I wouldn't do for her."

Love. It always boiled down to love. But how did you know when it was real? Drogan and Cassie loved her, or they had until a crisis tore through the family, turning it inside out. Changing roles and altering relationships. A frown or silence where she'd once received a smile or a hug. Had they ever loved her for herself? Or had they liked having a younger sister who worshiped them, was blind to their shortcomings, a little puppy who sat at their feet, wagging her tail for the tidbits of affection they threw out?

The phone rang, shocking her out of her musings, and she lifted the receiver before her secretary could screen the call. "Yes."

"Hello. Who, other than you, is on the line right now?"

Her heartbeat responded to the sound of his voice and began a rhythmic pounding in her chest. "Hi. Just you and me. Why?"

"Then it's safe to tell you I'm full of you, that you've taken a seat in my head and pushed everybody and practically everything else out of it. Sharon, tell me I'm not dreaming."

She didn't see the point in being coy, but she didn't want to be out on a limb, either. "I could ask you the same question."

"I want you to listen to me. I'm thirty-nine years old, and I've had enough disappointments for half a dozen men, but I've also had enough experience to realize that there's nothing ephemeral about this thing between you and me. It's real, Sharon. At least for me. What about you?"

"Oh, Rafe. Be careful with your words."

"Sometimes, Sharon, I think about you, and you . . . you take my breath away."

His words catapulted her back to that night of love in his arms when his fingers roamed over her naked flesh, possessing her, staking his claim, making certain that she would want no other man. That night when his lips, his whole body, set her afire.

"Hey. You still there?"

"Yes," she whispered, getting a grip on her mind. "If you want to talk to me like that, please wait till we're together."

"Didn't you ever feel that you were overflowing, that you'd burst if it didn't come out?"

"Didn't I . . ." She controlled the laughter that would have told him her nerves were on a wild rampage. "Rafe, you had me in that state perpetually the last . . . Ooops." She slapped her hand over her mouth. "I'm hanging up. This is getting out of hand."

"All right. I know what you mean. I didn't choose the best time for this conversation. When can I see you? How about after work? I'm in Woodmore today."

"Five-thirty? It's cold, so I drove today."

"I'll tail you. How's your mother?"

"She came home today, so my routine will probably change. I have a lot of things to work out."

"You know I'm with you in this . . . and everything else. By the way, the interest in Scenic Gardens quadrupled this past weekend, thanks to that story in your paper. I've had three closures and four down payments today alone. I can't believe it."

"That's great. Call K.C. and tell her."

"I will, now that you mention it. See you at five-thirty."

"Uh . . . Still doing research on Wade Field?"

"*What?*" The question evidently surprised him. "Why, yes. I was out there this morning. Trust me, Sharon. I will do as I said. See you later."

She hung up just as a light rap sounded on her office door. "Come in," she said, and leaned back in her chair. Ross, Wilson, and Mack walked in, in that order. She got up then and moved over to her conference table.

"What do you have for me?" She listened to their reports and suggestions for the layout, the relative importance of different news items and stories. "Sounds good to me. I want to keep the editorial page as it is, but I want an op-ed page for guest notables to have their say, and I want Wilson to manage it."

Ross popped his fingers, and a smile lightened his cheeks. "It's a great idea, but how often do we run this new page?"

"Weekends. If it flies, we'll add Wednesdays. Can you handle that, Wilson?"

"Yes, ma'am. I'll do whatever you want me to do. Thanks. I won't let you down." He looked at Ross. "Thank you, sir. If I run into any problems, I'll come see ya."

Mack sat there, tight-lipped and obviously irritated, but he kept his thoughts to himself. As they left her office, however, Ross's voice drifted back to her.

"You're as good as they come, Mack, but when they passed out personalities, you got the short end of the stick. Wilson's easy to work with. Shape up, man."

"She doesn't like me," he grumbled.

"With your attitude," Ross said, "who the hell could blame her?"

After closing the door, she picked up the phone to call Cassie. She'd probably regret it, but she ought to find out if Cassie had any ideas about taking care of Mama at home. She could manage it herself, but her older sister had a right to help make decisions about their mother, provided she wanted to.

"Cassie, this is Sharon. I thought I should tell you—"

"Ross phoned me this morning. I hope she's planning to get a full-time housekeeper. She's got no right to pull out of the hospital with no plans for—"

"Cassie, Mama's care is not a problem. I just thought you'd want to be involved in any decision about her health."

"What's there for me to do? She's said to hell with modern medicine. I'm an artist, not a doctor."

Same Cassie, but at least she hadn't hung up. That was something! "You want us to interview the housekeeper and the nurse together?" she asked, hoping that Cassie would agree to cooperate with her.

"Look, I uh . . . She gave you the paper, didn't she? And she'll probably give you the house, the car, and her bank account. You look after her. I'm not rich. I have to work."

When she could get her mouth closed, she said, "You sure you mean that?"

"Of course I mean it," she shrieked. "You've got everything. I never dreamed you could be so insensitive." She hung up.

Sharon stared at the phone. For half a minute, Cassie had behaved as if they were sisters. Maybe there was reason for hope. She shook her head. Nothing, not even anger or jealousy, could explain to her satisfaction Cassie's strange behavior. When they were children, Cassie's clothing was always clean and neat, never mussed, like that of her playmates. She spoke in well-modulated tones and would walk half a block rather than scream for a person's attention. And in no case did she lose her temper and shriek. In fact, she'd always seemed to enjoy being so perfect that she made others around her seem inferior. She had the unpleasant feeling that Cassie needed help.

But the kind of help Cassie needed wasn't to be had on a psychiatrist's couch. At that moment, she paced the floor of her office, rubbing her arms and intermittently wringing her hands. Her second trip to the water cooler in the last half hour didn't relieve the dryness of her mouth. She went back to her desk and dialed her husband's number.

"Kix, I know you said you can't take off from work till after the first of the year, but I'm . . . I'm suffocating in this place. Can't we go away for the weekend?"

"Honey, what's the matter? I've been watching this restlessness in you, and lately it seems to be veering out of control. There's no one to substitute for me here during this season. You know that. Yesterday I had guests from as far away as Atlanta. They're here around Easter and again around Christmas. If these people make a long trip and I'm not here . . ."

She had to get away. She *had* to. "Don't you care that I'm . . . I'm . . . that I need to get away? Kix, this is unbearable."

"What's unbearable, Cassie? What are you talking about? Open up and let me know what's going on inside of you. I can't help you if you won't let me."

"You don't understand. You can't. You can't." Now she'd said the wrong thing.

"I can't understand? Is it written in Russian or Greek? If you say it in English, French, Spanish, Italian, or German, I can damned well understand it, and when you can say you speak and understand *more* than five languages, you can act as if I'm your inferior. Wake up, Cassie, before I no longer care."

She laid her forearms on her desk and rested her head there. How could a woman tell her husband that if he didn't get her out of the path of another man, she'd wind up in that man's bed? She ran her hands through her perfectly coiffed hair. If Mama hadn't given that paper to Sharon, she wouldn't be working so hard to make a name for herself, to prove that she was Sharon's equal. And she would never have met that man, because she would have been home at five o'clock on Saturday and Sunday afternoons. But would she ever have recognized the wasteland she'd made of her marriage?

She tried to figure out what it was about that low-class man that could attract her, a lady, a member of one of the town's most prominent families. An ill-kempt man, arrogant and strident, who eschewed what she regarded as normal niceties with women. Yes, he had mesmerizing good looks, with bedroom eyes and curly lashes, but when it came to looks, Kix didn't take a backseat to any man. So it wasn't the looks.

A long, tired breath escaped her. Maybe it was hopeless. When he'd had his tongue in her mouth and his fingers torturing her nipple, she'd wanted him inside of her badly enough to ravish him against his will if he'd been reluctant. She couldn't imagine where she'd gotten the strength to walk away from him. Never had she felt that way about Kix or any other man. She didn't even like sex; indeed, she disliked it. But that man . . . He'd sworn to have her, but she was damned if he would.

After prowling around her office for an hour, unable to get her mind on her work, she stuffed her unfinished designs into her briefcase, put on her coat, scarf, and gloves, and left the building without telling anyone where she'd gone. "I'm losing my mind," she said as she got into her car, started the engine, and drove off. She had to see Mama. If she didn't, she'd be fair game for the town gossips, but right then, she needed to get away. Anywhere.

However, having been indoctrinated from her youth with the Puritan work ethic, she couldn't justify to herself the waste of so much time when she should be working. She remembered that she hadn't finished her Christmas shopping and latched onto that as a reason for leaving her office. Finding herself on Highway 52 to Danvers, she parked in one of the shopping malls that sprawled along its sides, locked her briefcase in the trunk of her car, and went inside.

Standing in front of a men's clothing store, she released a harsh expletive. What did she care how Judd whatever-his-last-name-was would look in that six-hundred-dollar oxford-gray business suit? She caught herself as she was about to stamp her foot. Why couldn't she get him out of her mind? Later, in a bookstore where she'd gone in hopes of finding an encyclopedia of cooking for Kix, she felt a spray of warm liquid on her right leg, looked down, and gasped.

"I'm so sorry, ma'am," the woman said. "I don't have anybody to leave them with, and I tell you, trying to shop with three little ones is a chore. It's just milk, so I'm sure it'll wash out. I'm sorry."

Cassie stared at the woman. Three children under six and one in her belly and the idiot actually looked happy. She tossed the book on the counter and left the store. It was foolish to react that way, but wherever she went, somebody was putting babies in her face. She passed Radio Shack and turned back as an idea surfaced. Kix loved to sing in the shower; she could get him a radio to play while he showered and shaved.

"May I help you, ma'am?"

"Thank you. I'd like . . ." Her lower lip dropped and her eyes widened, and she imagined that she looked half-wild when the store clerk asked, "Ma'am, is something wrong? Are you all right?"

"Yes. Yes. I'm f . . . fine."

She bolted from the store and didn't stop running until she'd locked herself in her car. With her head cradled in her arms and resting on the steering wheel, her whole body shook. *Oh, Lord. He's everywhere. I can't get rid of him. The first time in my life I go in that store and he's standing ten feet from me. Thank God he didn't see me.* It occurred to her that she didn't know where he'd parked, so she'd better get out of the parking lot. With trembling fingers, she ignited the engine, revved it mercilessly, and knocked over two wastebaskets and a no-parking sign on her way out of the parking lot.

Half an hour later, she parked in front of her mother's house and leaned back against the seat. Relieved. He hadn't followed her. She got her briefcase out of the trunk and started up the walk. Always look the part was her motto. You never knew who you'd find in Mama's house.

"Well, hello. Are you here all the time?" she asked Ross when he opened the door.

"Somebody has to make up for your shortcomings," he growled. "You'd rather Marge was by herself?"

"Spare me, Ross. I'm not in the mood for any pontificating from you." She started past him, but he waylaid her with a hand heavy on her arm.

"Get rid of all that attitude, Cassie. Marge is sick, and what she needs now is peace and as much happiness as we can give her."

A tart remark about his meddlesomeness sat on the tip of her tongue, but she noticed the unshed tears glistening in his eyes and caught herself. "I'm not the ogre you make me out to be, Ross. All I want is what's rightfully mine." She brushed past him, unwilling to let him know that she'd felt chastened by his words.

She hugged Marge, who reclined in the chaise longue, and grudgingly acknowledged Eloise's presence. "You ought to be in the hospital where you can get the best care, Mama. I don't like knowing you're here where there aren't any doctors or nurses."

"Ain't no doctors and nurses gonna give Marge any better care than me," Eloise said. "They can't do nothing for her, but I can. I can give her love and comfort, which is what you should be doing."

"Your opinion is the last thing I need," Cassie said, and was proud that she hadn't said what she was thinking.

"Now. Now." Marge said. "You look wonderful, honey, and I'm . . . I'm so glad to see you. Eloise is right. The doctors have said there's nothing else they can do for me except dialysis, which, according to them, isn't worth more for me than an additional six or eight months. So I'm not putting myself through it."

She gasped. "Mama, how can you do this? What about your family? Get another doctor. Glick doesn't know what side is up."

"Glick and half a dozen others? They're all stupid? No, Cassie. And as for my family, those who care will stick by me. I've talked with Drogan and Sharon, and they're trying to accept this. I want you to do the same."

"Oh, for goodness' sake. Drogan is preoccupied with his own problems, and Sharon can afford to accept it; she stands to gain everything." Irritation began to surface in her, and she waved her hand to encompass all she saw. "I'll bet you've given all this to her, this and—"

"Shut up, Cassie. Shut up if you don't want to feel my hand across your mouth."

She glared at Ross, who'd sprung from his chair and was standing over her, fiery anger blazing in his eyes. "Don't you dare," he said in a voice that was little more than a snarl. "Don't you even think it."

"Don't what?" Marge asked.

For a minute she contemplated those two words. That voice hadn't sounded like Mama at all. "Nothing," she said. "Nothing. I . . . I have to get back to my office."

"Come see me again soon," Marge said, and raised her arms for a hug.

She stared down at her mother. "I . . . uh . . . I will." Maybe she was losing her mind. Mama's hug was as weak as a damp dishcloth. She rushed out of the room and hurried to the front door, but as she reached for the doorknob, Ross's hand covered hers.

"I told you not to bring up that business of a will to Marge and you did it, anyway."

She glared at him. "I didn't use the word. And what business have you got interfering with my relations with my own mother?"

He popped his fingers, a habit that she hated in anybody who did it. "I care about her, and that's more than I can say about you. All you care about is what you'll get when she dies, and you don't even mind letting her know it."

"Stop it. You don't know what you're talking about. How do you know what I'm going through? Mind your—"

He interrupted her. "I warned you that if you did it, I'd tell Kix, and I will. You go on, young lady. But you'll get yours."

Her gaze locked on his back as he treaded slowly away, then she tightened the woolen scarf around her neck and left the house. Her family and Mama's friends danced around in her mind like little children playing hopscotch, not caring about her and her problems. If only she didn't feel so alone. If she could just tell somebody how she ached inside.

All she had was her skill as a designer, her only way of enhancing her status and making a mark for herself. And she had nothing to show for the day's work. Nothing. She hadn't done one bit of work all day, and she'd never get ahead like that. She tightened her coat against the damp cold and got into her car. Maybe she should go home, but a teenager could figure out that what she wanted and needed wasn't there. She was tired of faking it. She loved Kix, but . . . She knew the problem was in her, otherwise the whole world wouldn't be so hot after sex, but she didn't know what to do about it.

When she stopped her car, she was in front of the building in which she worked. She got out, hunched her shoulders against the wind, and entered the building as other employees filed out, having finished for the day. She strode past the night guard and other night workers without glancing their way, ducked into the elevator a split second before the door closed, and relaxed. This was a place—elegant, with soft beige walls, recessed lights, tan broadloom carpeting, green plants, and airy rooms—where status meant something, and it suited her, gave her a sense of importance.

In her office, she turned on the lights and prepared to work, then remembered that she hadn't eaten lunch. She got a tuna fish sandwich, an apple, and a bottle of ginger ale from the machine at the end of the hall, stored that in her desk drawer, kicked off her shoes, and smiled. Why hadn't she thought of it that morning when not a single idea came to her? If she saw a picture of one more bride with calla lilies or baby's breath, she'd be sick. With bold strokes, she sketched plain white clematis and surrounded them with pale yellow centered white autumn clematis, stood, and looked down at it. Fantastic! Laughter bubbled up in her and poured out. She felt like dancing. She loved working when no one was around to bother her.

She'd better call Kix in case he phoned her at home and wondered where she was. "I haven't done a thing all day," she said when he asked why she was still in the office, "so I'm working a little late tonight. Honey, I can't let the day go by and not get a single thing done."

"How late, Cassie?" His voice carried the sound of testiness. "This is getting to be a habit."

"No, it isn't, hon. I—"

He interrupted her. "Look! I work eleven hours every day because I have to. From ten in the morning till nine at night every day except Monday, but when nine comes, I take off this apron and this chef's hat, and I come home to you. No matter what, I come home to you, and you know I'll be there."

"Kix, please. I . . . You don't understand."

"No, I don't understand. All I'm asking is that you be there for me. After the hassle I've been through all day, I need a little gentleness, some warmth, some love, and a little appreciation from my wife. I don't need to walk into an empty house."

"We . . . we need to support each other, and my career isn't important to you."

"That isn't true, and you know it. I'm proud of you. I love seeing your designs on cards and your sketches in magazines, but you don't take pride in what I do. You don't give me any support."

"Yes, I do. I . . . But . . . Oh, why can't you understand?"

"What do you want me to understand? Tell me."

"That I need my niche. I need to be somebody special. But you won't help me. You won't speak to Mama about that will. I was over there this afternoon, and when I started to mention it to her myself, Ross threatened to slap me."

"*What?* You started to . . . Woman! Have you lost your mind?" Harsh. He'd never spoken to her so harshly. She almost cringed. "Aren't you ashamed of yourself? How can you be so callous toward your mother? She's dying, for heaven's sake."

"She's not. Damnit, she's not. You're just like the rest of them. You want to see me grovel. I won't do it."

"Will you stop the histrionics, please? When I married you, you knew how to be tender and caring. What's happened to you, Cassie? The last three or four months, since Mama's been sick, you've been almost a stranger. I don't know you at all. And Cassie, right now, I don't care if you work all night." He hung up.

She stared at the phone. He'd actually hung up on her, and he'd never done anything like that before. He looked up to her. Well, she wasn't going to worry about that. When his testosterone started acting up, he'd come crawling. She sharpened a crayon and got busy.

"You planning to spend the night here? It's snowing."

"Oh!" She grabbed her chest and whirled around toward the door. "*You!* Where'd you come from? Get out of my office this second." Her heart pounded out an erratic rhythm, and her breathing accelerated.

He ignored both her question and her directive. "I'm working. I figured when you bolted out of Radio Shack this afternoon like a scared rabbit you'd go home and ease your guilt with your husband."

When she couldn't find her voice, he let a grin slip over his face. "But you didn't do that. You drove straight here. I don't think you like that guy."

Drummers had begun a maddening paradiddle in her head, her body heat shot up, and she wanted to pull off her jacket. He started walking toward her desk, and she jumped up. But he was between her and the door, so she headed for her bathroom.

"You might as well face it, Cassandra." His voice was low, masculine and . . . oh, he was so sure of himself.

She whirled around. "Don't touch me. You hear. Leave me alone."

He stood there as if she hadn't spoken, a mocking grin on his face. "You've got an exalted opinion of yourself, and it's gonna be your undoing. You know I work evenings and weekends, and don't tell me you didn't know I'd come in here tonight if I saw a light in your office. I've done it before. You saw me in Radio Shack, and you know I saw you."

"I'll have you fired. I . . . I . . ."

He narrowed his right eye, but his smile remained in place. "Go ahead. Try it. I haven't done a thing."

Tremors raced through her, and when she couldn't control the trembling of her bottom lip, she tucked it into her mouth until she could steady herself. "I'm going home, so get out of my way."

He shrugged as if her leaving meant nothing to him, as if she came cheaper by the dozen. "Okay, if that's the way you want it. But wouldn't you rather feel my tongue dancing in your mouth, my lips pulling on your nipple, and my—"

"Shut up. You . . . you . . ."

"Don't you want to burst wide open with me inside of you? Don't you want to know what it is to be a woman, Cassandra?"

"Please leave m-me alone. I want—"

"What you want is here. I'm what you want, and you won't rest until you get me."

"Don't. Ju-just go."

She wouldn't give him the satisfaction of seeing her cry. Never. But his scent, his aura, and his tough masculine persona hooked her, suspending her on a precipice above a misery of endless depth. She raised her head and looked at him, the personification of man. It was a gargantuan mistake; her nipples tightened until they pained her, and heat seared her feminine center.

As if he could see inside of her, he said, "I'll soothe everything that ails you, and whatever I do, I do it thoroughly."

With her self-confidence splintered by her raving libido, she turned her back to him, ashamed that he knew how badly she wanted him. She didn't wipe the tears. His fingers gripped her shoulders and slowly turned her to face him.

His voice deep and masculine but soft and beguiling came to her as if from beyond. "Open your mouth, baby, and take me in. I want you twice as badly as you want me." His tongue rimmed her lips, and God help her, she tasted him, the taste she'd longed to have again, that she'd dreamed of, that had kept her awake at night. His fingers stroked her arms, not rough as she'd imagined, but gentle, yet firm. "It's useless, baby. I want my tongue in your mouth. Open for me."

She shook her head from left to right, denying him, but her lips parted, and at last she had him in her. She sucked his tongue into her mouth and, with her hands behind his head, pressed him to her. He moved her hands and pulled off her jacket, and she couldn't wait to feel his grip on her again. Rough and masculine. Holding her as if she were his prisoner. She felt his hand go into her blouse, ripping the button, and didn't care for that or anything but the feel of his fingers on the flesh of her hardened nipple. When he pulled her breast from the confines of her bra, lowered his head, and sucked her nipple into his mouth, screams tore from her throat. She'd never let Kix do that for fear he'd make them sag. Her hands went to his head, pressing him to her, encouraging him, begging for more until she felt contractions in her womb and hot fire in her loins.

"Do something to me," she pleaded. "Take me. Take me. I can't stand it anymore."

He jerked her blouse and bra from her shoulders, lifted her above him, and kissed first one taut areola and then the other as if he enjoyed the taste of her. Then he buried his nose in the valley between her breasts, licked their sides, and inhaled deeply the scent of her skin. Nearly beside herself with desire, she grabbed at his belt buckle, but he stilled her hand, letting her know that he was in command, and lay her on the carpet beside her desk.

After locking her door—something she realized she hadn't thought of—he stood over her, staring down at her. And she wanted him to stare, to admire her beautiful breasts. As if he'd read her mind, his lips curved into a half-smile, and he lowered himself to his knees beside her and stripped her.

"Spread your legs."

She did as he ordered, and he hooked her knees over his shoulders and tantalized her with his educated tongue until she thought she'd die, that she'd explode from the fullness that fomented in her. She tried to control her rocking hips, to hide from him the need that began to consume her like a flame sucking up oxygen. Tried not to respond to sensations she'd never before experienced, to loving she hadn't permitted her husband to give her.

"Take off your clothes. Take them off," she said.

He took his time getting out of his shirt, and while her half-glazed eyes feasted on his thick chest and prominent pectorals, he slowly kicked off his jeans.

She gasped at the sight of his bulging sex, hidden from her eyes by a tiny scrap of G-string.

"Like what you see?" he taunted before turning his attention to her erected areolas with the surety of a butterfly zeroing in on the nectaries of a rose. Teetering toward loss of control, she stopped trying to halt the twisting of her body and the swaying of her hips as he suckled her.

He handed her a condom. "You want me, so take me," he said, and his voice, guttural and strained with passion and desire, excited her. "I said take it."

"But I . . . I can't . . . I don't know what you want me to do."

He leaned over her, stroked her jaw, and whispered. "No. I don't suppose you do."

Hot with want and nearly petrified with anxiety as to what he might do next, she let her breath out slowly as his tongue began its journey at her neck, eased over her breasts, arms, belly, and the inside of her thighs, skimming and torturing until her inferno of passion threatened to explode in her loins.

"Damn you," she screamed. "Damn you. Stop playing with me. Ooooh," she moaned, as his finger invaded her.

"Don't tell me what to do."

His fingers found the nub of her passion and danced their wicked dance, playing her as a harpist plays a harp, and she thought she'd die if he didn't get inside her.

Suddenly, he hulked above her. "Take me in, baby. Now. Hold me in your hands and take me in."

Shudders raced through her as she took his rock-hard velvetlike steel into her fingers and led him to her impatient portal. Her body swung up to meet his thrust, and she felt her eyes widen as he drove into her. Whatever gentleness he'd shown vanished as he gripped her hips and rode in and out of her. But she didn't care. Thrill after thrill shot through her as he possessed her body and finally lay claim to her five senses, for he was all she could hear, see, smell, taste, and feel. He pounded into her, and she fought to resist him, to hold back the tide of emotion that consumed her.

He demanded that she submit to him, but she didn't want to, didn't want to give up that last bit of herself, but he hammered at her will, forcing her to yield. Heat seared the bottom of her feet, and she swelled to the bursting point.

"Please. Please."

"Please who? Call my name. Let me know you know who I am. Say it."

She realized she couldn't control him. If only she could hate him. "Judd. Oh, Judd. Please. I can't bear it."

"Then stop fighting me and I'll give you what you want."

She grabbed his hips to force him, and suddenly the sensation of his lips on her nipple, his fingers toying with the nub of her passion, and his steel driving within her brought a scream from her throat. He drove into her until she threw her arms wide and capitulated. Then she tightened around him as he flung her into ecstasy. Seconds later, he roared his own release.

Stunned by the enormity of what she'd felt, she draped her right arm across her eyes and sobbed.

He looked down at her. "You all right?"

She nodded. "I'm just . . . I never knew."

He separated them. "I'd give anything right now for a cigarette. How long have you been married?" She told him. "And this was the first time for you? You realized now that you've been cheating your husband?"

"What would you know about it?"

His laugh, harsh and knowing, stung her conscience. "Plenty. You think you're better than I am, and you probably think you're better than he is. You've never given yourself to him."

"Would you please either change the subject or . . . or don't talk."

"Let me tell you something, Cassandra. No woman is better than the man she lies beneath, and the man above her is no better than she. Once they go to bed, they're forever equal. You don't want to have an affair with me, baby, because I wouldn't put up with your nonsense. Not for a second. So this is it for us."

He leaned over, kissed her cheek, got up, and began dressing. Suddenly, he covered her with her jacket.

"You're one hell of a woman in bed, but you and I are the only ones who know it. If you want to straighten out your life, let your husband in on it. If you resist him the way you tried to resist me, I bet he gave up long ago."

"Why don't you shut up?"

He laughed, and to her surprise, she liked the sound of it. "Don't tell me to shut up." A grin settled around his mouth. "You haven't moved because you want more, but I have to work." She stared at him as his face, beautiful by any measure, broke into a smile. "You could at least thank me for giving you your first orgasm."

She wanted to hate him, but she couldn't, and she heard herself telling him so. "I thought you were crude, but you aren't. Are you?"

"And that attracted you? Oh, I can be crude when it suits me."

She digested that as he dressed in what seemed like slow motion.

"Have you always lived in Woodmore?" she asked as casually as possible, not wanting him to know how curious she was about him.

With his gaze so knowing, so fierce, she couldn't assume her normal posture with him. He'd leveled the playing field. "I've never lived here. I grew up in Winston-Salem, but I live in Danvers. I've been chief electrician here at Cutting Edge for several months. He winked at her the way a man does when he is familiar with a woman.

If he was trying to shame her for her superior attitude, he succeeded. "I don't think I like you," she said.

His laugh was harsh and without mirth. "That's going to trouble me for years to come." Suddenly, he stopped pushing his T-shirt into his jeans and stared down at her, his features softer, and spoke with compassion. "Go home, Cassandra, and take care of business."

Home? After what she'd done? She didn't know how she could face Kix again. "I can't . . . I . . ."

He grabbed her, pulled her up, and shook her shoulders. "Don't trash his life just because you're hell-bent on trashing yours. Use what you learned to make it better, but keep your guilt to yourself."

He left then, and she went into her bathroom, ran some warm water in the washbowl, and scrubbed herself from head to foot.

T welve

"I'm going to close up my house for now," Sharon told Rafe when they met after work one afternoon about a week after Marge went home. "Eloise says she'll look after Mama, but Mama is my responsibility, and I'm going to stay with her for as long as we have her. She'll object, but I have to live with myself. I've hired Lizzie to come back and do the cooking and cleaning, and a nurse will come in for two hours every morning when that becomes necessary."

"I'm with you all the way. I hope she won't mind seeing a lot of me. When are you moving?"

"Tomorrow afternoon. I'll tell her when we get over there."

He tailed her to Marge's house, and as they headed up the walkway, holding hands, she glanced down at the red-and-gray logo of Gourmet Corner on the box in his right hand. "More goodies from Kix?"

"Yeah. He sent dinner for six when I told him I was sure Gert and Ross would be there in addition to Eloise. Your mother has wonderful friends, and I think Kix adores her as much as any of them do."

She opened the door with her key. "He certainly does. He didn't meet Mama till he wanted to marry Cassie, but he loves her as much as I do. That man has a story to tell."

"He's interesting, all right," Rafe said as they walked into the kitchen. "He told me that he dragged himself through school on a shoestring and later traveled all over the world on tramp steamers. Once, when a chef on one of the boats became ill, the captain gave him a job cooking. He got off the boat in France and enrolled in the Cordon

Bleu cooking school. When he returned to the States, he was a certified head chef."

"And what a chef," Sharon said. "If I'd known he was sending dinner, I'd have brought a couple of bottles of wine."

"He sent two bottles. I'd like him for a close friend, but I have the impression lately that he's unhappy and, considering my relationship with you . . . well, I don't think this is the time to cultivate his friendship."

Somehow Kix's unhappiness didn't surprise her. She didn't see how a man couldn't remain untouched by his wife's erratic behavior. "Cassie's going through some kind of crisis, and I hope she finds her way out of it soon."

They walked down the hall, and he put his arm around her shoulder, gripping it, just before they walked into her mother's room.

"Uncle Ross was right; you're a queen holding court," she said to Marge, and clasped her in a warm hug, but the subtle changes, the weak response, didn't escape her. *Mama was always so strong, so full of life.*

Rafe enfolded Marge in an embrace. A loving embrace, she realized. *How could I not care for him?*

"Gee, Aunt Eloise, I didn't know you were here." She kissed her godmother. "Anything for me to do?"

"You can take your weight off your feet," Eloise said. "I was just figurin' out what to have for supper. Marge ain't got much appetite 'less it's somethin' her son-in-law sends here. She'll gobble that up."

Told that Kix sent dinner, Eloise took out her knitting and pulled up the rocking chair beside Marge's bed. "Marge is giving me knitting instructions," she explained. "Keeps me busy and her interested in what's going on."

Sharon didn't like that, and with his knowing glance, Rafe confirmed her opinion of the implications. "Aunt Eloise, I'll be staying here for a while, help you keep Mama company."

"Something wrong with your house?" Marge asked her.

"No, but I've made up my mind, and that's that."

To her surprise, Marge laughed aloud. "Darned if Ross wasn't right. He said you'd developed a thick layer of toughness. I'm proud of you. That's what you need in this life: compassion and guts. Where's Ross? I got so used to him that I miss him when he's not here."

"It ain't time for him and Gert yet," Eloise told her. "Give 'em another half hour. Now look what I did. I dropped two stitches."

"Give it to me," Marge said. She pulled the stitches up and put them back on the needle, but her lack of energy was evident to all of them.

The doorbell rang repeatedly. "I'll get it," Rafe said and went to open the door.

"Ain't nobody but Gilford Ripple," Eloise assured them. "He ring that bell like he own the place, and child, you know he can smell free food clear from here to California. Being a minister of the gospel don't license a person to be a deadbeat."

"I heard you, Sister Eloise, and I'm sure I don't have to tell you that you'll have to pray about that remark."

Eloise looked at Rafe, who entered the room behind Ripple. "Rafe, you an educated man. What is the meanin' of the word deadbeat?"

Rafe looked around and, unsuspecting, said, "A person who usually tries to get something for nothing and doesn't believe in paying his way. Why?"

Eloise rocked back and forth. "I rest my case."

Marge raised herself up, and Eloise propped the pillows behind her back. "Y'all stop meddling with Gilford. If he wasn't like he is, what would the Woodmore gossip mongers talk about? He's not sleeping with anybody's wife, and as far as I know, he's not hitting on any of the sisters, so if he tries to get a freebie now and then, what's wrong with that?"

"You tell 'em, Marge," the reverend said. "But don't think I haven't been tempted a time or two." He allowed himself a beatific smile. "Bless the Lord. I remember, though, when getting me to look pass those sisters shaking themselves in my face was almost as hard as dragging a bear away from a pot of honey. I tell you, the ladies sure do make it hard for a man of the cloth."

Marge sucked her teeth. "If Satan tempted the Lord, do you know of a reason why he should exempt you? Besides, I'm not so sure you looked passed all of 'em."

"Now, Marge," Gilford said, "it's true my eyes lingered on some of those lovely bosoms, but I didn't yield to the temptation."

Rafe, who reclined on the arm of the overstuffed chair in which Sharon sat, locked his hands behind his head and leaned back. "You bragging or complaining? If you tell me you walked away and *stayed* away every single time, I wouldn't believe you. What happened? Did you get your hand slapped?"

"Do you know you're talking to a man of the cloth?"

"Sure thing," Rafe said, "but, man, you protest too much. Nobody expects you to be perfect."

"Trouble with the rev here," Eloise sang out, "is the ladies likes his looks. 'Course, he do, too. If you ax me, he cursed with his good looks."

Gilford Ripple crossed his knees and slapped his thigh. "Why, Sister Eloise, I didn't know you were such a keen observer of life. We ought to talk sometime."

Laughter poured out of everybody in the room except Gilford Ripple and Eloise, who stopped knitting and rocking. "I declare if you ain't full of it, Rev." She folded the knitting and got up. "Sayin' you good lookin' ain't the same as sayin' you irresistible. You very resistible. Wonder what's keepin' Ross?"

Gilford looked at Rafe. "You're still young, son, but if you don't already know, I tell you, women were put here on this earth as payment for any sins we men might commit." He leaned forward. "Or even *think* of committing. But, Lord, they sure are something sweet."

"Will the real Gilford Ripple stand up?" Marge said, jostling her friend.

Sharon observed the people around her. It seemed that as they joked and teased, Marge became more animated and stronger. Happiness does that for a person, she decided.

As if he had similar thoughts, Rafe asked Marge, "Do you play chess?"

Her face brightened with pride. "Ross and Kix have been teaching me, and I'm surprised how much I like it. You willing to play with a beginner?"

"Sure. I'm not a master, but I'm pretty good."

"There they are," Eloise said as the doorbell rang.

Rafe's eyebrows shot up. "They?"

"Gert and Ross. Gert's car is in the shop, so Ross gives her a lift."

"Wait for me, Sister Eloise. I have to be going. Just let me say a word of prayer with Sister Marge."

After a brief prayer, he followed Eloise to the door.

"Girl, you got a houseful," Gert said to Marge before taking a good look at Rafe. "I saw that spread on you in the paper, and I've been anxious to meet you." Sharon introduced them. "You're a lot better looking in person. How are you, Marge, honey? Let's order pizza. I'm starving."

"Whew," Marge said. "Now that we're all out of breath from your speech, have a seat."

Ross had been standing by the bed, looking down at Marge. "What did you eat today?"

"She eat pretty good," Eloise said as she walked back into the room. "Pretty chipper, too."

Ross patted Marge's shoulder and walked in the direction of the telephone. "I'll order a take-out, and we can eat." As if he'd forgotten something, he walked back over to Marge's bed. "Sorry I was late getting here, but with two men out at the plant, I had to go over there and help out. What would you like to eat?"

"I'm glad you could come at all," Marge said. "Everybody's here now . . . except . . ."

"Kix sent dinner for six, so we're feasting tonight," Rafe told Ross, and Sharon knew he'd cut Marge off to prevent her from becoming morose about the absence of her other two children.

"It's roast duck l'orange and all the trimmings. Kix said Mrs. Hairston likes roast duck."

"She's not the only one," Ross said. "I'll set the table."

"Why can't we serve ourselves and eat in here with Mrs. Hairston?" Rafe asked.

Ross slapped his fist in his palm. "Right on, man."

The following evening, as she planned, Sharon moved her winter clothing and basic necessities back to the house in which she grew up. Sitting in the room that she shared with Cassie until her sister went away to college, she fought hard to resist a trip into the past when Mama was strong and healthy and life was easy. She lifted the receiver of the old black rotary phone and dialed Drogan's number.

"Hairston residence. Mrs. Hairston speaking."

She didn't want to speak with Imogene. "Hi. This is Sharon," she said more brusquely that she'd intended. "Is Drogan home?"

"No, and I don't know when he'll be home."

She stared at the receiver, certain that she hadn't heard correctly. "I beg your pardon?"

"I said I don't know. I'm busy, Sharon. Good-bye."

Dumbfounded, she hung up. She had begun to contemplate a life with Rafe, but the marriages of her siblings seemed headed for the rocks. Shaken, she prowled around the room, turning back the edge of the crocheted linen cover on the dresser, fingering her graduation photo, wiping specks of dust from the windowsill. Mindless wandering. *If Mama were her old self . . .* But she wasn't. Sharon shook her head. No, Mama wasn't the iron woman they'd always believed her to be, and from now on they had to solve their own problems, deal with their own shortcomings, and battle their own misgivings. *I'm not Cassie or Drogan, and how they deal with their spouses doesn't affect my relationship with Rafe.*

She sat down and dialed her brother's office number. "Hairston speaking."

"Hi. This is Sharon. I'm moving back with our mother, and I'll be staying with her till . . . till the end. I just thought you should know."

After a long silence, he said, "Well, you know what they say. Possession is nine-tenths of the law."

"What are you talking about, Drogan? I don't understand."

"Course you do. If you're living in the house, the courts are more likely to give it to you."

"You give me a pain, Drogan, and I'm sick of your innuendos. You made your bed hard; lie in it. Sorry I called."

"You've got a lot of mouth lately. When did you start speaking to me like this?"

"When you ducked your responsibility and began trying to push me around. I no longer worship you, Drogan, and it's liberating. Mama is very weak. I wouldn't stay away from her too much if I were you."

"What does everybody want from me? I can't be there and here, too, and Imogene's in her own world."

"I don't want anything from you, and I don't need you for one thing. But you'd better come see Mama."

"Damned if you're not full of yourself."

"I'm not swapping insults with you, Drogan. Stop blaming me and Mama for your problems and get a life. Be seeing you." She hung up, feeling the way she did after cleaning out her closets in the spring.

Drogan stared into space long after the dial tone droned in his ear. Sharon. Imogene. Mama. All of them were slipping away from him. His gaze caught the stack of bills on his desk. Imogene hadn't charged her diamond tennis bracelet to either one of her credit cards. He wasted hours trying to find it so he could have it appraised, because he wasn't even sure now that the receipt he saw gave the actual cost. When it hadn't appeared on the October bill, he'd waited for the next one. It wasn't on that one, either, and he suspected she'd destroyed the receipt, because he couldn't find it. Where would a woman who hadn't held a job in over four years get twenty-one hundred dollars in cash to spend on a bracelet? He sure as hell hadn't given it to her.

He folded his bedroll, put it in his coat closet, cleared his desk, locked it, and headed home for the first time in a week. Anger flared in him, and feelings he'd buried over the years surfaced unexpectedly. His foot pressed the accelerator; he couldn't get home fast enough. He hadn't thought himself stupid enough to let a person make a fool of him. Well, he'd soon find out.

She opened the door before he could get his key in the lock. "Drogan, honey, you came back. I was so worried. Is everything all right now?"

She reached up to kiss him, but he couldn't make himself bend over to receive it. In a few months, he'd be thirty-five years old, and his life was about as satisfying as ice-cold stew. He'd made a mistake, and he was willing to confess it, ask for forgiveness, and try to mend his marriage, though repairing it would have to wait until he got to the bottom of that business with the bracelet.

"I want to talk with you, Imogene. Seriously. Come in here, please, and let's sit down."

"Darling, you sound so serious."

And she could drop the sweet talk; he wanted none of it. "I *am* serious. For the past three months you've spent three and often four days a week shopping in Winston-Salem. You get home well after dinnertime, always too tired to be good company and half the time too tired or too disinterested to make love. You follow?"

She moved over to him and prepared to sit on his lap. "Stay over there where we can look at each other while we talk." He ignored her pout and her threat of tears, no longer susceptible to her manipulation.

"Like a spoiled teenager, instead of insisting that you behave like a married woman with responsibilities, I turned to another woman—" He ignored her loud gasp. "And carried on an affair for almost two months. I hated it, and I hated myself, so I broke it off. I know it won't be easy, but I hope you can forgive me. I make no excuses; I knew it was wrong, and I'm ashamed that I did it."

She was standing now, her hands balled into fists and her lips trembling with rage. "You sit there and casually tell me you've been sleeping around? How dare you!"

"I haven't slept around, Imogene. I had an affair with one woman, and I'm sorry. I told you about it because I want us to have a clean slate and try to find our way back to each other. No secrets."

"I never dreamed . . ." she sputtered. "No wonder your mother didn't trust you with the paper; she probably always knew she couldn't trust you, that you weren't worth—"

He interrupted her. "Don't say it. Don't say anything you'll be sorry for. I don't blame you for being mad about my having an affair, but you are angrier because I no longer spend every dime I earn making sure that you'll be the envy of all your friends. I decided to be sensible, pay off our debts, and save something for our future and for our children, if we're fortunate enough to have any. For that, you scorned me."

"Nothing you can say about me will add up to what you've done. Shopping isn't a crime, but cutting out on your wife is the worst one."

He crossed his knee and looked her in the eye. "I've confessed my sins. What about you? Have you got anything to tell me?"

"What do you mean? Are you suggesting that I"—she poked her finger in his chest—"that I've been playing around like you?" Her top lip curled in an angry snarl. "As far as I'm concerned, the highfalutin Hairstons have bit the dust. You're no better than anybody else."

She hadn't answered his question but instead had attacked him. It was a ploy he knew well. "I never thought we were better than any other family, and anybody who's familiar with Mama would laugh at what you just said."

He let a grin drift from his mouth to his eyes, purposefully disarming her, and watched her relax. "People who live in glass houses, Imogene, should be careful about throwing stones."

The color drained from her face. "I don't know what you're talking about."

He leaned back, crossed his knee, and swung his foot, ready for the kill. "I don't suppose you do, but I'll be glad to enlighten you. Where did you get the twenty-one hundred dollars to pay for that diamond tennis bracelet?"

Her eyes widened, and her bottom lip dropped, but she quickly recovered. "Oh, that! Honey, that's not diamond."

"No? Mind if I look at it?"

"Oh, darling. I don't even know where it is. It's . . . not . . . it's costume jewelry."

"I see. You paid that much money for costume jewelry? Didn't you tell me you didn't wear fake jewelry?"

"It was twenty-one dollars. I bought it because it was so pretty, I—"

He held up his hand. "All right. I thought you were going to tell me you put it on one of your credit cards."

She blanched visibly. "I uh . . . I paid cash for it."

He smiled, all the while staring at her. "I don't doubt it."

She stretched long and lazily like a cat. "Honey, I'm so tired. Let's go to bed. You are staying here with me tonight, I hope. A married woman gets used to . . . well, you know."

"Yeah, I know." He couldn't decide whether to sleep with her and let her think she was off the hook or make her find that bracelet. It didn't escape him that she no longer appeared to be angry at his having slept with another woman.

He leaned back against the sofa, stretched out his legs, and closed his eyes, and immediately he heard her tripping up the steps, as he'd known she would. He gave her a minute to commit to whatever thing she'd planned to do and dashed up the stairs in time to see her put her pocketbook in the bottom dresser drawer. He grabbed the pocketbook, opened it, and dumped its contents on the bed.

To his horror, she sailed into him, pummeling him with her fists, kicking and scratching him.

"Give me my stuff. You've got no right to go in my stuff."

He grabbed her hands, locked them behind her, and turned her with her back to him so that she couldn't kick his shins, already bruised and in pain from the thrust of her pointed-toe shoes.

"You might as well cool off. I gave you the chance to tell me everything, but you lied. Now I'm going to find out what you've been doing if I have to tie you to that door. And if you hit me again, I'm taking you back home to your parents and leaving you there. You got it?"

She slumped to the floor, and her whimpers mushroomed into loud heaving sobs. Once, he'd have capitulated, apologized, and let her seduce him until he spent himself inside of her. But not this time. She grabbed his legs.

"Turn me loose, Imogene. In fact, it's best that you don't touch me."

Her billfold yielded her three credit cards and driver's license, which he confiscated. He found a handful of receipts and stuffed them into his pocket. Suddenly, his blood seemed to curl and his heart skipped beats when his gaze fell on a small white leather box. He fought to control the anger that furled up in him and threatened to possess him, even as fear of what he'd find caught him in its clutches. Then he saw the little black book that bore in gold-tooled letters the word *appointments*.

"Let me explain," she begged.

"The best you can do for yourself right now, Imogene, is keep your mouth shut." He put the little black book and the leather box into his pocket and headed down the stairs. As he stood beside the sofa, putting on his leather jacket, tears cascaded down his cheeks. It would all have been avoided if he had agreed to manage the paper when Mama asked him to do it. As the door closed behind him, he couldn't remember his reason for refusing.

A blue sapphire ring banked by six diamonds. He put it back in its white leather box and tossed it into his briefcase. His trembling fingers leafed through the little appointment book. Jay's. She'd penciled it in three or four days a week beginning as far back as September the twenty-third.

Nine o'clock the next morning found him in Winston-Salem at 1624 Cord Street, the address he obtained through a directory service. "I want to hire a model," he told the receptionist, and bluffing his way, added, "I'd rather have Imogene."

"Ah, you have good taste. Imogene will cost you five hundred an hour, but we have others a lot cheaper than that."

Goose pimples popped out on his arms, and his nerves rioted throughout his body. Five-foot-four-inch-tall models were a rarity. Even he knew that. But since he didn't know what he'd walked into, he had to be careful.

"Perhaps I could see her portfolio. I want to know exactly what I'm paying for." The receptionist rang a bell, and he tensed.

A well-dressed, clean-cut man appeared. "You want to see a portfolio? Which girl?"

"Imogene."

The man opened a safe and handed him a black binder. "Look through this. I'll be back in a couple of minutes. She's hot stuff, man."

Sweat matted his hair, trickled down the side of his ears, and drenched his palms. He had to work hard to control his chattering teeth. Glancing around, he saw that he was alone and made a run for it. Minutes later, he was in his car speeding toward Woodmore. He made it to Highway 52, stopped at the first gas station he saw, and tried to calm himself. He'd never done anything like that before, and if he ever got the nerve to open the folder and look in it, he'd mail it back to its owner. Five hundred dollars an hour. What the hell kind of modeling was she doing? He needed to go to his office and get to work. Instead, he drove to his mother's house.

"I'm glad to see you," Marge said when he walked in, "but aren't you supposed to be working this time of day? What's the matter?"

"Nothing. I had to go to Winston-Salem and thought I'd stop by to see you before I go to the office. Where's Sharon?"

"She's somewhere around. She'll be going to the paper for a few hours soon as Eloise gets here. Have a seat, son. She needs to be at work, but I tell you it's good to have her here. Sure you're all right?"

No, he wasn't sure. And coming there was a mistake. He'd forgotten that Mama was always able to see straight through him. He leaned over and kissed her forehead. "Just dropped by. See you soon."

She squeezed his hand, and he thought she clung to his fingers. Maybe he should've stayed longer, but he didn't want to see Sharon. Hell, he didn't even know why he'd gone there in the first place with his mind so full of Imogene and her treachery. He walked back to Marge's bed.

"How many different kinds of modeling would you say there are, Mama?"

"High-fashion clothes, gloves, stockings, hair, makeup, shoes, all kinds. Models stand beside cars, furniture, all—"

He held his hands out, palms forward. "Okay, I get the message. See you soon." His heartbeat slowed to normal. Maybe he'd been imagining things. Imogene had a great pair of legs. Maybe she'd been modeling stockings. He went to his office and tried to make up for the hours he'd wasted being miserable.

He'd been working several hours when he suddenly stopped. When he'd kissed Mama's forehead, she'd been too warm. He dialed her number.

"Hairston's residence," Eloise said. "Marge is 'sleep right now."

"This is Drogan, Eloise. When I was there this morning, Mama seemed a little too warm."

"What else is new? She like that all the time now."

He didn't know what to say to her. "Well, if she's asleep, I'll call later."

"You do that."

Marge was not asleep, though she'd closed her eyes. With so many things to do, she had to keep her thoughts together and her mind clear. A way had to be found to pull her children back together. She reached for the phone on her night table and punched in Gilford Ripple's number. "This is Marge. I want you to come over here and bring a little cassette recorder. All right?"

"Sure, Marge. Be over there in a couple of hours."

She put the phone back into its cradle and dozed off to sleep.

"How's Marge today?" Ross asked Sharon when she arrived at the office around noon.

"A little weak, but she's alert and chipper. I'm cooking Christmas dinner. Why don't you eat with us? Mama will love that."

"I kinda depended on that," he said. She wondered at his sheepishness and what had happened to change him so much. Quiet and withdrawn. So unlike himself.

Rafe met her when she left the paper at five o'clock and tailed her home, as had become his habit since she'd moved back to her mother's house. They rarely had a moment of privacy for themselves, but if he minded that, he didn't let her know it.

"Kix wants to know how many you're having for Christmas dinner. He said he'd like to roast a goose, since that's Mama's favorite." He'd begun calling Marge Mama, and her mother seemed to like it.

"I'll let him know tomorrow. It's a pity he can't come. No matter how busy he is at the restaurant, he gets by to see Mama every morning on his way to work."

Rafe put their dinner on the kitchen counter and detained her with a hand on her arm. "Is there anything wrong between him and your sister?"

She supposed her face held a look of surprise. "I don't know. I haven't talked with her in a week. My brother and sister don't waste much time on me these days. Drogan was here this morning, but I didn't see him."

His arm eased around her, strong and loving. "Don't let it worry you. They'll come around. Can I have a kiss? Gentle, though, honey, because I'm starved for you."

She turned into his arms, parted her lips, and knew again the pleasure of his hands roaming her body as he claimed her with his tongue and his male power, gripping her body to his until she could feel him in every atom of her being.

"Y'all find someplace else to make out," Eloise said. "Sorry to bother you, but I got to give Marge a little cranberry juice. Her mouth gets dry." Her face bore a look of regret. "Can't y'all find some place other than the kitchen? It's like Highway 52 in here; everybody comes in and out of this kitchen."

Rafe patted Eloise's shoulder. "Thanks for your concern, but that had gone as far as it could go."

She slapped her hands on her hips. "You don't say. I guess times is changed since I was courtin'. Ain't no men I ever went 'round with acted like there was any such thing as a limit. Thunder and lightnin' wouldn't stop some of 'em. Nothin' would 'cept the mention of my daddy's name. That'd put the fear of God in 'em. My daddy didn't leave no hair on the hog."

Rafe leaned against the doorjamb and grinned at her. "I hope there were a few times when you forgot to mention daddy's name.'

Eloise threw her head back and let out a whoop. "Y'all go way from here. I declare. Y'all sure is somethin.'"

Sharon sat on the edge of her mother's bed while Rafe tried unsuccessfully to interest Marge in a game of chess.

"It takes too long," she said, "and Gert'll be here pretty soon wanting to play pinochle." She turned to Sharon. "Did you call Cassie and Drogan and ask them to . . . to come over for Christmas? I know Kix has to work, and . . . and something's wrong between Drogan and Imogene."

Sharon's eyes widened, and she supposed she gaped at her mother. "He told you that?"

"Well, he didn't say so, but he wasn't himself when he came here last. Yesterday, I think it was. He acted like he'd taken a knockout punch. Not like himself."

Sharon locked gazes with Rafe, sharing a moment of mutual unease. "I'll phone Cassie. I'm sure she'll be here unless she's having dinner with Kix."

"You tell her I want her to come."

She considered letting Ross call Cassie, but she'd promised her mother, so she excused herself and went to her room.

"Mrs Hairston-Shepherd speaking."

She wished Cassie would find a warmer, more gracious way of identifying herself when she answered the phone. So cold and artificial. And that, Sharon realized with a stab of pity, was the problem with Cassie. Her sister had donned so many affectations that the identity of the real woman was anybody's guess.

"This is Sharon. Mama told me to call you."

"She . . . why? What's the matter?"

At times she would enjoy shaking her older sister. "She wants you to come for dinner Christmas day. Kix is sending the food. Are you coming?"

"I'll . . . try."

That didn't sound like Cassie. "Are you all right?" she asked her. "I mean, is anything wrong?" In recent months, they'd lost touch with each other, and she didn't dare ask her sister even the simplest personal question.

"I'm fine. Why does she want me to—"

What a question? With diminishing patience, Sharon took a deep breath and told herself to convince Cassie for their mother's sake. She interrupted her. "Cassie, Mama gets weaker every day. She's still lucid and conversant, but she tires easily. And she's less alert today than she was yesterday."

After a telling silence, Cassie said, "She's got you, hasn't she?"

She ignored that. "And Kix wants me to tell him how many of us he's cooking dinner for."

"I'll come. What time."

Exasperated, Sharon counted to ten and didn't care if Cassie heard her. "You could spend the day. Don't you know this will be Mama's last Christmas?"

"That's ridiculous!"

"Go ahead and stick your head in the sand. I have to call Drogan."

She fared better with Drogan, who readily agreed. "I'll try to see her before then."

"I assume you're bringing Imogene."

"I . . . uh . . . she's probably going to Virginia to see her parents."

"You be sure and come now. Kix is sending the dinner."

She wondered at Drogan's silence. Finally, he said, "Cassie doesn't know how lucky she is, and if you tried beating it into her head with a stick, you wouldn't make a dent. She's got a husband who'll do anything to make her happy, and she thinks she's too good for him. If he left her, I'd send him a note of congratulations."

"Drogan!"

"You don't know what it's like being . . . Look. I'll see you." He hung up.

She walked with plodding steps back to her mother's room and back to Rafe. Rafe, whose presence in her life, she realized with increasing certainty, was nothing short of a blessing. He'd said he would stand with her through whatever she faced, and though she didn't need to depend on him for her inner strength, knowing he was there for her was joy in the morning when she awakened and a source of peace when she went to bed at night.

Rafe. The only solid thing in her life. She had thought them a strong, loving family, but the first crisis rended their ties, shredding their relationships, making a lie of what they'd thought of themselves and of each other. With their feelings laid bare, pretense didn't suffice, nor was it needed. Her siblings didn't feel unqualified love for her, and she no longer held them in worshipful esteem.

She didn't know to what extent Mama's illness and retirement precipitated the instability in her siblings' marriages, but she suspected that her ownership of the paper was at the root of it. What she understood least was the lingering resentment of her siblings toward their mother, especially when they had to know that she was enjoying her last days.

"What did they say?" Marge asked Sharon as soon as she entered the room.

"They're coming."

"But not Imogene?"

She shook her head. "Drogan said Imogene would probably spend the holiday with her parents."

Marge nodded her head in that slow way that said she recognized a truth. "I see. Before you marry a person, you ought to know whether that person satisfies all of your needs, not just your . . . your libido. Never marry a person who idolizes you. That's usually phony, and anyhow, it's bound to get tiresome."

"Mama, are you talking about Imogene?"

"I'm just talking." She dozed for a second, opened her eyes, and said, "It takes two to bust up a marriage. If it's not working, demand what you need, 'cause if you don't, the other person may not know what's missing for you. Ed was a wonderful husband and father. Even after twenty-five years, I've never once thought of anybody else."

"I hardly remember him," Sharon said.

"You're just like him. You look like him, and you've got his personality. Ross always said he spit you out. Where's Ross?"

A glance at Rafe and Eloise told her their concern matched her own, that at times Mama's mind wandered.

"He ought to be here soon. You remember Gert's car is out of commission, and Uncle Ross picks her up from her office?"

Marge rolled her eyes. "You sure Gert's car is in the garage?"

She responded with a chuckle, partly at the idea that Gert would make a play for Ross and partly in relief that Marge's sense of humor remained intact.

Sharon's left shoulder lifted in a shrug. "Who knows? A lonely woman . . ." She let it hang.

Marge's smile had the radiance of a sacramental blessing, stunning in its brilliance. "Well, you're not lonely, thank God."

"No," Rafe replied, "and if it's up to me, she won't be."

Marge turned her head to them, her movements so slow as to give the impression of one heavily burdened. "Nothing you could say would have made me happier, Rafe. I'm so glad she has you, because she's going to need all the support she can get."

"Why do you say that, Mama?"

Her eyelids drooped as if she were weary. "I know my children well."

At the sound of the ringing doorbell, Marge became alert. "Is that Ross and Gert?"

"I'll see," Rafe said.

"How's she doing?" they asked in unison as they neared Marge's room.

She didn't hear Rafe's answer, but if they'd asked her, she would have told them that her mother had taken a step back. She'd gotten used to Ross's new habit of standing beside Mama's bed, scrutinizing her as if imprinting her in the cells of his brain.

He looked down at Marge then and smiled. "How you doing, girl?"

And to her amazement, Marge returned his smile, raised her hand, and let it fall back on the bed. "You're just like that geyser in Yellowstone National Park, *Old Faithful*. You never did get to see it, did you?"

He popped his fingers several times and shrugged. "Naaah. Never could get away."

"You go. Drop everything and go. I'm glad we went to San Francisco. That was one of the real highlights of my life. You knew I wasn't well enough to go by myself, didn't you?"

He nodded. "I had to be sure you'd be able to enjoy it."

"Well, I sure did. Where's Gert?"

"Right here, Marge. I thought Ross was going to get us picked up for speeding. Would you believe he took Parkway Street at seventy miles an hour? I kept telling him he was breaking the law."

Marge seemed unimpressed. "When Ross breaks the law, he does it with style. Rafe, please call Eloise and see if she's home."

Sharon didn't want to seem anxious, but her nerves shimmied beneath the surface of her skin with the wildness of Harlem dancers in the heyday of jazz.

"Aunt Eloise will come here before she goes home, Mama."

"Good. You make sure Drogan and Cassie come see me Christmas. You hear?"

"I'll do my best, Mama," she said, but it wouldn't surprise her if one or both of them failed to show up. If they didn't come, she'd wouldn't find it easy to forgive them.

Thirteen

With the smell of bayberry and pine wafting through the house, Sharon inhaled deeply, opened her arms wide, and greeted Christmas morning. Their Douglas fir stood eight feet tall, and in all her thirty years she'd never had so much fun and experienced so much joy decorating a tree as on that Christmas Eve. It began when, on impulse, Ross lifted Marge out of bed, put her into the wheelchair, and wheeled her into the living room. She and Rafe had tried to inveigle Mama into letting them take her there to watch the tree trimming, but she'd refused. Eloise had also failed to convince her. Ross arrived, and to their amazement, she readily assented when he asked if she'd like to help decorate the tree. Along with Rafe, Eloise, and Ross, Sharon hung the bells, family heirloom trinkets, tinsel, and lights on the prettiest tree she'd ever seen in their home. And to their delight, Marge participated, pointing out vacant spaces and, weak though she was, joking and laughing at their antics.

That Christmas morning, she and Lizzie, the housekeeper, cooked, served breakfast, tidied the house, and took care of Marge's needs. She found herself praying that Drogan and Cassie didn't do anything to dissipate her euphoria. She looked up, folded her hands, and prayed, "Lord, please let this be a perfect day." And it was.

On his way to work early that morning, Kix dropped by to wish Mama Merry Christmas, and around ten, Rafe arrived with chestnuts to be split and roasted in the brick oven that her father built over a quarter of a century earlier in the corner of the garden. By noon, Marge had a full court, enjoying the jostling and teasing with which Rafe, Eloise, Ross, and Gert peppered each other. The Gourmet Corner's minivan—Kix's newest addition to his business—arrived at one o'clock with the Christmas dinner, and her anxiety increased. She paced the living and dining rooms, glancing at her watch every few minutes. Surely they wouldn't disappoint Mama on Christmas day.

Her exasperation had reached fever pitch when Ross met her in the hallway. "Aren't Drogan and Cassie coming?"

"They said they would."

"I'll give 'em half an hour, and then I'm going to find them. Nothing's going to ruin this day for Marge." He popped his fingers, ran them through his thinning hair, and looked at her. "Do you realize there's not a single present under that tree?"

"What? Do you know I didn't think about that? I didn't even buy a present for Rafe."

He tapped his finger against the side of his head. "The subconscious can really mess you up. I didn't think about that, either. I guess none of us could think past today."

"You think Mama will notice?"

He shook his head. "I doubt it. She's forcing herself for our sake. Not that I think she's uncomfortable; she's not. Marge is happy, and that's all that keeps me going." At the sound of the bell, he swung around and headed toward the door. "I hope that's one of 'em."

"Well, Ross, why am I not surprised to see you here. Having dinner with us?"

"Wouldn't miss it," he said to Cassie. "Merry Christmas. Marge is in her room."

Sharon had followed Ross to the door, and while seeing Cassie relieved some of her fear, it occurred to her that her sister's presence could make a debacle of their Christmas gathering if she decided to subvert it.

"How are you, Cassie," Sharon asked, and the woodenness, the formality with which she greeted her only sister, nearly brought tears to her eyes. But she didn't see a way to breach the chasm that Cassie had opened and which she widened each time they spoke.

"I'm . . . I'm all right. What's Kix sending for dinner?"

Strange that Cassie didn't know. "A roast goose. He sent the dinner in his new van with his uninformed driver. Very impressive, let me tell you."

Cassie's bottom lip dropped, and both her eyebrows shot up as her face mirrored her surprise. And though she wanted to know whether it was the van or the driver that had surprised her sister, Sharon didn't ask.

Cassie recovered quickly. "Hmm. I'd better go see how Mama is," she said, leaving Ross and Sharon to stare in her wake.

Sharon wasn't used to seeing Ross perplexed, but as he ran his fingers back and forth beneath his jaw, shaking his head, she surmised that his thoughts paralleled her own.

He confirmed it when he said, "Don't you think something's wrong with Cassie? I don't remember seeing her look like that."

"Right. Practically no makeup, her hair not styled, just combed straight down and—"

Ross popped his fingers. "And no arrogance. She wasn't that subdued when she was ten. I'd give a lot to know what's happening with her."

"Me, too, but I wouldn't dare ask her. Maybe Drogan knows something."

However, Drogan hadn't been in contact with Cassie. He arrived a few minutes later, bringing a large bunch of holly wrapped in clear cellophane paper. He handed it to Sharon with the explanation that after bruising his fingers with its needle-pointed leaves, he'd wrapped it to protect her delicate hands. So much like the banter they'd shared from their youth onward that she dared to hope.

"Don't tell me your calloused fingers can feel a prick," she was about to say when she realized that his eyes bore no warmth. So instead she said, "I'm glad you're here, Drogan. Mama's been asking for you."

With a nod to Ross, he said, "How's it going, man?" and joined the others in Marge's room.

Ross's hand on her shoulder was all that prevented her from going after Drogan and shaking him. He'd come to do his duty, but she shouldn't expect more. Well, she had prayed that they would be there, and they were. For that, she was grateful.

"What is it?" she asked when she saw that Ross had followed her to the dining room.

"I know we planned to eat in Marge's room, but maybe she can sit at the head of the table in her wheelchair."

She didn't think much of that idea, for she didn't suppose her mother had the strength. "I'm . . . uh . . . not so sure that'll work, Uncle Ross."

His gray eyes stared into her brown ones. "If she's willing . . . if she can sit there for just ten minutes, we lose nothing, and it will make her happy."

She often wondered at his thoughts and feelings about Mama, and she hoped she'd one day have the courage to discuss it with him. "Uncle Ross, if I could have only one wish, I'd ask for a lifelong friend like you."

He lifted first one shoulder and then the other one. "Friends aren't something you wish for, and . . . well, you don't make 'em, either. They just grow on you like weeds among the grass till after a while you're one and the same." He fixed his gaze on her. "I got to the place where I knew what Marge was going to say before her words got out." As if he were in wonder, his head moved from side to side. "One hell of a woman! I tell you, she's one hell of a woman." He whirled around. "Better go see what everybody's doing."

Her heart went out to Ross as it dawned on her that he was losing the person closest to him. But how did you put your arms around a proud and crusty but soft-centered man who kept his distance and tell him you loved him and that you were there for him?

"Ross is gonna bring Marge into the dinin' room," Eloise said as she entered the kitchen, her face bright with smiles. "I tell you that's the nicest Christmas present I could get."

"Did she say she'd let him do that?" Sharon asked Eloise.

"Yeah. A minute ago, Gert said she realized Ross can get Marge to do things, 'cause she always listened to him when she was at the paper. She's used to trustin' him."

"Uncle Ross is turning out to be a very interesting man. Much as I've been around him, I realize I never knew him."

"Ain't he, though?" Eloise said. "'Deed he's so interesting Gert can't get her car out of the garage, though she and I both know she could buy that garage."

"Now, wait. I thought you and Mama were teasing her. You don't think she's interested in Uncle Ross, do you?"

"Why not? Old man Hayes done took so much Viagra, he walks like a penguin, and Gert said it ain't done him a bit of good, neither. He still don't know in from out. So what can she lose with Ross?"

What indeed! "No idea. But I don't get the impression Uncle Ross's mind is in Gert's direction." She put a bowl of holly in the center of the table and stood back to admire the effect.

"Me, neither, but you tell Gert that. She always got to have somebody, but she barkin' up the wrong tree now. Ross is like a horse; you can get him to the trough, but you can't make him drink the water."

"We can serve the dinner now, Miss Sharon," Lizzie said, "and it looks as good as it smells. That must be *some* restaurant Mr. Kix runs out there on Wright Road."

"Let's play some music. What would you like to hear, Mama?" Rafe asked her as Ross settled Marge at the head of the table."

"Did Paul Robeson sing any Christmas music?" Marge asked. "I always loved Paul Robeson. So elegant, and such a beautiful voice."

Rafe looked through the records, cassettes, and CDs. "If he did, you don't have any. This is always a nice one." He put a record on the turntable, and soon Robeson's great bass baritone gave them the greatest interpretation of "Old Man River" that was ever recorded. At its end, Sharon gloried in the happy smile on her mother's face. Wanting not to tax her mother, Sharon asked Drogan to say grace, and soon they chatted and ate, joked and teased, as if nothing had impaired their relationships. Rafe played more Robeson's songs, and a smile formed around Marge's lips when Robeson began to sing "I Still Suits Me."

Marge patted Ross's hand. "That's my favorite Robeson song. When he sang it in the movie, he was singing it to his nagging wife."

She held a slice of goose breast on her fork and looked at it. "This is so good. All of my children are here, Ross. They're all here with me. Isn't it nice?" She chewed the meat as if she truly enjoyed it. "Ross, did we fire Mack? I don't remember. Did we?"

Ross adjusted the bib Marge wore. "Not yet, but Sharon warned him."

"Oh. My Cassie looks like she did when she was a little girl and wore her hair long like that. Cassie was always so beautiful. They all took their looks after Ed, you know. Drogan got that *and* a good dose of Ed's charm."

"Sharon, honey, do you remember Nat King Cole's "Sweet Lorraine"? Ed used to sing it. I forgot the words. Drogan, sing it for me." She turned her head to look around the table. "Drogan has a nice voice."

To Sharon's surprise, Drogan sang it at once without waiting to be cajoled. "And when it's raining, I don't miss the sun," he sang, and Marge smiled at Ross. "They're all smart and talented. I love holly," she said. "It's beautiful."

"Drogan brought it with him," Sharon said.

Her eyes closed briefly as if she were fighting sleep. "Good. Good. It's a happy day."

"Best meal I ever eat," Eloise said as she, Rafe, and Sharon straightened the dinning room and cleaned the kitchen after the dinner. Lizzie had gone home to give Christmas dinner to her own family.

"I'd better run along," Cassie said to Sharon soon after dinner. "I . . . uh . . . I didn't know Mama was so weak. I . . . uh . . . I have to wish Kix Merry Christmas. He'd already left when I woke up this morning. Merry Christmas, everybody."

Minutes later, Drogan walked into the kitchen. "That was some dinner. Kix outdid himself. I'm leaving now. Merry Christmas, everybody."

Sharon wondered what, if any, progress they'd made and whether their coming to have dinner with her and Mama signified anything more than respect for obligation.

She voiced those thoughts to Rafe later that evening when Marge had gone to sleep, and they sat alone in the living room.

"If that's why they came, it's not a bad thing. They're still in touch, and so long as they are, it's possible to mend fences. We've had a wonderful day. Let's enjoy what's left of it."

She sat with him, contented in silence, thankful for their Christmas and for Mama's ability to enjoy it. She leaned her head on Rafe's shoulder and breathed a sigh of contentment.

"I decided to pass on Wade Field."

She pitched forward, her head grazing his chin. "You did? You can't imagine how glad I am. That is one issue that would have split us up." She let her fingers stroke his cheek.

The carelessness of his shrug didn't fool her. He'd given up something that he wanted.

"It wasn't altruism on my part," he said. "It's just too expensive to sink a basement there, and a modern building such as I had in mind needs one. The water level is too high."

"I don't care what your reason is. I'm happy that you're not going to ruin that lovely field."

His fingers stroked her right arm. Up and down. Up and down. And she wondered if he did it deliberately or if he thought she had become immune to his touch. He reminisced about the day as his hand moved along her bare arm.

"Too bad you were busy. I spent a lot of time laughing while Gert and Eloise exchanged barbs, and Mama encouraged them. What a trio they must have been! On the face of it, they have nothing in common."

"That's what Drogan and Cassie think, but they love each other, and it's unequivocal."

"So I gathered." His hand ceased crawling up and down her arm and suddenly gripped her belly and tugged her closer to him.

Immediately, her nerves tingled with exhilaration, drowning her in a puddle of desire. He tipped up her chin with his left index finger, and she stared at the hot want mirrored in his eyes.

"Rafe," she whispered. "Honey, I—"

"Kiss me. Baby, I'm so hungry for you."

At the intensity of his manner, butterflies battled for space in her belly, and she could only stare at him in wonder as she breathed his breath, smelled his heat, and felt his hunger. The desire in his eyes excited her, and she opened to him and parted her lips for the sweet torture of his tongue. And he claimed her, possessing every crevice of her mouth, prowling over her body with his hands, swirling his palms over her erected areolas, and stroking her thighs until shivers of need betrayed her tingling body.

"Don't you know how I long to bury myself inside of you and live again?" he whispered. "Once in my entire life I've been complete, whole and fulfilled. That one time in your arms I finally knew who I was. Don't you need me? Baby, don't you need to make love with me?"

How could she with Mama right there in the house? She said as much. "I need you, but I . . ." It didn't make sense, and she let it hang. He lifted her into his lap and let her feel his need. Not thinking, she rubbed her breast until he moved her hand and did it for her. When she crossed her legs in frustration, he stood with her in his arms.

"Which is your room?"

"Right over there," she whispered.

"Are you sure? If you're going to be uncomfortable, it's no use."

"I need you as badly as you need me."

He strode into her room, closed the door, and lay her on her bed. As he stood looking down at her, she thought about his power, his strength, and the sensation he'd created moving inside her and held her arms up to him. He pulled the caftan over her head, knelt beside the bed, dragged the bikini over her hips, and tossed it aside.

Leaning forward, he kissed her belly and then moved to her breast.

She held her breath until his lips captured her nipple and began the torture that would make her do anything he wanted her to do. When she began tugging at his clothes, he stripped, eased into her seething tunnel, and took her on a wild, ecstatic ride to sweet oblivion.

Hours later, sated and sleepy, she threw an arm across his waist and lay her head on his shoulder. She wanted to tell him that she didn't want him to leave her. Not then or ever. But how could she do that when he hadn't declared himself. Thwarted and a little vexed, she bit his shoulder.

"Hey! What's this?"

"Sorry, I don't know what made me do that."

He turned her to her back and gazed down at her. "Yes, you do. Let's have it."

"It seemed so unfair. I don't want you to leave me, but I don't want Lizzie and Aunt Eloise or Kix to come here tomorrow morning and find you here. I don't have the right to wake up in your arms. I just got angry." She attempted to turn away from him, but he wouldn't allow it.

"Do you want that right?"

"Don't ask me that. Why do you think I made love with you, or before for that matter?"

"Do you love me?"

What was it about men that made them demand certainty before they implicated themselves? She resisted pummeling his chest. "I'm not telling. You'd better go home before we both fall asleep."

"Sure you want that?"

"I am not in the habit of saying what I don't mean."

He pulled her into his arms and held her, stroking her back with gentle fingers. "Your mother's condition is deteriorating, and you're not getting any support from your brother and sister, though I can see that you need it. I'll be there for you in every way that I can, but I don't want you to confuse what you need from them with what you need from me. When this crisis has passed, think this over and tell me if you still want to wake up with me every morning. I'm not going anywhere."

"Is this your way of backing off? I don't remember proposing to you."

"Come on, now. I didn't mean to imply that you did. I know I want you, and I know where I want our relationship to go, but this isn't the time for critical decisions either on your part or mine."

"I don't disagree with that, but waking up mornings and looking over at you sure wouldn't make me miserable. I was going to apologize for biting you, but I won't. You deserved it."

A smile creased his face, and he bent to her lips. "At least I'm warned that if I get you, I'll have a hellion. Who'd have thought it?"

He wasn't in bed with her when she awoke the next morning, but she flung her arms wide and laughed aloud. One of these days, he would be.

When Drogan awoke that morning, his thoughts centered on his aloneness. With Imogene visiting her parents in Suffolk, Virginia, he'd weathered Christmas without her for the first time since they met at a vegetable stand six years earlier. Giving her Catholic faith as a reason—one that he grudgingly accepted as valid—she'd refused to sleep with him until he married her, and he'd been shocked to realize that she was a virgin.

He sat up and pulled the covers up to his shoulders. Imogene had handed him her virginal prize with the pseudohumility of a Columbus presenting Queen Isabella with the New World. He had required neither her virginity nor her humility, but she reminded him constantly of her precious gift to him.

Cold air from the open window chilled his face, arms, and neck. Reluctantly, he rolled out of bed, showered, and cooked his breakfast. He could thank Mama for teaching him how to take care of his basic needs, such as cooking, making his bed, ironing his shirts, and changing the oil in his car.

The radio blasted out a song by Ricky Martin, and he rushed to it and flicked it off. He didn't care about another man's troubles; he had his own. He started to straighten up the kitchen, looked around at the two bags of refuse that had to be discarded, the pots of withering plants on the windowsill, the trash he'd swept in the corner, and the dim ceiling lightbulb that he ought to replace, and threw up his hands. "To hell with it." He'd do it later.

He had to do something about Imogene. Sitting in front of the television, he didn't see the Ravens' touchdown or the twirling batons and dancing cheerleaders at halftime. The shambles of his marriage drove everything else and every other thought from his mind. He accepted his part in it. Imogene claimed that marriages fared better when the wife stayed at home and took care of the children and her husband. The women in his family held responsible jobs, and he respected them and took pride in their accomplishments, but he'd taken Imogene for granted.

The doorbell rang, but he heard it and didn't hear it, so centered were his thoughts on the mess he and Imogene had made of their lives. He'd tried to give her everything she desired, never hinting that he thought her demands excessive. Not once had he talked with her in a quiet moment and shared with her his feelings, concerns, fears and misgivings, or his reasons for behaving as he did.

He got up and walked from one end of the living room to the other, knocking his right fist into his left palm as he paced. *What a mess!* When he stopped catering to her whims, she found a way to get what she wanted. He still didn't know what kind of modeling she did or the value of the ring that white leather box held, because he hadn't gotten the courage to have it appraised.

The incessant peel of the doorbell got his attention, and with feet of lead, he dragged himself to the door and opened it.

"Hi. What a nice surprise!. I didn't think you'd be here," Imogene said as she breezed past him. "How was Christmas?"

Still sweeping the dirt under the rug, was she? Well, he was through with that. "If you didn't expect to find me here, why didn't you use your key?"

Ignoring his question, she pulled off her gloves, unbuttoned her coat, and turned her back to him so that he could help her out of it. He gritted his teeth and, like an old batsman swinging from habit, did what she wanted him to do.

She turned to face him with a smile that didn't glow. "Thanks, hon. I'm just dying for some coffee. Why don't I make us some?"

He stared down at her luscious mouth, her full bosom with the nipples hardened and pointed from the cold, and felt himself stir. She knew it, damn her, and moistened her lips with the tip of her little pink tongue. Three and a half weeks of celibacy threatened to undo him, to make him her willing victim and the dupe of his own libido. The hunger sliced through his guts, but this time, it was a craving, a yearning for loving that was genuine. Unaffected. For months, all he felt after making love with her was an emptiness, a feeling that his insides had been hollowed out.

He shoved his hands into his pockets. "You want coffee? Go ahead and get yourself a cup. I already had some."

The glow left her face, but he knew he'd see it again as soon as she regrouped, for he was learning that Imogene was and always had been a consummate actress. It was D day, and he knew it, because she meant to continue as if there were no chasm between them, no crisis hovering over them, and he didn't intend to let her do it. Maybe she was scared; he knew he was. Walking aimlessly around the living room, he felt chilled, went into the hallway to turn up the thermostat, and decided to get a sweater.

He was proud of his cashmere sweaters and kept them folded in the bottom drawer of their chest-on-chest. When the drawer failed to yield to his strength, he opened the one above it in the hope of easing the traction, and his gaze fell on a red velvet box that protruded from beneath Imogene's lingerie. He pulled it out, opened it, and felt the bottom drop out of him. He leaned against the chest of drawers, a victim of hyperventilation, sweat beading his forehead and dampening his neck. Anger welled up in him, and he opened the drawer wide. Six more boxes, and only God knew whether she'd stashed away more. His sweater forgotten, he took the boxes, got the portfolio and white leather box that had remained in his briefcase, went into the living room, tucked all of it beneath a pillow, and dropped himself on the sofa beside it. Drained.

"I brought you a cup, too, hon," she said, placed the tray of coffee and hot-buttered croissants on the coffee table and sat down as close to him as was possible without sitting on top of him.

"I don't want any. You help yourself."

Not surprisingly, her eyes widened, for if he said no to coffee, he was either sick or running to catch a plane. "You don't want any?"

He shook his head. "No."

She put her cup on the tray and pushed it away from her.

He hadn't thought about what he'd say to her; the severity of his pain hardly let him think at all. He reached for the portfolio but put it back under the pillow, still fearing what he'd see. But a glimpse of her face and the innocence she portrayed sent a wave of furor streaking through him. He grabbed the white leather box, opened it, and waved it in her face.

"What the hell is this, and where did you get it?"

"Give me that. You took it out of my pocketbook. Give it to me." She reached across him, grabbing at it, and when he held it firm, her fists pounded his chest.

"I thought I warned you not to hit me again. You don't want me to defend myself. Trust me. I gave you the opportunity to tell me what you'd been doing, to come clean with me as I did with you. You didn't accept it. So either sit over there and take your medicine or start packing."

"You wouldn't. I can get you anytime I want to, and we both know it."

He would have laughed if he hadn't hurt so badly. "You tried that a minute ago, and I got hard as a rock, but since you weren't offering what I needed, I passed it up." He opened the box and took out the diamond-encircled sapphire ring.

"How much did this cost, and what did you have to do to get it?"

"It's not real, for goodness' sake."

He let a smile soften his mouth. "Really? Junk jewelry in a leather box? Is it all right if I flush it down the toilet?"

Her mouth opened, and he could see her fear. Fueled by his anger, he took the red velvet box from beneath the pillow and opened it. "Hmm. Pearls. Now don't tell me these are fake. Mikimoto does not sell fake pearls. I bought some there for you. Remember? And we haven't even gotten to that twenty-one hundred dollar tennis bracelet that you claimed was fake."

He ignored the tears cascading down her face and threw the remaining boxes in her lap. "How many men did you go to bed with in order to get all this stuff?"

When the heat of her hand nearly blistered the side of his face, he gave silent thanks. The spontaneity and force of her reaction was proof that at least she hadn't done that.

"How's Jay these days?" he asked her, and in spite of it all, he had to fight with himself to keep from pulling her into his arms, as she seemed to shrivel in size at that most damaging evidence of her culpability. He handed her the portfolio. "Want to open that for me?"

She pushed it away and dropped her hands into her lap in an act of surrender. With little to lose, he opened the portfolio and stared at the pictures of his wife, nude in every conceivable kind of pose. He worked hard at controlling his temper, as he gazed at the ruins of his marriage.

"You want a divorce?"

He shook his head and ignored the cramps that cut through his stomach. "I told you I wanted us to open up to each other, clean the slate, and get on with our lives. It may be too late now. I . . . Hell, I don't know. I haven't been an angel, but I haven't embarrassed you. Where are those pictures published?"

"A lot of magazines. I'm not sure which ones," she said in words barely audible.

"How'd you get into this?"

"Keisha said we would model for art students. Only they weren't students, and when I wanted out, they blackmailed me, threatened to tell you and Keisha's husband."

"I don't believe you. You were enjoying it just like you enjoy parading around me without your clothes. Maybe you didn't like it at first, but the woman in these photos is an exhibitionist and proud of what she's showing."

"I . . . I didn't mean to get so involved, Drogan. At first we only had to stand still and not move while they painted us."

"Who is 'they'?"

"The . . . uh . . . the . . ."

Exasperated, he interrupted her. "The men. Right?"

She nodded. "When we found out they had cameras all over the place, we wanted out, but they wouldn't let us quit."

He turned to face her. "What do you mean, they wouldn't let you quit? You could have stayed home."

"They threatened to tell you . . . and . . . I guess the more we did it, the easier it got."

"But you lied. You said you were shopping. Have you ever seen one of your pictures in a magazine?" She nodded. "And how did you feel?" He was hurting her, but why shouldn't he when he was dying inside.

"I . . . uh . . . I just . . ."

"For five hundred dollars an hour you lolled around butt naked in front of a bunch of cameramen."

"What are you going to do?" she asked in a subdued, self-pitying voice that he detested.

He didn't know the answer to that until he heard himself say, "I'm moving into the guest room until I feel better about this, if I ever do. I don't want Keisha's number on my phone bill. And if I find out you've been with her, I'll have a nice long chat with her husband."

He wrapped the portfolio in brown paper and addressed it to Jay's Modeling Agency, then changed his mind, threw it into the fireplace, and watched it burn. He'd pay Jay for the portfolio, but he refused to return to any man those pictures of his wife. He wished he hadn't seen them.

Stressed out, nerves shot, and unable to concentrate on his work, he put on a leather jacket and went outside to brave the biting wind. When he returned forty-five minutes later, she hadn't moved, and her gaze beseeched him unashamedly, but he couldn't give her the assurance he knew she wanted. He shook his head, bemused. Pictures of his wife photographed nude in a hundred different sexy poses for anybody who cared to look. Seeing them had deadened his emotions; he felt nothing for her, though he knew he was not without guilt.

As he hung his suits in the guest-room closet, he thought of the price he was having to pay for refusing to manage the family paper, and cold shivers plowed through his body. He wasn't proud of himself; he'd played a major role in the debacle his life had become. And, Lord, how he hurt! He didn't know it was possible for pain to gnaw a man's insides until he wanted to scream for help. He stopped his fist a second before it crashed into the mirror and splintered the image of himself that he saw there.

He looked around and saw Imogene standing in the doorway. "Just . . . just leave me in peace," he said.

"Drogan, listen to me. Please listen. Even if you send me away later, please let me say it."

He sat on the edge of the bed, opened his arms, and let them fall to his side. "Go ahead. Even a condemned man is given a chance to speak."

She spoke with her head bowed, and he told himself to ignore the compassion that welled up in him. "I . . . I always felt so inferior to Mama, Cassie, and Sharon because they did important things and I couldn't. I never forgot that Sharon has a Ph.D. and that Cassie has at least one master's degree. I hardly got out of high school. I wasn't important."

"If I had needed that in a woman, Imogene, I could easily have married such a woman."

"Please hear me out, Drogan. I couldn't even carry a baby to term, and most any woman my age can do that. When your mother and sisters talked about their work and what was going on in the country and the world, I could hardly keep up. You took me to all those places they'd never been and bought me jewelry and things they didn't have. In that respect, they weren't my equal. Then you stopped. Sharon always looked like a country cousin, then she got the paper and a man, fixed herself up, and looked like a model. I couldn't any longer make myself feel good by saying I was pretty and she wasn't."

Impatient to hear the end of it, he pounded his fists on the bed. "Where is all this leading?"

"It's . . . I don't expect you to sympathize with this, but I felt special and important with those men staring at me and not allowed to touch. The money . . . it made me feel superior to go in those expensive stores and buy things Sharon and Cassie couldn't afford and see the store clerks smile and rush to wait on me. They didn't look down on me. Drogan, I was somebody special."

In their four years of marriage, she hadn't shared with him the things about her that were important, and he hadn't been sufficiently observant to realize that she hurt. His mother was slipping away from him, and his wife, the woman he loved, was . . . maybe already gone. He lowered his head till it rested in the palms of his hands and shook with the sobs that racked his body.

"I'm sorry. Drogan, I'm so sorry. If I could take it all back, I would."

But she couldn't. Neither could he undo his infidelity. He raised himself up, walked past her without looking at her, and headed for his car as the biting wind numbed his coatless body.

"Drogan, what on earth are you doing here without a coat?" Cassie asked as she opened her front door and saw him standing there.

He didn't answer, only strolled past her into her living room and sat down. She couldn't imagine what could have propelled him out in below-freezing weather without a jacket or coat.

"Are you all right?" Suddenly she grabbed her chest. "Is it? Is it Mama?"

He leaned back in the chair and closed his eyes. "Nothing like that. I just had a wallop that—Cassie, I feel like I've been gutted."

"Yesterday, at Mama's, I thought something was wrong, but I figured you felt bad about it being Mama's last Christmas. I had to admit, though, that she seemed happy."

"I think she is, too. She had us and all her cronies there, and she enjoyed it. She said she missed Kix, but she knew he had to be at the restaurant. She—"

"What's the matter?" she asked him when his voice seemed to die away and his hand rubbed back and forth across his forehead. "Something's killing you."

He sat forward and rested his forearms on his thighs. "And you, too. I don't want to dump on you, because I suspect you've got your own load. It's just that . . . Cassie, I love Imogene, but I don't know. I just don't know."

Sheer black fright gripped her, and the muscles of her stomach clenched, paining her. "What . . . what's happened with you and Imogene? Did she have an . . . an a . . . affair?" She could hardly force the word from her lips.

He shrugged, as if it didn't matter, but she knew better. "She didn't, but I did. She posed nude for some girlie magazines. My God! You should have seen those pictures."

"She what?"

"You heard me. All those shopping trips." He shook his head. "I can't believe I was so gullible."

If he wanted her to grieve for him, she was sorry. She had all she could do to deal with the mire of her own misery. Time was when the three of them were close, caring and supportive. But that was . . . "I'm going to make some coffee. I don't have to ask whether you want some."

She came back a few minutes later with a mug of coffee for each of them and a saucer of miniature doughnuts that she bought at the supermarket.

"Drogan, I'm not judging you. You'll do that to yourself. But is what you did any less offensive than what Imogene did?"

"I never said it was. I told her about it and asked her forgiveness, but she lied about this. Besides, a man doesn't want his wife bare-assed, naked in front of who the hell knows how many Peeping Toms."

With her own guilt bearing so heavily on her that she couldn't function normally, she had neither the right nor the desire to upbraid him for his infidelity. And that was what he'd come for, she realized. He wanted absolution. Well, he'd have to get that from Imogene and the Lord.

"He who is without sin can cast the first stone," she said, paraphrasing the biblical passage to the best of her memory. "That's all I can say about it."

He stretched his legs out in front of him and hooked his thumbs in his belt. "If I could just figure how we got into this mess. She never once said she wasn't happy, but to hear her tell it this morning, she's been miserable."

She jumped up and shook her fist at him. "Why didn't you pay attention to her? You got yours, didn't you? Why didn't you know she wasn't satisfied, that she . . ." She clapped her hands over her mouth and flopped back down into the chair.

She knew he understood her when he said, "That was never a problem. It was . . . Wait a minute. That's the issue between you and Kix, isn't it?"

"What do you mean?" she bluffed. "The real problem started when you wouldn't manage the paper. After that, you'd have thought a tornado ripped through this family. Until then, we were close. We cared about each other. Now we're at each other's throats, unless we want something, that is. Our marriages are a wreck. Everybody's suffering."

The pain inside of him gnawed so violently at his insides that he had no solace to give her or anyone else. "Except Sharon. How can you say it's my fault? You could have managed the paper and continued your art work. Why did it devolve on me to take over from Mama? I don't know beans about a newspaper. You at least got your bachelor's degree in the social sciences. Mine's in computer sciences."

"You wanted to be the man in the family, but . . ." She threw up her hands. "Oh, give me a break. I've got my own problems."

"Yeah. I imagine you have. Coming here was a mistake, Cassie. I'll let myself out."

She took the saucer and cups to the kitchen, rinsed them, and put them in the dishwasher. Ordinarily, she would be at the office the day after Christmas, when she'd have the place to herself, but she hadn't dared go for fear that Judd might find her there. He'd called their encounter a one-night stand, and her mind wanted it that way, but her body . . . If he touched her, she'd be in trouble.

After dragging herself upstairs, she prowled around, straightening closets, tidying drawers, and changing the linens in the bathroom, until she exhausted herself. Not knowing what else to do, she headed to the bathroom for a shower and stopped; she'd had a bath a couple of hours earlier. She paced the floor, struggling to gain control of her emotions.

If only she hadn't given in to it, hadn't lowered herself in her own eyes, hadn't betrayed the one person who loved her and would do anything to make her happy. If she could just stop hating herself and get on with her life. She might have to do that without Kix, because she knew she couldn't live with him and not tell him.

A week had passed since her indiscretion with Judd, and fortunately for her, Kix had worked late every night to serve the holiday crowd, and she had either been asleep or pretended to be when he got home. The previous morning, while pretending to sleep, she surreptitiously watched Kix step into a blue G-string as he dressed for work. She had never realized that a man's body could be sensuous, mouthwatering, until Judd stood before her proudly naked. And she hadn't allowed herself to enjoy looking at Kix's body because she hadn't understood that his body was for her pleasure. She'd thought it was only for his enjoyment. Was this her punishment for the occasions she had exposed her nude body to him and basked in the pleasure of having him want her when she knew he didn't have time to consummate his desire, or when she pretended to be asleep? An unfamiliar ache settled in her vagina as she gazed at his strong, muscular physique, his washboard belly, broad shoulders and tight buttocks. Her mind raced back to the first time she saw him. Her head had snapped around in a double take of the tall dark man with light-brown eyes and an infectious smile that displayed glistening white teeth and a tiny dimple on his left cheek. Lord, what had she done to herself?

She turned over on her belly and buried her face in the pillow. She realized that her attitude toward sex had changed, and she shivered with fear; if Kix approached her, she'd want what he offered, and she'd have to pay the piper.

Fourteen

Sharon awoke late that Sunday morning to see sunlight streaming through the Venetian blinds of her bedroom windows. Anxious that her mother may have needed her while she slept, she grabbed a robe and raced to Marge's room, only to find Eloise, Kix, and Ross sitting around the bed, drinking coffee. Kix came by every morning on his way to work, and Eloise used her key as she pleased, but Ross's presence so early in the day surprised her.

Embarrassed by the possibility that they might think her negligent, she greeted them, kissed her mother's forehead, and went to get dressed.

"Wait a minute." She turned as Ross's voice reached her.

"She's smiling, but she's kinda poorly this morning."

So her impression had been correct. She tightened the robe around her body. "I sensed that, too, Uncle Ross. Do you think I should call Dr. Glick."

"Well, if you want to, but what can he do? No point in upsetting her."

Observing him closely, she decided that he didn't seem his usual self. But since Mama wasn't quite right, either, that no doubt explained Ross's seeming anxiety. She patted his arm. "I'll be back soon as I get some clothes on." She stopped, turned, and walked back to him. "How'd you happen to come so early today?"

His shrug lacked its usual careless air and instead suggested the helplessness that they both felt. "Couldn't sleep."

His pain shouted out to her, and without thinking, she enfolded him in her arms. To her surprise, he accepted the comfort she offered.

"It's rough, Sharon. It's rough." She didn't look at him, but rushed to her room, dressed, and concentrated on staying calm.

"What are you doing?" she asked Ross when she returned and found him putting Marge into her wheelchair.

She'd never seen his face ashen and drawn, and her heartbeat speeded up when he didn't look at her as he settled Marge in the chair, took the blanket from the bed, and secured it around her.

Marge patted Ross's hand. "I want to see the garden. The sun is so nice this morning. Ed loves the garden."

"Where're you going?" Sharon asked Kix when he took her arm and walked with her into the hall.

"I'm calling Cassie and Drogan. This is serious." Standing at the phone, he dialed with one hand and held her tightly with the other. "Cassie, this is Kix. I'm at Mama's house. Honey, I think you'd better get over here. It doesn't look too good. Would you rather I came and got you? All right. I'll call Drogan. No. No. I'll be here when you get here." After calling Drogan, he asked her for Rafe's number.

She repeated the phone number, clutching his arm as she spoke. "You . . . you think . . ." She couldn't bring herself to say the words.

He nodded. "I'm sure of it. Rafe, this is Kix. Man, I think you want to be with Sharon right now. No, but it's imminent. She's right here with me." He handed her the phone.

"Head up, baby. I'll be there in half an hour."

"Thanks. I . . . thanks."

She'd never known the wind to be so calm, the sun so bright, or the sky so blue as on that Sunday morning, two days after Christmas, when they all sat on her mother's porch in the total quiet of that cold December day.

"It's so . . . so . . . bea . . . beautiful," Marge said, her voice soft and urgent. "And my children . . . Ross, they're so beautiful. Wonderful. Ross. Eloise, where's Ross?"

It didn't surprise Sharon that Ross sat at the end of the swing beside the wheelchair, holding Marge's hand. All at once, his arm went around her shoulder, tightened, and he kissed her cheek.

"I'm right here, Marge. I'll never leave you."

She glanced around, seeming to rest her gaze on each of them. Then she leaned against Ross's shoulder, her smile sparkling, brilliant, and slipped away from them.

*　*　*

Later that afternoon, as neighbors and friends filled the house, Ross sat alone in a corner of the living room.

"Come in the kitchen with me, Uncle Ross," Sharon said, taking his hand, and to her surprise, he followed her.

"It's the only place in this house that isn't crammed with people. I need them around, but I'd like to be able to break down in private."

"You mustn't do that, Sharon. She left here happy, and a lot of weeping would make her mad." He leaned back against the counter. "She once asked me why I never got married. I told her I was married to the paper."

She whirled around and waited expectantly for the words that would follow; waited because she didn't think she had the right to ask.

"I've been in love with Marge for over thirty-five years. There was never anyone else for me. But you know? She never guessed it. I'm proud of that. I was your daddy's best friend and her friend, and it never once occurred to me to cross that line and risk either his friendship or hers."

Though stunned by his admission, she had the levelheadedness to clasp his hand in a gesture of condolence. But somewhere in the recesses of her mind, she'd known it, at least since the late stages of her mother's illness, but she hadn't put her finger on it.

"She knew you loved her."

"Yeah. But she didn't . . ." He stared into her eyes. "Sharon, she didn't know the half of it. She couldn't. Nobody could."

She cried then, for the first time. Cried for him, for her siblings and for herself.

"Don't, Sharon," Ross said. "Be thankful you had her for your mother. I'm grateful that she was part of my life." He straightened up and braced his back with both hands. "Let's go see what's going on."

He didn't fool her. She knew he needed to change the focus of his thoughts, and she quickly stood and took his arm, urging him toward the others. She didn't want to see him break.

In the dining room, they found Gert standing in the middle of it, lecturing to Eloise and three generously proportioned sistahs from Marge's church. "I don't care what anybody says, celibacy is against the laws of God. Forty years, you say?" Gert asked one of them. "Girl, I'll bet you my house you got vaginal atrophy. You're sinning against nature."

One of the other woman looked at Gert, adjusted herself in the chair, and rolled her eyes. "Wouldn't bother me none. What did nature ever do for me? I spent almost half of my life looking for a husband. When I finally found one, he spent the other half of my life in the gym, jogging and staying so fit that he was ready to fall asleep at the sight of a bed."

"Shoulda give him some Viagra," Eloise said. "That's Gert's cure for everything wrong with a man."

"Pshaw," one of the women said. "You can load the gun, but what good is it if the man don't know how to shoot it? What do you do then?"

Gert permitted herself a genuine hoot. "If Marge was here, she'd say, 'You can't get blood out of a turnip.'"

Ross ran his fingers through his thinning hair and shook his head in what had to be a reprimand as he looked at Gert. "Something tells me she kept you under control. If this is what people mean by girl talk, give me magpies, and I mean the ones with feathers."

Sharon headed for the living room to find Cassie. She couldn't bear to watch Eloise, Gert, and Ross struggle to deal with their feelings, making small talk and trying unsuccessfully to amuse each other.

"Where's Kix?" Cassie asked her.

It occurred to her that those were the first words her sister had said to her all day, a day on which normal sisters would have clung to each other.

"He and Rafe went with Drogan to make the arrangements. I wish Imogene was here."

Cassie's eyebrows eased up slowly, triggering Sharon's curiosity with their signifying movement. "And why, may I ask, do you wish our dear sister-in-law was here?"

"Because Drogan needs her. Cassie, he loves Imogene."

"Yes. I suppose he does." Her voice carried a wistfulness that Sharon thought unlike her sister. She patted Cassie's shoulder and went to speak with the Reverend Ripple, but she couldn't rid her mind of the thought that some kind of problem weighed on Cassie, one not amenable to an easy solution.

The following Wednesday afternoon, they left Marge beneath a blanket of white roses, calla lilies, and white carnations and trudged back to their cars as snowflakes drifted over them.

"Mama was such a romantic," Sharon told Rafe. "She would have loved this." For an answer, he squeezed her arm.

Drogan, Imogene, Cassie, and Kix walked together in the silence of their thoughts. Behind them, Eloise and Gert held hands as they followed Ross, Sharon, and Rafe to Rafe's car. "No long black limousines," the Reverend Ripple told Sharon. "Marge said skip all the heavy stuff and act like you're just saying so long for now."

Ross opened the back door of Rafe's Lincoln Town Car and held it for Eloise and Gert, got in, and closed it. "Yeah. She would have loved every second of it, right down to that idiot poem Mack read."

Sharon stood beside the front passenger door, looking in the direction of Kix's car. "Excuse me a minute, Rafe." She walked down the hill until she reached the dark blue Oldsmobile that Kix bought a few days before Thanksgiving.

"When can we all get together?" she asked her siblings. "I'd feel so much better about . . . about Mama if the three of us could just sit down and . . . and talk. I—"

Cassie dabbed at her reddened eyes. "I'm not ready for that. I . . . I can't handle that right now."

Sharon looked at Drogan, hoping that he would take the reins and pull them together, but he offered nothing of himself, not even a smile. And she knew it had all been for show—his greeting guests so graciously prior to the service, reading aloud the family letter with such expressiveness, comforting Cassie and her at the bier.

She imagined Drogan had a full plate with Imogene and the scraps of his marriage, but couldn't he see that she also needed him? Impulsively, she reached up and kissed his cheek, went over to Cassie, hugged her, and tried to ignore their wooden responses.

"I hope we can get together soon," she said.

The events of recent months had taught her that she could rely on her own fortitude, but the seeming indifference of her siblings less than a hundred feet from their mother's fresh grave was as much as she could handle, and she gave thanks for the strength of Kix's fingers at her back.

She headed to Rafe, grateful to have him in her life, and he walked to meet her, opened his arms, and enfolded her to his warmth. "I see it didn't go as you'd have liked, but from what I've seen of them these past few days, they're not only dealing with grief and their relationship to you; they're struggling with their troubled marriages."

* * *

Cassie was also struggling with herself, trying to come to terms with her adulterous act with Judd, for in spite of her intolerance, she had always been a principled person. And Kix's considerateness and caring during her grief only added to her sense of guilt. And though it cost him a sizable share of his yearly income, he hadn't hesitated to close Gourmet Corner for a week out of respect for Mama.

"I'm going to reopen tomorrow," he told her as they lay in bed that night. "I hope you don't think I'm rushing it, but Mama would understand that I need to minimize my loss. If you'd rather not be alone, come stay in my office at the restaurant. You can rest on the sofa. It's up to you."

"With so much to do, how can you get ready for all those New Year's Eve reservations in such a short time? You'll be half-dead."

"My assistant chef's been taking care of the preparations. I'll only have to cook." He raised up on his elbow and looked down at her. "Do you realize this is the first time you've ever expressed concern about how things went with me at my work? Do you?"

How could she answer him except to admit that he was right? Yet if she posed as a repentant wife, he'd think it false, and maybe it would be. She had never treated him right, and Judd had washed her face with that truth. Still, she wanted to find a way to show him the contriteness she felt without inviting the intimacy she dreaded. Intimacy that would expose her need for a man, a need to which Judd introduced her and which Kix didn't know she felt.

"You've got plenty cause to complain, Kix, but right now, I'm running on empty. When I can, and *if* I can, I'll try to make it right."

He turned out the light on the night table beside him and kissed her cheek. "Tomorrow is New Year's Eve. Let's hope the coming year is an improvement over this one. If you can't sleep, come over here in my arms. Night."

She wanted to snuggle up to him for the selfless comfort she knew he'd offer, but he was human, and they hadn't made love in weeks. She couldn't risk fanning a fire that he might not be able to control, so she remained apart, alone in her loneliness. Sleep wouldn't come, and she lay there, restless and afraid to turn over for fear he'd take her into his arms. What she needed lay beside her, but she dare not take it. She ached for the feeling that she was dying, flying, sinking, and soaring through space. She crossed her legs in frustration, needing the sexual release that he could give her. But if she risked it, he would know everything. Oh, Lord, what had she done to herself?

The next morning, not knowing what else to do, since she knew if she lounged in his office Kix wouldn't get his work done, she went to her own office. Almost immediately, a soft knock on her office door caused her head to snap up.

"Come . . . in."

"A leopard doesn't change its spots."

"What are you doing here?" she gasped as Judd stood in the doorway, almost unrecognizable in a business suit, shirt, and tie. "Can't you leave me alone?"

"Hello, Cassandra. I'm not working today. I took a chance I'd find you here. I heard about your mother, and I came to tell you how sorry I am."

"Oh. Uh . . . thank you. Thank you."

He waved a hand as if to depreciate the merit of his action. "It was the least I could do. I couldn't be there." He stood at the door, his stance nonthreatening, almost calming, a different Judd from the one she'd known.

"I didn't take lightly what we had here, Cassandra, but I meant it when I said I wouldn't pursue it, and I don't think you want me to. I wish you the best. If you can get it together with your husband, and I hope you can, you'll be a happier woman."

As she stared at him, she realized that although he still looked like God's gift to womankind, he didn't knock her out of commission as he had before. But she didn't congratulate herself, because she knew at once that it was his roughness, his earthiness, that had attracted her. In that business suit, the coarseness was less evident.

He wanted to leave her with a good feeling, so she forced herself to smile. "No. I don't want to take it any further." Her strength surprised her. "I don't know whether to thank you or curse you."

"I deserve both." She couldn't contain her curiosity about his changed demeanor and ventured a guess. "Have you ever done anything like that before? Taken a woman just because you wanted her and she was . . . was willing, the circumstances be damned?"

His gaze bore into her, but he camouflaged his feelings. "No. I have some sense of propriety, Cassandra, and I don't make a habit of going after other men's wives. With you . . ." Seeming to muse over his next words, he paused and then said, "I haven't been able to explain it to myself." He touched his forehead in a quick salute. "Be seeing you."

The swagger was absent as he walked out. She was glad he'd come, for she discovered that she didn't fear being alone with him. She leaned back in her chair and let the feeling that she'd dropped a yoke wash over her, realizing that she no longer wished she'd never seen him or that she hadn't given in to what she felt for him, because he'd taught her more about herself than she'd learned in her previous thirty-two years. She only wished that knowing him hadn't meant being unfaithful to Kix.

That night, longing to experience again what she'd felt with Judd, she struggled with the legacy of her infidelity. Kix stripped down to his underwear and headed for the bathroom to take his shower. She leaned against the banister, ogling his strong chest, hard biceps, and the print of his sex in the G-string, and liquid accumulated in her mouth. At that moment, she wanted him to catch her at it, but unaccustomed to such attention from his wife, he didn't look her way.

A week later, Sharon walked into Attorney Keith Lubbock's office and took a seat in the reception room.

"Go on in, Ms. Hairston," the receptionist said. "The others are already here."

She stepped into the conference room, rectangular shaped and dominated by a long mahogany table and chairs that rested on an enormous green Aubusson rug. She didn't like the setting, and especially not the heavy green velvet drapes at the windows.

"Have a seat, Ms. Hairston. Now that we're all here—"

With a glance around the table, she saw those she supposed Marge had remembered in her will. *This ought to be interesting,* she said to herself as she looked at Cassie's face, drawn and sullen with obvious displeasure, and Drogan's defeated slouch. A stranger would wonder why, so soon after their mother's demise, a brother and two sisters sat so far apart, not even glancing at each other.

He began to read:

"To Pastor Gilford Ripple I leave my music system and ten thousand dollars for the church.

"To Gert—Gertrude Williams I leave my fur coat, gold watch, my jewelry, and any of my clothes she wishes. They're too short and too small for Eloise.

"To my beloved Eloise—Eloise Rouse, I leave my pinochle cards, my car, porcelain dinnerware, silverware, linens, 3M and IBM stock certificates, and the contents of my bank accounts. Even this cannot repay her for feeding me and my children after Ed died and at times when I was completely broke.

"To Ross Ingersol I leave the remainder of my stock certificates, my books, my television, and my eternal love and devotion.

"To my beloved son-in-law, Kix Shepherd, I leave my collection of porcelain, cloisonne, and crystal vases for his restaurant, my cookbooks, and all of my CDs, cassettes, and records."

"The remaining contents of my home are to be sold for the benefit of the senior center or given to the center as Eloise sees fit.

Sharon watched, sadly, as Cassie crossed and uncrossed her legs and Drogan ground his teeth, something she hadn't seen him do since his early teenage days, when he was learning to replace his temper with charm.

"To my three children . . ." Cassie's hand clamped over her mouth, but the gasp had already escaped. "I leave this house and the acre of land it sits on. These are to be sold for the highest possible sum and the proceeds divided equally among them. God bless all of you."

Without a word, Drogan strode out of the room, and it didn't surprise her that Cassie followed his example almost at once.

"My assistant will be at the house from ten to twelve mornings and four to six in the afternoon every day this week. Thereafter, you must collect your things by appointment. The property will be put up for sale in one month."

Ross started toward the door, saw Sharon, and walked over to her. "Whatta you know about that? Cassie was going crazy thinking Marge didn't have a will, and now I'll bet she's mad as a hatter."

"Why would she be angry?" she asked him, realizing he knew something she didn't.

He shook his head as if bemused. "Well, she thought the house should be hers and Drogan's, but Marge did the right thing, just like I knew she would."

"Do you think they'll contest it?"

"Yeah, but it won't do 'em any good. Old man Lubbock knows his business, and I suspect that's why she called on him." He stuffed his hands into his pants pockets, his diffident demeanor so unnatural to him. "I didn't want anything, Sharon, and I'm surprised she left me all that. The TV would have been enough, just something that had been hers. That's all I'd want."

She took his arm and walked into the reception room. "Mama left you more than material things, Uncle Ross. Far more."

As his eyes glistened with unshed tears, a smile struggled for a place around his mouth. "Yeah. She did, didn't she? I wouldn't take anything for it. Nothing in this world."

Clasping each other's hand as if clinging to a lifeline, Eloise and Gert joined them. "Sharon, you can have any of the things Marge left me. I don't ask for nothing. She was my friend. My sister," Eloise said.

"Same here," Gert said. "I think Cassie and Drogan feel they didn't get their due, but considering how they acted the last few months, they've got a lot of nerve."

She knew Gert was right, but she felt for them nonetheless. "I want Mama's wishes carried out to the letter, but if they want my share, they're welcome to it."

"None of that," Ross said. "Carry out your mother's wishes. She knew what she was doing. Come on. The old Cadillac's seen a few years, but she rides like she was just christened."

"Thanks, but I drove. I'll see you at the paper in about an hour." She hugged Eloise and Gert, walked down Fifth Street to Courthouse Square, got into her car, and sat there. A genuine reconciliation with her brother and sister now seemed unattainable. And it pained her to see Ross sad, deflated, so unlike his tough, strident self. Suddenly, she realized that since Mama passed, he hadn't popped his fingers in her presence. She turned the key in the ignition, moved away from the curb, and headed over to the Woodmore Building on Eighth Street.

For the first time since taking over the paper, she wanted freedom at midday to wrap herself in something warm, stroll along Pine Tree Park at the edge of Salem River, the narrow stream that wound its way through Woodmore, and open her arms wide to a few hours of indolence. As her mother's constant companion for the last month of her life, she'd reveled in her love and courage and had gained the strength she needed for the days ahead. She hurt for Drogan and Cassie because they didn't have those memories, hadn't witnessed Mama's awe-inspiring courage, and their months ahead would be rockier. She couldn't help them; they wouldn't let her.

Drogan hadn't thought much about their mother's will except to resist Cassie's ill-conceived attempt to make him pressure his mother about it. Granted, she had a right to remember her friends, but from where he sat, she'd given away what was rightfully his. Sharon stood to make a fortune with the paper, and now she had a third of the house and the land it stood on. He picked up the phone and called Lubbock.

"I'm going to contest my mother's will, so nobody gets anything of hers until I get a settlement."

"Well, son, she said you'd do that, you and your older sister. But I advise you not to, because if you lose your case—and you would— your share goes to the county. As much as we need around here, which way do you think a jury would lean?"

"Are you saying—?"

Lubbock interrupted. "I'm saying I've already written a brief for the court contesting your case if you decided to go that route. And your mother left a taped message to be played in court if any of you went to court to break the will."

He jumped up and walked as far as the telephone cord would allow. "What right did she have to give her car, stocks, and bank account to Eloise Rouse? The woman can't even speak a proper sentence."

"Sorry, son. The answers to that and the rest of your questions are on that tape."

He hung up and prowled around his office, examining his options. *You brought this on yourself,* his conscience nagged. *You had your chance, but you were used to having your cake and eating it, too, and you thought you could duck the responsibility of the paper and still share in its proceeds. You've done that your whole life. This time, it backfired. Take your medicine.*

He dragged his fingers over his tight curls as he wandered around his office, fingering the art objects collected during his many overseas jaunts, trips that cost him a small fortune and which he now wished he'd had the wisdom to forgo. The thought diverted his attention to the target he needed as a receptacle for his anger. He stuffed his papers into his briefcase, got his laptop, and headed home.

Finding the house empty and with no idea as to Imogene's whereabouts, he picked another target: Sharon.

"This is Drogan," he said when she answered the phone. "I hope you're going to do the right thing and split your share of the house and land between Cassie and me. She gave you the paper. Isn't that enough?"

Her silence should have told him what to expect, but he was so used to associating her with timidity that her response came as a shock.

"You have no idea how happy I am that you can no longer intimidate me. Oh, you can still hurt me, but the pain won't be so deep. A lot of things happened to me since Mama became ill, and learning the real you has been the hardest to endure. In Mama's last days, you went to see her when I suggested it was time you did. Kix visited her every morning, cooked her dinners and sent them to her, sat with her and held her hand. While he did this, you sulked.

"No, Drogan, you can't have my share. Earlier today, I was going to give it to you. But not now. Mama's wishes will be followed to the letter no matter what tricks you and Cassie try. 'Bye." The dial tone droned in his ear, and he slammed the phone in its cradle.

He kicked at the overpriced carpet that he hated but which Imogene had insisted he buy. Lubbock would probably sell the house and land for three hundred and fifty thousand. Half of that would put him way ahead, but in a three-way split, he'd get fifty-eight thousand less—enough to add a room to his office, buy half a dozen computers, and expand his business to in-house hands-on computer training. He could have done that already if he hadn't spent that much on a summer in Greece, catering to his wife's whims.

Darkness gathered, and he glanced at his watch. Five o'clock. He wanted to smash something. His life hadn't approximated normalcy in months, if indeed it had ever been normal. *I won't stand for this any longer. Either I have a marriage or I'll free myself for one.*

A few minutes later, his temper dissipated and replaced by sadness, he heard her key turn the lock, stood, and treaded toward the hallway, where he knew she'd be hanging her coat. As she reached for it, he lifted it from her shoulders. She turned and looked up at him, her face plastered with a mixture of hope and anxiety.

"I didn't want to come home, so I walked till I got so cold I couldn't stay out any longer."

He leaned against the closet door and gazed down at her. "Why?"

"It's so lonely here, and so cold. I know I brought it on myself, but it . . . it's killing me, Drogan. I didn't need all the jewelry, not even what you gave me. But when I wore it, I thought about the women who didn't have it, and I felt like somebody."

"Let's go in the kitchen and I'll run some hot water. Your hands are so cold." He hadn't thought it a time for them to dig into the mire of their marriage, but as he considered it, they had always had problems but had shoved them under the rug, so to speak. Their troubles surfaced when Mama gave . . . when he rejected Mama's suggestion that he manage the paper. He had to start calling it like it was. Even so, he'd gotten a raw deal in that will.

She followed him to the kitchen, and he put her hands into a bowl of hot tap water. All the while, she stared up at him with eyes wide, and her expression tortured.

"I don't beat women, Imogene, so loosen up."

He watched her shake herself the way a bird dries its feathers after a bath and realized she didn't know she'd done it. He wondered at the symbolism. Instead of commenting on his remark, she said, "How did it go this morning at Lubbock's office?"

His mouth filled with bitterness, but he hastily swallowed the poisonous words and settled for a restrained reply. "I got screwed."

"I suppose Sharon walked off with the lion's share."

"She damned well got enough. I don't want to—" He'd nearly said he didn't care to discuss it, but he had to. His life was bound up in it, and so was hers if they settled on a future together.

She trailed behind him as he climbed the stairs, almost tripping on his heels until he stopped, throwing her off balance, and turned around to face her.

"What is it? Come on out with it."

"I . . . we . . . I can't go on like this. I fouled up things, and I'm sorry, but I can't crawl, Drogan, because if I do, you'll walk all over me. Much as I love you, I'd rather we just split."

He reached for her hand and walked with her to the guest room he'd used for the past month. "*We* fouled up. When did you last see Keisha?"

"The day you showed me that portfolio. She called me a couple of times after that, but things aren't so good at her place, either."

"You mean with her husband?" She nodded.

"I've never spoken a word to him."

"I know. He followed her several times and found out."

"If we stay together, would you be willing to adopt a child?"

"I'm only thirty, Drogan. I'd like to try for one of our own with the doctor's help before we do that. If I have another miscarriage, then we can adopt; that is, if you still want to."

"Do you think you can be satisfied with what I make and take a vacation every two years so I can save some money?"

"If . . . if we can patch up our relationship, I want a fresh start. I'm . . . My daddy said I should stop being a baby." She looked him straight in the eye. "You encouraged my foolishness."

"Yeah. I did. What about you? Do you have any grievances against me?"

She took in a large volume of air and blew it out so slowly that she had to be procrastinating. "I . . . uh . . . What about that woman? Are you still seeing her?"

He shook his head. "I broke it off for good before I told you about it."

Her next question was one to which he'd search for an answer, only to have it elude him. "Why did you need her? I have to know."

He didn't want to hurt her, but if he answered as truthfully as he could, he would. Yet it was that or more of the same, and he didn't want that.

He went with his gut feeling about it. "This will hurt, but if we're to have a chance, I have to say it. When we make love, I do everything I can to meet your needs, to see that you're completely satisfied. But you forget you have a partner who also has needs. You get yours, and you're ready to sleep. I can't count the times I've felt as if I've serviced you and I'm no longer important." There! He hadn't understood it till he heard himself say those words. "And it intensified when . . . well, in recent months when you were always tired and . . . and less interested."

She sat forward. "Since we're being frank, how was she different?"

"Imogene, for goodness' sake!"

"I want to know. Tell me."

"All right. She experimented, searched for ways to please, asked me what I wanted and needed, and provided it."

She sat back, and he could see the air seeping out of her, as it were. "I'm sorry, but you insisted."

Her hand went up. "No. No. No. It's okay. I get the message."

After a long silence, she asked him, "Are we going to make it?"

"I don't know. You said you love me, and I know I love you, but we, both of us, have to rebuild trust. Let's start by trying to be friends. I can only say I'm not moving out."

"Me, neither, and don't expect me treat you as if you were the pastor of my church."

"Yeah, I know. You'll deck yourself out in your Victoria Secret getups and declare war." She shrugged, as if to say, What do you expect?

What indeed! That was half of their problem. "This isn't about sex, Imogene. It's about you listening and not hearing what I say, though I suspect I haven't heard you, either. It's about you looking at me and not seeing the man in front of you. It's about you wanting—the biggest house, biggest car, designer dresses, flashy jewelry, expensive vacations, membership in every exclusive club—wanting and never concerning yourself with the cost."

He grabbed the back of his neck and held on to hide his shaking fingers. "Imogene, this is about me working my ass off and coming home dead tired, disappointed, and miserable, only to find you in your latest designer evening gown, my tux laid out on the bed, and a dinner of potato salad and hot dogs on the table. You wanted to stay home and be a housewife. Okay, but you don't see that I'm dead inside, that I need you. You give me a minute to get indigestion, and you're pacing the floor for fear we'll be late to some function or other that offers a blues singer with no teeth, a rusty voice, and an out-of-tune guitar."

He didn't look at her because he didn't want to see her misery. He'd started, and he had to get it out. "I'm sick of running out every night to this gala, that stupid party, that opening"—he waved a hand—"whatever. Just so you can show off. You want to be Mrs. Drogan Hairston because maybe some other woman will envy you. But to hell with Mr. Hairston and his needs."

It poured out of him, resentment he'd never articulated or understood, ill feelings he'd harbored until they bordered on self-hatred for not going after what he needed. "You plan everything for your convenience, right down to when's the best time to have sex so you can get pregnant. Never once in these four and a half years have you turned over in the morning and said, How're you feeling, honey? If you notice I'm there, it's because you want something and your hand goes straight to my groin. No, thank you.

"I know I must've let you down a lot of times. Now's the time for you to tell me where I've failed you. Imogene, we don't know each other."

She didn't look at him, but kept her gaze downcast. "I . . . I don't know what to say. I wasn't used to your kind of life. My folks are poor, and I'd never made more than two hundred a week, so I thought I was doing like your friends and . . ." She dropped her hands into her lap and released a labored breath. "That's not quite true. It's not the only reason. I've been selfish. My folks told me at Christmas that I've always been like that. I've been living out my fantasies, the dreams I had as a young girl when I saw those movie stars and socialites on television all dolled up, consorting with rich, handsome men."

"Have you ever loved me, Imogene? Have you ever just wanted to be with me, to hold hands strolling through Pine Tree Park, where no one would see you with Drogan Hairston? Ever wanted to sit alone with me and not say a word. Listen to soft music? Watch the sunset with me? Just us. Have you?"

Tears trickled down her cheeks, but he braced himself against the urge to hold her and shield her even from his own tortured confessions of longing.

"You . . . you don't know how you're hurting me."

He ignored that. "Did you know I cried when you lost our babies? Did you? No, because you locked our bedroom door and wouldn't let me in while you grieved alone, as if I were responsible."

Furiously, he rubbed the back of his neck, then softened his voice and his stance. "Imogene, baby, why can't you tell me what it is you need that I'm not giving you? I don't mean things. I mean in there." He pointed to her chest. "Deep down, where you feel it. The thing that makes you whole. What is it? If you don't know and if you don't tell me, you'll never be happy with me. I'm not talking about some romantic notions like candlelight and music. I'm talking about life, yours and mine. I want you to demand something of me other than sex and the things money can buy. I want to be a man to you."

She wiped her eyes, and he couldn't tell whether she was acting or hurting. "I'm . . . I don't know how to answer that."

He paced around the bed, unable to believe she said it. "In this past month, I found out I could do without sex, so you can't use that as your fix-it panacea. If you don't love me like you mean it, I'm out of here."

"Are you saying you'll give us a chance?"

"I don't know. If anybody had told me I could hurt like this, I'd have laughed."

"Maybe it's because Mama—"

With a wave of his hand, he interrupted her. "You're grabbing at straws. This business with Mama and Sharon brought it to a head because it's made me look hard at myself and at my life. I have stopped smiling when I don't feel like it. If people don't like me, my real self, to hell with them. I am no longer going to live a lie, and believe me, baby, it's liberating. If you can't handle this, we can part here. I'll soon be thirty-five years old, and half of my life's been used up worrying about what people think of me and being likable. But from now on I'm not faking one single thing. If you have anything against me, *anything,* please say it now. I want the slate clean."

He heard the phone ringing and didn't care if it did, but she sprang to it as if it were a welcome lifeline.

"Hello. Hairston residence." After a short pause, she said, "Just a second," and covered the mouthpiece. "It's Cassie. She says she has to speak with you."

"We're busy, so tell her some other time. I don't feel like listening to Cassie's harangue. It's enough right now to deal with my own feelings."

"He said he'd call you. Okay?" She hung up.

He walked over to where she stood and loomed over her. "I did not say that. Hell, we're right where we started an hour ago. You just don't seem to hear me. I am not sweeping anything else under the rug. You hear me? I'm through living a lie."

He threw up his hands and walked away from her. "Maybe we'll make it, and maybe we won't. It's not going to be easy. One thing is certain: I am not going to any other woman for what I need and don't get from my wife. No more. If we can't meet each other's needs, we'll have to split."

Fifteen

Cassie paced the floor of their living room, unable to contain her rage. Anger at Drogan for not talking with her, at Sharon for having more than her share, and at Mama for giving it to her. "Will you please stop this and look at yourself," Kix said. "Cassie, why can't you let me in? For months you've shut me out. Don't you know that whatever hurts you hurts me?"

She loved Kix, more than ever, maybe, and she didn't want to hurt him more than she already had, but she couldn't stop the awful downhill slide. Yet the bottom was nowhere in sight. Pain welled up in her, the pain of guilt for her treatment of her mother and for her folly with Judd. Tears gushed from her eyes, startling her as they cascaded down her face. She heard her sobs, then her moans, and felt the strong arms of her husband enfold her.

"It's all right, baby. I'm here for you."

She sobbed until the tears dried. Still, he stroked her back and her arms, all the while whispering words of love and comfort. She looked up at him, and shock reverberated throughout her body as the blaze of desire that filled his eyes transfixed her. She stared. Mesmerized.

Heat flared in her, for she knew what was behind the blaze in his eyes. The stirring in her feminine center, the ache to feel again the heat of a man storming within her, made her reckless.

"Kix!"

As if he knew he'd poleaxed her, he captured her mouth and flicked his tongue over the seam of her lips more aggressively than he'd ever done. Thinking only of the heat—newly discovered and treasured—that seared her love tunnel and forgetting that she had never made sexual demands on him, she pulled his tongue into her mouth and sucked it like a woman starved. And indeed she was, for now she knew what he could give her, and she hungered for it.

Stunned, he backed away and stared at her, then pulled her into his arms and let her feel his arousal. She knew she'd have to face a reckoning, but excitement roared through her, and she didn't try to slow him down when he gripped her hips with one hand and pressed her center with his bulging need. When she didn't demur, as she usually did, he hesitated and then tested the water, first brushing her breast, and when she didn't object, he squeezed her nipple.

Lord, it felt so good. If he'd only . . . She arched her back for more, and he yanked the shirt over her head and slipped his hand into her bra. Wild with want, she cupped her breast, and a scream flew from her lips as he covered her nipple and sucked it into his mouth.

"Oh, Lord, honey. Oh, Lord," she moaned, and pressed his head to her breast, forgetting that she never allowed him that liberty. Minutes later he had them in bed, their clothes scattered over the floor. Helpless in the onslaught of the abandoned loving of a man long deprived, she lost control of her body as it swayed beneath him like a sapling in a storm while he kissed and licked ever inch of her.

"Take me," she moaned. "I can't stand it."

Frantic for relief, she took him in her hands and planted him inside her. He drove into her like a man crazed with need, and she took him, rocking wildly beneath him in time with his rhythm until he sucked her into a vortex of ecstasy. In her dazed state, she barely knew that he splintered in her arms. Vulnerable. Hers as he'd never been before.

In nearly half an hour of complete silence, their bodies lay joined like a tangled heap of old clothes while they slid down from the first high they'd ever reached together.

Finally, he braced himself on his elbow and stared into her eyes. "You want to tell me what's happened and why?"

Trapped beneath him, she couldn't even turn her head. "Now?"

"Yes, now. But first I want you to know that this is what I've always wanted and needed from you, a chance to love you and have all of you. Somebody beat me to it. You tell me why you let it happen and what is he to you now?"

As he lay buried inside of her, she looked into his eyes and told him the truth. "I tried to make you take me away so I wouldn't do it, but it was my fault that I didn't resist, didn't let you help me. I realize I always had this notion that I'm better than everybody else, that—"

He interrupted. "Yes. Including me."

She nodded. "I don't think he would have bothered if I hadn't treated him as if he were dirt. I think he wanted to prove to me that I'm no better than he. It was so perverse. An attraction to someone who was the epitome of what I dislike and scorned, considered beneath me and arrogantly dismissed as unworthy of my courtesy."

"Are you listening to yourself?"

"Yes, and I'm ashamed. I know this is it for us, and I'm— Only God knows how sorry I am. I hated myself ever since it happened, and I . . . I have no defense. No woman ever had a better husband than you."

He separated them. "Will you see him again?"

"At work, I have to, but only in passing."

"And you think that's the end of it?"

"Yes. For both of us. He . . . told me not to ease my guilt by telling you and making you miserable, but I . . . I couldn't live a lie with you." She wished he wouldn't look at her so intently and that she didn't have to see the pain in his eyes.

Suddenly, as if he only then grasped the magnitude of what she'd done, he gripped her shoulders. "How'd you let it get to that? Do you think I haven't known that you deliberately wouldn't give yourself up to me. Afraid you'd lose control of yourself *and* of me. After months and months of trying to get the response from you that I needed, I decided that maybe you couldn't give more and accepted what you gave, but—"

"You knew what I was missing, didn't you? Why didn't you show me? Why didn't you make sure that I—"

"I tried, dammit, but you wouldn't even let me touch your breasts, the one place I knew would make you knuckle under. But you let him do it, didn't you? Didn't you? How'd he manage it? What else did he do to you?"

Chills streaked through her at the memory of her transgression. "Kix, please. I don't want to talk about it."

"Really!" The harsh testiness in his voice sent shivers throughout her body. "He didn't ask your permission to do what he wanted to, did he? Of course not. You let him suckle you. What else? Did he get his head between your legs? Did he—"

She couldn't stand it. "Stop it. Please stop it. I hate myself as it is. I'm . . . I'm so ashamed. If I could undo it, I would."

"But you can't." He gazed down at her. Quiet. As if deep in

thought. Then he narrowed his eyes. "I hope you remembered to use protection."

She barely recognized her voice as the words seemed to teeter out. At least she could tell the truth. "I didn't, but he did."

"Funny. These past few weeks, I thought you were sick. No makeup, hair hanging down. This will take some healing, provided I can manage it, and I don't know if I can. You understand that, don't you?"

"I have no choice but to accept your decision."

He fell over on his back, stretched out, and locked his hands above his head. She didn't say a word. She didn't know this side of Kix and couldn't anticipate what he'd say or do next. He spoke dispassionately.

"Don't think I exonerate myself in this, Cassie. After months of disappointment, I quit trying to make you see that lovemaking means sharing your body and your soul with your lover, holding nothing back. I should have persisted, but I didn't want to hurt or offend you. You said don't play with your breast because that would make them sag. And you always stopped the foreplay and forced my entry when I knew damned well you weren't ready.

"I treated you with kid gloves, submitted to your whims, when I should have put a stop to it and showed you what I wanted and what you needed. But I love you, and I wanted you to need me, to give yourself to me the way I longed to give myself to you. You gave me my conjugal rights, but that's all. I never had *you* until tonight. Never! That's as much my fault as it is yours."

When she awoke the next morning, her first thoughts were that Kix had slept with her in their bed—albeit on the very edge—and that she hadn't gotten up and taken a bath.

"You can come over here to my office in the church, the three of you together," the Reverend Ripple told Drogan several days later, "or I'll have this tape printed out and sent to every newspaper and radio station in a hundred miles of here. Round up Cassie and Sharon and be over here tomorrow at one o'clock."

"What's on it?" Drogan asked him.

"I haven't the slightest idea." She taped it a month before she died and told me to play it for you within two weeks of her death. "Maybe

The Woodmore Times won't print it, but every other paper will. Hairstons are news."

Shortly after one the next day, Ripple offered a short prayer, cleared his throat, and flipped on the cassette. Marge's voice, still strong, though soft, surrounded them.

"Drogan, my firstborn, by now you think you made a mistake when you didn't agree to manage the paper. Actually, you did the right thing. You're better at what you do. Stick with it, but son, stop being so charming and you won't have so much to live up to. Besides, charm is cheap; even snakes are experts at it. Being handsome will get you in enough trouble, as I'm sure you already know.

"Cassie, my child, pull your nose out of the air, and for Pete's sake, ease up on your poor skin. One of these days you're going to scrub it off. Try luxuriating in your femininity, wallow in your sensuality, enjoy being a woman and you'll find your water bill will be much lower. Give Kix a break; he needs it. I'd love to be around to see him do somersaults when you finally embrace him totally.

"Sharon, you don't have to worship Drogan and idolize Cassie in order to love them. Besides, they don't deserve it. And you'll have to love them, frailties and all, because neither is going to own up to having any. Accept their faults and you'll be happier. Remember, they haven't changed; it's the situation that changed.

"Drogan and Cassie, you're both going to be furious about my will, but be honest with yourselves and you'll see that I've treated you equally. Sharon earned the right to own the paper; you passed up the chance. I'm proud of all of you, and your father would be, too. I love you all."

After minutes of quiet, Sharon stood. "She didn't say good-bye."

"No," Reverend Ripple said. "She told you good-bye the day she left here. Let's bow our heads. Father, I know that in your own time and your own way you will unite them, and I beg you to do it before they wreck what's left of their feelings for each other. Amen."

Nothing's changed, Sharon realized as they filed out of the reverend's office without speaking. On the street, before they headed for their separate cars, Drogan nodded to each of them. "I'll . . . after I get things together, maybe I'll . . . be seeing you."

Cassie stood beside her white Lexus with her hand resting on the door handle and looked at Sharon. "She couldn't have been more blunt. See you."

But when Cassie got home, she found a note stuck to the refrigerator. "As much as I loathe what you've done, I had a sense of triumph last night when you didn't jump out of bed and wash away all evidence that I'd been inside of you. Another thing. Unless you're on the pill, you may be pregnant, because we were in such a hurry, I didn't remember to use a condom. Let me know how you feel about that prospect. Kix."

In her relief that he might not leave her, she didn't care if he'd made her pregnant.

After months of calling Drogan and Cassie, leaving a message, and getting no response, Sharon abandoned her efforts to mend their relationship.

"It takes strength for a person to admit he's made a mistake or that he's mistreated another person," Rafe said as they sat in her living room an evening in July. "Would you like me to talk with them. I want to; I hate seeing you brood about them."

"Thanks, but when the time comes, I'll speak with them. It's worse today because it's Mama's birthday, and Aunt Eloise always made black bottom pies and put birthday candles on them. We loved that pie."

"I'm going to call her; it's time I got that soul-food dinner, and I want black bottom pie, too."

She pulled her gaze from his long tapered fingers. She could look at his hands and get thoughts she wouldn't share with a soul. As if to cleanse her mind of it, she switched to an impersonal topic.

"Mama once said she'd like the paper to sponsor some annual scholarships to get more of our young people interested in studying beyond high school. So I've decided to give three scholarships in her name every year."

"Great idea. How're you going to package it?"

"High school seniors will compete in a citywide essay contest, and the awards will be announced at a reception on Mama's birthday. The problem is that if Cassie and Drogan aren't there, this family will be the town's favorite topic for years."

"I'm sure they'll come around before this time next year, so I wouldn't worry about that angle."

"Wonder who that could be?" she said mostly to herself as the doorbell peeled repeatedly.

Rafe got up. "I'll get it."

"Well. Well, well," she heard him say. "We were just talking about you. Come on in. Come. Come."

Sharon jumped up and sped to the foyer. "Cassie! Kix! What . . . I mean, come in." She glanced down at Cassie's left hand, snugly clasped in Kix's right one, and looked inquiringly into her sister's face.

"Today is Mama's birthday," Cassie said, "and I just . . . All day, that's all I could think about. I've been so upset, and then Kix said maybe I'd feel better if we got together with you. Oh, Sharon, I was so relieved. I hope you don't mind."

Mind? She opened her arms, and to her amazement, Cassie reciprocated the gesture and clasped her tightly. Sharon's glance landed on Kix and the tears that pooled, unshed, in his eyes. I wish Drogan was here," she said. "Then everything would seem like normal."

"Let's start from here," Rafe said, and his eyes widened as the doorbell sounded again. He walked back with Drogan and Imogene in tow.

"It's Mama's birthday," Drogan explained. "Seems like today was harder for me than the day she left us. I've never been so lost. All I could think of was what she said on that tape. Not a word about how awful I acted about the paper and when she was sick. It's eaten my insides from the time I got up this morning. We went by Cassie's, and when nobody answered, we came on here."

"Cassie and Kix are here," Rafe said when she couldn't open her mouth to respond.

They cried, laughed, and cried some more. "I guess the Lord took his good time just like the reverend said," Drogan observed as he wiped tears from his eyes.

Imogene appeared to linger at the fringe of the group, as if she didn't belong. "How's it with you two?" Sharon asked Drogan as he walked with her to the kitchen to get coffee.

"I don't know. We're trying to straighten it out, but I'm beginning to think we might not make it. I guess we both have too much to forgive and forget. I haven't given up yet, but, well, frankly, it doesn't look too good."

"What's the problem? Anything you care to tell me?"

He shrugged, and a frown clouded his face. Thoughtful and, she realized, depressed. "Apart from lack of trust, it isn't anything that can be fixed. There's nothing to build on. We don't have in common enough of what's important to us, and we're realizing we never did.

It's a question of whether we're able to live with it. I don't know. Doesn't look too good."

She put her arms around him. "Don't give up too soon. It deserves your best shot."

He nodded. "Sure."

Several hours later, sated with loving, happy and fulfilled as she lay in Rafe's arms, he asked her, "Do you think everything's all right with you, Cassie, and Drogan?"

"No. But we've made a beginning, and six hours ago I hadn't counted on that. It ought to get easier with time."

Wrapped in his loving arms and at peace with everyone in her life, she went to sleep with a smile on her face.

WHEN TWILIGHT COMES

GWYNNE FORSTER

ABOUT THIS GUIDE

The suggested questions are intended to enhance your group's reading of Gwynne Forster's WHEN TWILIGHT COMES. We hope you have enjoyed this story of the strength and importance of family bonds. It is our hope that all readers will be able to understand and identify with the Hairston family as they make their way through life's gains and losses.

You can contact the author at:

Gywnne Forster
P.O. Box 45
New York, NY 10044
e-mail: GwynneF@aol.com
website: www.gwynneforster.com

DISCUSSION QUESTIONS

1. In your view, is Marge typical of the strong black women around whom the black family has historically revolved, who nurtures and supports her children singlehandedly? If not, in what way is she different?

2. Marge makes a decision that precipitates the disruption of family relations. Considering the personalities of Drogan and Cassie, did she do the right thing? If not, why and what should she have done?

3. Prior to the time Marge gives the paper to Sharon, do you detect any evidence that relations between the siblings may be fragile? What is the clue? Give examples of the superficiality of these ties as depicted in their childhood relationships.

4. Considering the nature of Drogan's business, should he have agreed to manage the paper. If not, why? How do you characterize his attitude in refusing? In this context only, is his behavior typical of men raised without a father and who have always relied on their mothers?

5. Drogan sees himself as head of the Hairston family and wants to be regarded as such, but he refuses the opportunity to assume the role. Is he justified in doing so? In what respect?

6. When Marge gives the paper to Sharon, Drogan and Cassie react in anger and disrespect. In this and other areas of their lives, they fail to see their faults. Name ways in which this character flaw impacts on relations between family members.

7. What accounts for Cassie's exalted impression of herself and her intolerance for those she considers her inferior? Is her fanaticism about personal cleanliness compatible with this character trait? What does this tell you about her? About her relations with her husband? What drives Cassie?

8. Cassie considers her husband socially beneath her. Why do you think she married Kix?

9. What accounts for Imogene's deviation from satisfied, dutiful wife and homemaker to a woman who disrespects her husband and leads a double life for monetary gain?

10. Why does Drogan lose Imogene's esteem? As his wife, should she have supported and encouraged him, gotten a job? Does she exhibit immaturity? Lack of love?

11. In your opinion, did Imogene marry Drogan for money? Status? If yes, how is this revealed? If not, why not?

12. Do you think Drogan mistook his needs in a mate when he chose Imogene? Or did he fail to understand himself and his true needs. If yes to either, is this more typical of women or men?

13. Is Drogan justified in having an affair? Why does he terminate it and confess his deed to his wife? Why is Imogene's reaction upon learning of it so mild? In view of his infidelity, is Drogan too hard on Imogene when he discovers her nude modeling?

14. Do you think there is a solid basis for the rebirth and preservation of Drogan's marriage? What is lacking? Is the author right in suggesting that the marriage may not prevail?

15. What is it about Judd that attracts Cassie, and why could she release herself with him when she hadn't done so with Kix?

16. Why is she vulnerable to a man other than Kix, and how did her passion—once unleashed—entrap her?

17. Is Judd Cassie's salvation? Does her experience with him lead to a healing of her relations with her family? With Kix? Does it alter her estimate of herself in relation to others? Why?

18. Should Kix forgive her? Why? Kix says he is in part responsible for Cassie's infidelity? Do you agree? Why? If not, why not?

19. Does Sharon have personality faults that contribute to the breakdown of relations between her and her siblings? Would the bond between Sharon and Rafe have withstood his erecting buildings in Wade Field and her opposition to it? Should a woman sacrifice her ideals for the promise of love? What happens when she does this?

20. Who suffered the most from the rupture of relationships between family members? Of the three siblings, whose character developed the most as a result of the family crisis?

21. What does Ross's role in this story symbolize? What do the relationships between Marge and her friends Gert and Eloise symbolize?

22. Did Marge know that Ross was in love with her? If not, why did she lean on him so heavily during her last days?

23. Why is Marge's posthumous message to Sharon an indictment of all three children? Did Marge treat Drogan and Cassie fairly in her will?

24. What, in your opinion, is the likelihood that Drogan, Cassie and Sharon will be able to love and support each other as siblings should?